T̶ ̶ed blood ̶ the floor of the v̶n confirmed s̶e wasn't his f̶t. There ̶ ̶ ̶ies hidden somewhere. She was in a un̶ ̶ ̶ion to confirm that without the legal strictures of interrogation and defense counsel. But he was stronger than she had originally judged, and it had been a long while since she had moved in these ways. A little less strong, reaction time a little slower, she was out of practice, and the confines of the van limited her options more than she had foreseen. She should not have let him get her into the van; that was an error in judgment.

Things may have already gone too far, but no time to think about that now. For now she felt her forty years of conditioning kick into fight or . . .

That was it, fight. There was nowhere to run.

Becky Masterman spends her days working in a forensic science publishing house and her nights writing stylish, exhilarating thrillers. *Rage Against the Dying* is her debut novel. Becky lives and works in Tucson, Arizona.

RAGE
AGAINST THE
DYING

BECKY MASTERMAN

An Orion paperback

First published in Great Britain in 2013
by Orion
This paperback edition published in 2014
by Orion Books,
an imprint of The Orion Publishing Group Ltd,
Orion House, 5 Upper St Martin's Lane,
London WC2H 9EA

An Hachette UK company

3 5 7 9 10 8 6 4 2

A CIP catalogue record for this book
is available from the British Library.

ISBN 978-1-4091-2693-5

Printed and bound in Great Britain by
Clays Ltd, St Ives plc

The Orion Publishing Group's policy is to use papers that
are natural, renewable and recyclable products and
made from wood grown in sustainable forests. The logging
and manufacturing processes are expected to conform to
the environmental regulations of the country of origin.

www.orionbooks.co.uk

For Frederick J. Masterman,
my husband and writing partner, finally

ACKNOWLEDGMENTS

My gratitude to Helen Heller and Hope Dellon, who are more collaborators than agent and editor. I still can't believe my good fortune in getting these two magnificent minds on my side.

My apologies for playing fast and loose with Tucson geography, though I tried to stick pretty close to law enforcement procedure and forensics. The following experts gave advice either personally or through their own reference books: Anil Aggrawal (paraphilias), Ronald Beckett (mummies), Diane France (anthropology), Vernon Geberth (serial murder), Harold Hall (psychology), Steven Karch (toxicology), Rory McMahon (investigations), Michael Napier (interrogations), Scott Wagner (pathology), Richard Walton (cold case investigation), and especially James Williamson, retired Tucson detective, who read the manuscript for accuracy, took me through the forensics lab, and showed me how to shoot a gun. Anything that's incorrect is sheer willfulness on my part.

While adapted for the purpose of the story, NamUs is a real public database that matches missing and unidentified people. I applaud the work of Michael O'Berry and Kevin Lothridge of the National Forensic Science Technology Center who created this concept, and I thank them for giving me permission to use the site in a fictional context.

I thank fellow authors for their gentle critiques: William Bell, Mickey Getty, Frederick J. Masterman, and Pat Mauser McCord.

And finally the intrepid members of the Catalina Mystery Book Club who inspired the character of Brigid Quinn and provided backup at the Hanging Tree Saloon: Carole Cascio, Jean Cliff, Frema Goldshine, Molly Landi, Ina Mapes, Margaret Parnell, Marilyn Raue, Joan Roberts, Phyllis Smith, and Margaret Thompson.

RAGE
AGAINST THE
DYING

PROLOGUE

From his idling van atop the Golder Ranch Road bridge, Gerald Peasil examined his next girlfriend. With his elbow leaning out the open window, and his face resting on his forearm, the slide of his lips back and forth on the hair of his arm aroused him a little, that and the salty sour odor of his skin. No hurry to introduce himself. Savoring the anticipation of meeting was part of the thrill.

The little woman would have been poking among the rocks in the dry riverbed below, too busy to spot him. She didn't have all the qualities that her picture promised. Sure, wisps of gray hair snuck out from under her khaki canvas hat, and she leaned on her walking stick whenever she stopped to examine a rock, but her body was so erect she could almost pass for hot.

The idea of a hot granny frightened Gerald a little, but no matter. It had probably been a lifetime since she got any, and she'd welcome the attention of a younger man. With his free hand Gerald rearranged himself through his thin nylon workout shorts and thought about his own mother. Mom used to grab him there really hard to discourage him from touching himself, until he got big enough to smack her across the chest with her prize Amway skillet. Dad thought that was pretty funny, only told him he should pick on someone his own size. But anybody telling Gerald not to touch himself from then on was asking to swallow their own teeth.

Gerald turned the van left at the end of the bridge and eased down the steep hill that stopped at the edge of the dry riverbed, what they called a wash here. He paused again and looked up and down the wide expanse of sand that was the color of wet concrete.

It was mid-August hot and not a dry heat by any standard. The summer monsoons had pummeled the desert in the last couple of days, so the usually dry sand showed dark rivulets where the rain saturated the ground. Another storm like the one last night, especially in the Catalina Mountains to the east where the river started, and the wash would fill with water, would "run."

But today you could walk in the riverbed, as the woman was. While Gerald watched, she shifted her exploration to underneath the bridge and faded from his sight. He was unconcerned; she couldn't see him either and that gave him all the time he needed to plan what he would do next, and next, and after that.

Gerald put the van in gear and turned at the end of the bridge down the dirt road that led to the very edge of the wash. He stopped just before the packed dirt became tractionless river sand and maneuvered a careful three-point turn so he faced back up the hill. That way the back of the van was open to the wash for ease of loading, and, if they had unexpected company, he'd be able to get the hell away. He didn't worry about whether she could hear the engine. A second dirt road that ran along the side of the river meant other cars sometimes came this way, so she wouldn't be alarmed at the sound of his. Besides, she was likely hard of hearing. At that thought Gerald blew a little puff of air out his nose, in a kind of laugh.

He jerked up the emergency brake, got out, and made sure the blue plastic shower curtain was smoothed out on the floor of the van and the restraining straps within easy reach. He picked up a set of pliers that had fallen from their niche on the side of the van. A place for everything and everything in its place. When he had tidied up and made his preparations, from a small box he pulled a roll of duct tape and yanked off a six-inch piece that he stuck lightly on the front of his sleeveless T-shirt so it would be at hand when needed. Then he pushed the doors shut but didn't close them altogether.

Gerald stopped once more to check out the hillsides on either side of the wash. Just a few prefab houses clinging to the side of the hill. Sweet location, from a made-to-order wet dream. There wouldn't be the fuss there was sometimes getting them into the van. He fingered the square piece of foil attached to a string around his neck and stuffed it down under his shirt.

His rubber flip-flops skidded on the fine gravel covering the slope into the wash, but he recovered. Tucking an oily strand of hair behind his ear and adjusting himself one more time made him feel presentable enough to approach his date.

The woman appeared not to notice him as she picked up rock after rock with her bulky garden gloves, examined them, threw some away and put others in a dusty olive green backpack resting on a larger stone. That was a good sign, her ignoring him. You could tell they were a little fearful if they didn't look at you. Fear was a good sign.

As he watched she bent down and one-handed a rock that looked to be about five pounds. Did a couple curls with it. Maybe not so old after all?

But then he got closer and saw that, yes, this was the one he was looking for, and she was ripe. Face not wrinkled, but lined a little with the dryness of the desert, and a trace of softness along the edge of her jaw. Gerald sucked in a sudden breath as he thought about running his nose over that jaw. Freckles sprinkled the part of her chest that showed above the neckline of her T-shirt. So thin and frail he wondered if her hips might break when she spread her legs. Fantasies of cracking bones aroused him again. She took off her hat and wiped her face with it. The hair that looked gray on first sighting from the bridge glowed white in the mid-morning sun.

The reflection of the sun in her hair made Gerald think about how goddamn hot it was. At least a hundred and five, maybe more. More humid than usual, too. You could almost feel steam rising off the wet sand. His head itched and he scratched it, picking the residue from under his nails as he picked his way through the hardening mush of the riverbed.

A trickle of sweat ran down his inner thigh, matching a sheen of moisture where the woman's denim shirt formed a V between her cushiony breasts. Ten degrees less would make this a whole lot more comfortable. Most guys of his persuasion did their work at night, but when your specialty was older broads you had to take advantage when the opportunity arose. All the older ones had been to the early bird special and were in bed by the time darkness fell.

His thoughts for a moment took him far away from the wash, to other sites and other women. Returning, Gerald was surprised to discover the woman looking at him. No "hi," no friendly wave, just observing him with an unblinking gaze. Her left hand that held the stone paused in mid-curl. She was so still she creeped him out, made him want to back away, to nix the deal. But then he remembered there was more than just satisfaction at stake here.

"Hiya," he said. The urge to tug on his balls was unbearable but he knew it could be off-putting in a new relationship.

"Hello." Her rich, elderly vibrato made him swell. Hers was an odd voice, not high and airy like most old ladies, but almost as deep and strong as a man's. She looked down briefly at the boner pushing up from underneath his shorts. Her head jerked involuntarily, and gave a little tremble. Maybe she hadn't seen a hard-on for a long time. Maybe she was excited.

"You okay down here?" Gerald asked. Back and forth in the sand he bent the rubber edge of his flip-flop, casually, to show he was relaxed, to put her off guard until he could get closer.

Her eyes crept to the right and left of him, scanning the mesquite trees on the side of the wash with the intensity of prayer. She started to speak, coughed once, unsuccessfully, but managed to croak, "Fine." In the sand her walking stick swizzled nervously.

"It's a hot day and it's noon," Gerald said. "You could get dehydrated before you know it, and no one around." With that he took a step closer, not directly but a little to the right like a coyote side-stepping to figure out the best approach to his prey.

5

The woman didn't deny she was alone. "I've got water in the bag." She indicated the backpack nearby, then turned her head to look at the bridge above and behind her, at a single car going over and going gone. Funny how most of them never screamed for help, like they'd rather be dead than embarrassed if they turned out to be wrong. She turned back to him, startled, as if afraid she'd looked away too long. "I want to get back to my rock hounding. Please."

"What's with the rocks?" Gerald asked, shaking his head, taking a step closer, a little to the left this time.

"I like rocks."

"Are you a—what do you call it—"

"Geologist?" The woman asked. She was very still again. You could almost imagine her tongue where it stopped after hitting the *t* sound.

Step closer, little to the right. "Yeah, a geologist," he said.

"No . . . please, lea—" she stopped in mid-word, as if knowing that begging Gerald to go would make what was happening to her too real. As if it would rub her face in her own vulnerability.

"Well, that's good." Gerald wasn't much for small talk. He had kept angling toward her while they spoke, right and left, like the rivulets in the sand, so she wouldn't get scared and bolt. Sometimes even the ripe ones could give him a run for his money, and it was too hot to chase her.

But standing flat-footed, alert yet indecisive, gripping her walking stick, this one let him come within about four feet. Her steadiness made Gerald falter again. Then he remembered hearing about people being paralyzed by fear. She looked like that. Maybe he'd just pick her up under his arm like a stiff cardboard cutout and carry her back to the van that way. He puffed another laugh. Later, when he had her secured, he'd have to tell her that one.

The hand that held the rock suddenly shifted, getting a firmer grip.

"That looks heavy," Gerald said. "Let me help you with that."

"No," she drew out the word, made it sound a lot like please.

He was near enough now. Fast as a nightmare Gerald closed the gap between them and knocked the rock from her hand so she couldn't drop it on his foot. He took a few steps back again to gauge the effect.

Still unmoving, she might as well have been another rock for all the reaction she had. This wouldn't be any fun if she didn't get scared. Was she some kind of retard? Gerald licked his lips. He'd never done a retard before. Maybe a more direct message was necessary. He tugged on the string around his neck to raise up the foil-wrapped condom attached to it. Not like he needed a condom—there would be no evidence to be found—it was just to make them think he wasn't going to hurt them. The woman studied the little package resting on the outside of his T-shirt.

Maybe now she understood.

The woman's eyes widened.

"Why?" she said, fear now taking up what he knew would become permanent residence on her face.

Gerald only grunted with his final dash forward and the effort of grabbing her arm by the wrist and wrenching it behind her back. With his other hand he tore the duct tape from his shirt and clamped it over her mouth.

The woman flailed ineffectively at him with her walking stick, really just a dowel of the kind you got at Home Depot, not much heavier than balsa wood. When she did connect with his hip, the stick swinging behind her, he could hardly feel it. He knew the fifty feet or so to the van was the most dangerous time. If a car went by, and if the person happened to look, they would see struggle. But she was small, and weaker than he thought when he saw her lifting the rock. The most she could do was drag her feet, which she did mightily. Gerald punched at the back of her knees with his own to buckle her, and that made the rest of the way go faster.

One more sharp knee to her backside and into the van she went, messing up the shower curtain. He could tell she noticed the dried blood underneath it. The duct tape kept her from screaming as she tried to get very small against the back wall. That gave Gerald a moment to close the doors to the van, to get her secured before taking them both to his place near San Manuel, about a forty-five-minute drive north.

Now that they were safe in the van, the woman cowering and so in shock she didn't realize her hands were free to pull off the tape, Gerald took a more leisurely look at her. The canvas hat had been left in the wash, and the wisps of pale hair he had spotted were falling among thick white waves almost to her shoulders. The only sound for a moment in the van was her noisy breathing. Somehow she had kept a hold on the dowel, and pointed it at Gerald, not knowing it was about as threatening as a chopstick. He held out his hand, palm up, kept his eyes on hers.

"Give me the stick. Come on, sweetheart. Give me

the stick. I'm not going to hurt you. I just wanted to come in out of the sun. Talk about rocks." Gerald puffed a laugh and grabbed at the stick, then sucked his breath back again. A sharp sting on the palm of his hand made him release the stick. He gazed in surprise at a gash that ran from the bottom of his index finger to the top of his wrist. As he watched, blood seeped up through the cut. What had caused that? His blood had no connection to what he imagined happening in the van. He struggled to put the blood in context and then saw that it wasn't just a dowel she held. It was a dowel with a blade attached to the end, a blade that formed a triangle with a razor on one side and a point at the end.

He saw the blood before he felt the real pain, and felt the pain before he felt the rage when the woman ripped the duct tape halfway off her mouth and the exposed side grimaced.

She was thinking. In the shaved moment while she watched the pain reach his consciousness, watched him process the absurdity of an attack by a woman who two minutes ago had been immobilized with fear, watched the rage flash in anticipation of his own counterattack, she was thinking.

The dried blood on the floor of the van confirmed she wasn't his first. There were bodies hidden somewhere. She was in a unique position to confirm that without the legal strictures of interrogation and defense counsel. But he was stronger than she had originally judged, and it had been a long while since she had moved in these ways. A little less strong, reaction time a little slower, she was out of practice, and the confines of the van limited her options more than she had foreseen. She should not have let him get her into the van; that was an error in judgment.

Things may have already gone too far, but no time to think about that now. For now she felt her forty years of conditioning kick into fight or . . .

That was it, fight. There was nowhere to run.

ONE

Ten days earlier . . .

I've sometimes regretted the women I've been.

There have been so many: daughter, sister, cop, tough broad, several kinds of whore, jilted lover, ideal wife, heroine, killer. I'll provide the truth of them all, inasmuch as I'm capable of telling the truth. Keeping secrets, telling lies, they require the same skill. Both become a habit, almost an addiction, that's hard to break even with the people closest to you, out of the business. For example, they say never trust a woman who tells you her age; if she can't keep that secret, she can't keep yours.

I'm fifty-nine.

When I joined the FBI there weren't many female special agents and the Bureau took advantage of that. A five-foot-three-inch natural blond with a preteen cheerleader's body comes in handy for many investigations, so they were willing to waive the height requirement. For a good chunk of my career I worked undercover, mostly acting as bait for human traffickers and sexual predators crossing state or international lines.

I did the undercover work for nine years. That's about five years longer than usual before agents burn out or lose their families. Because I never married or had children I might have done more time if it hadn't been for the accident that necessitated fusing several vertebrae. It could have been worse; you should have seen what happened to the horse.

The surgery made problematic many job requirements—leaping across rooftops . . . dodging knife thrusts . . . lap dancing. I could have taken disability but couldn't see what life would look like outside the Bureau, so the second half of my career was spent in Investigations. Then I retired.

No, that's not the whole truth. Toward the end I was having a little difficulty making decisions. Specifically, a couple of years ago I killed an unarmed perp near Turnerville, Georgia. Contrary to what you see in movies, FBI special agents seldom use deadly force. It causes the Bureau embarrassment. Look at Waco, or Ruby Ridge. As for the agents, they're not trusted so much anymore and the defense can use it against them in court, paint them as a rogue who might plant evidence or slant the facts to fit a case.

There was an investigation by our internal affairs group, the Office of Professional Responsibility, which cleared me with a decision of suicide by cop. The civil suit by the relatives of the guy I shot took longer and was more expensive. That's another thing you don't see in the movies, that the evil serial killer has a large extended family, including a sister with a limp who teaches special needs children and who testifies that her scumbag brother is the sweetest person who ever lived.

The family claimed I shot him because I was afraid he wouldn't get convicted. They lost, but it left a bad taste in everyone's mouth. By time time my career was over and they reassigned me to the field substation in Tucson, which everyone told me was a lovely place but that felt a lot like Siberia, only hot. I hated the agent in charge and lasted a little less than seventeen months before opting for retirement, which is what they were hoping for in the first place.

Now that's the whole truth. Mostly.

For a year I gave retirement my best shot. I joined a book club, but the other women started ignoring me when they found out I never read the book. I tried yoga at the advice of a therapist who said it would help my "anger issues" but was kicked out by the Bikram instructor after she wouldn't let me drink water in a humid room with a temperature of one hundred degrees. I'm the one with anger issues? Namaste, my ass.

I kept going to the gym every other day to at least stay in shape, which had always been pretty good, and absolutely necessary given the work I did. I had to be able to improvise, to be flexible. I had taken special ops training from a Navy SEAL named Baxter. That was his first name. I can't remember his last. We were very close and he was wise, for a trained killer. Whenever I picture Black Ops Baxter he's cracking crass jokes about teaching me to use my cleavage as a weapon. He's dead now, Baxter is.

Come to think of it, like the kid in that movie, I might know more dead people than live ones.

But back to my retirement: it felt like I was still undercover, temporarily posing as a Southwestern Woman of a Certain Age. If anyone asked me what I did for my work, I told them I investigated copyright infringements. That always killed the conversation because everyone has copied a video at some point.

I'm still gifted at disappearing into whatever environment I encounter, fading into the background, happy to succeed at what other women my age dread.

That's who I am, and that's what I hid from my next-door neighbors, from my beloved new husband, and sometimes from myself. No one likes a woman who knows how to kill with her bare hands.

As I said, retirement didn't work out that well except for, also at the advice of my therapist, auditing a class on Buddhism at the university. That's where I met the Perfesser. And shortly thereafter stopped seeing the therapist.

Mutual attraction was fairly immediate. During the first lecture I watched the intense Dr. Carlo DiForenza pacing back and forth in front of the class lecturing like a caged tiger who had eaten the Dalai Lama. In the middle of Carlo's review of the cyclical nature of karma, one of the girls, wearing a tube top that squeezed her out the top like toothpaste, pressed her elbows together and said, "Oh, you mean, like, 'wherever you go, there you are.'" The professor's pacing stopped and he blinked out the window without turning toward the speaker, a tiger distracted by a gnat.

"Contrary to what that bumper sticker says," I drawled, "it's not precisely true."

Carlo finally turned to the class and zeroed in on me. His grin shot to my loins. "Go on," he said.

"It's my experience that it takes about a year to catch up with yourself, so you don't have to worry as long as you keep moving."

He started blinking again. I expected I was going to be treated to a condescending retort. Then his grin returned. "Who are you?" he asked, emphasis on the "are."

14

"My name is Brigid Quinn," I answered.

"We should speak of this over dinner, Brigid Quinn."

Most of the students tittered. Tube Top only looked chagrined to have been trumped by an older woman.

"I hardly think that's appropriate in the middle of class," I said.

"What the hell," he had replied. "After this term I'm retiring." He was a lot more aggressive with me in those days. I was a lot more honest with him until I fell in love on our first date. I'll recall that date later if I'm feeling a little stronger.

Within the year, I married Carlo DiForenza and moved out of my apartment and into his house north of the city. With a view of the Catalina Mountains out the back window, the house itself had been decorated by Carlo's Dead Wife Jane in the style of my crazy aunt Josephine—that is to say, red-fringed lamp shades and faux Belgian tapestries with depictions of unicorns. The large backyard had a life-size statue of Saint Francis sitting on a bench. That was all right; I had never decorated any place I'd lived and this fit the kind of person I wanted to be like ready-made slipcovers.

The house came with a set of Pugs, which are sort of a cross between Peter Lorre and a bratwurst. The dogs were given to Carlo by Jane just before her death from cancer five years before; she figured caring for them would give his life purpose after her death. We kept intending to name them.

But the best part of the deal was Carlo.

It, the marriage I mean, all happened so fast I could hear my mother whispering one of her platitudes, "marry in haste; repent at leisure," but I knew what I wanted.

What I actually had I wasn't quite sure even now, but that meant he hardly knew me, and as I'd never known another way to live I was comfortable with that. One may say this is not the basis for a good relationship, but I'd learned my lesson: keep the violence in the past and focus on learning how to be the ideal wife. Ideal Wife was the woman I would be now.

Carlo took his time as well. He learned not to sneak up and hug me from behind and would place his palm ever so gently on my cheek so I would lean into it instead of tighten. He never tried to pry out of me the reasons for my fight-or-flight behavior, and I was certain he agreed it was best not to know. I was slowly relaxing, learning to trust him, and life was perfect except for those times in the middle of the night when I was over-whelmed by anxiety, when my heart would start to pound in habitual terror that he would leave me, that I would lose everything I had at last found.

That first year we made love, walked his Pugs, seduced each other into our favorite cuisines (him sushi, me Indian), watched movies (I discovered an appreciation for indie mind benders, he for things blowing up), and collected rocks.

I particularly liked the rock hounding. Besides being pretty, rocks don't change, and they don't die on you. My best local place for rock hounding was a quiet wash about a half mile down the hill from our house, under a bridge where Golder Ranch Road crossed it. The sum-mer monsoon season, a flooding rain that brought the desert all of its yearly eleven inches within a few short months, tumbled the rocks from the surrounding moun-tains to gather there.

On the day I'm recalling, in early August, I had walked to the wash by myself, filled my backpack with twenty pounds of anything that looked unusually colorful, and trudged back up the hill, feeling a little woozy with the hundred-degree temperature but glad for the workout.

Soon I sighted our backyard at the eastern edge of the Black Horse Ranch subdivision. We're a recent anomaly, surrounded by the real desert dwellers. People with horses. People cooking meth in their trailers. When it rained you could smell horse manure, and sometimes trailers blew up.

Does that sound critical? After spending most of my life in urban apartments I actually loved this rural area the way you love a sloppy old uncle who tells good stories from the war. I loved the smell of horse manure, and the occasional bray of a donkey coming from an unknown location when the wind is very still, and the reminiscent bark of gunfire from the direction of the Pima Pistol Club.

But like I said, what I loved most was Carlo. Tall as Lincoln with a slight Italian accent, Roman beak, mournful Al Pacino eyes, and a bad-boy smile to contradict them.

When I lugged the backpack into the kitchen and dumped the rocks in the sink to rinse them, Carlo was making hummingbird juice, mixing water and some strawberry-colored powder. Without my asking him to, he had hung the feeder on the white thorn acacia tree in the front yard where I could watch the hummingbirds from my office window.

The sight of him fixing the feeder for my pleasure made my heart . . . swell to overflowing is supposed to be a worn-out phrase, but for me it's a brand-new feeling.

This may seem an unusually strong reaction to a man filling a bird feeder. If you have led a relatively peaceful life you will not appreciate its value and treasure it the way I do, not understand what it feels like to go day after day with that vibration in your chest, as if you carried inside of you a violin string that has just been plucked but now the string is silent and still because the threat of violence is long past.

Now I was living in peace with a man so gentle and sensitive he gave sup to hummingbirds. Does this seem precious? I don't give a rat's ass.

"What do you have to give me?" he asked, pouring the juice through a funnel into the clear plastic container. His low voice and the glint in his eye made the question a double entendre.

"Just some pretty rocks, Perfesser. You'll have to tell me what I have."

I turned to the sink where I'd dumped the stones, rinsed them off one by one, and placed them still wet on the dark granite counter for Carlo's examination.

The rinsing heightened the vivid colors, smooth blood red, vanilla ice cream, round and speckled green like a dinosaur egg, silver shot with black specks. We opened the color atlas of minerals in the southwestern United States to see what we had.

Carlo was no more a geologist than I was. Rather, before becoming a philosophy professor, and before marrying Jane, he'd done time as a Roman Catholic priest. Father Dr. Carlo DiForenza could explain either linguistic philosophy or comparative religion so simply a learning-disabled bivalve could understand.

Carlo and I sat side by side on the stools by the breakfast counter where he leaned his gaunt frame over the stones like a giraffe protecting her young. His thin fingers tickled the rocks as he admired each one individually.

"Pudding stone," Carlo said, pointing out the picture in the book. "See the quartz plugging it? I can imagine the megasurge of heat that boiled the granite into a juice that mixed all these elements together. Then a plunge of temperature that hardened the elements into a single mass with each mineral distinct. Gorgeous, Brigid. Oh, and you found some more shot with copper."

I squirmed a bit and leaned closer. Plugging, megasurge, plunge, juice, shot—is it just me, or did Carlo talk dirty about a billion years of geologic activity as if they were one hot night of sex? Plus I got a kick out of watching him stroke the rocks.

The geo-erotica started working on us both. We went from stroking the rocks to stroking each other's fingers stroking the rocks, and I made a lame joke about getting our rocks off and then I started licking his fingers and then Carlo started murmuring Bella, Bella, which is what he calls me when he's feeling romantic and I didn't care if he used that so he wouldn't accidentally call me Jane because I knew in my heart that this time Bella meant me. That's how it goes when you have a lot of life behind you, no self-delusion.

He didn't mind that I hadn't showered yet. We slipped off the stools onto one of Jane's faux Persian rugs. Turkish. Oriental. Whatever. And kissed. But the Pugs stared, and lovemaking on the floor didn't have quite the charm it once had. We moved into the bedroom and tossed aside

Jane's pink satin comforter with the blue trim.

The sex was spectacular, but don't worry about my going into details of the act. You may be younger than I, and won't like to think about someone outside your generation making love. For you the image may be embarrassing, vulgar, or comic.

Carlo and I were none of those.

While he dozed afterward, as always, in grateful lust I thanked him silently, from the center of my soul, for letting me live in his normal world. For giving me this new self, different from the one defined by any of the other women I had been.

But gratitude for the present invariably came with memories of the past where I'd learned my lessons. One of the things I brooded about: Paul, gentle, widowed Paul of the cello and the truffle oil, of the two cherubic preschoolers, Paul repulsed by me despite his best efforts. As gently as he could even though he thought I couldn't be hurt, *See, Brigid? You stare into the abyss of depravity, and sooner or later it begins to stare back. The abyss is where you've lived for so long you'll never escape it. I fear it too much to live there with you. I can't expose my children to you.*

I was still terrified to think I might destroy my relationship with Carlo the way I had destroyed my relationship with Paul and determined that I would do nothing to make that happen.

Paul was the last man I tried to be honest with, twenty-two years ago. I still wonder what made me leave that crime scene photo on the kitchen counter. I didn't expect the children would find it.

TWO

Paul was right, your past doesn't die. Hell, it doesn't even wrinkle.

About a week after the rock-sex episode, I'm sunk into the overstuffed cushions of Jane's shiny brown brocade couch, sipping coffee from a Grand Canyon souvenir mug from one of their vacations while pondering how hard it could be to bake something, a pastry or something. As I paged through one of Jane's cookbooks her scent wafted up at me, honey and flour, and I wondered whether she would approve of me. Not for the first time I resisted the urge to just once go to my e-mail, key in *Jane@otherworld.com,* and ask her.

The doorbell interrupted my thoughts with "Eine Kleine Nachtmusik" and I cringed. I hate music, but I couldn't figure out how to reprogram the doorbell.

I found Max Coyote on my front porch. Deputy Sheriff Coyote was half Pascua Yaqui tribe and half Columbia University anthropologist on his mother's side. He and I worked a few cases together when I was still with the Bureau. Unlike many in law enforcement, he didn't think FBI agents were total assholes and was part of the reason I stayed out here. We had become friends of a kind; I'd even told him about Paul over one too many Crown Royals, but this would not be an invitation to dinner.

The Pugs frisked and barked. "Hey guys, it's just your uncle Max," I said as I opened the screen door.

"Carlo home?" he asked, walking in and looking around comfortably, the way you do when you know people well enough that it's okay to be nosy.

"He's checking the price of gin at Walgreens. You here for poker or philosophy?"

Max and Carlo had met at a house party and hit it off, maybe were better friends even than Max and me. They would get together once a month and teach each other what they knew about Bertrand Russell and Texas Hold'em. Max was quite good at complex thought. Carlo kept losing his shirt.

Max didn't answer right away, pausing instead to stoop and rub each grateful Pug between its bulgy eyes with his thumb before he moved aside one of the too-shiny purple pillows that lined the back of the couch and settled down. He had been at the house enough so that he no longer made fun of Jane's peacock feathers in the oriental vase, but he did pick up the cookbook I'd been looking at and sniffed the stain on the bread pudding recipe.

"How's the cooking coming along?" he asked.

"I'm still discouraged by ingredients like crème fraîche," I said, taking the book from him and thwumping it shut. I put the cookbook on the coffee table but something about him made me stay standing. "Why are you stalling?"

He sighed, looked mournful, but that was his default expression so I wasn't too concerned yet.

Not too. Having lived in a world where the news was usually bad, I asked, "Why do you want to know where Carlo is?"

22

Now focused like a man on a mission, he again ignored the question. He put a hand on each of the Pugs that flanked him. I had the odd sense he was prepared to use them for cover if I threw something at him. "We have a serial killer in custody," he said.

I'd been in the business so long those words could still send a pleasant little reverb up the back of my skull. "Good job. Who?"

He spoke cautiously, like an actor still learning his lines. "Long-haul trucker, name Floyd Lynch. Border Patrol picked him up a couple weeks ago about seventy miles north of the border on Route 19, heading to Las Vegas with a load of video-poker machines. Routine stop, but there happened to be a cadaver dog at the checkpoint who alerted to a dead woman in his truck."

"In the trailer?"

"No, the trailer with the poker machines was clean. The body was in his cab. Both the sheriff's department and the FBI got called to the scene."

"They ID the woman?"

"Not yet. The trucker says she was an illegal."

They use dogs to locate aliens who don't make it across the desert. My mind was rushing about trying to figure why he was here telling me this while I let him take his usual time. I said, "Now I'm remembering. I think I saw this on the news. It died fast."

"The FBI kind of made that happen."

"But that was two weeks ago."

"The FBI took over the interrogation."

"Priors?"

"None. He never got so much as a traffic ticket."

"You want a Diet Coke?" I walked across the expanse of

open room to the kitchen area and pulled two cans out of the fridge without waiting for his answer, talking as I did so. "I assume you're here because the victim has some connection to me."

He paused, and then didn't answer my question. "You couldn't tell much from the victim. The body was mummified."

"Curiouser and curiouser. Smell much?"

"No."

I nodded, making a mental note to get more celery before I closed the refrigerator door. "Did he confess to killing her?"

"Not at first. He said he had found the body just off the side of the road, that it had been dressed in shabby clothing, the shoes already stolen, an illegal alien who hadn't made it across the desert. He said he was just using it."

"Using it. Nasty." None of this explained why Max took this long to tell me, let alone why he was telling me at all. This should have been maybe a phone call in a bored moment, not a special visit. A nerve sparked on the side of my neck. I handed one of the Cokes to Max and popped open my own, but still couldn't bring myself to sit down. "So far this isn't a serial killer case, Max. You've got one victim and he denies killing her." I didn't have to tell Max that would only amount to a class 4 felony, desecration of a c+orpse. A little jail time. "Not to be all self-absorbed, Max, but what the hell does this have to do with me?" I sipped from the can.

"When the techs went over the truck they found a compartment with scrapbooks and journals." Here Max measured out his words more carefully than he had before, if that was possible. "And postcards."

Some soda splashed on Jane's rug when my hand jerked. "Were they addressed?" I asked.

He shook his head. I shrugged. "Lots of people buy postcards. Even truckers."

He took a deep breath and said, "The journals were all about the Route 66 murders."

Route 66, the biggest sexual homicide case in my career, and the case I had failed to close. The case where I lost a young agent who became the killer's last-known victim. She was the only victim who was never found. I didn't want to ask the obvious question, the one I'd wanted an answer to for seven years. So instead I said, "A groupie. This, this what's his name?"

"Floyd Lynch."

"He could be a groupie." Even serial killers have fans. It's celebrity reality at its most debased.

"The journals really seemed to implicate him. He knew a lot, names of the victims."

"That was in the news."

"The writing was all, 'I slashed her Achilles tendon so she couldn't run, I raped her, I strangled her slowly and felt the bone in her throat give way'—"

"That was all in the news, too. He could have been fantasizing, making it his own."

"—'I sliced off her right ear.'"

That blasted the story I was making up. No one but law enforcement knew what the killer's trophy had been. No one had ever found any of the ears. "We withheld that," I admitted.

"That's what they tell me." Increasingly nervous, Max shifted on the couch and cleared his throat. His voice went soft and gentle to calm me. I hate it when people do that. It's never a good sign. "Then, Brigid, when the techs told George Manriquez, the ME—"

"I know the medical examiner."

"—about the journals he got the facts of the case and put them together with his examination of the body found in the truck. Despite the mummification he had detected a crushed hyoid bone, slashed Achilles tendon, missing right ear. It was all there, the whole MO."

"The mummy on the truck," I said.

Max nodded. "Just like the Route 66 victims."

Unable to come up with any other explanation, I finally asked the question, my heart pounding in anticipation of the answer. "Is it her? Is the mummy on the truck her, Max?"

His answer was both relief and disappointment. "No. It's not Jessica Robertson's body. At least according to Lynch."

"Oh," I breathed, a very small, empty nothing of an oh. So close to finding her after all this time, and yet she wasn't there. I fumbled my way to the recliner that faced the couch, and folded into it when my knees gave way.

And then he added more hurriedly than before, "But he says he can take us to her."

Even with this information I didn't trust what I was hearing. "Just like that, he confessed?"

"They had him boxed in and offered life."

"The fucker made a deal." The violin string I hadn't felt in a long time vibrated in my chest, and I felt my ire rise. "Where is she?" I was ready to grab my bag.

"Allegedly, in an abandoned car. Off the old back road to Mount Lemmon."

"Has anyone informed her father yet?"

Who knows how they all thought I'd react? His mission accomplished and observing my failure to freak, Max relaxed his spine and let himself get sucked a little into the overstuffed couch. "Don't worry. We're waiting for verification before we do that, but it was time to let you know. Your involvement in the case, I mean. I spoke with the special agent on the case, you know Laura Coleman?"

"I met her while I was doing time in the Tucson office. I thought she worked fraud."

"She switched to homicide after you left. She thought we should tell you and bring David Weiss in."

"David Weiss knows already?"

My tone must have gotten its edge back then, and Max struggled to extract himself from the back cushions, sit up a little straighter, and return to his soothing voice. "Yes. Since he was the profiler on the case he's flying in tonight to do a competency test so we can make sure we've got all the ends tied up for life without parole."

"I want to come to the dump site," I said.

But before Max could respond, I heard the garage door go up and the Pugs both whisked off the couch to greet their master. Carlo's deep voice of all things normal preceded him into the kitchen area. "Honey, the Tanqueray was ten dollars more than at Sam's Club so I just got a few other things, Breath Busters for the dogs and a salami." He stopped at the sight of Max and me staring back at him as if we'd been caught trying to hide something, which in a way we were.

"Walgreens sells salamis?" I asked.

"Hello, Max," Carlo said.

"Hey, Carlo."

"Is something wrong?" Carlo asked.

Max opened his mouth to speak but I got there first, shifted to normal for Carlo's sake. It was a knee-jerk reaction.

"Everything's fine, honey. Max was just saying he needs a poker and philosophy session."

THREE

The death toll on the day I talked to Max was officially six, if you didn't count the new mummy found on the truck. There were five murders before Jessica, all girls from the ages of eighteen to twenty-three, their naked bodies left in degrading positions along or off State Road 40, what used to be called Route 66. A lot of travelers wanted to get their kicks hitchhiking the famous route from Chicago to LA, kind of like the Appalachian Trail, only paved. The girls who were killed over the course of five years never won their bragging rights.

The killer operated between Amarillo, Texas, and Flagstaff, Arizona, and only killed one girl every summer. It was how he spent his summer vacation.

You could tell the same guy murdered all five girls because his MO was very distinctive. Slash their Achilles tendon to prevent their escape, rape them (condom, no DNA), strangle them slowly, and remove their right ear postmortem, as a souvenir that would help him relive the event later. Then dump the body on a different road on a different night for us to find, sometimes a few miles from the supposed pickup spot, sometimes as much as a hundred miles away. We kept some of this from the media so we'd know a copycat or a false confession, someone who wanted to atone for another sin or get the fame without the wet work. There had been a few of those, but while they knew some of the details, they didn't know all. That was why I asked Max all the questions about Lynch. No one had ever before told us about the ears.

The car the killer used each time was always rented under a different name and abandoned somewhere distant from the body. When the car was found you could tell it was the primary crime scene from the blood on the floor of the passenger seat, where he slashed the victim's tendon, and in the backseat, where he raped her and sliced off her ear.

It became an obsession with me, these killings, as most serial cases do. After the second murder I had a hard time thinking about anything else all year, and as each summer approached I would look forward to the next hunt with an equal mixture of fear that another victim would be claimed and hope that the killer would be caught.

You can talk all you want about professional detachment. But you never really know obsession until it's one of your own that gets taken. You never really experience death until it's someone you know.

On top of the bad back that put me out of commission for the undercover game, I was now too old to make a convincing hitchhiker. But Jessica, fresh out of the academy, small like me, could pass for a fourteen-year-old runaway. I trained her myself. Weiss and I trained her. Between us she learned both how to tell a scumbag and defend herself against one. That summer I convinced myself she was ready to play with the bad dogs. Or was she? Did I just want to catch that guy too much?

*

Absurdly, the next morning I found myself putting on lipstick.

I had told Carlo I was just going along for a ride at Max's invitation. So when three very official vehicles stopped in front of the house to pick me up at six thirty, Carlo looked understandably speculative. I picked up my hiking stick and regulation southwestern tote bag, big enough to smuggle a Mexican but more often used to carry a couple bottles of water, gave Carlo a public peck, and headed down the drive to meet them.

A tallish gal in the dark standard-issue FBI suit despite the already-scorching heat got out of the passenger side of the middle car like a praying mantis unfolding, introduced herself with a firm handshake and the kind of intense gaze that makes you suspect there's something you still don't know.

"I'm the case agent, Laura Coleman," she said. "I'm so pleased to see you again, Agent Quinn." It was nice that she called me Agent Quinn even though I'd been decommissioned. As an additional gesture of respect or seeing I had the stick for going over the rough terrain, she opened the back door for me. Maybe because I'd chosen cargo khakis and a short-sleeved cotton blouse for the outing and because the temperature was already hovering in the nineties, she relented and took off her jacket before getting back in.

The vehicle behind us was a crime scene van. The vehicle ahead of ours carried Floyd Lynch. I know I shouldn't have, but before I got into the jeep I walked up to the vehicle in front where a U.S. marshal sat in the driver's seat. The passenger seat window came down, a hand came out.

"Royal Hughes, the public defender," he said.

"I guessed. Brigid Quinn."

Hughes flashed satisfied teeth in a metrosexual smile, toned down some for the occasion. "I know," he said.

What a cutie.

In the back, behind a security screen, cuffed and wearing his orange jail garb, was Floyd Lynch. Slim but saggy body, curly brown hair, a ski nose, and little Bolshevik glasses. Late thirties, but hard-lived. More like an accountant than a serial killer, but that's what they always say, don't they? Except for those reptilian, affectless eyes that no amount of boyish charm can disguise if you know what to look for. He looked at me looking at him through the window as if he were a snake in a zoo, as curious about me as I about him. Then his mouth made a little self-effacing grimace and his head bobbed at me before he looked away. I was tempted to tap on the glass but sensed the two men in the front seat getting a little edgy at my nearness so I refrained.

At that point I knew he had killed seven women altogether, including the one found in his truck. He had tortured and raped them and gazed into their eyes, letting them hope for life while he strangled them slowly, and now he was going to show us the last crime scene. Because of that small act, his taking us to the body dump site, there would be no fair retribution for all the pain he had caused the victims and those who loved them. Jessica Robertson was going to be used as his ticket out of the death penalty. The life she lost, this scumbag gained in trade; she would have hated that, and so did I.

I wanted Floyd Lynch dead six times, and slow, and painful, but this trip was going to ensure the son of a bitch got a life sentence instead, and you could see he thought that was a fine deal. I imagined myself putting my pistol up to the window and watching the glass embed itself into his face with the bullet. I imagine things a lot. The fantasy temporarily eased my impotent rage at the injustice of our legal system.

Max stuck his head out of the driver's side of the jeep, gestured at the open back door. "Come on, Brigid, the AC is getting out."

I got in and there in the backseat beside me was Sigmund (aka Dr. David Weiss). We looked at each other. I don't know what he saw, but over the last five years since I'd left the Washington Bureau the man had gotten a little old. Beard shot with gray, and his ears could have used a trim. His chest had become his belly and he needed to give in to a larger shirt size. He represented the best and worst of my time in the Bureau, all my nightmares, and the closest thing to a friend.

Emotions in a jumble over what we would see this day, I wanted to hug him till the juice ran. But the circumstances and present company didn't call for it, so instead I buckled my seat belt while I said, cool and soft, "So nice to see you again, Sig."

His eyes twinkled from a million light-years away, in that way that always made me think he was an extraterrestrial who found us all damn charming. I could tell he understood what I was feeling, but he was careful to express no sympathy or affection, knowing it was the only thing I couldn't take.

"Hello, Stinger," he said, and the mere use of our nicknames for each other made me look away and then lean toward the front seat.

"No Three-Piece?" I asked Max.

"No cameras," Max replied.

The Tucson Bureau Special Agent in Charge Roger Morrison was named Three-Piece after his persistence in wearing a vest with his suits well into the nineties, not having gotten the memo that they went out with shoulder pads. Max's "no cameras" comment referred to the man's well-known ability to smell celluloid and only show up whenever the news crew did.

I was sitting behind Coleman, so I couldn't see if she reacted to the jibes tossed back and forth about her boss. Max put the car in gear and our macabre little caravan headed toward the Samaniego Ridge of the Catalina Mountains.

FOUR

From where we live, it's an hour-and-a-half drive up to the summit of Mount Lemmon if you go the nice paved route on the south side. Our destination on the old back road approaching from the north, with bumps connected by ruts, takes longer. As we headed up Route 79 to get around the Samaniego Ridge on the way there, Coleman was quiet. I didn't get sullen vibes, just tense and brittle. Sigmund was quiet, too, but more comfortably so, looking out the window at the harsh beauty of the high desert. I named what I could, mesquite and prickly pear, barrel cactus crowned with hot-pink flowers as big as your fist, green-leafed ocotillo sporting red coach-whip blossoms, and white-capped saguaros. I didn't know the names of all these things a year ago—Carlo got me an Arizona field guide and binoculars for my last birthday.

I tried to make a little small talk with Max and Laura Coleman, not very successfully, then steered the conversation in the direction of the crime scene, which is where we all wanted to be anyway. "So have you ever seen this car Lynch is talking about? How did it get there?" I asked Max.

Unlike most of us, Max is not a transplant. "It was kind of a rite of passage when I was in high school, to go up here at night. No one knew when or how it was abandoned. Seems it crashed off the side of the road and slid about thirty feet into the arroyo without rolling over. The driver was never found. We sat around it telling ghost stories about the driver coming to take his car back, drinking beer, smoking a little dope. That's all I know."

"And nobody ever looked inside?" I asked.

"Sure we did. Sat inside, too. But that was over twenty years ago. Kids stopped going, got more interested in computer games. Easy to imagine nobody looking in that car in the past fifteen years."

"Who was the owner of record?"

"I can't remember his name, not an Arizona man, and, like I said, they never found him alive or dead. It's a local mystery."

That's when the road got bumpy. Coleman tried to say something about Floyd Lynch but had to stop for fear of biting her tongue. I wished I'd peed once more before leaving the house.

We were all pretty much silent as we bounced our way up the mountain, where the climate grew more temperate and offered pine trees instead of the drought-hardy vegetation in the valley.

About two-thirds of the way to the summit, Coleman pointed to the car ahead and said Lynch was lifting up his cuffed hands, gesturing. Within another second or two we had all pulled into a line on the narrow shoulder of the right side of the road.

The crime scene techs behind us were all efficiency, getting some small pieces of equipment and two body bags out of the van, along with slings to bring them up from the arroyo into which the rest of us looked as we waited. Lynch was explaining to Coleman the configuration of a saguaro with eight long arms jutting in all directions and a rocky outcropping that helped him locate the spot.

Max introduced me and Sigmund to U.S. Marshal Axel Phillips, all boots and a big gun. Phillips responded politely but without offering to shake our hands. You could tell he kept his attention on Lynch, doing his job. When the techs came up to us with their equipment, I recognized an older one I had seen before on a case, Benny Cassell, and a younger one guided by Benny, introduced as Ray Something. I had a hard time focusing on anyone but Lynch, but I could tell Sigmund kept his eye on me.

The way down into the arroyo was steep and I was glad I brought my stick, which enabled me to gently shrug off Max's offer of a hand down when I slipped on a pebble. Lynch asked if the marshal would undo his cuffs but was refused, while Phillips angled his shotgun just a little more conveniently to kill his man if he had to while keeping a precarious balance. I hoped he had his safety on.

Max went first, followed by Floyd Lynch, his elbows jutting out for balance, followed by Phillips. Those three chose the way down, followed by Benny and Ray, followed by me and Coleman, all in more or less single file. Sigmund brought up the rear as if he wanted to watch all of us at once. One by one we stopped at the bottom to find a car that must have gone off the road at least three decades ago. Phillips echoed Max, said he'd known about the car, everyone who grew up in the area and had traveled this way more than once had, but probably no one had been around to look inside for a long time.

"I remember the place being filthy with all the trash we left behind," Phillips said. "Looks like it's been cleaned up."

I looked at the car, recognized it as a Dodge Dart from the seventies with the paint long removed by sandstorms and sun. I kept repeating to myself, it's evidence, it's only evidence, while another part of my mind whispered all these years you've been looking for her this is where she's been.

Even close up, through the filter of the dust covering the windows, you couldn't see much. Benny removed a digital camera from his equipment bag and took shots from every angle. Then he and Ray donned latex gloves and, given a nod from Coleman, tried to open the driver's-side door.

Lynch pointed with one hand, which, cuffed, drew the other up like marionette's arms connected by a single string. "She's—"

"Let the men do their work," Coleman said.

The door creaked open a couple inches, then stuck. Ordered around by Benny, and cursing under his breath, Ray scrambled quickly back up to the van and returned with a can of WD-40 while the rest of us waited, feeling useless.

Ray sprayed the hinge through the gap, worked the door some, sprayed it some more. With a groan the door of the long-closed-up vehicle finally opened all the way. I could feel us all brace, but if we were expecting that overpowering smell of putrefaction, there was none. Instead, it smelled like grandma's housecoat folded away unwashed after her death. Not unpleasant, just distinctly human.

The front seat, the old kind from before bucket seats where the bench extended unbroken by the gear shift jutting out from the steering column, was largely filled with what looked like dry garbage. Old crumpled newspapers, rags, quite a few beer cans that added another aroma to the scene. Benny snapped more photos.

"Now we know where all the trash went," Max said.

Benny and Ray pulled garbage bags out of their pockets and, while the rest of us waited, silently removed the trash out of the car with a care approaching that of archaeologists on a dig. Ray moved to the other side, slipping a bit down the steeper slope on which the car leaned and, with a little more effort, popped open the passenger door as well to get to that side more easily.

While they worked Lynch stayed silent and apart, breathing only lightly, yet tensed, the way you expect a jack-in-the-box to look coiled in the dark while the music is still playing. His eyes drifted around the group without moving his head as if he didn't want us to know he was looking. I watched his gaze come to rest on Sigmund, maybe wondering who he was and what he was doing here. Sigmund stared back at him, as he would at something smeared on a slide, before turning his attention back to the car.

After a while Lynch lifted his cuffed hands to his face and stroked it with his nails going up and his fingertips going down. It must have been a habit; his cheek was slightly scabby with all the stroking. He was unable to stay silent.

"I threw the trash in there so if some hikers came by and tried to look in, you couldn't see," Lynch said. He spoke in a careful monotone, but with an underlying current, an excited man trying to appear calm.

When the trash on the front seat was nearly clear, I could see first a couple of planks that entered my consciousness as big logs of beef jerky and then morphed into naked legs. The whole body was naked and brown like that, dark leather curled up like a monster fetus. Benny looked at me, and then at Max, who nodded. Benny took photos of the body.

I couldn't find my voice to ask before Max did. "That's her," he said.

"No." Lynch had started breathing faster, out of sync with the rest of us who were holding ours. He stopped stroking his face. "I tried to tell you." With the same flat tone as he had spoken about trash, no more no less, "That's just the lot lizard. It's been there a lot longer."

I hadn't meant to speak to Lynch except through Coleman or Hughes, his lawyer, but seeing this other body that Lynch referred to as a lot lizard, a prostitute who hangs out at truck stops, this surprised me. "You mean you killed another woman and hid the body rather than posing it?"

"Yeah, the first time," he said.

"When?" I asked.

He paused. "Just before the second one," he said, with no apparent sarcasm.

Coleman said to me, "You didn't know?"

I shook my head. "How could I?"

"Sorry, you're right. It only came out in the interrogation. I should have mentioned on the way here."

"Eight victims, then," I said. "Eight including the one on his truck."

Lynch nodded, "You want the one in the back."

40

Benny pushed the seat forward on hinges that had suffered from a fine dust that could get in anywhere, even a closed-up car. But he managed to expose the backseat, with trash like in the front. This was cleared as well, and, as if by prior agreement, trying not to appear all dramatic about it, the others stepped back to let me have the first look.

At first glimpse the pain that I thought had finally eased up hit me in my gut, forcing me to bend and brace my hands on my knees, looking down until the blood came back to my head. Then I toughed up, because nobody, not Lynch not nobody, was going to see me react. It's only evidence, I thought again, pretending I was bent over so I could better peer into the dusky interior of the Dodge.

She, her body, that is, was naked like the one in the front. The flesh was rippled in some places, shiny at the tops and dull in the valleys. Instead of being carefully curled up she seemed to have been thrown more casually onto her back, her knees pushed up to get the door shut and her upper torso at an uncomfortable angle against the other door. The head was nearly detached from the rest of the body from the lack of support as the corpse aged.

After Benny did his thing one more time with the camera I got a flashlight from him and shined its light on the face. The lips had lost their plumpness, making the teeth more prominent in the slightly open mouth. The lids had receded from the eyes, which were as dull as the surrounding flesh, like a clay statue. It didn't much look like Jessica, it hardly looked human, but I wished I had something to cover her with just the same.

The hair was dark straw, but not so long that you couldn't see one of the ears was missing. That made me shine the flashlight at her ankles, and confirmed that at least one had been slashed at the back, at the Achilles tendon.

"This is a Route 66 victim," I said.

"Can you tell it's Jessica Robertson?" Coleman asked.

"It's Jessica Robertson, all right," Lynch said. All attention turned to him again and you could tell he liked it that way.

Again I spoke directly to Lynch. "Did you know this woman was an FBI agent?" That was another thing we kept from the media.

Coleman started, "He said he knew, Agent Quinn, she told—"

"She said so; she thought I'd let her go because of that," Lynch interrupted, and he seemed for a moment to become a little more animated, shuffling his feet as if this would help him keep the floor. "This is what I get life for, bringing you out here. That's what you call quid pro quo."

Royal Hughes, the PD, pressed his lips together and turned his head, trying not to show his distaste. "It's probably better if—"

I thought of this shmuck who had taken eight lives and thereby ruined those of everyone who loved them, while his only concern was escaping the consequences of his homicidal lust. "Quid pro quo," I moved my lips and tongue slowly as if the words took up more space in my mouth than words usually do. "Do you know what that means?"

Lynch said, "It means I show you the bodies and I get life."

"And where did you get that phrase, Floyd? It sounds vaguely like something I heard," I snapped my fingers a couple times as if I was trying to remember, "in a movie once."

"*Silence of the Lambs,*" he offered eagerly.

"That's right!" My voice dipped near a whisper. "Because you sound like Hannibal Lecter talking to Clarice Starling. Do you think you're Anthony Hopkins?" I pointed to Coleman. "Do you think this is fuckin' Jodie Foster and we're making a movie here?" In retrospect I guess my voice might have started to grate. I guess maybe I looked like this is what they'd been waiting for, like I was going to go for him because Benny and Ray got still, Phillips looked edgier than before and glanced at Max, and Sigmund put his hand on my shoulder but removed it quickly when he felt the response of the muscle underneath.

Royal Hughes clenched his abs and raised his palms like he was doing push-ups against the air. "It might be . . ." I could tell he pursed his lips to say "wise" but changed his mind, ". . . better if you didn't speak to him."

It wasn't Hughes's words but the thought of Sigmund's touch that grounded me again and I focused instead on keeping my head from trembling after the sudden adrenaline burst. Jessica deserved better than pissed-off grandstanding.

Even Lynch had quailed at my reaction, and he was under armed guard who now looked ready to turn his weapon on me. "I'm just saying," Lynch said, then shut himself off again and concentrated on gnawing a small wart on the back of his left hand.

"I think you should stay quiet now, Floyd," Coleman said.

He nodded.

I wasn't conscious of it at the time, but in retrospect I remembered that was the moment when something felt wrong. Then the moment moved on.

Coleman took me a few steps away as if to speak privately, though I knew it was partly to remove me farther from Lynch's vicinity. "He does that a lot, quoting from movies and books," she said. "The books in his truck had things underlined that he used in his interrogation." Then, "Can you tell it's her?" She asked me again.

I studied the face again. "Enough to testify," I said. "But the ME has the dental records already, I assume?"

"You assume correctly, Agent Quinn. Do you want to be there for the autopsy?" she asked.

"I should, preliminary tests should be ready, what, tomorrow afternoon?"

Coleman nodded, her voice level to a fault, professional. "I'll make sure they work on it tonight. Let's say three unless I call you."

"Okay, I'll be there. I know it's not protocol but I think it's best if I notify NOK."

Coleman nodded again. NOK, next of kin. My relationships with some of them were known in the Bureau because most agents avoided them, passing them off instead to professional victim's advocates, passing out cards of therapists. When a case wasn't closed, I remained the advocate for the victim.

Benny and Ray put plastic bags on all four hands. Lynch asked why they did that. The techs didn't respond.

"In case there's any tissue or blood under the nails," Hughes told him.

"Ouch," Lynch said, but it wasn't at the memory of Jessica having scratched him. He lifted the hand with the wart. There was blood on it. Careful not to make contact, Hughes handed him a Kleenex as if he was used to this happening.

The techs first lifted the body from the front seat, inadvertently detaching the head in the process and leaving behind a layer of skin that had stuck to the upholstery. Some of the trash adhered to the body.

"It's been there a long time," Coleman explained, glancing away. "Floyd told me thirteen years. She was twenty-three and he was twenty-five when he killed her."

"Is that in his journals?"

"No, he told me. He only started keeping a record with the next victim, the one we think of as the first Route 66 kill."

I dipped my head at the body being placed in a black bag. "Does he at least know this victim's name?"

"He says no."

I turned and looked out across the arroyos that became a canyon leading into the heart of the mountain. I looked away not because I couldn't take watching Benny and Ray delicately sorting the pieces and loading them into separate body bags and hoisting them up the side of the hill. I was wondering what was going to be worse, this or calling Jessica's father.

FIVE

The rest of the group started up the hill in pretty much the same order they'd come down it, but Sigmund gave me a look and bent over to pick up a piece of trash the techs had left behind. "Sloppy," he said. He straightened and handed it to me like a memento of the occasion, then tucked my hand in his arm, pretending to help me over the uneven ground and up the steep slope of the hill. "Ah Stinger, a sad triumph it is," he said, as we slowly started after the others. The sound of his voice comforted me, but I didn't feel a need to respond.

Then, "That Agent Coleman is one smart cookie," he said, when we were lagging far enough behind so no one could hear our conversation.

We had worked so long together, him in profiling and me in undercover, that in the past it had always been the Sig and Stinger show. I felt a twinge of jealousy. Silly.

"How can you tell?" I asked.

"She was trying to interview me all the way from my hotel to your place. All about if I knew of any other case where a serial killer had switched his modus operandi from rape and strangulation to necrophilia." Sigmund never said MO like the rest of us. I think he may be too proud for acronyms.

"What did you tell her?" I asked.

"That it was new to me, but that there was that other case where the killer went from simple execution-style killings with a .22 to mutilation with a knife and drinking his victim's blood. She said she was familiar with that case. She asked, too, about my theories regarding trophies and souvenirs, that sort of thing. She had done her homework, and wanted my opinion of Floyd Lynch."

"Did you give it?"

"You know I detest professionals who give an opinion without ever talking to the alleged perpetrator. In addition to that, in my case I have to be cautious because there's bias, being so familiar with one of the victims."

One of the victims. I wanted to say that detachment was all well and good, but we were talking about Jessica here, not some generic victim, and it hurt not to say so. But agents didn't talk about their feelings like that, even me and Sig. If he knew what I was thinking he didn't let on but continued seamlessly, "I told Coleman I would not comment at all until after the full battery of competency tests and then only in a written report."

"And how did she react?"

"She tried to disguise it, but she was frustrated. She seems ambitious. Wanted to move faster. She reminded me of you."

There was that twinge again. "Is that why she was a little stick-up-the-ass in the car?"

"Possibly. And perhaps we both intimidate her a little, too. We *are* respected and famous, aren't we?"

"Absolutely, in a washed-up kind of way. So what *do* you think? Is he sane?"

Sigmund pulled his glasses down and twinkled at me over the rims, declining to answer.

"If you want my opinion, I think he's skeevy in spades," I said.

He gave in with a nod. "An abomination of all things human. Yet for a sexual sadist, lacking in that certain psychopathic je ne sais quoi?"

Only Sigmund could dig me out of the pit and lighten me up a little even at a time like this. "Yeah, that," I admitted.

"I picked up on it, too. And yet remember Harry Winthrop?"

"A real twerp. It was hard to imagine him cutting off male organs and sewing them to female torsos." But I wasn't in the mood for reminiscing. "Come on, I won't tell anyone what you tell me, what does your gut say?"

"My gut, as you call it, is conflicted. He's different from the man I expected to find. And yet it's all there, the body on his truck killed in the same fashion as those of the Route 66 murders, the journals, the confession, knowing where the body is. I might have entertained the possibility of a copy cat, but he did know where the body was. If the dental records match, we'll even be sure that, of the two bodies in the car, he identified Jessica's body correctly. It's cut-and-dried."

"Open and shut. How's Greta?" I asked, changing the subject in that kind of mental leap that only friends are capable of.

"She divorced me shortly after you left."

"What the fuck?"

"She said I was too introverted to feel strongly. While I never met her therapist I would suppose those were his words she was quoting."

Bullshit. Anyone who knew Sigmund, who knew what

he had been through during his time crawling around in the muck and stench of killers' minds, knew that he had done all the feeling there was and he was just all felt out.

"How about you, have you married well?" he asked because he knew it would be the next line in small talk.

"Gosh yes." I smiled and felt my face go warmer at the mention of him. "I'm crazy about Carlo."

"Gosh? That is linguistically uncharacteristic of you." He glanced at my face. "As is blushing."

"Stop profiling me," I said, but couldn't help but explain, "The man used to be a priest and I'm working at cleaning up my language."

He shook his head in disbelief as if this revelation was more bizarre than any encountered in his career. "Stinger Quinn, going Stepford."

"The name is DiForenza now," I said, sounding as smug as I felt.

We approached the lip of the hill where the cars were parked, and, once begun, I hated to stop talking with my old buddy. I asked him over for dinner, said I'd take him back to his hotel after.

Even as I said it I thought about how with Sigmund, Carlo, and me, it could only be half a conversation, nobody saying what was really on their mind. At the time I thought I had divided my lives that successfully. I hoped he would say no. Sigmund knew that, too, and like a typical man didn't try to make excuses for it.

"No," he said.

"Are you coming to the ME's tomorrow?"

"No again. I'll visit Morrison because I haven't spoken with him yet and I should have followed protocol, but Agent Coleman wanted me to be here this morning."

"Was she worried I'd go all ten-eight on Lynch?"

"Of course not. We all knew you would maintain admirable restraint." He lowered his voice as we got closer to the others. "Agent Coleman, on the other hand, could use a trifle more restraint. They might have ended it, but at some point I feel confident she and Hughes have had sexual relations. They're trying so hard to not show it their body language makes them look like same-pole magnets."

"Good old Sig, I can always count on you for some profiling parlor tricks."

He disengaged my hand from the crook of his elbow and patted it in brotherly fashion before opening the door on my side of the car. "So tomorrow I'll talk to Mr. Lynch. And this evening you, Stinger, have a phone call to make."

SIX

Max turned off on Golder Ranch Road to drop me off while the other two cars continued south on Oracle back into the city. As we pulled up to the house I thought of the man and two dogs who awaited me inside. While it had been great to see Sigmund again, and despite the pain of seeing Jessica's body, maybe even because of the stress of coming face-to-face with that part of the past, as I walked back up the driveway I imagined myself pounding on the door and yelling, "Sanctuary!" That's how good it felt when Carlo opened the front door and gave me his grin.

For a second his look faded into what I imagined was my own before he said, "Couch time," and we all moved to the living room where the Pugs could more easily get at my face. I was doubly glad then that Sigmund was not here to see the reunion of the pack.

After an early dinner (pasta with pesto, spinach salad) and before it was time for the Pugs' evening walk, I took the rest of my wine into the extra bedroom that had been Jane's quilting and scrapbooking room and that Carlo had agreed could be my office when I told him I needed a space of my own the way men have their garage. I didn't tell him it was because I couldn't quite let go of that particular woman, Special Agent Brigid Quinn. Plus, one of these days after I learned how to be a better wife than Jane ever was, I planned to set up a little private-investigating business.

I had my desk that I brought from my old apartment, cluttered with mostly magazines I meant to read and housewares catalogs with cooking utensils that mystified me, and my laptop. A swivel desk chair. Some banker's boxes with old tax returns and other nonoffensive files. A metal cabinet with a lock, purchased after Paul left me, for the rest.

There were a few pictures on the walls to remind me of my successes in foiling evildoers, like the one of President Reagan congratulating me for preventing a terrorist attack that no one will ever know about. Another frame held the award I got for bringing down the Thai slavery ring. Another for infiltrating the Palo Mayombe cult and in the nick of time saving a boy from being boiled alive in a cauldron. I had mixed emotions about that award because there was already another kid dead in the cauldron when we showed up; it was also the time I shot the unarmed perp.

Jane's quilting materials were in a box in the closet along with her sewing machine.

I sat down in the desk chair, put my feet up on a nearby banker's box, and stared at the cell phone I'd left on the desk. I thought about my outburst on the road to Mount Lemmon. If it was just a matter of dealing with Jessica, I probably would have been able to keep a better grip on my feelings. After all, she was dead and feeling no pain. But there was her father Zach Robertson to keep me ever mindful of that event.

Zachariah Robertson had been a decent dentist in Santa Fe with a wife who loved him enough, a son who didn't give him any trouble, and a daughter who had just joined the FBI. I never told him how much I regretted recommending Jessica for fieldwork too soon because I was eager to get her trained as my replacement. How I regretted I was a little too old to pose as a convincing teenage hitchhiker. As with all of my victims' loved ones, I just told him to call anytime of the day or night.

He did. After Jessica's disappearance that night on Route 66, seventy-nine miles west of Tucumcari, New Mexico, his calls went from hopeful shortly after zero hour to despairing after six months. He started showing up at his dental practice still too drunk from the night before to keep his hands from rattling around in his patients' mouths.

Even after two years went by, he kept calling me. That's how I found out Elena and his son Peter had left him, about three years sooner than it usually takes for the family of a murder victim to break apart. Then Elena got cancer and died without seeking treatment. Zach didn't stay in touch with Peter much after her funeral.

Last time I talked to him he was mostly a drunk hermit who seldom bathed in a cabin in the upper peninsula of Lake Michigan.

I tossed off the remaining wine, took a deep breath, and called him.

He answered on the first ring, just the way he had when all this first started. "You always wait for me to call you," he said straight off, and then with a wobble in his voice, "You must have found her."

"We did." I didn't tell him everything right away, wanted first to gauge how much of it he'd remember in the morning.

"What, what about who did it? Do you know?"

"We do. We know everything now, Zach." He sounded only moderately soused so I told him everything I knew, everything that had happened in the last twenty-four hours, and in the time before that what I knew of it. I didn't pull any punches, hadn't in years. And he didn't need to ask any questions because I anticipated all of them.

When I finished speaking, I heard what I thought at first were ice cubes sloshing in his glass, but then realized he was typing on his computer while he listened to me.

"What are you doing?" I asked.

"Damn, you can't get to Tucson direct from anywhere," he said, after the typing finally went quiet. "American Airlines Flight 734 arriving at two P.M."

"No, Zach."

"If you're not there I'll take a taxi to the medical examiner's office."

"Zach, listen."

"I won't be any trouble. I never once, once blamed the Bureau, even right at the start, did I?"

He had told me so many times how he never blamed the Bureau, by which he meant me. "No, Zach. You never did."

"Even that night, that night you spent with me."

It was more like forty-eight straight hours I spent talking him up from suicide when he called from halfway across the country and told me his sweating palms were stained white by the fistful of sleeping pills he was holding.

"No, not even then. But you don't want to see her, Zach. Not this way."

"Oh yes I do." His courage failed him, finally, and he started to cry. I don't have much respect for whiskey remorse, except when it comes to someone in Zach's shoes, so I waited patiently until he was finished.

Then, wiping my own nose on the palm of my hand, I said, "I swear to you, when this comes to trial you'll get your day in court. You can read that statement you wrote such a long time ago. Remember that statement? Keep thinking about that. You still have it, don't you?"

He hung up.

And that's what happens to many victims' loved ones, the part you never see after the media gets bored, or after the movie when the credits roll. When the bad guy is caught, the actors playing the family have Closure, knowing justice has been served. The actors playing the detectives turn their back and walk triumphantly off camera. People watching the show throw out their popcorn, wipe off their greasy fingers, and go home, maybe at the most feel a little tremble of fear imagining there's someone hiding behind the other car when they pull into the garage after dark, but of course there isn't and life goes on as before, *tra la*.

When it's real life they, some families of some victims, spend the rest of their lives waiting to die. The end.

Only suckers believe in Closure.

SEVEN

At two the next afternoon I picked Zach up at Tucson International (one terminal, two concourses, twenty gates). I watched him come down the escalator into the baggage claim area, his body slowly clearing a dip in the ceiling, coming into view from the bottom up, shoddy hiking boots to balding crown. He wasn't much taller than me and was a lot skinnier. And though he was six years my junior, I don't think it's vanity to say he looked older than me.

The moving staircase gave way abruptly to the stationary floor, making him falter into my embrace. So as not to face reality head-on, he whispered into my hair, "Yee-ha. That last bit was like riding a bronco."

"You come in between the mountain ranges, the wind funnel makes it choppy." Besides being genuinely affectionate, the hug allowed me to give him a quick sniff. Last time I'd seen Zach personal hygiene had not been a priority. But he'd cleaned himself up for Jessica's sake and even had a new short-sleeved blue shirt on. I could tell from the perpendicular creases in the denim that it hadn't been out of the package long. I couldn't smell alcohol either. He must not have had a drink on the plane and that may be why he pulled away quickly, so I couldn't feel his fingers flutter like moths against my back.

I let his body go but kept his hands still in mine a moment longer, let him look into my eyes without looking away from him the way so many others had. "Don't do this, Zach. You don't have to see her. We got the confirmation from the dental records."

"Did I ever tell you I thought of being a forensic dentist there for a while?"

Yes, he had told me that, on four or five occasions, along with how he didn't blame me for Jessica's death. Zach retrieved a small canvas bag from the carousel and we walked from the terminal to the parking lot, where I got him situated in the car, handed him the bottle of water you always give to new arrivals in the desert, made him drink some, and headed up Palo Alto Drive, turned left onto Valencia, right on First, for the relatively short drive to the medical examiner's office downtown.

Max Coyote and Laura Coleman were already there, and Dr. George Manriquez met us almost instantly upon arrival in the lobby.

"Dr. Manriquez," I said, the situation calling for formality despite my having known him during my brief time with the Tucson Bureau, and stepped back to let him prepare Zach for what he was about to see.

"Mr. Robertson," he said, indicating a couple of small armchairs placed at an angle to each other in a far corner of the lobby, "Please sit here for a second."

Zach followed his instruction while the three of us, me, Max, and Coleman, faced each other pretending not to listen.

"Mr. Robertson," George said again, once they were both seated. "No one understands better than I do that this is real life, not drama, so I want to prepare you a little. We have no mystery here, no indirect lighting like in TV shows. You're not going to see your daughter, that is, anything that looks like your daughter. This is some dark brown skin covering a skeleton. Have you ever seen a mummy?"

"In books, yes," Zach said, nodding. "We . . . we went to Pompeii once but I know those bodies aren't the same." The memory of some vacation bowed him like a weight.

"Yes, those are plaster casts, but still, that's something how the remains you're about to view will appear. Do you have any questions you want to ask me? Anything at all."

Zach wiped the back of his hand across his mouth, seemed to decide not to ask, then asked. "Is there . . . is there any smell?"

"Not really, or not that disagreeable one you may be thinking of. A little musty, perhaps, but you won't be shocked by it. It's the sight that is likely to be disturbing."

Zach's head drooped and I noticed the knuckles of his laced fingers were white. I wanted to go to him but knew he was in good hands with the sweetheart Manriquez.

After a long enough pause to show Zach that there wasn't anything more important to him than this, George stood and put out his hand to help Zach up. Then he led us all down a corridor to the autopsy room.

They could never get the smell out of a room like this, a combination of disinfectant and old diaper, like a government-run day care center. On a plastic gurney rested the body of Jessica Robertson covered with a sheet. It was all purposefully clinical, like Manriquez had said, no shadowy corners, no instruments suggestive of cutting flesh, no background music. Zach was placed on one side of the gurney flanked by me and an autopsy assistant burly enough to catch him if he dropped. George stood on the other side. Max and Coleman hung back.

With a final glance at Zach for permission, George drew the sheet from the top of Jessica's head so Zach could see her dried hair and a bit of dark brown flesh on her forehead. When Zach appeared to be able to take that much, George drew the sheet down to just below her chin.

I had my head tilted enough to see Zach out of the corner of my eye but felt more than saw the tremor that passed through him like a private earthquake. There was a single soft groan. Other than that he was incredibly composed, worked through his own thoughts and memories without sharing. Then he lifted his index finger and delicately stroked the shriveled brown lobe of her left ear, still preserved over the years by the mummification process. He stroked her ear the way you would a thing that was terribly fragile but too amazingly beautiful not to touch. He couldn't see the side of her head where the other ear had been cut away. Then he pulled his hand away and the medical examiner pulled the sheet back up.

"I won't see her again," Zach said.

"No," agreed George, whether he understood or not. He looked at the assistant, who apparently had been given prior instructions, and then paused until Zach was led out to the waiting area. I was so proud of him.

Even with the weight of the corpse still in the room, we all breathed a little deeper.

As Max and Coleman came closer to the gurney, George said, "I moved here from Miami about ten years ago looking for a change of scene. Too many immigrants washing up on the beaches, I said. All that happened was I went from Haitian floaters to Mexican mummies. With the summer heat I've got a whole refrigerated truck out back full of unidentifieds that they picked up off the desert."

But then he went on with his job as he pulled the sheet off with less ceremony than before, this time all the way off the corpse. The body was in the fetal position as it had been when first placed in the car. The head was positioned where it would have been in life, though it was no longer attached to the torso. "This mummification happens quite a lot, naturally formed in the desert where the humidity is so low. You know, like the other body in the car." He was referring to the prostitute who must have frequented truck-stop parking lots, who Floyd had dismissed as a lot lizard, his first victim.

"I didn't have much time to look at the other one," I said. "Was it the same MO as the others?"

"I concentrated on this one first. All I can tell you is that the other corpse has both its ears. I can give you a better report when I've done the autopsy on the other."

I asked, "What about the body found in Lynch's truck? Are there any similarities of cause and manner of death?"

"Like I said, Jessica Robertson's body seems to have been naturally mummified. The one in Lynch's truck had some help. It's all in my report."

Coleman and Max nodded. "Help me out, Doc," I said. "I'm trying to catch up."

Manriquez didn't seem to mind at all, and started in eagerly, "He used something called Natron. It's commercially available, a mixture of four kinds of sodium: carbonate, bicarbonate, chloride, and sulfate. You pack it in and around the body so it dehydrates and makes it inhospitable to the bacteria that would usually decompose the tissues. Plus he removed the organs, which accelerated the process. All that was left was the bones and dried soft tissue."

Like many medical examiners, it turned out there was nothing he enjoyed talking about more than his work. I was aware of Zach waiting by himself and needed to get this over with, but my curiosity was piqued. "You say this Natron is commercially available?"

"It's used in those little desiccant packages they put in things to keep them dry. Mr. Lynch apparently isn't stupid, and knows how to look things up on the Internet. That's how he found out how to do it. Agent Coleman could confirm from her interrogation, but I would guess he put the body in a ventilated box out in the desert while it was drying. There was no evidence of predator scavenging."

"Lynch said it only took a few months until he could use the body without smelling up the truck," Max said.

"How long did Lynch have it in his truck?" I asked.

"About a year and a half," Max said.

Manriquez nodded that it agreed with his findings on approximate time since death and added, "He didn't try to move it so it stayed pretty intact. Of course once it gets that old you can hardly pinpoint a date, but I found enough dried semen on it to show he had it quite a while."

"Sure it's his?" I asked.

"We've had time to do the DNA analysis that matched it to Lynch."

"Back to Jessica," I said. "Cause and manner of death?"

"It's hard to find ligature marks because the way the head was angled it had fallen off the body anyway. And of course with the eyes dried you can't see the typical petechiae though it might show up in histopath. But no need to go that far, the hyoid bone is definitely crushed, the Achilles tendon slashed, and the ear removed on this side." Manriquez shook his head. "After the confession I read the autopsy reports on the Route 66 murders. That's when I discovered the body in the truck had the same mode associated with it. So I checked the body of Jessica Robertson for semen and found some on various parts, just like the mummy in the truck. Preliminary tests don't exclude Lynch. We've put a priority on the DNA analysis to confirm."

I thought again about Zach alone out in the waiting room and wanted to get back to him, but Coleman was talking now. "In his interrogation Lynch said he'd been using Jessica's body for several years but got tired of driving up the mountain road and worried someone would spot him. So he started experimenting with animals and ended up with the body he had on his truck when we caught him." She turned to Manriquez, "Would you send me both the reports, for Jessica and for the other body found in the car?"

"Sure. I've got it over here." Manriquez walked to the far end of the autopsy lab where the other body waited on a gurney, covered with another green cloth. Max and Coleman turned their attention to it as Manriquez withdrew the cloth. I saw the dark tissue that was speckled here and there with yellowed bits, pieces of trash that had stuck to it before it completely dried. I left the others gazing at the body, Manriquez enthusiastically waving his hands as if he was going to levitate it. He was saying, "This one was fairly intact, like that of Jessica Robertson."

Max said, "Intact? The heads came off when they took them out of the car and this one is in pieces."

Manriquez said, "I'm talking hard-tissue damage."

"Hey, I gotta go," I said, still standing next to Jessica's body, but no one heard me.

EIGHT

I took Zach to the Sheraton nearby, at the corner of Campbell and Speedway, got him situated in room 174, ordered him a Salisbury steak and mashed potatoes from room service, and made small talk until they arrived. I sat in the chair at the desk and he sat on the edge of the bed nearest me. I wanted to slip him one of the Valiums I kept in my tote, but thought better of it since I saw him looking at the liquor list on the room service menu. He didn't seem to want to talk about his experience at the medical examiner's office. He assured me he would be all right, preferred to be alone. I didn't believe him, but what can you do? He was a grown man.

"You shouldn't have been there," I said again, at the same time stalling and wanting to go, like the last friend at a wake.

"No, you see, I had to do it. Kind of go to the bottom."

He didn't have to explain about going to the bottom. I understood, and knew I couldn't follow him there. I said, "I'll make the arrangements for Jessica's body myself. Will you be taking her back to Michigan?"

"No, that was never her home. I guess she's gotten used to this area. She should stay."

I could have mentioned my husband was an ex-priest and could assist with a memorial service, but neither

Zach nor I had believed in that for a long time. "When are you planning to fly back?"

"I don't have a return ticket yet." There was the same stoop to his bony shoulders I had seen when he arrived, but now his eyes had a kind of a glitter that unsettled me when he said, "Just leave me here for now, okay, Brigid?"

"You're not going to do anything stupid, are you?"

"Like kill myself? There's only a butter knife with that food you got me, and you put me on the first floor." He almost smiled. "We've been through a lot together, haven't we? You know me better than anyone I've ever known."

Yes. I knew Zach long enough not to try saying lame things like, "God never gives you anything you can't handle." So instead I said, which was nearly as foolish, "Will you sleep?"

"No." He smiled as if the question would have been meaningless at any point in the last seven years but now was utterly absurd. He pushed himself off the bed and went to the window and pulled aside the curtain to look out at the parking lot, spoke without turning.

"Brigid?"

"What, Zach."

"Lynch made a deal, didn't he?"

It was the one thing I hadn't told him, and I should have known he'd notice the omission. I didn't answer.

"I want to see him, too," he said.

"No, Zach." And this time I meant it. "I promise to call you when we get a date for sentencing, and you can read your statement in court."

He could tell I would hold firm, and turning from the window, he stared at me as if he had seen nothing but his daughter until this point. "It's been a long time, but you look good. The sadness is still there underneath, but falling in love has given you a nice glow. And the desert climate has been easy on you."

"Maybe, but the cost of moisturizer is killing me," I joked. I often joke when I feel awkward.

"You need to go," he said.

"I really don't," I said, walking over to the tray that had been placed on the desk. "Look, I got you some coffee. I'll pour you a cup. You like it black with fake sugar, right?"

He shook his head, unable to hide his mild annoyance at my attentiveness. "If you won't go away I've got something to show you." He tottered—good lord, he tottered and he was only fifty-three—over to the bed where he had tossed his black carry-on. Unzipping a side pocket, he took out a picture of Jessica and handed it to me. It showed her next to a multicolored image that took up two-thirds of the photo, leaving her a small figure on the side. "This was the last picture I had of her, taken at the hot-air balloon festival in Albuquerque. It's not the best picture, but it's the most recent."

I studied the picture, a neatly laminated five by seven, without taking it from him, without knowing what to say. They say a woman is good at knowing what to say at moments like this, but that's one of the women I've never been. After a few seconds he seemed to recognize that nothing more would be said or done about his photograph, and leaned it against the lamp next to the bed.

I thought that was all, but he went into the same pocket and drew out a dozen postcards. Now this, this I knew before he said another word. Zach had been getting these postcards periodically throughout the months and years after Jessica's disappearance. There had been four of them: a picture of a grinning alligator from Florida, a lone trumpet player in New Orleans, Hello from Carlsbad Caverns, a close-up of a scorpion—I remembered them all. And all had the same message, "Having a wonderful time with my new friend. Wish you were here. Love, Jessica."

I remembered all the time we lost with laboratory analysis and document examiners. Looking for fingerprints, hoping for DNA on the postage stamps that were always peel and stick, tracking down the post offices, interviewing the postal workers there, rushing off to the locations mentioned on the cards looking for clues. The text and address were printed out from a computer somewhere and attached to the card with clear tape. Yes, we checked both sides of that tape for trace and impression evidence, too.

I had known some truly disgusting assholes in my career, but whoever sent these postcards after Jessica Robertson's death was the worst I had ever known. It hadn't been enough to torture, rape, and murder her. This killer, maybe because the victim was an FBI agent, was prolonging the horror by taunting and torturing the family as well.

I thought about the man I had met the day before, who had confessed to the crimes. I could imagine him doing something like this, and I hated him with fresh hate.

"You've still been getting these?" I asked, stupidly, holding them in my hand, not bothering to look at them individually.

"I know I was supposed to send them to you as soon as I got them, Brigid. But it wasn't doing you any good, was it?"

"No. We were useless."

"And once Elena left, and there was no one around to cry, I sort of started to look forward to them." Zach stared at me as if asking if I could understand how he felt. I said I did. That encouraged him. "This way, I got to pretending that they really were from Jessica."

"When did you get the last one?" I asked.

He riffled through the cards and pulled one out, showed me the postmark. "This one. A couple of months ago."

"They . . ." I stopped, timing that to Floyd Lynch's movements, knowing he would have mailed it more than a month before getting caught.

Zach shushed me. "I love you, Brigid," he said.

"I love you, too, Zach," I said. It was one of those knee-jerk moments when they say it and you say it and nobody knows what it actually means. But it can't hurt.

"Now get the hell out of here and leave me alone," he said in his toughest guy voice, holding out his hand to take the cards back from me.

After mentioning the mashed potatoes looked pretty good, I told him I'd check in with him in the morning and take care of any paperwork to release Jessica from the medical examiner. I also asked if he wouldn't mind my taking the postcards.

Apparently after seeing Jessica's body they weren't so important to him anymore, and he gave them up. I put them into the side pocket of my tote bag, handling them with the same respect as if they were from Jessica after all.

I certainly didn't prefer to be alone, but couldn't face Carlo just yet, couldn't pretend. On my way out of the hotel I called Sigmund on his cell phone to go out for a drink. He would know how it felt to be with Zach and Jessica after all that time, and I could hear about how the insanity tests were going.

"They're not going at all," he said when I asked him. "Morrison said no need, insanity's not even on the table, and if any assessment needs to be done he'll call in someone local. He apologized for the miscommunication."

"He just sent you packing?"

"It was his call, after all. He was very polite, and quite embarrassed. I didn't know that Agent Coleman hadn't cleared it with him. As a matter of fact, I inadvertently mentioned that you had attended the expedition yesterday, and Morrison was annoyed by that, too. Apparently he doesn't want you in the picture either, so Coleman violated protocol on that count as well. She may be in some trouble."

"I hate Morrison."

"So you've often said."

"You could get involved anyway. You've got the clout."

"That was always one of your problems: you never played your assigned position, always running into left field." Sigmund never watches sports but can speak it.

"Still, you want to get together?"

"I'm sorry, Stinger, I should have made it clear, I'm not there. I got home an hour ago. It's seven thirty here. But let me know if I can help you out."

Nice to see you, too, Sig. We said good-bye without any of those empty promises of keeping in touch.

More reluctantly I called the Bureau office and got

Coleman. I was surprised at her eagerness to meet me, which was expressed as, "Agent Quinn. Oh my God, yes. Now?"

"I just dropped Zachariah Robertson off at his hotel so I'm still in the city," I said. "Want to meet at that Greek restaurant near your office?"

"Can't. That was the last fraud case I worked and I'm about to bust them for money laundering."

"I heard something about that, but the gyro platters are so good," I said, but she wasn't listening.

"Larry?" Her voice turned away from the phone and I heard her ask someone for a place around Campbell and Speedway. I heard a man's voice say, "Pretty sure it's open now." She gave me directions to a cop bar near the Sheraton and added, after listening again to whoever on her end of the line was giving directions, "It's Emery's Cantina. I'm leaving the office right now."

NINE

There are designated cop spots, places where everybody might not know your name, but where you can be sure they'll cover your back because there's a shotgun behind the bar. The Naugahyde elbow rest on the bar is cracked in places, the lighting is bad, and you try not to think about the kitchen. People besides cops go to these places, of course, like silent elderly couples on fixed incomes who appear to have said everything they have to say to each other decades before. Everyone knows it's a safe place with reliably standard fare and dollar happy hours. This one turned out to be close to the hotel, about a mile north from the Sheraton on Campbell in a freestanding old building close to the road, one of the few in Tucson that hadn't yet been torn down for a strip mall.

I got there first and recognized a couple deputies from the sheriff's office, if only by first name. Wally and Cliff both stopped grinding their burgers just long enough to lift a greasy palm in greeting, as did the bartender, one of those cheerful lugs who look like an overweight baby.

At the bartender's direction I took a table against the wall that was painted to look like crumbling adobe. A waitress came up before I had a chance to unstick the little white band that kept my paper napkin folded around the silverware. The waitress was in her late twenties,

I thought, though young people look younger the older I get. She had a runner's build and was African American. If I was still living in DC that last thing wouldn't be worthy of remark, but there aren't many black people living in Arizona.

I could have waited for Coleman to arrive so I didn't seem in such urgent need but holding up my palms like two scales said, "Vodka in one glass, ice in another." Customary maximum at cop bars is generally two light beers; the cops glanced over when they heard me order. I ignored them and looked around the place, noting the Special Olympics and Toys for Tots appreciation certificates on the far wall and the usual mass of photographs of customers mugging cheerfully. It felt good to get away from Zach and meet somebody for cop talk.

Coleman must have been booking it because she showed up before my drink was gone, so I didn't have a chance to order a second without her knowing. When she sat down and leaned her black satchel against a leg of the chair, she looked at my glass. Though I spooned some more of the ice into the vodka glass I didn't feel as if I had to justify myself.

After registering my alcohol she looked around at her surroundings, at the other cops in the bar, and didn't seem entirely comfortable with it all, too low class or too barish for her.

"So why did you leave Fraud for Homicide? Usually people go the other way," I asked.

"I just felt that was what I had to do." She gave a mild shrug to go with her nonanswer and turned up one corner of her mouth. For someone so eager to get together she was evasive, her eyes pausing only in the vicinity of mine. Under the pretext of raking her fingers through her short curls she passed a hand over a pale copper birthmark on her right temple as if she considered that birthmark her only flaw and wanted to hide it. Other than that my only impression was that in high school she might have been the sort of girl who rode on floats.

The waitress came back. "Do you know what else you want?" she asked, as if there was a statute of limitations on how many times she would come to the table. Funny how, after spending the past two days with a serial killer and assorted dead bodies, neither of us had the courage or energy to object to the pressure of an assertive waitress. We defaulted to taco salads. As Coleman closed her menu, I spotted the name on the cover. "Emery's Cantina," I remarked. "Is that ironic?"

"No, why?" asked the waitress.

"Cantina. Emery. Emery sounds about as Mexican as … Moishe," I suggested, the vodka stimulating my creativity.

"The Mexican theme is a common leitmotif in the Southwest," she said with a carefully straight face as she extended one hand palm up toward the bartender. "That's Emery, the owner. He's Hungarian. I'm Cheri. I'm not." Said Hungarian was leaning across the Formica bar comforting some clearly off-duty cop who was also not following the two-light-beer rule. I heard, "a taxi."

I raised my glass and clinked the remaining ice. Coleman asked, "Do you have any wine, Cheri?"

"The house burgundy's palatable after the first glass," she said.

"Iced tea, please."

"Oh come on," I said. "Give it a little effort."

"Okay, a light beer. Any brand."

Cheri went off to put in our order.

"Leitmotif?" I asked, not because I cared but to end a small uncomfortable silence that Coleman could fill only so long by arranging her jacket over the back of the chair, fussing with the napkin around her own silverware, and using the napkin to polish her glasses.

"Everyone in Tucson is either getting a degree or writing a book," Coleman said, and pointed back over to the end of the bar where Cheri, after bringing us the beer and a second vodka, now sat reading an introduction to criminal justice textbook propped against one of those jars of pickled pigs' feet that no one ever eats.

"I know that. What I meant was, what's the difference between a leitmotif and a plain motif?" I asked her.

"I don't know," she admitted and, for the first time since we'd met the day before, smiled. But she still wouldn't quite look me in the eye, and passed her hand again over her birthmark.

I guessed this had something to do with trouble over not getting authorization from Morrison for Sig's and my involvement, but she wasn't ready to tell me yet. We talked about the office some, people we both knew, drank a little more, talked a little more, ate our salads when they came, but Coleman took a while to get to the point of why she had agreed so eagerly to meet me, and it wasn't to bask in my fame or apologize for her lapse in following procedure. There was a line being drawn and she wanted me on her side of it.

"So what did you think of Lynch?" she asked. She seemed to pin me with her eyes, trying to catch my reaction before I spoke.

The feeling I had at the scene after being with Lynch came back to me, but I tried to ignore it. I said, carefully, "Narcissistic, conscienceless, repulsive. Every inch a sociopath. Though not totally the one I expected."

"What did Dr. Weiss think of him? I read his profile of the Route 66 killer in *Criminal Profiling*. Did he think Lynch matched it?"

I felt my first genuine smile of the day. "You have to say the whole title to get the full impact: *Theory and Practice of Criminal Profiling: An Interdisciplinary Case Study Approach*. Sigmund will be so tickled to know somebody read it."

"Sigmund? It *is* David, isn't it?"

"David, sure, we've known each other a long time, since he was brought in to help set up the Behavioral Science Unit in the seventies. We called him Sigmund for Freud; you know how everybody gets a nickname."

"I saw you two talking yesterday. I just wondered if he had an opinion."

I felt like the lights went up. I knew now that she hadn't gone around Morrison because she just forgot procedure. I knew that with Weiss having been dismissed I was the only one she could turn to, and I wondered why. I dipped my upper lip in my drink to indicate my control while I thought about how to respond. I didn't tell her Sigmund refused to say much at all. "I don't know, there were a few surprises. For starters, we would have expected a stronger guy who could lift a hundred pounds deadweight overhead into his cab. I always pictured Route 66 being smarter, too, but that's all conjecture of course. Why are you asking me now?"

Coleman took a deep breath. Her body clenched as if

she was expecting me to reach over and wallop her. She reached into her satchel and pulled out a sizable report that she placed in front of me with the care of being in the presence of an explosive device. Then she finally spilled. "Because I think we have a false confession."

You don't navigate Bureau politics for forty years without knowing what's what. All the collegiality I'd been building for Coleman evaporated as I leapt to the implication of her words. It was all fucking bullshit and I told her so.

TEN

"So that's why you did the end run on Morrison and called in me and Weiss without getting authorization. You went to Morrison first and he wasn't buying it. Then you tried to get Weiss on your side early on, but he wouldn't discuss the case without assessing Lynch first. Now Weiss is out of the picture so you're trying to use me to back you up. Did you really think you could pull that shimmy on me?"

"Please," she said.

I wasn't finished. "Worst of all, you let me call the victim's father and tell him we caught the guy." I imagined Zachariah Robertson, how I had just left him in a hotel room with a laminated picture of his dead child. With that image fueling my anger, I leaned across the narrow table and lowered my voice. "You don't, you *do not* bring a father in, show him the remains of his daughter who was tortured to death, tell him you finally found the killer, and then next day tell him never mind. Do you have any feeling at all for what that man has gone through and what it would be like to tell him sorry, our bad? Nuh-uh, Floyd Lynch is the man. He did it."

"Would you please just listen?"

I was inclined to continue ranting, but couldn't think of anything else to say at the moment without repeating myself. So I drained off my watered-down vodka and contented myself with glaring, while I put my hands under the table where no one could see me dig at my cuticles. I guess over the past couple of years I'd allowed myself to get a little too relaxed and I was no longer used to this crap.

Coleman took my silence as temporary acquiescence. She began with an apology for insulting my intelligence, which was the least of my concerns, then opened the report on the table and turned to a page with two columns: on one side, under the heading "Route 66 Killer," the profile of the Route 66 killer that Sigmund had compiled, and on the other side a profile of Floyd Lynch.

"I found nineteen points," she said. "I used this table David Weiss did as a template and found nineteen points that didn't match."

I took the report from her and scanned the page, saw a few characteristics I'd already spotted in Lynch. "Okay, so he's not as physically strong as we assumed. He doesn't seem to be as well organized, and is less articulate than we imagined. Big deal, we were wrong. We're not always on the money." I threw the book on the table. "Besides, Weiss says himself in his book that profiles don't get convictions. Only evidence gets convictions. And we're up to our ass in evidence. Lynch kept journals with all the details. He took us to Jessica Robertson's body."

Coleman squirmed a bit. "I know all this."

"The semen on her body matches him. He had a victim on his truck killed in the same way, with the same postmortem mutilation. He knows about the ears and that was our hold-out information. Nobody but those connected to the case knew about the ears."

Coleman looked about ready to leap across the table to physically shut me up. "He doesn't know where the ears are," she said.

"What?"

"Remember the point Weiss makes about the importance of trophies and souvenirs, how they're priceless treasure to the killer? Floyd Lynch couldn't tell me where he kept the ears. He says he forgot."

That gave me pause, but I had a counter. "He's just not telling you."

"He told us everything else."

"He wants to keep them for himself forever. Even if he goes to prison for life he'll always know where the ears are."

"That's what they all said when I told them. Morrison, Adams Vance the prosecutor, even Royal."

"Royal . . . ?"

She was caught off guard. Sigmund was right. I hoped she'd never try to go undercover. She stuttered a bit, "Hughes . . . the public defender."

She recovered and went on. "They all say it's a small point in a huge mass of damning evidence. They want this catch so bad. The publicity is enormous, the director himself called to congratulate Morrison, so he won't back down. Remember there was that highway-serial-killer initiative the Bureau instituted a few years ago."

"So now you're hoping I'll do your work for you. You should have been a brave little soldier and forced Morrison to authorize a further investigation. You know, follow protocol."

Coleman looked away at that remark. "Look, we found Jessica's body. As far as Mr. Robertson was concerned, that's the main thing, isn't it? That's why Robertson was here, because he insisted on seeing it."

"You should go back to Fraud where you belong, dear."

"Please don't call me dear—it's condescending and I don't deserve it."

She deserved it, all right. I ignored her and went on, "Sure, we honored Zach's wish to see Jessica's body. But it's been seven years of wanting not only his daughter, but wanting justice. It's bad enough that Lynch is going to escape the death penalty. Zachariah Robertson's suffering is beyond anything you can imagine. You're not going to make it worse because you didn't have the guts to press a case you think is right."

"Can I get you anything else?"

Coleman and I both jerked upright at the voice, as if we'd forgotten we were in a restaurant. I don't know how long Cheri had been standing there. We slapped on smiles that from the waitress's perspective might have looked more like snarls.

"Just the check, please," I said.

Cheri picked up our plates and left.

"You're no better than Morrison," Coleman said, crossing her arms and looking at me like that was the worst thing she could say.

"Bullshit" was all I could come up with on the spot.

But Coleman would not be distracted. "What about Floyd Lynch? What if he's innocent of the Route 66 murders?"

"Innocent? Coleman. The man fucks mummies."

Everyone in the room looked over and I realized I wasn't using my indoor voice anymore.

80

"There's not even real evidence that he didn't just find that body like he says he did. We can't prove that he killed the woman on his truck. So you're going to put a man in prison for life for desecration of a corpse? Being repulsive isn't a capital offense," Coleman said quietly.

She was right. You convicted someone for their crimes, not their nature. I had said something similar more than once in my career. I looked at her posture, which managed to stay straight even when she was leaning over the table, and her naturally curly hair, and her professionally plain glasses, and I wondered if her analysis of the case showed the same perfection, the same attention to detail.

"Did you coerce him? Feed him the information?" I asked.

"I swear no. Morrison wanted nothing to go wrong, so we videotaped all the interrogations. You can see for yourself."

"Why do you think he would confess?" I asked, knowing from experience that it happened all the time for no damn good reason.

"I don't know that part yet," she said.

"Did you ask him?"

She relaxed again now that I was asking questions instead of attacking. "He's sticking to his story and he seems to know all the details. Seems, hell, he's got it down cold. It's all in here," she said, tapping the report, pushing it part of the way toward me again with the tip of her well-manicured finger that I bet she never chewed. "It's short, not the whole murder book, just what I thought was important for my analysis. Please look at it . . ." She paused, fixed me with a look and continued, "Especially this video." She opened the report and pointed to a DVD tucked into an envelope and pasted inside the cover. "This is the part of the interrogation I'm talking about, the part that I can't get out of my head. Look at it before you tell me to fuck off."

When I hesitated a moment more, she said, her self-assurance slowly returning, "I know you don't know me, and I'm asking a lot. But even if you don't care about sending the wrong man to prison for life, look at it this way. If Lynch didn't do the Route 66 murders, then the guy who did is still out there." Coleman leaned across the table again. If I'd had lapels I think she might have grabbed them. "Don't you see, Lynch knows the details of the case so well. If he didn't do the killings I'll bet he knows the man who did. Lynch could lead us to the man who really killed Jessica Robertson. A man who at any point might start killing again."

If she was right, she was absolutely right, and I really disliked that. I had one objection left. "Do you realize my being involved is not a benefit? Have I indicated that Morrison and I share anything but a mutual disgust?"

She ignored that, her face allowing itself to finally reveal just how stricken she was by the load she'd been bearing by herself. "Agent Quinn, I wanted Floyd Lynch to be the Route 66 killer so bad. I want it as much as anybody does. It would make the rest of my career, being the one who interrogated him. But I just can't get his expression out of my mind, when I asked him about the ears, I mean. I saw a different man. More pathetic than psychopathic. I think about it in the middle of the night. It's like there's this ton of evidence that says he's guilty, but I can't let go of the one piece of evidence that makes me doubt he really is. I'll do anything to get to the truth and it's driving me a little crazy. Has that ever happened to you?"

I didn't respond, and Coleman took it for yes. She said, "All I'm asking for is your expert opinion on whether the case deserves to remain open. That's all. If you think I have a point, I'll find the corroborating evidence and somehow force the issue, get Lynch to recant before he officially pleads guilty—I don't know how." She tried to give me a good hard stare, but her eyes drifted off. "And if you say I'm fucked up on this at least I'll get some sleep again."

"You don't have much time. Days?"

Coleman nodded and pushed the report the rest of the way across the table. "Promise you won't make up your mind until you've looked at the video."

Even in this case, the lure of the unknown was too much for me to resist. I put the report in my tote bag and told her I'd call her in a couple of days. All right, all right, the following day.

ELEVEN

I spent the drive back up to Catalina thinking about the day, about watching Zach hiding his grief, and standing over Jessica's desiccated corpse, and how what I thought would be a nice unwinding at the bar threatened to reopen the wounds I thought could finally heal. My emotions had been jerked around considerably in the past several days.

Carlo must have seen that I was preoccupied and offered to take me to Bubb's Grubb for ribs. I didn't want to tell him I'd already had the taco salad with Coleman so I wrenched my mind into the kitchen, bent on being that trifecta of Betty Crocker, Donna Reed, and last year's centerfold. I could do it; while during my career I was all fast food and TV dinners, cooking had gotten easier, once I'd had the epiphany that spaghetti isn't made with ketchup.

I made another salad with shrimp, walnuts, dried cranberries, and crumbled blue cheese on it (mine a lot smaller than his) and we ate in front of TV, which turned out to be not such a good move. We watched part of a program on the History Channel about the Etruscans, which I never would have watched on my own but kind of enjoyed. Then Carlo toyed with the remote (Carlo may be a genius but he's still a guy) and stopped at the local headline news:

"A thirteen-year-old cold case solved in Tucson, Arizona. Serial killer confesses to bizarre string of murders."

Shit. "Want some pineapple sherbet?" I asked.

"I'll get it in a minute. Let me see this," Carlo said.

There it was, including Morrison preening at a podium, fielding questions from the press, the answers to which I already knew. Abducted girls. Torture. Death. Mummies in trucks. Belinda Meloy, the local anchor who was as close to Robin Meade as you could get without cloning, came on.

"Have you noticed how female broadcasters are wearing skimpier clothes these days?" I asked, still trying to distract him. "That spangly thing looks like something I'd wear to a cocktail party."

Belinda said, "Floyd Lynch was arrested by the Pima County Sheriff's Department seventy-five miles north of Nogales on Route 19 after being stopped for a routine check by Border Security officials nearly three weeks ago. Since that time Lynch has confessed to eight murders, all young females." She turned and the camera went wide. "Special Agent in Charge of the Tucson Bureau of Investigation Office, Roger Morrison."

Morrison flashed a look that said he'd wanted to clear his throat but now there was no time for it. "Thank you, Belinda. The FBI Violent Crimes Task Force commends our agents operating in conjunction with county law enforcement under the highway serial murder initiative, which led to the arrest of Floyd Lynch without incident. The members of the FBI's Violent Crime Task Force and Highway Serial Killer Initiative include the Pima County Sheriff's Department, the Tucson Police Department, and the FBI.

This cold case, approximately twelve years old, is now officially closed."

After Morrison's carefully prepared statement a picture of me as the unsuccessful investigating agent all those years ago completed Belinda's report. They didn't have a problem with showing my face now that I wasn't undercover anymore. It was the formal portrait taken upon the occasion of my retirement.

"Look, that's you," Carlo said.

"Was that thunder?" That was always a good distraction in a land where annual rainfall measures eleven inches.

Carlo looked sideways at me where I sat in Jane's matching armchair. "Is this where you went yesterday?" he asked as a shot from a news helicopter showed the abandoned car.

"It's nothing, Perfesser. Max just asked me to tie up some loose ends, you know, give my opinion on a cold case. I'm done now. You don't want to talk about it."

That got a raised eyebrow but no further questions. We watched an episode of *Law & Order* because Carlo enjoys my telling him where they make mistakes. Then, "Let's walk the Pugs, O'Hari," he said. He calls me O'Hari (short for Mata O'Hari) because of my being Irish and having a mysterious past. I don't mind that as long as we keep it light.

We each took a Pug, leashed it, grabbed a poop bag, and walked around the block, the light barely dimmed in a long day. I introduced those nearly inconsequential topics that make up marriage. Whether to attend his grandniece's baptism in Des Moines (no). How the back fence needed a coat of Rustoleum (yes). Whether the brief sprinkle that afternoon counted as rain (hell no). It was all really normal.

When we got back there was a text message on my phone from Coleman, asking if I'd watched the video yet. It said, *U wch vid?*

"Go away," I laboriously texted back, not being comfortable yet with the common style.

Then while I had the phone in my hand I checked in with Zach. He was watching a movie, he said. No, he hadn't decided yet when he was going home, he said.

I looked out the back window at Jane's life-size statue of Saint Francis that sat on a bench next to a birdbath, and beyond that the now-darkening silhouette of Mount Lemmon, the sight that in the past had rested my soul. From our window you couldn't see the road we had taken up the northern slope, but just the same the mountain made me imagine mummies in abandoned cars and from now on always would.

Shaking off that thought, I lured Carlo to bed early and thereby managed to stave off any return to questions. I wasn't being manipulative. Truth is, even with the sadness, or maybe because of it, there's something about criminal cases that makes me frisky. He still looked at me with unasked questions, but after a few moments got into the spirit.

Afterward, while I listened to Carlo sleep, I thought I should get up and look at that video. Then I heard Sister Marie Theresa's voice from fourth grade religion class, "Sufficient unto the day is the evil thereof." When you're ten years old that doesn't make a lot of sense with or without the "unto" and "thereof." But today I understood Sister Marie Theresa. Today there had been enough evil. The video could wait until the early morning, when I was strong enough to confront whatever awaited me in it. I got up, took a sleeping pill to dam up my brain, and went back to bed.

TWELVE

At a decent hour the next morning I called Zach's cell number and left a message. When he didn't return that call I called his room number, thinking there might be something wrong with his phone. Then I called the front desk, where they told me he hadn't checked out. Thinking about maybe having to tell Zach that Floyd Lynch wasn't the killer and Carlo continuing to look at me funny made me nervous.

But I still couldn't bring myself to look at the video just yet. How to explain it? Like feeling a lump that was probably nothing, but not ready to show it to the doctor.

Carlo went out to sand and paint the back fence and I went to the gym and worked out with the free weights, but it wasn't enough.

That was the day when I decided to go down to the wash to find some rocks and clear my head even though it was Africa hot. And let a homicidal rapist get me into his van.

I pulled the same walking stick from the faux Louis Quatorze umbrella stand in the front hall that I had used when we went to find the mummies on Mount Lemmon. It's not like I'm feeble or anything, just need the stick for balance and as protection against the occasional rattlesnake. I put a bottle of water and my garden gloves in my dusty backpack and strapped it on. Cell phone in the pocket of my cargo pants. Headed down Golder Ranch Road to the Cañada del Oro Wash that runs underneath the bridge.

I have this little warning signal that has served me well in dangerous times. The nerve on the side of my neck sparks. I don't know why it didn't spark when I first glimpsed the white van, old and dirty, on the bridge, its driver leaning out the open window, staring down at the dry riverbed. Maybe my internal warning battery is wearing out.

Intuition aside, I should have noticed the van was illegally parked and that it looked all wrong. Instead I rested my backpack near the skeleton of half a tree that had been carried down the river during some flood long ago when the rivers still ran strong. I put on the garden gloves and began poking rocks with my stick, occasionally picking up a nice piece of rose quartz or mica-encrusted granite to put in my bag.

The van caught my attention again when it drove slowly down the packed dirt path leading off the wider road running close by the wash. As I pretended to examine more rocks it made a three-point turn to position itself for easy departure back up the steep slope. So far still not terribly suspicious; this was a public place where people sometimes exercised their dogs.

The man who emerged from the driver's side wasn't the throw-stick-let-dog-run type, though. With the nerve now sparking in the side of my neck big time, and my continuing to act as if this day was only going to be about rocks, I watched him as he opened the back doors of the van, arranged something I could not see, and closed the doors without shutting them altogether. Then he turned to watch me.

After glancing at his license plate for later reference, I refocused on the wet sand at my feet, poking my walking stick here and there to dig out smaller rocks. But I could feel him when he started to move, slipping down the bank of the wash, pretending to look around, but relentlessly coming closer and closer.

Another nerve nestled in the pit of my stomach, one I hadn't felt for a long time. It had been years since I was in a position like this and I was, frankly, afraid. Then I turned to him because now it was too late for fear.

The assailant stood within about ten feet of me. He was nearly six feet tall, approximately one hundred and forty pounds, thin frame, jerky movements, red-rimmed eyes and blotchy skin indicating chronic stimulant abuse. Lank hair that was not so much long as uncut. Early thirties. A sleeveless University of Arizona track shirt, a piece of yarn around his neck, orange nylon shorts with trim that once was white. No underwear. Green flip-flops with the rubber breaking around the toe from a habit of bending it back and forth as he was now. But the most telling thing, worse than the boner that told me he wasn't about to ask for money, was a strip of duct tape plastered against the front of his shirt.

I prepared for his next move, which was some inane conversation about geology, with which he hoped to put me at ease. While this went on I considered my options:

1. Run like hell and hope he didn't catch me.
2. Disable him here and call the cops.
3. Find out who he was.

I should have gone for number two. What the hell was I thinking? Maybe it was when he pulled on the yarn around his neck and drew up a foil-wrapped condom from under his shirt. That made me mad. So when he suddenly stepped forward and knocked the rock I was holding out of my hand, I decided to go for number three, try to find out how many times he had done this before and where the bodies might be hidden before he could lawyer up. There was some logic operating, you see, I wasn't just pissed off.

I let him wrench my arm behind my back, slap the piece of duct tape over my mouth, and force me toward the van with enough struggle to be convincing. Once inside the van I caught my breath and had second thoughts, thinking I might have done something stupid. During the trip into the van I was better able to judge his strength and balance against mine, and it was closer than I had anticipated. Plus it felt like I was about to wrestle in a phone booth.

But Black Ops Baxter's training kicked in. The man grabbed for the dowel that I was holding toward him like you do with a snarling dog, and cut his hand on the blade attached to the bottom. When he recovered from his surprise and charged at me, I was concentrating so hard I could feel the air he displaced. I feinted to one side, so he hit the back of the van. I twisted faster than he'd expected, buying time to get some distance and leverage to use my stick in a way that would do more good.

He managed to roll to one side where his tools were held against the wall and pulled the pliers off. If he got one good shot at me with those I'd be done.

My blade got there before he could secure his grip, as I hooked the tool through the joint and popped it out of his way. Now it was his turn to stop and regain his breath. Unlucky for me, when we had stopped moving he was still blocking the door.

"Round and round we go, where we stop nobody knows," he said. He sucked at his palm and seemed to lose focus for a moment, as if fascinated by the taste of the blood.

I started to speak and realized the duct tape was still hanging from one corner of my mouth. I loosened it and grimaced with the pain as it reluctantly gave up my cheek. I slapped its sticky side against the metal wall, then reached up and fingered a tendril of my white hair which had fallen when my hat came off in the struggle outside. Put him off guard, get some information. "You were attracted to this, were you? You like older women?"

"Actually you're a little young for me," he said, in a crouch, swaying. "This time is different."

"How old do you usually like?" I asked, doing a little swaying of my own so I wouldn't stiffen in the cramped van.

"Old enough so when they go missing people don't do AMBER Alerts and put them on milk cartons. Women no one will miss."

"Ever tell anybody what you do?" I asked.

He shook his head with what looked like regret. "Not lately, unless you count the Internet. But nobody takes you seriously there. Everybody talking all kinds of shit, mostly." He opened his mouth to speak again, then shut it.

So it was my turn. "How do you do it?"

"You really want to know?"

"Sure do."

He whistled like this time really was going to be different. He didn't know the half of it, but my admission had made him chatty. "You know how most guys do stuff that gets messy? Okay, I might get a little blood, you saw it on the floor, but mostly I don't do that. I break their bones instead."

"You break their bones. That sounds familiar."

"Can't be. I'm the only one who does that. It's my 'signature.'"

"Unique," I said to encourage him.

"Totally. You know, you've got some balls for an old broad. This is going to be more fun than I figured."

"It's clever, too, that you've got your setup here in the van."

"Yeah, want to know what I call it?"

"Tell me."

"Squeals on wheels." He laughed. He was uncharacteristically talkative for a serial killer, like it felt good for him to share this with someone.

I smiled as if impressed by his wit. "You could do me right here and no one would know."

The man shook his head, shifted to a more comfortable position. "Fuck no, that would be too risky. I . . . wait . . . you think I'm stupid. It's not like you're going to get out of this. You're the stupid one."

"You may be right. But how can you be sure?"

"Number one, we're still in my van, and, number two, I'm bigger than you are even if you did get lucky with that blade just now."

While he had been talking, I had begun circling the

bladed stick with one hand while the other, fingers up and thumb out, framed him. There was enough head room for me to rise up on one knee while the blade circled slowly, smoothly, in a slow-motion way that focused me to the point where I could feel the weight of the air between us. I was killing a little time while I figured out how best to disable him. Distract him with one or two more minor cuts and then break his collarbone, I decided.

He watched me, thoughtfully wiping his palm on his nylon shorts as he said, "Hey, those look like ninja moves. Get it? Old lady ninja. Ha!"

"I'll give you old," I whispered and darted forward. I swear I hadn't intended to do this, but he rose up at the same time and my blade sliced at just the wrong spot on his thigh. He watched like a rubbernecker at his own accident as the arterial spurt shot a good six inches and pooled in the grooves of the floor. "Oh shit," I said.

"Help me," he groaned as he fell back against the door and passed out.

"What do I look like, a paramedic?" I said to no one, but threw his body down flat, tore the yarn from around his neck, shook off the condom, and formed a tourniquet around his thigh above the wound. My garden gloves made tying the string difficult but instinct kept them on. With some effort I rolled him over on his back and sat cross-legged beside him on the shower curtain to avoid getting slimed by the blood pooled on the floor.

He was coming around slowly, still alive but too groggy from the plunge of blood pressure. I didn't have time to waste on the usual EMT process. Instead, I snapped the bone in his little finger and he bounded back with a shout.

"Hurts, doesn't it? Listen," I said. "I've accidentally

severed your femoral artery. No, don't bother to look. I put a tourniquet around your leg to slow the loss of blood, but if I don't tie off that artery within—" I checked my watch, "—thirty minutes you'll die anyway. Now tell me where you put the bodies."

"I'm bleeding to death."

"Yes, but slowly. Tell me where the bodies are."

"There, there's a sewing kit up on that shelf."

"First talk, and I'll keep you from losing your leg. I know how, but you're going to have to work with me."

"They'll get you for this."

I considered that he might be right, but he didn't need to know. "It's self-defense. Or at worst accidental manslaughter. Tell me where the bodies are."

"I'll say you attacked me."

"Look at you. Then look at me."

The man groaned.

"I'm getting pissed and you're dying. Not a good use of time. Now tell me where you threw the bodies, you sick fuck."

"Bodies . . ." He paused as if considering what to say. Then he started to whimper something and I leaned forward, close enough to be repelled by the sour smell of stale beer, to hear something that sounded like, "Yer dead . . ."

Which seemed fairly confident for a man in his condition. But I had overestimated his weakness and let down my guard. He lurched to his left side and head-butted me, making me see a flash of tiny lightning. While I shook myself, he managed to roll over, pinning me under his weight, but couldn't do much more than that. His hands tried to hold me, but weakened by his injury, they couldn't get enough purchase to do any good. His teeth the only weapon left to him, he clamped down on my upper arm. I shrieked but was pinned against the wall, legs crossed, no way to throw him or get out of the way. The coarse denim of my blouse wouldn't hold long to keep him from breaking the skin. I needed to do something fast, but the pain was distracting me as, in the way of a coral snake, he ground his jaws.

Already mentally counting the cost of my deed, already mourning the loss of the peace I'd found in the desert, I moaned with regret as I twisted to force my upper body down toward his legs.

I allowed myself one whispered "goddamn," then held my breath and closed my eyes and mouth tightly, in anticipation of the blood that would gush when I reached down with two free fingers and pulled the tourniquet away from his leg.

I've done it again, I thought afterward, and this time I don't even have a badge. I'm fucked.

THIRTEEN

What was it made me take a chance like that? Questioning him before he got a safety net in the criminal justice system and Miranda rights, that logic dissipated in the smell of warming blood. Logic. That's right, I was trying to find out where he'd put the bodies. Or was it also, just a little, wanting to reassure myself that I was still physically strong enough to take down a guy like this without help?

Plenty of time to think about all that later. For now I crawled to the back of the van where I could avoid the blood still running through the grooves in the floor and allow myself to recover from a mild shock, concentrating on bringing my breathing rate down so my heart would follow suit. Trusting there was no one outside the confines of the van to hear me, I screamed as loudly as I could, which settled me some. Then it was time to face the music. I hate music.

First taking off my blood-soaked garden gloves and hooking them over the top of my cargo pants, I unsnapped my side pocket and pulled out my cell phone. It was important to appear cool and in control of the situation, like I was still a professional. I cleared my throat and practiced a couple times, "Hi, Max? This is Brigid Quinn. Hi, Max? This is Brigid Quinn," until I could say it without choking. Max was programmed in, and my thumb shook over the Call button for a moment, thinking of how to spin this.

Then I thought, maybe not call Max first, maybe call Carlo instead. Explain everything to Carlo right off the bat before anyone else got to him and gave him the wrong notion of what had happened here, of what I had done in self-defense. I paused further, immobilized by the thought of Carlo coming down to the wash and seeing me awash in blood.

No, that wouldn't work. Instead, I thought, I could sneak home, get cleaned up, and then, without the blood, explain rationally and calmly what had happened in self-defense.

I paused yet again.

In that pause, while I sat on the floor of the van gazing at the filthy dead thing, I remembered the moment when Paul, of the cello and truffle oil, looked at a crime scene photo and told me he couldn't bear to have me in his world.

I'm sure there are other people who have experienced The Moment themselves. The kind where you've been one sort of person up to this point in your life. Then you're in a doctor's office, or at home, or at work, and someone, someone you might have always trusted, walks into the room and makes what is likely an offhand remark they'll never remember, but the comment rocks you at your deepest, unhinging whatever you had been. You think you're so tough, never realizing how fragile you are until you break. It happens that easily, that quickly. Paul was one of the moments. This was another, and beyond that, nothing can explain or justify what I did.

With an unbearable ache in my gut I thought about losing Carlo, and thought I would not, could not, survive the loss of the one happy thing in my entire existence. I'd waited too long for him and I would not drive him away the way I'd driven away every other civilian in my past. If I lost my husband I would not survive, and I would not take that chance. It would be so much simpler not to tell Carlo or anyone else about this.

How about I just say I panicked? And I went a little nuts. I tore my eyes away from the body, closed the phone that made the same soft click as a permanently closing door, and put it back in my pocket. And I put into play what was arguably the stupidest mistake of my life.

I considered my options, came up with three, decided. Made a plan.

Phase one: I opened the doors of the van and peered out. After the murky interior the light bouncing off the sand blasted my eyes. Then the wash came back into focus. I hopped out, unkinked my back, and got the liter bottle of water out of my backpack. I took off my gloves and dropped them in the sand. I washed some of the blood spurt off my face, then poured water over my blouse to spread the blood evenly through it, so it looked like darker denim. Rather than doing it in the sand I did this over a bit of scrub bush under the shelter of the bridge to hide the trace evidence in case they did a careful scene processing. Picking up my hat from where it had dropped in the struggle, I gathered up my bloodied hair into it. It didn't take a mirror to tell me that anyone seeing me now, at least from a distance, would merely see a bedraggled woman, wilted from the heat.

A car drove over the bridge heading west but didn't slow.

Phase two: I put my gloves back on, climbed in through the back of the van expecting to have to search the body for the keys, but I was in luck. He had left the keys in the ignition to make his getaway faster. I checked above the visors and in the glove compartment for a wallet, insurance card, vehicle registration, anything that might identify him and raise questions. All I found was an eight-by-ten manila envelope slid between the driver's seat and the transmission console, which I tossed on the ground outside the van so I wouldn't risk getting any blood on it.

Going back into the rear of the van, I opened the latch of a small cupboard attached to the wall. Among the contents was a pink Barbie Doll lunch box which I tried not to think about as I nosed around inside to find a box cutter. That would do nicely. I flicked up the blade of the box cutter, dabbed it in the man's blood, made a couple experimental cuts in his wrists, and tossed it near the body to make it look like he sliced his own artery.

I nearly missed my walking stick, lying in one of the grooves, the raw wood stained now with blood that would never come clean.

Knowing every second was a chance taken, I looked around the interior as best I could trying to spot any other clues that I'd been there. It seemed clean enough.

Phase three: I got into the driver's seat and peered through the front windshield to see if anyone had been watching me. Finding the coast clear, I turned on the engine and turned the van onto a dirt road that ran along the top edge of the wash. Luckily the wash and the road veered hard left, and I traveled around the curve until I felt the van would be well out of sight from the bridge where I was known to do my rock hounding. Also luckily, here the river had caused a higher drop from the edge where the water had rushed around the bend in times past, carving out the sand at the curve.

I carefully maneuvered the van closer, closer to the edge of the wash where there was an opening between the mesquite trees that clung stubbornly to the earth despite the erosion of the sand beneath them. When I felt the tires begin to sag dangerously on the driver's side, leaving the vehicle in drive, I pulled up the emergency brake, crawled over the console and out the passenger side. It would have been more convenient if I were on the left bank of the river and could punch the gas with my walking stick. Instead, I released the brake, pushed on the open passenger door, and prayed for the strength I needed as well as maximum rollover so the drop and tumble would justify the condition of the corpse.

The technique worked. The van fell the eight feet or so into the riverbed, twisting as it dropped so that by the time it hit the softest sand it was lying on its roof, the engine still humming. Holding my breath, practically holding my heartbeat, I stopped long enough to listen if any observers had noticed the accident and were screaming and running toward the wash. There was no sound except one delayed thump like a sack of cement mix falling in the back of the van. The scumbag's body, I reasoned, which must have caught on something before making the drop.

It had taken less than fifteen minutes to reach the point of no return from my decision.

Ideally it would be at least a week before the van was discovered, decomposition and insect activity obliterating the slashed artery. If not, this could be judged a suicide of a derelict John Doe. They wouldn't look closely enough to see some of the cuts were post-mortem; he'd be stored in the morgue fridge and no one would ever ask for him.

I went over the scene carefully in my stocking feet, leaving the tracks that showed my presence in the wash but dragging the backpack behind me to obliterate his footprints near the bridge. That brought me back to where the van had originally been parked, and I saw the manila envelope on the ground. Staying to look inside, removing it from the scene, both were risky. I picked it up and put it in my backpack.

When I hefted the backpack over my shoulder, I noticed it was lighter than usual. I had been in the wash about ten minutes before the perp showed up and had only gathered a half dozen or so rocks. Questions would be asked if I returned home after such a long time with so little. I picked up the rose quartz and a few others.

Phase four: rather than taking the main road home, I trudged up out of the wash about a hundred yards past the bridge and crossed Lago del Oro Parkway. Morning rush hour was past, so the dozen cars it comprised and any hope of their providing rescue was long gone. If some other woman had been down there, she would be lying in the back of the van right now, broken. Because it had been me, the man was broken instead. That comforted me.

Other women. Unfortunately, I had accidentally silenced the asshole before I could find out about those other women. But more important, there wouldn't be any others, ever again.

Listening to my ragged breathing and trying for a time to cleanse my mind of death, I looked again at the nearby mountains about three miles to the east. They had that whole purple-mountains'-majesties thing going for them. That thing I thought I was going to defend in my more naive days as an agent.

I made my way across the arroyos separating Lago del Oro Parkway from the edge of my housing development. Only a quarter mile as the crow flies, but it was some rough going, sliding down the gravel on one side of a narrow gulley and having my back spasm as I dug with my stick into the other side for the climb back out. There were about six of these, each one higher up than the last so that at the very top you're looking back into a small valley that the river had carved over millennia.

Other than that there was nothing, nothing but desert scrub highlighted by occasional orange-red blooms blasting from the top of a barrel cactus and the track of horseshoes, but my nervous system couldn't seem to get out of hyperalert mode. Peering through scraggly tree branches and behind low hills, I kept my stick ready and stayed on the balls of my feet. Every sound, from a motorcycle roaring on the road that ran parallel to my route to the rustle of a rabbit in the brush made the nerve on the side of my neck spark.

I could have disabled him in the wash and then called for backup. That's what I should have done.

The 10 percent humidity and dehydration began to affect me, making me a little woozy. My blouse was already dry, stiffened a bit by the blood saturating it. I craved water but wouldn't open my lips to drink, aware that the dead guy's blood cells, a few of which had probably collected in the corners of my mouth, were likely infected with something.

Despite the wooziness, when I came to the last arroyo before the house, I buried my bloody walking stick in the softer sand on the side toward the top, where it would not likely be washed away in the next hard rain.

When I finished, and started once more to pull the backpack over my shoulder, I remembered the envelope. I was mildly curious about its contents, but needed to get into the house and cleaned up without Carlo seeing me. Phase five: Carlo. I foolishly thought that this would be the greatest challenge, not to bring a scumbag to justice, but to forever hide from my husband and the world the ghastly thing I had just done. Killing the guy, that was the easy part.

FOURTEEN

I snuck in the side gate, through the outside door that leads into the garage, and from there inside to the laundry room. I could hear the shower going on the other side of the wall in the master bathroom, thank God. It gave me precious moments to toss my backpack on the claw-foot mahogany foyer table and the cell phone onto the kitchen counter, rip off my clothes, including blouse, hat, shoes, underwear, and gloves, and dump all into the washing machine; throw in half a bottle of bleach; and turn that sucker on. I'd toss it all in the garbage later, but no use providing more evidence than was inescapable.

The Pugs, who must have been having their morning nap in my closet, rushed me. Rather than jumping on my legs the way they always did, they approached cautiously, interested in the new smell I had brought home. I spoke as fiercely as I could while keeping my voice low, "Stop! Stay!" Unaccustomed to sharp tones, they sat back on their haunches and eyed me suspiciously as if concluding I actually was that stranger I smelled like.

Trying to move as fast as I could, before Carlo came out and saw me with most of my body stained where the watered-down blood had seeped through my clothes, I started into the front bathroom, then stopped when I heard Carlo belting an aria in the shower of the master bath.

I don't know much Italian, but knew that this one went on like that for a while. At any other time the sound of singing would make my skin crawl, but this time it came as a gift. He knew all the verses and the orchestral accompaniment between them and wouldn't turn off the water until he got to the end of the song.

I went into the guest bathroom at the other side of the house and shut the door. My knees buckled from the shock and dehydration and I wanted to lean up against the sink, but would not take the chance of leaving any trace evidence, so I just stood and swayed a second. To keep from collapsing I stared in the mirror at the little tattoo of a white rose over my heart. Carlo never asked me about that tattoo either.

I thought about what I should have done. I should have left the van as is, come home and cleaned up, and explained everything to Carlo as gently as possible and then called Max. That's what I should have done.

It took a long time to get clean. I took a bottle of alcohol into the shower with me and poured most of it over my face. Only then did I finally open my mouth under the shower and drink my fill. I washed my hair and the rest of my body, not caring if the soap ran into my eyes. Blood seeping through the gloves had caked in my cuticles and dried on the walk home. It finally melted with my repeating the whole washing process a second time. Even so, when I stood again in front of the mirror, inspecting the reddening bite mark on my upper right arm, I let my fingers soak in a little more alcohol that I poured into the sink. Only then was I ready to leave the bathroom.

I had practiced again using my voice while in the shower so was able to call "Hi, Perfesser. I'm back!" loudly enough and without a tremor to reach him anywhere in the house. Luckily he was still in the shower himself and had moved on to something mournful that sounded like *Piangee, Piangee,* so did not acknowledge my greeting.

In no hurry for Carlo's first appearance, I finally allowed the exhaustion to take me, fell into the living room couch to further excite the Pugs, who, happy to have the real me back, threw themselves at my ankles like muscle-bound two-year-olds, making hum-smack noises with their tongues. Then they stopped their playful attack to sniff me again, likely detecting a residual whiff of dead scumbag. "Everything is just fine," I told them. As if puzzled still, without my being able to detect any signal between them, they left to cool their taut bellies on a part of the Mexican tile that was not covered by Jane's rugs.

A final sound of a flush, the water running, the foosh of air freshener, and Carlo emerged from the master area with an opened copy of *Islam Today* and a triumphant gleam in his eye. That little bit of normalcy reminded me why I did what I did. Though prepared for this moment, I felt my body go rigid with tension and concentrated on one muscle at a time, starting with softening the corners of my mouth.

When he saw me he squinted a bit, trying to figure out what was different while, still working on composure, I stared back at him.

"You're naked," he finally asked, sitting beside me on the couch and crossing his long legs. Overwhelmed with joy at the entire pack being united, the Pugs began a new assault on his shins. He brushed them off without taking his attention from me.

I recognized my last chance to speak the truth. The man in the van, covered with blood, mouth open in the final groan, snapped in and out of my head. I replayed the events in a flash and made them play out differently. But there was no turning back now. I felt my eyes flash open. "I tripped over a rock and got sand in my hair," I said, nuzzling Carlo's cheek and patting his thigh while wondering how long it would take for someone to find the van in the wash. "What a klutz. I'm glad you weren't there; you would have loffed and loffed."

Instead of chuckling at my phony British accent Carlo shook his head and pointed at my arm. "Must have been a bad fall. Is that a bruise coming up?"

I got up and went into the kitchen area of the great room. Using the microwave door over the stove as a mirror, feeling Carlo's eyes on my ass, I stood on my tiptoes and once more examined the crescent bruise on my arm, reassuring myself he wouldn't recognize it as a bite mark, then busied myself fluffing my still-damp hair. That way I could arrange some over the other darkening bruise on my forehead where I'd been head-butted and stall looking him in the eyes until I developed my alibi more completely.

Carlo came up behind me. I could see the reflection of his questioning look in the microwave door. The look was surprisingly unnerving for someone who has spent most of her life undercover, let alone someone who has just killed a man.

"Are you okay?" he asked.

"Is there any coffee left?" I asked, sniffing in the direction of the monster Cuisinart that didn't look like any coffeepot I'd ever seen outside of a Dunkin' Donuts.

"I think so," Carlo said. "Let me get you a cup." He pulled one of Jane's Bavarian porcelain cups, the kind with little feet at the bottom, out of the cupboard and poured me a cup of black, cold. While he was getting it for me I got my backpack off the credenza and dumped the rocks into the sink to rinse them off. The water bottle fell out, too, and I was glad I had my back to Carlo, hiding it from sight as I washed more blood off it.

I focused on my hands to make sure they weren't shaking when I turned to take the cup from him. Partly successful, the cup didn't rattle against the saucer as I sipped, but it had to follow my head a bit, which had begun moving back and forth at an alarming rate. I wasn't wimping—only a psychopath can take life without some reaction. Just as bad was having to hide the fact. Luckily Carlo missed my trembling, having turned to the sink to finish rinsing off the rocks I had left there. With his back still to me he said, "I can't believe you bothered to drag all these rocks up the hill after tripping."

"I'm in incredible shape for an old broad, is that what you're trying to say?" I said lightly, put the empty cup and saucer on the counter next to the sink to keep him busy, and went to blow-dry my hair despite the fact it was already dry. I crammed myself hurriedly into jeans and a blouse before remembering the bloody bottle that must have left some residue inside the backpack. I'd have to throw the backpack in the washing machine for a second run.

When I grabbed it off the counter I felt the bit of resistance inside and remembered the envelope. I glanced over at Carlo, who had settled into his chair with the copy of a life of Ludwig Wittgenstein he'd been reading. "If you want me I'll be checking e-mail, Perfesser."

He nodded, lost in philosophy. I went into my office, sat down on the swivel chair at the desk, pulled the envelope out, and looked inside, hoping to find something that would identify the man who had assaulted me.

What I drew out of the envelope was an unlabeled DVD disk on top of a photograph printed off a color computer on plain paper.

Probably porn, I thought, and put the DVD aside to look at the photograph. In the first moment I don't know what I saw. For the first moment my mind failed to register anything at all other than that, kind of a cerebral short circuit. Then I registered an unpretentious neighborhood street, neat sidewalks, graveled yards. Sage in bloom, like a burning bush consumed with lavender flame. A woman with white hair pinned up. After that I was aware of a muscle twitching once, hard, at the corner of my mouth.

I was staring at a photograph of myself.

Once the shock passed of seeing myself, and understanding that the attack in the wash could not have been just a coincidence, I looked at the image for details. The clothes were what I'd been wearing the evening before when we walked the dogs. I had taken a long shower to get the smell of the medical examiner's office out of my skin and put on that red T-shirt. Someone had driven by and taken my picture without my being aware. I wracked my brain for a memory of the white van going by, but there was none. Our tidy middle-class subdivision was small, if two cars went by it was a busy evening. I would have remembered a crummy white van. And I would have remembered a driver who looked like the man I killed.

I picked up the DVD that I had discounted as just porn and inserted it into my computer. While it loaded, I got up to close the door to my office. The DVD was a short clip, just the news report from the night before about catching Lynch and about my involvement in the Route 66 murders. And there for that brief second was my face on the computer, the formal picture in my black suit taken on the occasion of my retirement from the Bureau.

I thought of the man I had just killed, whom I had never seen before today. There was no way he could have seen the newscast the evening before and taken the picture within two hours of it. Someone had to know about me before then, and know where I lived. And then I thought of his words that I thought were preposterous bravado just before his final attack: "Yer dead." Maybe he wasn't talking about doing it himself. Maybe he was talking about the person who hired him, and how it wasn't over.

I played over the entire scene in my head, from his observing me from his truck to my accidentally puncturing his femoral artery and losing whatever chance I had to find out more from him. Was this connected to the capture of Floyd Lynch and my involvement in the Route 66 case, or was it a grand coincidence? No, I returned to the idea that someone would have had to know about me more in advance of the news report to track me down to that wash. No coincidence.

And even if it was, for safety's sake I needed to treat it as an assassination attempt. In asking the man in the wash where the bodies were, I had been asking the wrong question, and now he was too dead to give me the answer to the right question—who sent you?

I tracked back over the events in the wash, the way he liked older women, the way he broke their bones. But nothing clicked. Coming up blank on everything except for the certainty that there was something I did not yet know and that not knowing was dangerous.

There is a peculiar feeling at times like this. The closest I've been able to come to describing it is to say I drained out of myself. With hands that were now rock steady I opened the compartment next to my desk where the extra keyboard and broken monitor were kept. I reached way in the back behind the useless monitor and pulled out a box about ten inches long by six inches wide by three inches high. I opened the box and removed the FBI special, Smith and Wesson Model 27 with a three-inch barrel, from its foam casing.

The ammunition was kept in a drawer on the right side of the desk, the one with all my pens and what have you. This smaller box was also hidden toward the back, a box that had originally contained staples. One by one, without a tremble I pulled out six shells and loaded them into the weapon. I placed the weapon on the desk.

Now I was in control.

FIFTEEN

Or thought I was in control until a knock at the door made me jump a little. There had never been closed doors and knocking until this moment. There had never been jumping. "Not now," I said loudly enough to be heard through the door, then afraid I had spoken too harshly, added, "Perfesser Darling."

"It's your cell phone, honey. It's buzzing."

Everything normal. I got up, opened the door and smiled.

"Sorry, just thinking hard." I really did feel sorry, because at that moment there was something invisible yet more impermeable than a Kevlar vest slipping between me and Carlo. A lie wide enough to divide us. This is what I had tried so desperately, risked everything, to keep from happening, but it was happening just the same. Even in the stress of the moment, bigger-picture things like danger and death, there was this little pinch in my heart. Maybe that's what they mean when they talk about hearts breaking.

So far Carlo didn't seem to notice the difference. "That business you're involved with?"

"Uh-huh, that."

As Carlo handed me the phone, his eyes drifted over my shoulder and stopped. That would be where I left my

Smith on the desk. We both pretended it wasn't there.

I smiled my reassurance again and he turned away to let me answer the phone.

"Brigid," the voice said.

"Hello, Coleman."

"So, what do you think? Did you look at the video?" She sounded a little disappointed, as if she already knew the answer to that.

I forced my thoughts to something I temporarily couldn't give a shit about. "No, not yet. I've been a little preoccupied with some personal business."

"That's where ..." She sighed, knowing she'd gone over all that already. "I was thinking I'd go see Lynch's father out in Benson tomorrow. We didn't take the time to interview him and he's so close."

"That's premature. You need to develop an interview plan."

"You think I didn't already do that?"

In my distracted state I'd forgotten this was cross-the-t Coleman I was talking to. "So, go."

"Come with."

"No," I started, then thought about my being attacked in the wash two days after I got reinvolved with the Route 66 case. Visiting Lynch's father might not be such a bad idea. "Okay, why not. When do you want to go?"

"Swing by my office first thing in the morning since it's on the way. I'll drive from there."

I hung up (I don't care what they call it these days) the phone and sat for a while, wondering if I should hide the gun or keep it handy. I covered it with the manila envelope. Then I threw the backpack into the washing machine with the other clothes and made a mental note to wash them again, but for now I let the exhaustion wash back over me. I spent the rest of the day pretending not to brood while I made my plan for finding out who wanted me dead.

"You know what?" I said, going into the kitchen in the late afternoon where Carlo had just poured himself a glass of Chianti and put some Triscuits and a hunk of smoked Gouda in a plastic bowl. "I think I'm in the mood for a drink. I guess that fall stunned me more than I want to admit."

"Shall I fix one for you?" Carlo makes a good vodka martini, loads the glass with olives, making it more of a salad than a drink so I feel less like a lush.

I watched Carlo with the shaker while thinking of having, for the first time in my life, someone close enough to me to be in danger. I was part of a family, a pack if you counted the Pugs. I carried my martini out to the backyard under the pretext of relaxing, but actually to assess the perimeter of our property in case of attack. There were no houses in back of ours except for in the far distance, where the ground rose up to the mountain. On either side we were separated from the neighbors by five-foot cinder-block walls. The neighbors to the right were snowbirds who wouldn't be returning until the weather cooled. Someone could easily hop over that wall. Or simply unlatch the gate leading to our backyard, though the rusty latch made so much racket the Pugs would surely be alerted. They had followed me out and were sniffing for lizards by the bougainvillea. I should have a shepherd, I thought, or at least a hound. These guys put together wouldn't make one decent dog.

I walked out a bit to the life-size statue of Saint Francis

and wondered whether Jane bought it for Carlo before or after she bought the Pugs. By that time the drink settled me some and I was able to go back over my experience of the afternoon more calmly than before, like watching someone else's movie frame by frame. Old women. Condom on a string. Blood in the van. Broken bones. Other bodies. Photo of me. News clip on a DVD. Barbie lunch box.

Nothing.

Dinnertime came and there we were, just like always, cozily munching on chicken curry sandwiches that Carlo, trying to be subtle in his hovering, fixed for us. The Pugs sat at attention waiting for the empty dishes to be lowered at the end of the meal so they could clean up the chicken residue.

There was nothing on the news that night about a body being discovered outside the city, no ticker headline running across the bottom of the television that read *Former FBI Agent Sought in Tucson Slaying*. I had mixed emotions. If the body was found it might be identified. And knowing who it was would lead me closer to finding out who sent him. On the other hand, with every twenty-four hours that passed, decomposition and insect activity would destroy more and more evidence of my involvement.

Either way the time dragged. In the evening the phone in the kitchen rang twice, once from a telemarketer offering us reduced rates for credit card transfers, and once from Carlo's sister in Ann Arbor. Each time I was certain it was Max coming to get me after discovering the body. After that I unplugged the phone and turned off my cell so I could relax a little.

At bedtime, still with the events of the day replaying in my head, I kissed Carlo to reassure myself, though I noticed that our glances slid by each other in a way they never had before, as if I was afraid my eyes would reflect what I had seen that day and he sensed my secrecy. Just my guilty conscience working my imagination, I'm sure, but this is what it would have been like at the best of times, married in the Bureau: half-truths and sliding eyes. As it was, despite all my precautions, I couldn't keep from fearing that it was only a matter of time until Carlo would discover the woman I really was and look at me the way Paul had.

Carlo turned the ceiling fan on and the light off, and in the dark my thoughts shifted. If I hadn't tried to cover up the incident in the wash, if I had told Max about what I did, he would have found the envelope with the photos that showed I was a target. Then I would have had him on my side. If that were the case, I would have given anything to repeat the last ten hours, given anything but Carlo, that is.

Long after his breathing had settled into that quiet rhythm that told me he was asleep, I reached over and lightly brushed his hand through the sheet, my touch lingering on his man-size knuckles. When that didn't wake him I folded slowly, one millimeter at a time, my fingers around his thumb, trying not to imagine it disappearing, my ending up with nothing but a wad of bedsheet in my grip.

What do they call this, obsessing? I was obsessing.

I finally fell asleep to the sound of a pack of coyotes somewhere in the arroyos beyond our property. It was a chorus of barks, howls, coughs, cackles, and a high-pitched keen, like manic ghosts. Carlo told me once they do that when they've killed something.

SIXTEEN

Still rattled from my experience of the day before, brooding about who had hired the killer and how I was going to find out, yet knowing that I was going to have to appear knowledgeable about Coleman's continuing the investigation of Lynch, I pulled the DVD labeled "Lynch Interrogation: Session 12" from its pocket in Coleman's report. Because the case was so big they hadn't relied on just recording him but videotaped every session for posterity. The date on it was August 7, three days before Coleman had gathered us all together to go find Jessica's body.

To avoid Carlo's hearing any of the interrogation I got up and shut the door of my office, and for good measure kept the volume so low that I had to lean forward to catch the dialogue. The video loaded to reveal an empty room, standard interrogation, like a white box with two chairs and no table to hide their body language.

As I watched, the door to the room opened and a jailer led Lynch in, dressed in his orange prison suit and handcuffs. Lynch shuffled immediately to the far chair as if he'd done this enough times to know the drill. After spending so many hours in this room, he had also discovered the camera mounted in the corner near the ceiling. He waved at me, then apparently forgot the camera was there and lifted his cuffed hands to run his upper lip back and forth over the wart on the back of his hand the way he had when we were at the crime scene. When he bit down on it, he didn't show any pain.

I stopped the film and studied him more closely than I had been able to at Jessica's scene. There was the dark curly hair I remembered, the ski nose, and the wire-rimmed glasses. Now I noticed other details, how his upper lip was more prominent than his jaw. How his fingers showed he was a fine-boned man. I noticed again that scabby patch on one cheek that looked like it got picked at when he was bored with biting his wart. How his ears stuck out from his head.

After a few minutes Coleman and Max Coyote entered the room. I couldn't see them, but Lynch said hello to both. I heard the skreek of the other chair on the tiled floor as Coleman took the chair facing Lynch. Max would stand, leaning against the wall by the door, the usual stance. Lynch rose just enough to make a little bow, convincingly respectful without threatening Coleman, and sat back down. While he was the only one I could see throughout the interrogation, I imagined both of them sitting there with their little wire-rimmed glasses, looking like social studies teachers in conference.

Lynch lifted his hand to show a small smear of blood. Did he do this to create the sense that he had some control over his captors?

I heard Max open the door, speak to the jailer outside, and come back in with a tissue. He appeared briefly in front of the camera while he handed the tissue to Lynch and then retreated back to his spot near the door. Lynch dabbed the wart and balled up the Kleenex in his fist so the blood didn't show. When he was done, Coleman spoke:

COLEMAN: Good morning, Floyd.

LYNCH: Good morning, Agent Coleman.

COLEMAN: Did you sleep well?

LYNCH: Not too bad. My cell is bigger than the cab of my rig. Want to know something else?

COLEMAN: What's that?

LYNCH: I was thinking some, talking to you has made me think a lot, and decided I must've talked more to you than anybody else in my whole life.

COLEMAN: Why do you think that is?

LYNCH: Not much of a talker, I guess.

COLEMAN: Did you talk to the girls a lot, Floyd?

LYNCH: No, not much. I didn't want them to talk. *(Closes his eyes and with his fingertips makes a circular motion on his thighs, as if he's lost in the memories. The cuffs make his hands move in sync with each other.)* Girls never said anything nice to me.

COLEMAN: Please open your eyes, Floyd. *(He does, but looks slightly off to the right, a dreamy expression on his face.)*

COLEMAN: Is that why you switched to having sex with dead girls, Floyd? Because they didn't talk?

LYNCH: I thought we went over all that already.

COLEMAN: Do it again.

LYNCH *(looking like he'll resist, then giving in)*: Okay. When I found out I had an FBI agent in my car—

COLEMAN *(interrupting)*: In your car, not your truck.

LYNCH: That's right. Like I told you before, I would park my rig off road somewhere and use a rental car to pick up the girls. Then I'd get them into the rig and dump the car. But this one scared me, especially when I found out she was wired.

COLEMAN: How did you find that out?

LYNCH *(pause)*: I don't remember every line of the conversation. We're talking seven years ago, you know? *(Pause.)* Wait, I do remember that bit. As soon as she got in the car I got her mouth taped, her wrists bound, and slashed her ankle. She fought me, but I surprised her. She thought I was a woman, see.

COLEMAN: How did you do that?

LYNCH: I had a wig on and shit. And I raised my voice like this.

COLEMAN: Would you please repeat that?

I stopped the video, made a note: Do a voice comparison to see if it matches the one we have on file from the night Jessica got taken. Something, but still not compelling enough to force Morrison to review the case, let alone make Lynch recant. I started the DVD again.

LYNCH: I found out she wasn't really listening to anything on her headphones, that it was a wire. I figured she was a plant. So that's when I came up with the plan to play the CD and leave her wire in the SUV. To stall whoever was tracking her.

COLEMAN: And do you remember the music that was playing on that CD?

LYNCH *(rolls his eyes and laughs)*: Yeah, Kate Smith.

I stopped the video again. I'd forgotten. This was another one of those facts that we never released. So far this video was not swaying me toward the opinion of a false confession. I clicked Go again.

COLEMAN: Why in the world would you want to listen to Kate Smith?

LYNCH *(laughs softly)*: She reminds me of my mother. Anyway, I was lucky, they took a long time to get their act together, or they were too far away, or something.

COLEMAN: I think you must have told me before, but when did you first think of making mummies?

LYNCH *(Pause. He stares at her, blinking.)*: I can't remember.

COLEMAN: Try. There's a seven-year gap between Jessica Robertson's murder and the body we found on your truck.

LYNCH *(pause)*: I went back to the car again and again, and jacked off on the body. I liked that. I found out I liked that just as much as killing. *(He stops talking; his thumbs move in circles rapidly over the tops of his thighs.)* After a while the body dried out and I started thinking about how cool it would be to have a body with me all the time and not have to go up on the mountain and take the chance of getting caught. I experimented on animals and shit.

COLEMAN: I understand.

LYNCH: Do you, Agent Coleman? *(He stares at her with a sad frown, his eyes narrowing, his thumbs moving more rapidly over his thighs.)* No, I can see it in your face, Agent Coleman. You think I'm sick.

COLEMAN: Floyd, judging sick isn't my job.

LYNCH: But I want you to understand. I'm no different from everyone else.

COLEMAN: Why do you need me to understand?

LYNCH: Sex and death together. It's what everybody likes—like macaroni and cheese.

COLEMAN *(pause)*: Not quite the—

LYNCH *(interrupting)*: I bet you like those vampire shows, dontcha?

COLEMAN *(pause)*: No, I—

This part made me squirm. Coleman seemed uncertain. She was losing control of the interrogation and I felt embarrassed for her.

LYNCH: I seen a movie the other day where there's these zombie girls who dance naked in a joint and then eat the guys. I bet that movie made a lot of money.

COLEMAN: Floyd, let's get back on—*(His eyes close again and his head tilts back. His breathing is more noticeable, almost audible. He speaks softly, his upper lip pushing out with each word.)*

LYNCH: Guys standing in line to get ripped apart . . . because they want to have sex with dead girls.

COLEMAN: Floyd. Stop.

MAX *(moving into camera range, closer to Lynch)*: Floyd.

COLEMAN: It's okay, Deputy Coyote. Look at me, Floyd.

LYNCH *(eyes still closed but lids fluttering, his voice turns harsh)*: But you think I'm different. You think I'm a freak. You think this is some kind of a freak show.

COLEMAN: Look at me, Floyd.

LYNCH: No. *(Opens his eyes, stares at her with something other than the practiced mildness he has been exhibiting, with desperation.)* No. You look at me. *(He spreads his knees apart to show the camera a small stain on the crotch of his trousers, darker orange than the rest. Max moves within range of the camera. The next bits of dialogue fold over each other, everyone talking at once.)*

MAX: You disgusting asshole.

LYNCH *(ignoring Max, pinning Coleman in his gaze)*: What d'you see, Agent Coleman?

COLEMAN: It's okay, Deputy Coyote. It's okay.

LYNCH: What d'you see? Is that freaky enough for you?

(Long pause, Lynch still staring in Coleman's direction, his whole body hanging, not spent but sad. I can imagine Coleman facing him off, refusing to be affected. Lynch lifts his hand to his face and strokes the scabby patch with his nails up and down. Max moves back out of range, but I get the sense he's staying closer to Coleman now. Even with what I can't see the tension in the room is palpable.)

COLEMAN *(clears her throat)*: We're going to take a break now. You go get yourself cleaned up.

LYNCH: Sure.

It was okay with me, too. I blew out my breath, unaware till just then that I'd been holding it. No matter how many times you've seen this kind of creature in action they always have an effect on you. And then sometimes they don't, and that's even worse.

(Sound of Coleman's chair as she stands)

COLEMAN: Oh, one last thing while I've got it on my mind. The ears you removed. Were they a trophy, a souvenir?

LYNCH: I guess you could say that, yeah.

COLEMAN: The medical examiner reports said you cut them off postmortem.

LYNCH *(vague)*: I guess so.

COLEMAN: That means after death.

LYNCH: I know that. I read a lot of Jeffery Deaver.

COLEMAN: Where are they?

LYNCH: Where's what?

COLEMAN: The ears. What did you do with the ears?

(Long pause. Lynch pushes an invisible something away from himself.)

LYNCH: I . . . I threw them away.

COLEMAN *(pause)*: Where did you throw them?

LYNCH *(Pause. He has to think, and this time he's thinking hard. His voice goes up a half octave.)*: I don't know, some garbage can somewhere. What difference does it make?

COLEMAN: It's just that you know so many details, more than we even knew, like where the bodies were. You know about the postcards that were sent after Jessica's death and playing the Kate Smith CD, and you know about how the ears were removed. It seems like it would be important to you to remember this detail.

(Lynch's face is working against itself while he listens to Coleman's logic. He does not respond.)

COLEMAN: What's wrong, Floyd? Are you afraid if you say something wrong that you'll still get the death penalty? That won't happen, I promise.

LYNCH: I really need to go take a piss. Right now.

For the first time in twenty-four hours I thought of something besides killing a man. I backed up the video, reran it. Three times. Counted the pauses, one one thousand, two one thousand, three one thousand . . . more than three seconds each time. Managed to pause it at the precise moment Coleman asked him what he did with the ears. This is what she had given me the video for, so I could see it and judge for myself. Lynch's retinas dilated and his eyes cut left and down. His jaw dropped. But even if I didn't have those tells to go on, I felt certain he had to be lying.

More than lying. He actually went so pale the scab on his cheek appeared to darken. The look on his face was panic. And after Coleman pointed out how important was knowing the location of the ears, the look on his face was . . . fear.

I forwarded the video and the profile comparison to Sigmund Weiss.

SEVENTEEN

Subsequent generations may develop new distasteful terms for it but, shocking though it may be, the concept has been around for some time. Dr. David Weiss, JD, PhD in psychology, aka Sigmund, Sig for short, and I were fuck buddies once. Okay, twice. Three times if you count my going-away party, where we were so drunk we never succeeded in even removing our clothes.

The first time I had sex with Sigmund was when Paul dumped me; second was toward the end of my career, after I shot the suspect, when I couldn't remember if there was someone I really was and one night needed a connection to her.

Also, Weiss was smarter than me, and I always liked that. I like hanging out with people who make me skip mentally to catch up to them.

I did not marry the Perfesser because he subconsciously reminded me of Sigmund.

On the East Coast, Sigmund was three hours ahead of me, but that was no guarantee of his calling anytime soon. He always said he subscribed to some ancient rule, *Among mortals second thoughts are wisest.* Sigmund would watch the video, and think, and watch, and think again before calling.

So I killed some time. I got a package of ground meat

out of the fridge and mixed it with egg, bread crumbs, and chili sauce to give it a kick. Meatloaf was part of my rotating list of seven things I could make, including Shake'n Bake chicken, broiled fish, and baked pork chops with some barbecue sauce on them. I had been thinking of getting a grill.

I mashed and punched at the mixture while I thought of Floyd Lynch's face. I shaped it into a little football and put it back in the fridge for later.

Sigmund still hadn't called, so I fired up my computer and Skyped him.

"Bravely using the latest technology," he said, leaning back from the computer in his office and taking his time giving me the once over. I didn't try to stop him, didn't know how, though I hoped my recently killing someone didn't show. "I suppose you are not quite the Luddite I had taken you for, Stinger."

"Because I didn't sleep with a toaster when I was little the way you did?"

"Stinger is bantering. She always banters when she's under stress."

"Come on, the toaster crack is funny. You've just always been jealous because you can't take a joke."

"You hide behind your jokes." He leaned forward again as if he could see more of me that way. "This business is taking a toll on you. Let me see your cuticles."

I held up only the middle fingers of both hands, fingers that I hadn't worked over lately. He leaned back again, looking superior. "So I watched the video you sent. What a surprise." He didn't look surprised.

"When Coleman asked him what he did with the ears, he paused, you know that pause?"

"Yes, I know that pause. It was long."

"I timed it at three point five seconds. And then you saw him say he threw the ears away."

"Only his facial expression wasn't indicative of that. It didn't match the carelessness of simply tossing the ears into the garbage. It was an expression of panic. He was suddenly afraid we'd know he didn't do it. Either he doesn't know where they are, or he's afraid of telling us because whoever has them is the real killer. *Quod erat demonstrandum*," Sigmund said, which is his shorthand for *everything is apparent and speaking about it further bores me.* "He's not your man, of course."

We both knew that no killer who goes to that much trouble to enact a murder, with a repeated elaborate ritual, and then takes something from the victim to relive the pleasure afterward would ever throw these souvenirs in the garbage, let alone forget where he threw them. Think Dahmer with his body parts in the fridge. Think the Crown Jewels in the Tower of London. Either Lynch doesn't know where the treasured ears are, or he knows where they are but couldn't tell because of who it would incriminate.

"Are you as certain as I am?" I asked.

"More so. He would never forget where the ears are, if he ever knew. You still need to find those ears, Stinger. The killer has them. And I think that scares Mr. Lynch more than the death penalty. But an expression isn't enough, of course. You need evidence."

That's where I was stuck. "There's no *me* about this. I can't get near Lynch in any official capacity, and I wouldn't want to ruin the case by doing so. It's up to Coleman, and she's running into resistance. Coleman tried to tell Hughes about her doubts but even his public defender is swept up in the circle-jerk thrill of catching the Route 66 killer."

"Morrison's pressure. He wants this case for his self-published memoirs after he retires. I'm coming back out there."

"That's okay. It would just cause Coleman more trouble."

"You were the one who said I still have some clout."

"Not yet. Let me handle it and I'll let you know if I need help."

"They need to start from the beginning. There will be bigger holes in Lynch's confession than being afraid to tell you where the ears are. Who else is on the list?"

"There was no wife or kids. Coleman wants me to go with her to talk to Lynch's father, who lives east of the city."

"They didn't already do that?"

"No, they didn't. What do you think about doing a voice comparison? Check that bit where Floyd talks like a woman against the tapes we have from Jessica's wire?"

"That couldn't hurt. I'll have it done at the lab here. They should also ask Mr. Floyd Lynch again about that other body they found in the car, the one he called the lot lizard. He faltered when he spoke about her at the dumpsite."

"They, they. It's turning out to be Coleman and me, and I'm limited by being out of the business."

"Have you heard much about NamUs?" He pronounced it "name us."

"Not much. An identification database. It was being developed around the time I left."

"Civilians can look at it and add information without authorization."

I made a note on my pad to find out what was known about the prostitute and check it against the site. "Remember the postcards?" I asked.

He shifted his head and waved a hand to indicate it went without saying.

"Zach kept receiving them. He showed me maybe a half dozen more that he stopped bothering to send to us. Told me they comforted him because he could pretend they were really from Jessica."

"No." For the split of a second Sigmund's eyes narrowed and a rare wave of disgust passed over his face. It was so subtle I may be the only person in the world who could recognize it. Sigmund looked away from the screen. "We have to find that motherfucker," he murmured in what I knew was the direction of his office window. Obscenity with Sigmund was also rare. Then he recovered his composure and stared at the screen impassively. "They need to interview Floyd Lynch again under the presumption that this is a false confession, and find out how he got the information."

Sigmund didn't need to defend the possibility of a false confession. More than thirty people confessed to the famous Black Dahlia murder in LA, and over five hundred came forward claiming to have some involvement. Some false confessions were coerced under the pressure to solve the case, but there were other, voluntary confessions. Sigmund was thinking about the celebrity motivation, the wannabes. Henry Lee Lucas, who confessed to six hundred murders though there was only evidence of three. John Mark Karr, who confessed to murdering JonBenet Ramsey though his DNA did not match that at the scene and there was no record of his ever having been to Colorado where the murder occurred.

Robert Charles Brown.

Laverne Pavlinac.

Those two were convincing enough to be sent to prison until the real culprit was found. You could look it up.

In Lynch's case it would have been simpler than that. The apparent evidence of his guilt, combined with what might have been an obsession with the Route 66 killings, the lack of support from his public defender, and the threat of the death penalty, would have made a confession seem like the best option.

Floyd Lynch may have killed the woman found in his truck, or he may have found her already dead as he said at the start. He may have begun with a fascination for the Route 66 murders, and, when he was cornered, decided to take responsibility.

And voilà. The idiot goes to prison and the asshole stays free.

But it all went back to how Floyd Lynch knew about the details withheld from the public. That's what was different in this case. Barring the extreme coincidence that someone on the inside at the Bureau had leaked those details, which had somehow found their circuitous way to Lynch, it could only mean one thing. He knew the killer.

"It's been a whole seven years since the last killing," I said, hoping Sigmund would get my point and agree.

"No killings that we know of," Sigmund said. "He may have just changed his venue and mode, may even now be planning his next kill. Or he's stopped temporarily like the Grim Sleeper."

He had to remind me of the guy out in California who was dubbed that because he killed half of his victims in the mid-eighties, then took a break and killed the other half after 2002. I groaned.

"Don't deny you've already considered it. Besides, the Route 66 killer is enormously controlled. He was able to wait precisely one year before he killed again. That's frankly another point against Lynch being the killer. I don't see him as having very good impulse control." Sigmund picked up what I figured was the comparative profile that Coleman had compiled and gazed blankly at it. "I wonder what the real killer is feeling about this little man who has usurped his fame. It will either drive him deeper into hiding or inspire him to regain his glory. You need to get to Lynch, Stinger."

He was right; it was what I was thinking. I said, "Thanks for your help." I stopped picking at a hangnail, my whole body wanting to tell Sig about the real mess I needed help on. "Sigmund?"

"You can see I'm still here."

"Is it possible that somebody we put away is out on parole and we weren't notified?"

He thought, said, "No, they're very good about notifying us. Why?"

"Nothing. Just thinking."

I expected Sigmund to be the first to disengage from the conversation, but he did not.

"Now for the thing I don't know," he said. "You're different from when I was there."

"How so?"

"I can tell you're really troubled when you sound breathier than usual, as if you weren't breathing with both lungs. Are you terribly upset by the likelihood that Lynch isn't the killer? Are you feeling guilty?"

No, I'm having problems with a dead guy who I surmise is somehow connected to everything we'd just been talking about. I wanted so badly to tell Sigmund about it that I could feel the words forming in my mouth and had to bite down hard to keep them from coming out. There was something about Sigmund that made you want to confess and end the suspense. And then he could help me find out who might be after me.

Instead of spilling, I found myself giving a caricature of a casual shrug and actually batting my eyelashes. "Other than feeling jerked around by all this uncertainty, and hating the thought of having to tell Zach that the guy who killed his daughter is still out there, nothing. Nothing's wrong."

EIGHTEEN

Flowing between several different mountain ranges like a river of pavement and buildings, the Tucson area is tucked into the center of the Sonoran Desert. The Sonoran Desert is the largest, possibly the only, stand of saguaro cactus in the world. It's pronounced "swarro," and they're the kind of cactus you always think about when you think cactus, the kind that studs the landscape like a giant Gumby.

Now desert is mostly beige, that is to say rocks and sand. Only the hardiest of plants can survive, and you get to thinking, if that cactus can take it, so can I. I like the ruggedness of a place that can kill you, either by brush fire, dehydration, or drowning in a flash flood. Next to the desert, I feel soft and gentle.

Unlike Tucson, the area around the town of Benson, about an hour east from the easternmost part of the city, and at a higher elevation, sports less desolate-looking vegetation, with apple, peach, and pecan orchards. Benson has at least as many mobile homes as houses, and even a lot of the houses are prefab, their aluminum skirts hiding their lack of foundation like modest librarians.

As Coleman had suggested, I had met her in the parking lot attached to one of several skyscrapers in downtown Tucson, a twelve-story building in which the

FBI occupies the sixth. She was sitting in her car looking at her watch when I pulled into the space next to hers.

I couldn't bring myself to apologize for being fourteen minutes late, and besides, in that time she'd cranked up the AC so her Prius was bearable. Almost. Having taken my suggestion to dress in less intimidating attire, she was wearing black slacks and a white short-sleeved linen blouse. I guess that was as casual as Coleman could be. I pressed the button to shut off her radio, which was playing a song by one of those girls who all sound alike.

"Do you mind?" Coleman asked.

"Not anymore. Please leave it off. I hate music."

Coleman allowed that and as the Prius pushed the speed limit along I-10 East, she grilled me about my reaction to the video, and nearly crowed with triumph when I told her I not only saw the part about the ears but forwarded it to Sig Weiss, who concurred.

"So both of you think it's awfully suspicious," she said.

"That's right." I repeated how Weiss thought we should interrogate Floyd again from the supposition that his confession was false. "But we still need evidence. We need the big holes in his confession." I smiled at a thought. "We need to show Lynch the gun that isn't smoking."

Satisfied that for the time being she had Sigmund and me on her side, Coleman spent the rest of the trip briefing me on what she knew about Wilbur and Michael Lynch, Floyd's father and brother, respectively:

"Wilbur works?"

"On disability."

"Michael lives at home?"

"Yeah."

"Employed?"

"Started paramedic training, but I don't know if he ever finished."

"Mother?"

"Unknown."

"Call ahead?"

"Uh-huh."

"Resistance?"

"Not much."

And so on, with my thoughts half on Lynch and half on the dead guy in the wash, and whether this interview would help me discover a connection between them.

Coleman turned right on Palo Verde Drive into a trailer park, where I directed her to park a little ways off and we walked to the childhood home of Floyd Lynch. Dirt coated the roof of the trailer, its windows, a dirt bike with wheels the size of small blimps parked out front and the ragged umbrella with faded blue and white striping that tilted over a rusted metal patio table.

Wilbur Lynch stepped through the front screen door with his shotgun and did not invite us in. Tall and cowboy lean, his body belied the sixty-three years that Coleman had told me he had. His face, on the other hand, was lined with a lifetime of low humidity and Camel cigarettes, one of which fit a notch in his lower lip that looked like do-it-yourself cancer surgery.

Coleman flashed her badge while I put my hand on my tote as if I still had a badge to flash. "I'm Agent Laura Coleman," she said, "And this—"

I was about to interrupt her, but my disguise, hair down and Jackie-O sunglasses, was preserved by Lynch's own interruption.

"You don't look like FBI," he said, explaining his shotgun.

Privately I disagreed; I would have thought Coleman looked like FBI even if she wasn't. But we both did that little side head tic that gets past the allusion to our not being male, and Coleman shot me an arch look that said, "I should have worn the black suit."

"I wondered when you'd get here," he said, sitting down on a rusted chair by the rusted umbrella table and gesturing to the other two. We cautiously took two of the other chairs, taking care not to get scratched. "I thought you'd all be over to see me right after you captured him. I thought I'd be on the news." His drawl was easygoing, but he fixed his eye on us as if he wanted to make sure we noticed how much he didn't care. He put out his cigarette on the table and casually brushed the ash off with the side of his hand.

"I'm sorry about your son," Coleman said, without elaborating on the part she had played in putting him in jail.

Lynch smiled and took a packet of cigarettes out of his shirt pocket. "Well, good for you. I guess it's good that somebody's sorry." He tapped the packet so a couple cigarettes slid out and offered us one with an excessively smooth gesture that told me he was concentrating on keeping his hands steady. We declined, so he lit one for himself.

Once the cigarette was fitted securely into the notch in his lip, Coleman said, "Can we take it from that that you didn't have a good relationship with Floyd?"

"You could say that."

I picked up the slack left by his comment. "He grew

up here, though, right? Went to school, had friends?"

"I suppose. He always kept to himself, read a lot. He was a reader." Lynch left his upper lip cocked in a snarl as he said the word, as if that was the first step on the road to sexual homicide. "So he confessed. Don't send me the body." He made a heh-heh sound that was supposed to be a laugh.

"The fact is, Mr. Lynch, it may comfort you to know we're here because we think that Floyd didn't commit the crimes he confessed to," Coleman said.

Lynch turned his head away from us and stared at some buffle grass that hugged the side of the trailer. He looked like a man who expected little in the way of comfort, ever.

"And we're here trying to corroborate a few remaining questions," I said. "Can you think of a reason why Floyd would take blame for something he didn't do?"

"Nope." Lynch took a bitter drag off his cigarette, jerking his head as if his lungs alone weren't strong enough to pull in all the smoke he craved. "Because I think he did," he said after he exhaled it. "That boy always had bad blood."

"Bad blood?" I asked.

"Evil seed, I think they call it. Look, I don't know what you were expecting from me. Maybe somebody ashamed because his son is a serial killer. Maybe you'd like to see me wringing my hands and crying. Well, let me tell you something. I was glad when he finally left home and I didn't have to worry about him killing anyone close by." Lynch paused as if he were listening to an echo of his words, made the heh-heh sound again, and looked to us to laugh, too.

Coleman and I could not bring ourselves to comply.

"When was the last time you saw Floyd?" Coleman asked.

"He got his own rig about four years ago. Came around to show it off to us."

"Was your wife alive at the time?"

"No. Why, you wanna pin that on him, instead?" Lynch laughed, louder this time but with as little mirth as before.

"What did you think of Floyd's truck? Did he take you inside, show it to you?"

"Didn't go inside. I was hopeful, though. It's a big deal when a man can afford his own rig. I figured I could stop wondering when someone like you would show up with questions about him, heh-heh."

I could see now how the laughter was a cover, maybe had always been a cover, for the fears he had denied. Perhaps his son's capture was, in some part, a release. Maybe he really looked forward to a time when his son was dead.

Four years ago Floyd Lynch bought the truck. I did a mental calculation and figured at that point Lynch was tiring of going up the mountain to Jessica's body. Maybe that was partly the motivation for buying his own rig, so he'd be more comfortable storing a body in it.

"Did he just come to show you the truck? Is that all?"

Lynch thought back a moment. "He told me how successful he was, how he was making a ton a money."

"He didn't tell you anything about his life?"

Wilbur Lynch glazed over a bit. Almost as if he didn't realize he was speaking aloud, "Something."

"What's that?"

He seemed surprised to find us sitting there, had to go

on. "A box that he asked me to keep."

"Do you still have it?" Coleman asked. Her tone was a little too eager and I hoped Lynch wouldn't notice.

"I never thought about that box until just now."

"Could we see it?"

"He said it was just books."

"We'd still like to see it if you wouldn't mind too much."

He considered, possibly, whether it would be more to his benefit if he agreed or refused. "I'll see if it's still there." Lynch uncoiled himself from the chair and started into the trailer without speaking, apparently a little curious himself.

"Would you mind if we came along?" Coleman asked.

He didn't say no, so we followed him in.

The word "squalor" was invented for the interior of the trailer, ten feet wide and twenty feet long. Over time the dust had found its way in here, too, mixed with hair oil and thickened into a patina on the back of the shabby couch. Intersecting rings of various shade and depth where countless aluminum cans puckered the wood veneer coffee table. The kitchen area smelled like it was waiting to catch fire.

Lynch led us down the right hallway to a bedroom, where the roar of the AC window unit in the living room was quieter. The desert-frosted windows there made me feel encased. "He and his brother used to share this room before he left," Lynch said.

Pretty much the only thing in the room was a mattress that must have become a little cramped for two growing boys. A sheet lay wadded up on top of it. Both the mattress and the sheet were the same shade of gray. A small pile of clothes in the corner presumably served as the closet. The only other thing in the room was a stack of five boxes towering nearly to the low ceiling in the far corner, each one smaller than the one underneath it, an empty pint bottle of Jack resting on the narrow ledge formed by the largest box at the bottom.

Lynch pulled the boxes down and looked in each one, then handed them to Coleman, who gamely placed them in another stack in the other corner. When he got down to the last box he knelt down. This one was sealed.

A mason jar filled with alcohol and ears. Or vacuum-sealed in a baggy. Or at least something that connected Lynch to the man who tried to kill me.

He seemed to reconsider for a moment opening it, or at least opening it in front of us, but then took a Swiss Army knife from his right back jeans pocket and pulled out the blade. He wasn't about to just give up something that may have been of value. He neatly sliced through the single strip of packing tape and lifted the cardboard flaps.

The box was loosely packed enough so that Lynch could push the contents around with his blade. As the three of us leaned forward all we could see were some crime novels and porn and thriller DVDs.

"I told you he was a reader," Lynch said. He dug into the box, using the blade of his knife with a combination of curiosity and hesitation, like someone who doesn't want to reach bare-handed into a dark hole. He pulled out a few of the items and put them on the floor next to the box while Coleman and I stood watching him to see what he would find and what his reaction would be.

He drew out a DVD of a National Geographic program called *The Mummy Roadshow*, read the back of it still as if he were alone, and placed it on the floor next to the box. Then he found a manila folder, opened it, and paged through articles about serial killers that had been printed off a computer. I was standing just behind him, which allowed me to read some of the names over his shoulder: Ted Bundy, the Green River Killer, Jeffrey Dahmer, the BTK killer, Son of Sam, the Route 66 killer. Also a description of Natron, its uses, and how to order it. Also a printout of the home page of a site devoted to information and discussions about serial killers in general. Apparently unaffected by these things, Lynch put the folder on top of the video and looked back inside the box.

A glimpse of something tucked down on one side between the cardboard and the books got his attention, and he hooked it with his knife, pulling it out of the box and staring. It was just a shabby old dog collar, brown with silver studs, the leash still attached.

"What's wrong?" I asked.

"This collar. Had a dog. Barky. A good dog. The boys told me he ran away, but maybe I'm misrecalling." Lynch seemed a little dazed. He didn't say heh-heh.

"Did you still have Barky when Floyd came with his truck to visit you?" I asked gently.

That finally did it. He shed his careful façade as if he had been able to deny the unspeakable reality until this moment. "Oh fuck," he breathed in the voice of a very old man, the indignity that was his son too much on display in this artifact.

We were interrupted by the sound of boot heels ringing up the metal steps and the trailer door crashing open. "Hey Dad!" a voice called over the muffled roar of the AC unit. "You ready to hunt us some wetbacks?"

"We got company," Lynch called back, a little too quickly, from his kneeling position.

I glanced at Coleman and saw she understood why I had told her not to park in the yard. You never know what you'll hear if you don't leave your car in the yard.

The man who owned the voice skidded to a stop as he saw us, and stared.

I eyed Mike right back. His haircut, shaved to the scalp back and sides, with a longer patch on the top of his head, looked like a portobello mushroom cap. Largely due to the haircut combined with a menacing air, he was the kind of man who looks silly and scares you at the same time, the kind you doubt will someday grow out of his rage. I didn't ask what Floyd's brother might mean by "hunting some wetbacks" but felt confident he wasn't recruiting migrant farm labor.

He looked at his father rather than us when he said, "What are you doing back here?"

"They're from the Ef-Bee-Eye," Lynch said as precisely, as meaningfully as he could, but there was no telling from Mike's unchanged expression if he was able to spell. "They don't think Floyd killed those girls."

Mike strode back down the hall, speaking without turning around. "Come on, Pop," he said. "We're losing daylight."

Lynch rose and shouted after Mike, "Hey, did Floyd take Barky with him?"

I peered through the desert-frosted window where Mike had moved very quickly to saunter toward the dirt bike at the edge of the property. Lynch started after him.

I picked up the box before he could think about selling the contents on eBay and asked, "Would you mind if we took the box along, Mr. Lynch? You don't seem to have any use for this stuff."

"Mr. Lynch, what was in that box doesn't necessarily prove your son is a serial killer," Coleman said.

Lynch started to turn away, snapping as he did, "Oh, just kill him and get it over with."

I saw us losing control of the interview, gave Coleman a hard look. This wasn't an authorized visit and we needed to make the most of it. She stopped him and handed him a card, which he tucked in his shirt pocket without looking at it. "Mr. Lynch, do you know of anyone else who might have been associated with your son over the years?"

"Can't rightly say," he said, heading quickly down the hall to the living room as if he couldn't care less how long we stayed.

"Is there anyone who might benefit from your son confessing to the Route 66 murders?" I called after him as he went out the front door. "Did he ever mention any name at all?"

But Lynch had other things on his mind. Over the growl of the motorbike he set his feet wide apart and yelled at his son with raw fury, "You tell me, goddamit. You get off that fuckin' bike and tell me if Floyd killed my dog."

As we stepped down the rickety metal steps of the trailer, between the shouting and the motor, I was able to come closer to Lynch, take off my sunglasses. I hoped to catch him off guard when I asked without Coleman hearing, "Did he ever mention the name Brigid Quinn?"

All I was to him was an annoyance. He gripped me around the upper arm and his face came very close to mine. He tongued the groove in his lip.

"It's not my fault," he said, his breath muddying the air with its shame. "You have a kid who turns out to be a monster. Doesn't deserve to live. What do you do then? I shoulda drownded the little bastard when I had the chance."

NINETEEN

Coleman expertly turned on the ignition and the AC simultaneously. "Shit, we forgot to ask him if his wife was a fan of Kate Smith. That's what Floyd said."

"Textbook interviews only happen in the textbooks," I said. "Here's to Barky. May he rest in peace."

She said, "I never said Floyd was a nice man. Did you know he said he experimented by mummifying animals?"

"Yes, that was part of the video you gave me, but the family pet? I mean, come on."

"Still not a capital offense," Coleman said. She deftly maneuvered her Prius out of the trailer park and onto the main street of Benson. "I'm going to stop at that Burger King we saw on the way in to get a Coke for the ride back. Want something?"

"Yes. Don't go through the drive-through, park so I can go inside and pee. And please get me a Coke, too."

I did, she did, and we were back on I-10 in short order heading west while slurping our sodas. It's about an hour's drive back to Tucson proper, so she got chit-chatty the way people do on long automobile rides after interviewing a couple of jerkwads. It's a way of assuring yourself you're one of the normal people.

"How did you get into the Bureau?" she asked.

I slurped the remaining soda, jiggled the ice to make the most of it. "Family was a cop family, dad and brother in city police, sister joined the CIA. My sister Ariel and I played with Barbies, but they busted Ken for possession instead of going to the prom." Coleman laughed, I assume because she thought I was kidding. "How about you?"

"I joined right in the middle of the Route 66 killings," Coleman said. "I thought you got lousy treatment, by the way, then and, and later." "Later" would be code for when I shot the perp. "I thought you were one of the best," she said.

"I'm not dead yet," I said. Time to change the focus: "Beyond the ears, that whole interrogation video was something to watch. Good work. You spent a lot of time with that guy. Pretty disgusting, huh?"

"Not—" and stopped to clear her throat.

I was rapidly coming to recognize that Coleman always had something on her mind and that she always started by talking about something trivial first, like how I came to join the Bureau. Facing straight ahead, I said, "Coleman, you may have heard things about the kind of person I am. One thing I'm not is a therapist. We don't have limitless sessions to indulge in, so spit out what's on your mind. I promise not to shriek with laughter or twitter it."

Coleman took a deep breath. In my peripheral vision I could see her grip the steering wheel a little more tightly. "I read all those books, like the one by David Weiss, to get ready for the interviews. Before I started them, I thought to myself, kind of excited, 'ooh, here I am, I'm going into the mind of the monster' like they say.

"The scary thing is, it never happened. Like you said, I was expecting 'disgusting.' But after a while, I think it happened shortly after that session you saw, it felt like I was just talking to some guy, all right, some totally fucked-up guy, but not the inhuman monster I was expecting."

"What did you expect, somebody who laughed evilly while twirling his mustaches?"

"Couldn't he have looked at least a *little* like Charles Manson?" Coleman finally laughed, and it eased us both. "Well, yeah, yeah, I kind of did expect him to look that way. It was almost like, he was too much like one of us, Brigid. Kind of a pathetic jerk, but I was unnerved because he was a human being and I was expecting something else."

"Let's cut to the chase. He got you with the business about the popularity of vampire movies, how there's something of a turn-on in combining sex and death."

"No," she said.

"Yes."

"All right, yes."

"We're a depraved race. To some extent, Lynch is right. We might as well admit it."

I turned to look at her. She had drawn her lips between her teeth and her eyes narrowed, as if her face was closing in on itself for protection. I wondered what she would say if I told her how I'd killed the guy in the wash. I pretended I was sucking wet air through a hose, joked to lighten the mood, "Luke. Come to the dark side."

She didn't laugh that time, so I went for the more serious approach. "Hey, Coleman, don't worry about it. Liking the *Twilight* series is a far cry from draining someone's blood. We all embrace our inner serial killer at some point. Because, because," I said, rapping my knuckles lightly on my window to make sure I had her attention and accentuate the point, "that's precisely one of the things that will make you so good at this it will scare you."

Coleman gave a weak but semi-encouraged smile. "Except, how do you know if you're empathizing with someone not because of the killer in you, but because they're not a killer after all?"

"Your intuition, you mean."

She nodded.

"I've been there, Coleman. You said it yourself the other day. Sometimes you can be so certain who the bad guy is you don't sleep till you prove it, even if it takes decades. But every once in a while it works the other way, like now. After all that time you spent with Lynch, in your core you knew he wasn't a killer. You couldn't stop thinking about it. That was what made you ask about the ears, and that was why you noticed his reaction when no one else did."

She nodded again.

"So I say you go with your intuition. Just don't tell the men I said so."

Coleman grew quiet after that, maybe mulling over what we'd talked about for the rest of the drive. Thinking she might want to talk some more, I suggested we stop at Emery's Cantina for lunch. She agreed, and pulled in to the space next to my car when we got back to the Bureau office. I told her I'd be there as soon as I checked up on Zach at the hotel.

"How is he holding up?" Coleman asked, while scanning the parking lot like she was looking for someone, or hoping someone wouldn't see us.

I waggled my head. "That's what I'm trying to find out."

"Are you going to tell him that Lynch's confession is suspect?"

"Hell no, I don't want to tell him anything this time until I'm sure we have something solid to prove Lynch's confession false. We need to find the physical evidence, and we need to present it to Lynch in such a way that he'll tell the truth. Until we can do that, Morrison doesn't have to listen."

Coleman gave a little grimace. "Lynch signed the confession this morning and his hearing is scheduled for Thursday."

"Three days to recant before it gets in the news and Morrison looks like an even bigger jerk. I remember the guy hates to look like a jerk worse than anything, and he comes by it so easily. Shit."

"And despite what you say about following my intuition, the evidence in that box makes him seem more guilty than ever."

"No, it doesn't," I said. "Why would you research other killers, go to the trouble to print their stories and store them, if you were a famous serial killer in your own right? It makes him seem more like a wannabe. See you." I got out of her car.

TWENTY

I knocked at the door of room 174 first, and when there was no answer, I used the second key I'd gotten when I checked Zach into the Sheraton. He hadn't killed himself, but he wasn't around. Where was he going, how was he getting there (even at his lowest Zach wouldn't use a bus), and what was he doing? I took a brief pass over the room, nothing but his small canvas bag that contained a couple of shirts still in their plastic wrappers, another pair of chinos, and some underwear. Also the neatly laminated five by seven of Jessica balanced against the bed lamp. Electric razor, toothbrush, and travel-size toothpaste in the bathroom.

I wrote a note on the hotel pad next to the phone on the desk, nothing long or heartfelt, just "I was here looking for you. Return call, you idiot." And my cell phone number. I tore off the top sheet, rewrote it leaving out the *you idiot* and adding *please*. I was frustrated. What with Coleman pressuring me about Lynch, my fears that the body in the wash would be discovered, and my own intuition that someone would still try to kill me, I didn't need this. But then I thought, suck it up, none of that is as bad as losing a child. Nothing is as bad as losing a child.

TWENTY-ONE

Even with my stop at the hotel, I still arrived at Emery's Cantina before Coleman and took a seat at the bar this time. I ordered a light beer while listening to the conversation around me. They were talking about teeth.

A guy from the metro police who the others called Frank said he needed a root canal and did anybody know a good endodontist in the Northwest? Cliff, who I already knew, said he'd heard about root canals but didn't know what they were. Emery said no, he had a jaw like a rock, couldn't remember ever having been to a dentist. Looking superior, he added that he flossed twice a day. Cheri said she went to Gentle Dental because she liked the drugs.

Then they all looked at me like someone my age would certainly know dental work. "I get all my dentures made in Costa Rica," I said, a little resentfully. "They sound like castanets." They laughed, but it sounded kind of polite, like they weren't sure what part—castanets, Costa Rica, or dentures—was meant to be the joke.

Cheri, who was standing near me at the bar, said, "I hear you're famous." Frank and Cliff looked at their food.

My cell phone rang. The nerve sparked in my neck and I prepared my what-a-surprise voice for Max saying he'd found the body, which goes to show how it hung in the back of my mind like a nightmare. You know that nightmare where you kill someone and the worst part of it is knowing you can't turn back the clock and make it not happen? No? Well never mind. I took a deep breath and opened the phone, gave a cautious hello.

"Brigid, it's Laura. Are you finished at the hotel?"

"Yeah, I'm at the bar."

"How's Mr. Robertson?"

"Wasn't there. Where are you?"

"I just stopped in at the office for messages. I'm on my way."

While I waited for Coleman I did some quality brooding about how I wished I hadn't done what I'd done. How I should have called Max right after it happened, and not covered it up. There was no going back on that. But how if I hadn't done what I'd done I wouldn't have found the DVD that suggested my assailant was targeting me, and that it might be connected somehow to Floyd Lynch. I might be dead. Hell, Carlo might be dead. I wished I could stop looping; it was getting me nowhere.

Lynch. I went over the interview with Wilbur and Portobello Mike, pausing, backing up, but could not find a motive for their being involved. Rather, they seemed to distance themselves from their son and brother.

Seemed.

Round and round we go.

Before I was totally brooded out, a slash of afternoon sun invaded the dark interior and I saw in the mirror that Coleman had arrived. I gestured for her to come join me at the bar. The conversation in the room dropped a notch while the men pretended not to watch her El Greco body glide across the room. Coleman looked uncomfortable and ran her fingers through her tight curls to disguise that she was passing her hand over that birthmark on her temple the way she did when we first met.

"Is this okay, or would you prefer a table?" I asked.

She shifted a little shift as if she was trying to get more comfortable with either her underwire or her side arm and sat down on the vinyl-padded stool next to mine. "No, this is fine," she said. "It's just my parents are Mormons and I've never gotten totally used to sitting at a bar."

She ordered an iced tea from Emery, who was hovering less like a good bartender and more like a man wondering what was underneath the linen blouse. He rested his palms on the surface of the bar and leaned, not quite leering, in her direction. Even Cheri passed by and skewered him on a wide-eyed look, the kind of watch-yourself-buddy warning that confirmed my guess that they were lovers.

Emery put a basket of chips and a bowl of salsa on the bar in front of us. "On the house," he said with his accent and a courtly flourish of his hand, both comically self-deprecating and elegantly European, before drifting away to serve someone else.

"He must like you," Coleman said, indicating the chips and sounding a little wistful at the thought of having a bartender of one's very own.

"He doesn't know me. He's flirting with you."

Emery brought her the iced tea, rested a spoon on top of a cloth napkin, and moved the container of sugar packets closer to her.

Apparently feeling that the tea needed an excuse, "I'm

still working," Coleman said as she squeezed the lemon. She must have had Barky on her mind. "You have a dog?"

"We have Pugs."

"Are Pugs good?"

I wasn't sure what that meant, never having had dogs before, but answered, "Sure, they work fine. How about you?"

"We had a miniature schnauzer when I was little. Duncan. He used to sleep with me." Then the small talk was done. She was too intense to have a knack for it. "That interview was a dead end. None of it is making much sense."

"Neither does lust killing. These people don't think the way we do."

"Like you say, we need more."

"With interviews sometimes you can't tell what's important until later. You just keep as much of it inside your head as you can, and sometimes connections appear. It's like we're all garbage scows of information and sometimes your life can depend on the connections."

When Coleman rested her elbow on the bar and her chin on her hand, was it to cover a smile? She stared at me as if she was soaking up all the instruction I had to offer, but her eyes showed only a kind of bland patience. She may have admired me well enough, but she was no suck-up. So I pulled back on the patronizing. Lord knows Coleman had never played the over-the-hill card with me and she deserved the same respect. "Sorry, you already know all that. Your analysis really impressed Weiss, by the way."

"I still can't believe I met David Weiss. He was huge like you, you know, like—"

"Dinosaurs? Just kidding," I said before she could attempt to shovel the words back into her mouth. But then I noticed she didn't seem uncomfortable at all, so maybe I spoke too soon about the over-the-hill thing. I ignored it. "We joined the Bureau at the same time. He had already had his PhD in psych and was tapped for the new behavioral science unit. We called him Sigmund because—"

"Freud. That's so funny."

I hate when I repeat myself. They say it's due to stress. I finished my beer, said no to a second when Emery swung by. "What do they call you?" I asked, to change the subject.

"Snow. Only not to my face."

"As in ..."

"Pure as the driven." She rolled her eyes while I kept my face carefully bland, remembering the suspicion Sigmund had about her and the public defender. "I heard Dr. Weiss call you Stinger. How come?"

"Will they still call you Snow when Morrison finds out you've been working off the rez?"

Rather than address the Morrison issue directly, she slipped on an aphorism. "Sometimes you have to choose between following rules and doing the right thing."

Time to get her back for reminding me I'd repeated myself. "You sound like a refrigerator magnet. Nothing can fuck you up more than feeling noble."

She let that one pass, changed the subject again. "One thing I always wondered, Weiss spent so much time in his book on the Route 66 case but never mentioned Jessica Robertson."

"When he wrote the book she'd only been gone eight

months. He's a pretty cerebral guy, but I think even Sig was too close to her. A lot of people were."

"Why is that?"

"She was childlike, could pass for thirteen at a distance. Never got on anybody's bad side, which I'm sure you know is a quality unknown in an ego mill like the Bureau. One of those rare women who could be relentlessly perky and you didn't want to bitch slap her. You wanted to take care of her."

And that's enough about Jessica, I thought. Is that what the little bit of sharing about her dog and nickname had been about? Not small talk at all, but trying to get me to open up? Nice try, Coleman. I didn't add that I called Jessica Rookie and she called me Coach.

Coleman seemed to sense that I'd said all I was going to say and didn't press further. "I brought a copy of the section of the murder book that covers Lynch. It's in the car."

What she had given me the first time was her analysis of the case. The murder book itself was the sacred document and you weren't allowed to remove it from the office without authorization. I lowered my voice and gestured to her to do the same. "You brought it outside the office?"

She blushed. "Not the whole thing," she said. "Just the part specifically about him, his confession, his truck, that kind of stuff. But it provides a little more than what I gave you before."

Coleman was becoming an enigma. Rigid in some ways, yet . . . "Why Snow, you really don't operate by the book, do you?"

She was also getting better and better at ignoring me.

"I figured maybe we could go over it tonight at my place, and then we can interview Floyd again, say, tomorrow? Maybe we don't need any more evidence. Maybe he's been thinking about what he did. Maybe it will take less pressure than we think to make him tell us the truth. I've even been imagining, what if that body on his truck, what if the real killer gave it to him?"

"Whoa, girl. Maybe we're getting ahead of ourselves with this intuition business. Give me what you've got so I can take it home. I think better alone. I'll see if there's anything we can take to Floyd Lynch tomorrow that will make him change his story."

TWENTY-TWO

I had spent the rest of the afternoon bumming around with Carlo—Walmart, Home Depot, that sort of thing—and baked the meatloaf I had prepared that morning. For the rest of the evening I threw all my remaining energy into acting serene, aided by watching Schwarzenegger duke it out with Predator, which always relaxes me. Carlo had never seen the movie and he even confessed to enjoying it. So despite my wanting to get working on the material Coleman had given me, I wasn't able to do so until I slammed awake around four the next morning, hot-flash hot, thinking about the dead guy in the van.

Nothing to be done about that, so I quietly slipped out of bed, fired up the coffeepot, and headed into my office. With a pad beside me to jot down whatever action would be necessary, I poured through the slim binder, compelling enough reading to take my mind off the things I couldn't control.

Not even this was the whole thing. It was missing all the photographs, which Coleman had not taken the time to copy, and everything regarding the original series of Route 66 killings. This report went from Floyd Lynch's capture at 11:19 P.M. July 26 on page 1 to his signed confession on page 268. Along the way there were crime-scene-processing reports, lists of physical evidence found on the truck and on his person: Plastic bags lining the cab where the mummy rested while he drove. Trace evidence of Natron, which had been used to mummify the body. Body hair (only his and the mummy's) despite the plastic bags. A Jeffery Deaver novel, so worn it looked like he had read it over and over, not remembering the plot.

A printout of an e-book called *How to Kill Women and Get Away With It,* by Anonymous. The copyright was 2009. Along with the printouts we had seen the day before, another odd choice for an already-successful serial killer. I wrote, *"find out if the copyright is registered with the Library of Congress, if so under what name."*

A small battery-powered video player with, unsurprisingly, a DVD called *Zombie Strippers* inside, the one he'd described in his interrogation. Cheap watch. Extra pair of jeans and several T-shirts. Socks and briefs. Small toiletries bag of the kind he could take into a truck stop to clean up. Road atlas. GPS device. Cell phone. Trucking logs.

I stopped there. Truckers had to keep meticulous logs of all their activities and routes, I knew, even down to number of hours slept, since they could be stopped and checked at any time to determine if they were following safety rules. *Find out the dates on the logs,* I wrote on my pad. *Find out how long a trucker is expected to keep his logs. Find out if he kept his old logs anywhere. Compare to company GPS records during the time he was working for a company, if they had GPS systems in place then.*

Sudden flash of inspiration: I got my tote bag and pulled the postcards out that Zach had given to me. Sure enough, the latest one was sent in June, not too long before Lynch was caught. It had a postmark of June 7, sent from Las Vegas with a picture of the strip at night.

Bingo. *Check current logs to see where Lynch was on June 7*, I wrote.

By eight in the morning my list had grown: *check numbers programmed into his cell phone, find out trucking company Lynch had worked for from 2000 to 2007 when he bought his own truck, interview whoever he reported to during that time, talk to likely contacts at truck stops on his routes, get history of credit card purchases.* I thought a little more, then added: *go through trash found in car, check beer cans for prints and run against AFIS.* The chances of anyone following through on that were really slim, since most of those cans had been drunk by local teenagers, but someone had picked those cans up from the ground and put them in the car. And remembering my last conversation with Sigmund, I wrote: *find out more about "lot lizard," the Jane Doe in the front seat of the Dodge.*

I sent the list as an attachment to Coleman's private e-mail account so she could get started getting the information, along with a list of questions we could ask Floyd Lynch at an interview that afternoon. She responded immediately: *Got it gotta run meet jail 3 BTW you were right! Sort of.*

I went back to the murder book, started on the summaries of the autopsy reports, beginning with the Jane Doe found on the truck. Mummification, blah blah, extensive hard tissue blah blah, postmortem mutilation blah blah. Nothing I didn't already know.

I was about to get a caffeine dose when, after a warning salvo from the Pugs, I could hear a recognizable voice talking to Carlo at the front door. Like a criminal, I hid the pad I was writing on in my tote bag. I came out of my office to find Max Coyote standing somewhat at attention in the middle of the great room, hat in hand, but still in uniform and looking ready for business.

Like I said, Max and Carlo were friends. At any other time Max might have arrived for a game of cards or a discussion of existentialism. I would have fixed them sandwiches and listened to jokes that started with, "Sartre and a donkey go into a bar . . ."

But Max's presence here so soon after my experience in the wash could only mean one thing: someone had seen me—I'd been busted. Still, no use confessing outright. I forced the words around my heart, which had become lodged in my throat. "You coming to check up on me?" I joked.

Max looked a little pale. "You should see what we found down in the wash a couple hours ago. I knew you lived close by, so I thought I'd stop in and tell you myself."

I was cautiously relieved; it didn't sound as if he'd instantly connected me.

"Sit down, Max," Carlo said. "Can we get you some coffee?"

Max took his time getting settled on the high wooden stool that Carlo directed him to, and slowly placed his hat on the breakfast counter without noticing the rocks that had been set there to dry. The same rocks I had picked up the day I killed the guy he was going to tell me about. The rocks I had forgotten to move into the yard like I usually did. Why did I leave them on the counter? I tried not to watch the rocks while trying to keep the carafe from knocking against Jane's Bavarian china coffee cup as I poured his coffee. Instead, I watched him. Even at his most excited Max was so slow and somber your first inclination was to comfort him even if you were the one in trouble. He might have seemed a trifle intense just now, but with Max it was hard to tell. Despite his apparently not being here to arrest me, I nevertheless curled my fingers and imagined them black with fingerprint ink.

He looked doubtfully at the cup and saucer I had given him, as if his only problem was whether he could get his wienerlike fingers through the handle. After some deliberation, he wrapped his whole hand around the cup and took a solemn sip, heightening the drama of what I hoped wouldn't be bad news.

Making a small show of bravely hiding chronic back pain, a woman incapable of committing homicide, let alone staging a vehicle crash, I pulled myself up onto the stool next to his.

He ran his hand through his perfectly combed dusty-dark hair, as if the hat had mussed it, which it had not. "Wait till you hear this."

Before Carlo could profess curiosity, or I could force myself to breathe, Max spotted the rocks on the counter between us. "Did you get these from your usual place?"

He knew I went down to that part of the wash. I'd often left him and Carlo at the dining room table for one of their poker and philosophy sessions and come back before he was gone. I had to answer the question honestly or Carlo would know I was lying. Pointing to the rocks, "You bet. Look at the new specimens for my rock garden."

No "Did you see an overturned van?" just "Hm." Max turned the rocks this way and that with a rising excitement usually not given to rocks. "When were you there?"

Always tell as much truth as possible, but no more than

necessary. Liars always want to embellish and it gets them into trouble. I looked at the clock, stupidly. I told myself it must be time to inhale. "The other day. Why, what's up?"

"Don't you die in this heat?"

What was his game? "I try to keep under the bridge where it's shady. Isn't it funny how the temperature changes drastically when you're in the shade here?"

"I told her not to keep going down there," Carlo added inconsequentially and reached over the breakfast counter to push my hair away from my forehead to expose the faint remains of my bruise, while I jerked slightly, annoyed at being a specimen. "Look, she fell."

That qualifies as more information than necessary. Thanks, Carlo. Now I'd have to incorporate the fall into my story.

Max squinted at the spot Carlo indicated. More interested than usual, I thought, but maybe it was just the guilts working. I tried to look vulnerable.

"That must have been a bad knock," he said.

"Oh, it's okay, I've had worse. That looks good." I got off the stool to get my own coffee. I used the action to get control over my pounding pulse, hiding lips that threatened to twitch incriminatingly behind the coffee cup, trying to anticipate Max's questions and where they might lead: Did you see anyone driving a white van? Where are the clothes you were wearing when you tripped? I waited, mentally calculating the number of holes in my story. Why was he toying with me like this?

Regretting what Carlo might be about to hear, I still had to pretend ignorance. "So tell us what you saw. From the look on your face I'd guess it was something more exciting than a rabid bobcat."

"Found a vehicle upside down in the wash."

I let my eyes flare briefly, held his glance one count, two count, what an honest person would do, before looking away with feigned lack of interest. Pulse racing, take a deep breath through my nose to calm it, so my heart doesn't show up in my voice. Oh my God, this is what a murderer feels like. "That's not something you see every day. Who found it?"

"Clifton Davies. You know him, don't you?"

"Nice kid. Met him at your party, saw him at that place the other day, Emery's Cantina. You know the place?"

"Sure, been there a few times." But he shook his head with annoyance that I wasn't staying on topic. "Clifton was coming back from his night shift and saw some buzzards circling over the area, just was curious."

"Could the accident have happened after I left?"

Max shrugged in a tough-guy manner rather than admit to anything. This was a big event for him and he was choosing to keep me in suspense. "Where were you collecting rocks again?"

"Usual place, around the bridge where they wash up, and it's shady there, too."

"That explains it. Clifton found it around the bend in the wash north of the bridge."

"Ah, you're right, that explains it. If it was far enough around the bend from the bridge area I wouldn't have been able to see it." Too many words, stop spilling, turn the focus. "So why do you want to know?"

"You're the only person we know who goes there

regularly, so it kind of makes you a potential witness. But knowing you, you would have noticed something and called."

"Of course. What about the van, just abandoned after an accident?"

Focused on what he had seen, Max's eyes lit with the finding of death that we all feel despite the inappropriateness of the thrill. "Hell, no. It was disgusting inside. Stunk to heaven, guy dead for maybe what the ME thinks is a few days but maybe he'll be able to tell more after the autopsy."

"Oh my God." I turned in the direction of Carlo's voice, so concentrated on what I was saying to Max that I'd forgotten the Perfesser was standing there listening. He spoke in the hushed voice you save for church and funeral homes. "Less than a mile away from our house. And Brigid goes into that wash every day."

"Not every day," I said quickly.

Carlo's face went gaunt and pale. This was upon simply hearing of a body. I looked at that face and imagined his reaction upon hearing I was the one who made the body dead. Not to mention how. For the first time I felt maybe I'd done the right thing after all. But there was still Max, and he was just getting warmed up.

"The body was thrown into the back. Maggots were there and gone like even they couldn't take the heat. ME said probably a hundred and eighty degrees and with the wash running the other day decomp was accelerated; it was like a Crock-Pot in there. The bastard's stewed. Big fissures in his flesh where the gases broke through."

Cops love to talk about this shit the way little boys like frogs; it's a guy thing. But Carlo shivered and excused himself. Max was polite enough to wait until he was out of the room. "Made me gag," he confessed. "I've never seen anything like it except in pictures."

"So who is it?" I asked. "Anybody reported missing?"

"No clue right now. Even if he wasn't in such decrepit shape he would've looked like a bum, long hair, ragged Wildcats T-shirt, nylon shorts, no shoes. There was no wallet on the guy, no insurance card or vehicle registration. Ran a check on the license plate, though."

Come on, Max, don't stop now. Give me a name, give me a name. I tried to sound casual. "So was it stolen?"

Max shrugged. "Who knows? Registered in the name of Gerald Peasil but no guarantee that's who died."

"Unfortunate name," I said, trying to look semibored with the whole thing. "Did Gerald Peasil have a sheet?"

"Arrested for assaulting a hooker outside the Desert Diamond Casino about six months ago. And once for groping an elderly lady on the bus in Phoenix. That's it. I still keep thinking drugs, though."

"I don't know, two sexual assaults might not be coincidence . . . what do you think the ME will call it?"

"Right now, accidental. Could have died in the crash—" Max gave a weary crime-fighting sigh. "George Manriquez will try to slip his skin for fingerprints so we can compare against Peasil's but they're not even sure they'll have that. But I have to get back there. I left Clifton to take care of transferring the body to the morgue and getting the van hauled away, just wanted to see if you . . ." He stopped in midthought. Then his eyes narrowed, his mouth opened as if to say something he did not want to say.

Earlier in the conversation, before he said *van,* I had

said *van*. I shouldn't have known the vehicle was a van. I could almost smell him thinking, going back over our conversation, recalling the sequence, trying to remember who said *van* first. I stared at him as innocently as I knew how, silently hoping that he would get it wrong.

"... if I knew anything?" I said, finishing the sentence he had begun and shaking my head.

His expression adjusted, and when Carlo came back into the room he seemed to give it up. But the fact that he hadn't come out with what he was thinking was almost worse; it made me feel like a suspect.

"So are you staying around? Want me to fix you a sandwich?" I asked.

"Thanks, I better get back to the office and start my report," he said.

"Well, if you need me for anything, Max, you know where to find me." I gave him a cheery grin.

He looked at me speculatively. I looked at him more speculatively. Max left soon after.

"I think I'll walk down there, see what's going on," I said, after a little while, and started out the door.

Carlo looked mildly repulsed but didn't object. "Don't forget your stick." He glanced at the umbrella stand. "Where is it?"

I was sure the question was innocent. It wasn't like he was thinking of it as a potential murder weapon.

"It broke. That was the best thing you made me, with that X-Acto knife you put in the bottom. I'll have to get you to make another one." We stood there looking at each other a moment, both of us thinking, Why hadn't I told him it was broken before now? "You know, I guess I won't head down after all, it's probably all blocked off."

Murmuring something about poisoning an anthill, Carlo went into the garage. I got the suspicion that he wasn't believing me much anymore, either, that I was losing my knack. And I was going to have to figure out fast how to spin this whole thing to Max once he had more time to review our conversation. But at least I now had a name, one small lead in finding out who hired Gerald Peasil.

TWENTY-THREE

I had some of my own questions for Floyd Lynch, like had he ever heard the name Gerald Peasil? It would be taking a risk to ask him, but it might also be one step closer to finding out if they were connected to each other or to the Route 66 killer. And if so, how and why.

Maybe Coleman was right, maybe Lynch was finding out that sitting in a cell alone wasn't as much fun as he thought it would be. Maybe he was ready to talk and could answer these questions. So putting aside my worries about Max, I headed down to the county jail in the afternoon, a little earlier than my appointment with Coleman, to snag a few minutes alone with Lynch.

The jail, a cream-colored boxy structure with burgundy trim, was kind of attractive if you overlooked the coils of razor wire running along the top edge of the building. I left my weapon locked in the car, went through the scanner, signed in, showed my driver's license, and emptied the pockets of my cargo pants. They told me to take a seat in the waiting room. I waited with the rest of a small group in a plain though not totally depressing lobby, with nothing that could be turned into a weapon, just molded blue plastic chairs that were even a little cleaner than those at the Department of Motor Vehicles.

Most of the people joining me were women, with a few men, who were there to visit their spouses, children, felons. We all stared without looking, everyone folded into their personal drama. Most of them got up together and filed through the door to a public visitors' room while I still waited for Lynch to see me privately.

I waited about thirty minutes, until the time when Coleman was supposed to have shown up. Then I waited twenty more. Besides having my plans frustrated, I was annoyed at the tardiness of the rigidly efficient Coleman. I was getting ready to try calling her when Royal Hughes showed up instead.

"Royal Hughes, Floyd Lynch's public defender," he said, holding out his hand.

I shook it, did not bother to say my name because we had already introduced ourselves just four days ago.

"Is this a coincidence?" I asked.

"Not at all," he said, flashing those teeth. "They had instructions to call us if you tried to see Mr. Lynch."

I didn't bother asking who they and us was. "I was just meeting Agent Coleman here, so it's okay."

"No it's not. She's no longer on this case."

I tried to conceal my flabbergastedness. "Since when?"

He looked at his watch and I wasn't sure whether he was checking the date or just getting impatient. "Since three days ago when Special Agent in Charge Roger Morrison discovered she had brought you and David Weiss to the dump site and tried to set up an insanity test. She should have known better than to do that without authorization."

That meant that Coleman was further off the reservation than she had told me. She didn't have the authorization to proceed with any investigation at all, let alone set up interviews with Floyd Lynch's family or come to the jail to question him further. Why hadn't she told me this? And where was she so I could beat her up properly for blindsiding me again?

"So that's why she didn't show up? Why didn't she call and tell me?" I said it more to myself than Hughes.

Hughes gave an attractive shrug. "Maybe she's embarrassed."

"*Now* she's embarrassed?"

"Just go away and I won't report that she was going to meet you here." Hughes looked at his watch again and this time I was sure it wasn't about the date. I gripped his forearm gently before he could lower it. "Let me ask you something," I said. "Did Agent Coleman voice her doubts to you about Floyd Lynch's confession, and did she tell you why?"

"The profile, the ears," he intoned, not so much bored as weary. "She talked to anyone who would listen. But with our backlog, when you've got a voluntary confession on top of such a mass of corroborating evidence, you focus the tax dollars on the other cases."

I thought about what Coleman was going to tell me, what she had been so excited about in her e-mail message. Whatever it was, I was convinced it was the non-smoking gun that would exclude Lynch as the killer. I said, "You're going to put a man in prison for life who only fucked a mummy. And you're going to let the real serial killer off the hook."

"The case is closed, Ms. Quinn. On top of that, you were decommissioned four years ago and the case is not yours. Now why don't you go do something . . . retired."

That made me boil and I gave him my best retort. "Maybe you're right, it's a different world when the agent defends the perp and the defense doesn't."

Not good enough. Without seeming to take sufficient offense, Hughes started to move away from me. But he turned when I tested Sigmund's intuition with, "Whatever does she see in you?"

Hughes paused but didn't turn around until I said, with my voice low enough so no one else could overhear, "If you and Agent Coleman are having an affair I could blow the whistle and get you both in huge trouble."

He gave me a shocked glare and stormed out the door of the jail.

TWENTY-FOUR

It's true, if sex between an investigating agent and the defense counsel on the same case was known, it could cause a mistrial and get both fired. But I didn't like the thought of going there, just yet. I was still steamed about Coleman blowing me off at the jail, let alone not telling me she'd been taken off the case. Our Pure as the Driven Coleman, screwing the public defender, bringing in Sigmund without authorization, taking case files out of the office . . . I had my doubts about whether she could be trusted at all; she reminded me too much of me.

All that wasn't enough for me to throw her under the bus by blowing a whistle on her and Hughes. I pictured Coleman playing some kind of secret agent game. In my defense I must stress it was for this reason it had not yet occurred to me that she might be in danger.

For now I was focused on getting all the facts before I made an accusation that would make her lose her job. She was trying too hard to do the right thing. I phoned her cell, but it wasn't turned on. I e-mailed her that I'd had it and would be at her office to have it out with her the next day, but no response.

"O'Hari, what's wrong?"

Carlo and I were sitting on the back porch before dinner, having a glass of an inexpensive but passable

Malbec and enjoying the nice wet-dog smell of the desert due to some rain over the mountains in the distance. A bit of breeze brought the early-evening temperature into the high seventies.

I had finally gotten in touch with Zach Robertson on my way back from the jail. He had sounded as upbeat as he could get and eased my mind, so I didn't berate him for not returning my calls before. He said he had been taking care of having Jessica's body cremated and asked if I would spread her ashes on top of Mount Lemmon. I agreed.

"That's great," he said. "I researched the area and that's the highest mountain near the city. Jessica liked mountain hiking."

The conversation rambled a bit.

"When are you heading home?" I had finally asked.

He paused, and then said, sounding a little cagey or apologetic, "Tomorrow. I have one of those early-morning flights."

"You weren't going to say good-bye?" Sigmund and now Zach, I thought. What was it with these guys? "How are you getting to the airport?"

"Uh, taxi."

"At least let me pick you up. What time?"

"No need."

"I insist, Zach."

I heard him put his phone down, so I must have caught him in his room. He came back on shortly. "My flight leaves so early, six fifty."

"Fine. I'll see you at five thirty tomorrow," I had said.

Carlo put his life of Wittgenstein on his lap. My own Clive Cussler had been resting on mine for some time. It wasn't exciting enough to help me escape from real life. He reached over and lightly cupped my hand in his own. "What's wrong, O'Hari?" he said again.

So I told him. Oh, not about a man who was about to serve a life term for having sex with a mummy. Not about the serial killer who had obsessed me for the past thirteen years; who was likely still on the loose; and, if Sigmund's conjecture was solid, who might very well be killing even now. Not about how I suspected that someone had tried to have me killed and, failing, would try to do it again. And certainly not about killing Gerald Peasil and how I covered it up because I was still certain the Perfesser couldn't live with knowing what I was capable of.

Leaving out the gory bits, I told Carlo about a father who lost his child and who couldn't come to terms with her death. And how I couldn't stop feeling responsible for it all.

Carlo listened without speaking, without trying to quick-fix things. When I was done he slouched down in his chair a bit as if feeling the weight of it and said, "Life is so damn hard."

"You got that right. It sucks."

"And then you die?" He appeared to give that some thought, then shrugged. "I don't think of myself as a Pollyanna, but I have to say I've seen blessing come out of pain before."

"Careful, Perfesser, you're sounding a lot like a priest."

"Maybe." Carlo swirled the rest of his wine around and breathed in the scent. "Trying to derive meaning from hardship isn't exclusively Christian. There's Viktor Frankl. And I like what someone once said: 'there's a crack in everything, and that's how the light gets in.'"

I pointed to his book. "Wittgenstein?"

He shook his head. "Leonard Cohen."

And as with Sigmund, who already knew so much about me, I wished I could tell Carlo everything. I could feel the words expand in my chest and it took all my power to keep them there. I summoned a grin and flipped my fingers in the sign of the cross. "Bless me, Father, for I have sinned; my last confession was forty-five years ago," I said.

"Sorry, when you took me on as a husband you gave up the possibility of me as your confessor. You'll have to find another priest."

"You're not really a priest anymore, are you?"

Carlo's tone turned, not serious, but more thoughtful, as if I'd made him remember. "Actually yes, I am. I'll never be able to make that stop." Then he turned so he could see my reaction when he asked, "What about you, honey? Can you stop being a secret agent?"

"We're called special agents."

He gave a gentle smile. "Well then, can you stop being special?"

We both knew what he was talking about, and neither of us knew the answer. I heard the land line in the kitchen ring. Carlo took a sip of wine and said, with a little resignation, "We could let them leave a message."

I left him to go answer the phone, thinking it was Coleman and not wanting to miss the opportunity to tell her off for letting me think she still had any control over the Lynch case and standing me up at the jail. It wasn't her.

"Brigid," Max Coyote said, his voice a tad more

mournful than usual. "I'd like you to come down to the medical examiner's office tomorrow, let's say two o'clock."

"Why?" I asked, "Did you find something out about that other body they found in the car?"

"No, it's something else I want you to see," he said. And disconnected.

TWENTY-FIVE

I left Carlo with his first cup of coffee at five the next morning, took the Pugs along for the drive, and set out expecting to pick up a groggy or hungover Zach. But he seemed to be neither. He was moving much faster than I'd seen him move in years, with not quite a bounce to his step, but almost as if there really was such a thing as closure and he had arrived. It made me wish again that I could believe that Floyd Lynch was guilty.

There was a twenty-four-hour breakfast café on the way to the airport and I ran in and got us a couple of coffees and Danishes and continued to the airport.

I had a hard time getting a read on Zach's state of mind because he was involved with drinking his coffee while holding both Pugs in his lap. The male was contented to lay stretched out along his left leg while the female balanced on her hind legs on the right and looked out the window. Occasionally she would turn and lick Zach's unresisting nose, asking him if he agreed that all this was swell. Usually the Pugs would sleep in the backseat but today they seemed to sense, even if I could not, that this man needed a pack around him. The Danish went uneaten.

Zach finished his coffee and put the empty cup in the holder between us. Then without unsettling the Pugs overmuch he managed to get his wallet out of his trouser pocket, remove a card with the phone number and address of Desert Peace Services, and put it in my glove compartment. He saw my weapon there but didn't comment.

"They said they would have her, the remains, next week," he said, calmly taking care of business.

I could tell the same old Zach was in there somewhere because we were beginning our third time through this part of the conversation. "Are you sure you don't want me to hold on to them for a time when you can come back? We could scatter them together, Zach."

"No, I'd rather end it here," he said. As he spoke, he absentmindedly coiled and uncoiled one of the Pugs' tails.

I had grown accustomed to the little nerve in my neck sparking whenever he spoke in terms that used phrases like "end it here."

"Zach, just because we found Jessica doesn't mean, I mean you can still call me anytime. You got that?"

He caught his breath once, hard, and that was that. In a little while we were pulling up to the terminal at Tucson International. He told me where to let him out, and insisted—pleaded—that I not get out of the car to hug him good-bye. He opened the door while I helped extract the Pugs from his body and put them in the backseat. He pulled his small carry-on out of the trunk and waved me to go. I pulled away and when I glanced in the rearview mirror he was standing on the curb watching me.

TWENTY-SIX

It was way too early to go to the ME's office and find out what Max had discovered to link me to Peasil's death, and that had distracted me momentarily from tracking down Coleman. I was developing, practicing the story I would tell Max when I saw him and looking at it from every angle to see if it stood up. "Hey Max, remember that perp I once killed by accident? Funny thing, it happened again." No, that wouldn't do.

I was headed back home, tucked way inside my mind, hardly aware of getting from here to there. But about five miles away from the road that led home I spotted Catalina State Park and turned in on impulse, to exercise the Pugs and relax my brain a little by looking at some big sky. The man at the entrance station gave me a ticket for my dashboard to show I'd paid my entrance fee. He admired the Pugs and added, "Careful. Monsoon's predicted," but didn't try to stop me from going in.

I drove down the short road to the parking lot, saddled up the Pugs with the extra leads I kept in the trunk, stowed a bottle of water into my cargo pants pocket, wished I still had my hiking stick, tucked my hair up under a baseball cap for shade, and, seeing only a few cars parked with mine, also got my Smith out of the glove compartment. It was good to stay safe, but no one had been behind me coming into the park and I wasn't the sort of person to hide.

I walked across the street from the parking lot to what appeared to be the start of the main trailhead. The map of the park was simple: Romero Canyon straight ahead, Canyon Loop Trail up and to the left, and the Birding Loop to the right. The last would be the easiest on the Pugs.

To get to that trailhead I had to take off my shoes and carry them over the Cañada del Oro Wash, the same wash where, just a half mile or so to the north, I had killed Peasil on a drier day. With rain the night before, the wash was now running, but only up to my ankles in places. I imagined I saw one of Peasil's flip-flops near the edge of the wash but it was just some flattened coyote scat, filled with mesquite seeds.

A sign pointed me to a narrower trail that led through what passes for a grove in the high desert, scrubby trees not much taller than Carlo. They provided some shade, though, and we only stopped a couple of times for me to drink from the bottle and to hand down a palmful of water to the Pugs. Then rocks served as stairs leading up to a small mesa. The stairs were a little steep for the Pugs, so about halfway I hoisted one up in each arm and finished the climb that way, thankful that my back wasn't giving me any trouble.

When I reached the top, where someone had put a park bench so you could rest and enjoy the view, I looked at the mountain ridge ahead of me to the east. As so often happened at this time of year, clouds were building up rapidly over Mount Lemmon, crawling in our direction like black paws.

I sat down on the wood and metal bench set up as a memorial to some unknown nature lover, gave the dogs more water, and figured I had just a few minutes before I should start back to avoid the rain. You didn't want to be out in that kind of weather, when the lightning bolts came back-to-back and the water fell in sheets.

Though the network of trails on the map led all the way up and over the Samaniego Ridge, at this point the slope of the mountains was still a good distance off. The sun was losing a battle outracing the clouds but reflected off water slicing down the gullies and collecting in small pools. The reflection of the sun on the spots of water made me think of a giant smashing a mirror over the top of the mountain and scattering the glass shards. I wondered what Carlo would see if he was here, maybe dancing butterflies, and wished I could see it like that, too. Then I thought of my afternoon appointment with a badly decomposed corpse and figured the chances were against it.

While I was still gazing at the mountains, musing thus, one of the bits of sparkling mirror moved suddenly to the left. If I hadn't been looking at it I wouldn't have seen it, but as I watched it hopped again. The way it would hop if it were attached to a person who was jumping from one rock to the next, off any designated trail. The way it would hop if the sun was glinting off a piece of metal or binoculars. Or a rifle scope.

Silly me, right? Yet I squinted, and either saw or imagined the person connected to it, a long ways off. It moved twice more as if looking for the right spot. Then it stopped. Getting into position.

Outlandish as they may seem, like I had told Coleman, at a time like this you can ignore your instincts or go with them. Suspecting that Peasil had been sent by someone else to kill me gave me a little more confidence in those instincts. If I was right, I had several seconds to act. The angle of the shooter, if shooter it was, meant that we were exposed here on the small mesa. If we stayed low, we had enough cover to buy some time until I could figure out how to get the three of us out alive. On the other hand, dropping down would alert the shooter that I was aware of his presence. But if I was correct in my assumption it was either that or death. All that I thought in a flash with maybe a second and a half to go.

I'm not sure of the precise sequence of the next few events:

I slipped off the bench so I was on a level with the Pugs.

A gunshot cracked across the mountains.

I heard it punch into something with a splurting sound.

One of the Pugs screamed.

My head hit the other Pug, who yelped without as much anguish as the first.

The Pug that had screamed was now writhing in the dirt.

I drew my weapon from the back of my pants with my free hand and tried to find that reflection that I had seen before I hit the dirt.

All the while I was yelling, "Is he hit? Is he hit?" without knowing who would answer.

I had no cover unless you counted the flimsy bench. I was holding a revolver against what was certainly a rifle with a scope. Hardly an even hand, but all I had to work with.

First assess the damages. I risked exposing myself further by crawling the few feet to where the Pug was gnawing desperately at his leg, whimpering. "Hello puppy, hello you sweet puppy," I whispered, glad that he was still conscious but looking for the blood.

"Ouch, fuckin' goddamit," I said. Instead of the ricochet wound I was expecting I got stuck by a lump of cholla cactus embedded in the Pug's front haunch. The bullet must have hit a nearby cactus and turned it into a projectile. The spines had little barbs on the ends that wouldn't let go, and it was too deep to pluck out without getting it stuck further into my own hand.

Trying to keep an eye out for the shooter at the same time, I managed to double up a shirttail and get the hunk of cactus out of the dog's flesh despite his squirming with the pain. I knew it would take too long to get the cholla dislodged from my shirt so I didn't bother for now. I crawled back to the illusory cover the bench offered, tugging the stubborn Pug after me, and tied both their leashes to a leg of the bench.

Damn cactus removed from the damn dog, I could now turn my attention back to saving our lives. Novel situation, this. Mostly in the past I'd had to worry about myself, not two pathetic excuses for animals, both of whom I could outrun on a bad back day. I was, shall we say, concerned. One of them whimpered. "Shut up, I won't leave you," I said, while murmuring "Goddam fuckin' piece-a-shit," as I used a stone to get a bit of stubborn cholla out of my shirt so it wouldn't distract me from business.

That done, I rolled onto my stomach under the bench so I could look across the valley to the mountain from where the shot had come. I held my weapon with the muzzle pointing up alongside my head and waited.

I heard another shot, from a different direction, and was further alarmed to think I was being caught in a squeeze play. Then I realized, or at least told myself because it was what I could handle, that the second shot had come from the Pima Pistol Club adjacent to the park just south of where I was. As if to confirm, I heard another bark of what was unmistakably a pistol rather than a rifle.

My position didn't allow me to see anything useful, so I rolled back out on the far side of the bench, rose to my knees, and peered between the slats of the bench. Now that I knew what I was looking for, I had only to scan the area where I had seen the shooter. What I was looking for, among all the sparkles of light where the sun hit the water, was that one sparkle that moved sideways, like a slow-moving meteor among fixed stars. There was no glimpse of the reflection of the sun in his scope immediately, but then I saw it. He had moved a little down the mountain, to come closer, his scope blinking in and out of sight as the weapon moved up and down with each step.

The light stopped moving, and he fired again, this time with no hope of hitting me. The second round hit, if anything, a little farther away than the first.

If this was the same guy who sent Peasil after me, and now was taking care of the job himself, he might be a killer but he wasn't a professional sniper, wasting a shot that way. If he'd made the mistake of allowing me to see his scope, maybe he would make others. Maybe he would miscalculate the trajectory given distance, rising heat, and the drop of what was possibly a Steyr, a decent gun even in the hands of an amateur.

I checked the terrain again and the distance from where I estimated the shots to have come from. He had missed the element of surprise but he wasn't just going away, a testimony to his stupidity or determination; either quality made him dangerous. I could lie here and let him come closer, find out who he was and end this. But I was badly outclassed in terms of firepower and the closer he got the greater risk for me and the dogs.

"Stay," I whispered to the Pugs, and, keeping low behind the scrub at the near edge of the mesa, crawled a way until I could see where the edge dropped off onto a stone staircase like the one I'd come up on the other side. If he was coming after me he might come up those stairs. Better to grab the dogs and make a run for it back the way I came, though it was longer. Once I was a few steps down the hill, the mesa itself would provide cover. Then it was just a matter of hightailing it back to the parking lot before he could cut across the valley and intercept me, but I'd worry about that later.

I looked up at the sky. With any luck the storm would hit suddenly, as they often do, and the shooter would be flushed out of the mountain. But for now it worked against me; the clouds had started creeping across the sun and I couldn't always see him by the reflection off his scope.

I calculated the distance and figured if I was wrong, if the shooter was an expert with the gun I thought he had, he'd get the trajectory right and the shot would hit me within two seconds of his firing. But even if he had reloaded in preparation, if I moved just a little he'd have to get me in his sights again. A target alerted is a difficult target.

I raised up on my knees and peered again through the wooden slats of the bench, wondering where he was. The positive thing was that if I didn't know where he was, neither did he know my precise location. If only I could get him to react. I unwound the leashes from the leg of the bench. "Here we go," I said to the Pugs and started to rise to my feet. Then I stopped and dropped down again, when I realized I might have made a terrible mistake myself. "Wait a minute, pups," I said, my heart suddenly going bonkers in my chest.

Either I was correct in assuming that this wasn't an expert sniper . . . or he didn't care if he actually shot me.

I thought of the other shot coming from someone else at the pistol club. What if there were two people involved? The killer had sent Peasil to get me. Here was another one. Who knew how many people were in league? Maybe I was so preoccupied with what I would tell Max, I didn't notice I was being followed from the airport. Maybe not wanting to take any chances this time, a second killer was coming up from behind, by the steps I'd come up, to shoot me in the back. From the top of my mesa I looked at the big sky I had come to see, the stretch of the Samaniego Ridge to the east and the broad valley to the west, and had never felt so closed in, so trapped.

If I ran forward to the east end of the mesa I risked getting nailed by the shooter. If I went back down the way I had come, I might be running straight toward a second asshole.

"Small change of plan," I said to the Pugs, my heart

still thumping with the mistake I couldn't afford to make.

I looked toward the mountain again and in a brief break of sunshine through the clouds caught the light again. The rifle was still, and we were in a standoff, with only the unknown of what was behind me. I stood. "Hit me, you pussy," I muttered, and then aimed and fired.

In reply a third round hit a little closer than the first two. Wow. I felt the whisper of sand against my leg when it hit, close enough to take even my breath away. I dropped behind the safety of the bench and leaned against it, heaving with fear.

The purpose of my firing wasn't to shoot the sniper; there was no way I could at this range. I only wanted him to know I had a gun, too, make him, or his suspected compatriot, less likely to follow without knowing where I might be hiding in ambush. I took the leashes off the Pugs, who whined, upset by the loud noise of my gun and uncertain about what they were supposed to do. "Stick with me, guys," I said.

At that moment a microburst of wind, maybe forty knots, caught me by surprise, nearly knocking me over even though I was sitting down. My hat blew off and whisked out of sight. Then, as is the way with those winds, it was just as suddenly gone. I blinked the sand out of my eyes and studied the sky rapidly blackening from the east; I hoped it was a sign of things to come, a storm that I'd seen many times before from the safety of my back porch. A little weather could come in handy about now.

Like a sound effect for a B movie, a flash of lightning was followed too closely by a crack of thunder loud enough to rattle your fillings. Come on, come on, I thought, work with me here.

And then it happened. Over the mountain the cloud fell to earth in a sheet of rain that looked like a black magician's scarf making the mountain disappear from view. That put the shooter effectively out of the picture; he would have to worry now about getting off that mountain alive. I could just worry about whoever might be coming up from the rear.

The curtain of rain hadn't reached my mesa yet but it was coming this way. I had to move and I had to move fast. "Come," I said to the Pugs in a sharp command that I hoped brooked no resistance and took off running without looking back to see if they did.

Taking the chance that if someone was there they'd assume I would take the trail down, I slipped off the trail to the right of the stairs and butt-slid down the steep side of the mesa, the Pugs bouncing along with me like a couple of basketballs. It was the kind of thing that, if I'd still been in the Bureau, and lived to tell the tale, would make the guys howl with laughter in a bar.

By the time we started down the rain was close upon us, cold drops of water the size of blueberries splattering on us through the hot air. Then all the drops connected and it was just one big downpour, making my slide down a little slicker, a little faster. I bumped my tailbone against large rocks a few times, but we managed to avoid the more wicked cacti. I knew I was taking a chance at the bottom tucking my gun back into my pants, but there was no other option. I leaned over and scooped up both the Pugs so we could run faster.

Even then I stayed off the trail, instead making my

way through the scrub bush and around the prickly pear and cholla that with the wrong move could have immobilized me. I didn't see another person, the one I feared might be coming up from behind. It made sense. First of all, the rain made it nearly impossible to see anything at more than ten feet. Plus, that other person wouldn't want to come face-to-face with me any more than I wanted to run into him, partly because he would know I was a force to be reckoned with, and partly because he might not want to risk recognition. Maybe this was a person I knew.

With some luck on my side, I finally made it back down to the wash where all the trailheads joined and managed to wade across before it became a torrent that would sweep me and the Pugs downstream.

When I got back to the car, I threw the Pugs into the front seat, where they panted, slightly traumatized, a light steam rising off their backs. I shut my door and caught my breath, but left my Smith on my lap. I drove slowly around the parking lot peering through the windshield wipers at the other cars. There were two, with people inside waiting out the storm. The killer had twice as far to walk back to the parking lot as I did. He wasn't in either of these cars. He had hiked from a different trailhead.

I drove back to the house and reassured Carlo that we were all fine, just wet, got caught in the storm. He and I got busy with our own pursuits, my trying to get the more stubborn cholla spines unstuck from my shirt and finally throwing the thing away.

What was most on my mind was who had tried to have me killed, twice. I had put plenty of scumbags away for life without parole. A few convicted of lesser charges might get out, and a few of those had threatened me in the past. But I always received notification when that was going to happen, and it hadn't happened lately, Sigmund had said. I was still convinced this had something to do with Floyd Lynch, and my thoughts turned to his family. Two of them, with weapons and knowledge of the local terrain. A stretch, and why? To keep me from proving Floyd's innocence? If you could believe the elder Lynch, he'd be just as happy to see Floyd dead.

The most immediate concern: if someone wanted me dead bad enough to try twice it was likely they'd try again, or else go after people I loved. I thought again about the danger to my pack, this time imagining rattle-snakes in the mailbox and antifreeze cocktails tossed over the back fence for the Pugs. I thought about my dear Perfesser abducted. Tortured. Did I mention I have a sordid imagination?

I called Gordo Ferguson, an ex–Secret Service guy I knew who had opened up an executive protection firm here in Tucson. Gordo was the kind of man who could intimidate an entire rugby team, and if the rumors were right, once had. He owed me several favors, so I asked him if he'd watch over Carlo and the Pugs without their knowing.

Next. If life had been normal Carlo and I would have played a game of Scrabble before lunch. He would have beaten me. Then we might have settled down with our books in the afternoon, him to read the life of Wittgen-stein and me to finish the Clive Cussler action/adven-ture where the bad guys are bad and the good guys always win. In the evening we would have tossed a coin on watching an intelligent film or an action movie, and I would have won either way. I couldn't help but wonder if that life would ever come again and figured I was kidding myself that I could hold on to it. Even now I could feel myself slipping away from the Perfesser, preparing myself again to face the loneliness I hadn't before realized I felt. Pushing people away was one thing I could say I was good at.

When there was no response to repeated calls to Coleman's cell phone, I called her office a little before lunch, got the receptionist Maisie Dickens, a relentlessly cheerful person for someone who is the gatekeeper to so much murder and mayhem. You could be looking at photos of a mass grave when she asked you to sign a birthday card with baby ducks on it. It was a little creepy, actually.

"Brigid!" she shrieked, when she heard my voice. Maisie called everyone's name that way, as if she had heard they were dead and was pleasantly surprised to find them alive.

"Sorry, Brigid," she said when I asked for Coleman. "She's not here. She didn't come in this morning."

"Do you know where she is?"

"I sure do. The retirement center where her parents live called to say her mom was sick and asking for her." Maisie made her compassionate burbling sound. She probably had a sympathy card already stamped.

"Did she leave a message for me?"

Checking, "No, Brigid. If she calls in do you want me to tell her anything?"

"Just tell her I called."

"Okay, sweetie, I will."

I hung up. It took me a second to process, but I

wondered: what would be a big enough emergency that Coleman wouldn't do something, leave a message or call me on the way? Even if Coleman was going a little rogue on me, she was still rigidly efficient. I called back.

"Maisie, do you know what retirement center her parents are in?"

"No, sweetie, I have no idea."

TWENTY-SEVEN

To show I wasn't feeling particularly guilty, I arrived at the medical examiner's office fifteen minutes late, mentioned who I was there for, and was shown back to the autopsy room where George Manriquez had already opened what appeared from a distance to be a pastel-blue sea lion but smelled a whole lot worse than old raw fish. I could hear George talking into a microphone suspended above the gurney as I paused to get used to the smell, "Caucasian male, five feet nine inches tall, weighing approximately one hundred forty-five pounds at time of death. Time of death difficult to determine given advanced state of decomposition." He spoke in a less formal way to Max, "With the combined humidity and heat in the van, decomposition could have been much more rapid than usual."

"Give it a guess, Doc," Max said.

"Could be as little as forty-eight hours, as much as four days. Sorry I can't be as precise as they are in the movies."

"But this couldn't happen in less than two days, is that what you're saying?"

"That's right. Give me a little more time to call a specialist who can do the math on temperature inside the van relative to the insect activity and I might be able to come closer."

George finally glanced at me with curiosity. I'd been there a little too often for someone who had been decommissioned four years before.

Max wasn't totally cruel. He gave me some mentholatum to smear under my nose to counteract the stench of decomposition so dense you could feel it like oil on your skin.

But he did make me watch the whole thing while he watched me, from the external exam to the Y incision to the part where they peel the scalp inside out over the face and cut the top of the skull off with a Stryker saw, which sounds like they're drilling teeth from the back. Along the way Manriquez absentmindedly smashed a couple left-over maggots with a latex-covered thumb while he simultaneously talked to us and recorded his comments into the microphone. Even the assistant who was carrying organs back and forth to be weighed and photographed looked a little green. Nobody enjoys a decomp. I met Max's stoicism with my own.

"Here's the odd thing," Manriquez was saying, gently poking his right index finger through a rotting fissure in the corpse's left thigh. "It's harder to tell with the advanced state of decomp but I'm almost certain this wasn't done postmortem. Did you say there was a box cutter found on the floor of the van at the scene?"

Max nodded. "The floor was actually the roof because it had turned upside down, but yeah, there was a box cutter."

"I should have come to the scene."

"We tried to get you."

"The box cutter could have done this, or some other blade. I don't think it was an accident."

"You sure it's not suicide?" Max asked.

"Pretty tortuous way to go. If he wanted to bleed to death it would have been more efficient to cut his jugular vein. It's a lot closer to the surface and you pass out faster."

"He might not have known."

I wisely kept silent, waiting to hear why I'd been asked to attend.

Max kept his dialogue going with Manriquez. "Homicide?"

"I really do think so. Possibly accidental homicide, close-quarter fight in the van. Definitely keep it open."

"Okay, Doc. Keep him on ice. I'll check on NOK in case there's somebody somewhere who would claim the body. Can I use your office a few minutes?" Max asked.

Manriquez nodded and continued directing the assistant, who was sewing up the incision with heavy black thread while keeping her head turned from the corpse as far as possible and trying not to breathe.

Max gestured to me to follow him and we went down a short hallway into an office that, besides the simple furniture—a desk with an office chair behind it and two other chairs before it, thin upholstery with wooden arms—had only a donkey piñata hanging from the ceiling in the corner that looked like it had been there since the last guy. A short bookshelf contained pathology texts and atlases that didn't look just for show. On the desk sat an old computer, and the usual clutter you'd expect in a medical examiner's office: pads, a couple of pens, a box of microscope slides, and other biological paraphernalia. Otherwise, there were no personal effects, no medical school diplomas or pictures of family on the walls or on the desk. If there was a Mrs. Manriquez, little Man-riquezes, a life, it looked like the ME didn't want it to touch his life at the office. I'm not the only one who feels that way.

Max pulled out one of the chairs in front of the desk and motioned me to the chair next to it so we were angled toward each other.

I was getting all the various scenarios so tangled I wasn't sure what I could ask Max without incriminating myself, but had to take a chance. "How well do you know Agent Laura Coleman?" I began.

"Not well." He was obviously thinking of other things.

"When did you talk to her last?"

"The day we were here." He didn't ask why so I could make up a plausible story about my concerns, but changed the subject. "Close-quarter fight in the van," Max said, echoing Manriquez's conjecture.

"He said maybe it was that."

Max leaned forward, resting his elbows on his knees and lacing his fingers. "You knew the vehicle was a van before I said so. You knew it was there and you lied about it. I'm offering you the courtesy of not immediately calling this murder and taking you to headquarters for an official interview. You're going to tell me what the fuck happened and no lies."

I wasn't caught off guard. On my ride back from the airport I had got a better grip on the Max issue and fig-ured that I had jumped to a much greater conclusion than he would. Sure, he knew I knew the vehicle was a van, which meant I had lied about seeing it in the wash. But it would be a quantum leap from there to a former FBI agent murdering an innocent victim and then hiding the fact. Max had no reason at all to make that leap. That's why he said *interview* and not *interrogation*.

So feeling a little more confident, "I'm here to make my full confession, Max," I said.

He pushed his nose to one side with his knuckles and blew out, probably clearing some remaining stench from the autopsy room, and wiped a little mentholatum from the back of his finger onto his pants. But he adjusted quickly; the backseats of cop cars smell just as bad no matter how often they're hosed out. "Stop bullshitting and get on with it," he said.

I had heard enough lies in my career and gotten enough practice of my own. Now if I could weave enough of a story to win his trust without tying a noose . . .

I set it up carefully, connecting the truth with the lies in a story that I hoped was believable. I confided my relationship with Carlo and explained how he didn't know anything about my past. That was why I didn't want to talk in front of Carlo. "But yes, I had seen the van. I saw it the day before it was found and even looked inside. I saw the body. You were right, I knew the body was there.

"I pulled out my phone to call you, Max, but just went into a temporary slump, immobilized by seeing this kind of thing when I thought I never would again. Plus, I hated to have Carlo find out that I'd been even this close to violence."

I leaned toward him, mimicking his body language to show I was in sync with him, my hands resting lightly on the arms of the chair in an open, confiding posture. "I figured someone would discover it even if I didn't phone it in. And Cliff did, within forty-eight hours, before I had a chance to call."

Which part was lies and which truth? Even I can't tell anymore. But it all sounded like it could have happened, and he appeared to believe me. Or he was mentally putting me on the list of suspects. Either way, he gave a slow nod.

"I was wrong, I know," I said. "Really bad call, but you can't say I obstructed an investigation as much as postponed it for a day. I'll think about anything else I might have seen in that area and write up a report for you if you want."

Max seemed to relax a little, which made me relax. He said, "With all this rain the wash is a river. Our crime scene techs don't have much experience with aquatic environments. They say they figure the physical evidence has been flushed somewhere downstream, so even if they found something they couldn't guarantee it was connected to the primary scene. If the place where the van was found is actually the primary scene."

"You're right, just because the ME said it was the primary scene, all he could know is that the killing occurred inside the van. The van could have been moved from some distance away, the wash a secondary scene." Now that I appeared to be off the hook I wanted to be so helpful. "Jesus, where's Gary Sinise when you need him? If you're right about the guy being a derelict how hard are you going to press?"

"Oh I'll press, all right. Accident or murder, I'm thinking he's either a transient or there's more, maybe some connection with that meth lab that blew up in your neighborhood last week. Maybe this is drug- or gang-related."

"Yeah, this guy may have been one of those homicides who had it coming for years." I nodded just vigorously enough to imply I hadn't thought that myself, but that it was Max's idea. I wasn't necessarily in the clear; Max could be withholding all kinds of knowledge, testing me to see what else I knew. He was smart, and I respected him. But besides getting the focus off me, and showing a professional interest, maybe I could steer him onto the right track, Peasil as perp rather than victim.

"I've got the address his vehicle is registered to, and we'll send people up there to see if we can find anything else," Max said. "And I'll stop by the houses up the hill from the wash, see if they saw anything out of the ordinary that day."

He stopped and looked at me. I looked back. I've dealt with much scarier people in more dangerous circumstances.

"Are you done with me now?" I asked, going for the patient but slightly bored tone of voice.

He smiled. I noted it because I couldn't remember seeing Max smile before. "You'll be around in case we need you, right? Not going anywhere?"

Now that chilled me a little. I'd used those words too often myself on "persons of interest." His appearing to relax was a ruse. I nodded, saving my gulp for when my chin was down so he wouldn't notice.

"You see, I may need to talk to you again once the techs have finished going over the van. They're having a field day in there."

"How's that?"

"They've found lots of trace, sand with copper, a substantial number of unique prints, some hair. You'd think

203

all the blood was his but you never know. Could be his assailant. Kind of a mess with the decomposition."

"So are you done with me at this point?" I asked again.

"Nearly. One more thing." He reached toward the desk and took one of the little cardboard boxes that held a DNA swab. He pulled out the swab, which looked like a long Q-tip with cotton at only one end. "We've got your fingerprints on file through the Bureau but not your DNA. Want to open up for me?"

"Oh Max." That's what this whole conversation had been leading to, and why he brought me into this office. He probably had made sure in advance that there was a swab on the desk. "You got a warrant for this?"

"I was intending to keep it between us for now, but if you want me to go to the judge, give him your name, probable cause, and get paper, sure, I can do that."

What else could I do? I leaned forward and opened my mouth, hoping that none of the hair or blood they found was mine, or if it was, that all the mixed evidence would be corrupted into one great soup of undistinguishable DNA. Max swabbed the inside of my cheek, then carefully placed the swab into its little cardboard box and closed it. With a pen he marked a number on the box, rather than my name. I didn't mention I noticed, but I was grateful for that small favor.

He put the box in his shirt pocket and said, "You and I know some things about each other, don't we?"

He didn't have to elaborate. I could tell he was referring to some very specific thing, the questionable circumstances of my shooting the perp, and wondering if he had a vigilante on his hands.

"I suppose we do."

"Well, those things might make us think differently. Here's something. Something you might not know about me yet. I can take a lot before I go over the edge. I can take stupidity, for example. And even disrespect. Sometimes people think that because I'm always quiet and slow that I never get upset at all. But you know what really burns my ass?"

"What's that, Max?" I said gently, trying not to fan his flames.

"The feeling that I'm being suckered. Like somebody doesn't think I'm smart enough to know when I'm being suckered."

TWENTY-EIGHT

I couldn't blame Max for thinking I was holding something back, but I kept telling myself it was a long way from not reporting the van to actually killing the guy, and my story about hesitating before I called it in was plausible. Still, he would have to think that if I lied about one thing I might lie about others.

I had at least four days and probably more until the DNA tests were done, even if Max could discreetly pull some strings and bump my sample higher up in a long queue. But then the other trace would have to be analyzed, too, to make a match, and maybe there would be none placing me at the scene. One thing I could count on, Max would extend me the friendly courtesy of not voicing his suspicions to anyone until he had some solid evidence. I knew I could expect that from him.

For now I needed to focus on two things: finding where Peasil lived so I could make sure there wasn't anything more linking me to him, like the photo and news clip I found in his van, and tracking down Coleman, partly because I was pissed at her for going off the radar the day before, but also to find out what she might have discovered that made her send me the cryptic e-mail *BTW you were right! Sort of.* Right about what? And if she had evidence, who was she going to present it to before Lynch made his plea twenty-four hours from now?

I was already in the downtown area, so I drove the couple of blocks from the medical examiner's office to the Bureau. I pulled into the parking garage to keep the car at a temperature that would support life and took the stairs up to the sixth floor, partly for exercise and partly because I don't like the thought of being surprised in an elevator. I told Maisie I was going to see Morrison, and she buzzed me through the door without calling him first. She wouldn't do that with someone who hadn't worked there as I did.

I asked someone in a cubicle where Coleman's office was, went down the hallway, and found it open. No one seemed to be around so I spent a few seconds glancing around on her desk, in the top drawer, for something that seemed like an address book, or even a phone number scratched on a pad. In the course of doing that I bumped her computer and the screen saver appeared. Like any typical office worker, she had left it on.

Within a minute I had keyed Gerald Peasil's license into the vehicle registration site and come up with his address. Not quick enough to get out without notice, though. Special Agent in Charge Roger Morrison walked into the office just as I was backing out of the site.

"Maisie said you were here to see me," he said, and frowned at my hands hovering over the keyboard.

I slowly pulled my hands into my lap but didn't bother to come up with a reason for asking to see him. "I actually came to see Agent Coleman," I said.

"Why?"

Deciding pretended ignorance was the best plan for getting the information I needed, "I wanted to ask her a couple questions about Floyd Lynch and his involvement in the Route 66 murders."

"You've been informed that Agent Coleman is off that case."

I knew I might be getting her into hotter water than she already was, but I couldn't stop myself now that I was face-to-face with Morrison. "You're on dangerous ground, Roger. You're accepting Lynch's confession without a thorough investigation. You got questions that need answering."

That pissed him off to a degree greater than his usual pissedness. He tried to make his chest big. "What information has Agent Coleman shared with you?"

I didn't say anything, just showed him my best what-the-hell-are-you-talking-about face.

He paused, and his chest deflated a little. He was a little worried, I could tell by his hanging around and explaining. "I'm not sure why you're asking or why I need to make this clear, but she violated protocol. I shifted her back to Fraud for the time being. She's lucky I didn't suspend her."

"You're not concerned about where she is? Did she really go to see her mother?"

Morrison scoffed. "Who gives a shit? Frankly I think she's off licking her wounds, but this is the FBI, not group therapy. So take off your strap-on and get out of here before I have you arrested for using government property."

Talking to Morrison reminded me of one of the many reasons I'd taken early retirement. I resorted to the sort of thing you can only say when you're retired on full pension, and then only if you smile when you say it.

"I don't need a strap-on, Roger. I took yours."

TWENTY-NINE

What with the shooting incident during my hike, confronting Max at Peasil's autopsy, and my run-in with Morrison, it had been a lousy day. On top of that I was getting to feel like I was undercover in my own house, trying to show Carlo that nothing was troubling me. I stopped at the grocery store on the way home and wandered down a few aisles, tossing random items into the basket so Carlo would know I went to the store.

"Fresh ginger?" he questioned as he helped me put the groceries away.

Is that what that was? "You never know," I said and stared blinking at the rootish thing lying on the counter longer than I should have. He came up behind me and did that thing where his arms felt like a safety restraint in a carnival ride. I turned in his arms, gave him a kiss, and later snuck a box of baking soda into the pantry cupboard when he wasn't looking. I don't know what that's used for, either.

After dinner (Shake'n Bake chicken, microwaved frozen peas) I wandered out to the back fence with my glass of pinot gris to contemplate the mountains and the morass of deception into which I was sinking deeper and deeper. As I looked, a brown rabbit scampered by, its white tail failing to blend in with the landscape the way the rest of it did. Cruel evolutionary joke, that tail. It looks like a target. Then motion farther to the right caught my eye, and I watched a coyote trot across the ridge of an arroyo. It paid no attention to the rabbit. Like a big beige dog, this one seemed to be carrying a stick. It was too far away to see if it was the walking stick that I had buried out there when I realized I couldn't get the blood off it.

I ran back into the house, muttered, "roadrunner" to Carlo as he looked up from his book, grabbed the binoculars off the kitchen counter, and ran back out again. The coyote was gone.

I decided not to think about it. All in all, at that point I thought I was holding it together pretty good, notwithstanding the fear of an animal digging up my bloodstained murder weapon from where I had buried it and leaving it on the side of the road where someone might find it and report it to the police.

No, it wasn't until the following day things really started to go bad.

THIRTY

I had waited through the evening for Coleman to call me, e-mail me, but nothing. She could be licking her wounds over being dismissed from the case as Morrison suggested. She could be too embarrassed to tell me. She could be investigating some source that she didn't want even me to know about. I couldn't know any of these things, but at least I could find out where her parents lived and check that part of the story.

Today Floyd Lynch would be making his guilty plea in court, and as far as I knew, we had nothing. I'd go to the hearing in time to see what was going on, but until then I had time to cover my tracks before Max found out anything more about my involvement with Gerald Peasil.

I told Carlo . . . I can't remember now what I told him but I made up something and headed north to San Manuel, Peasil's last known.

Thinking while I drove, what if the guy was just talking out of his ass, Quinn? What if he was mentally ill? What if there are no victims? What if you killed an innocent man? Look at Floyd Lynch.

I have to admit, part of my reason for going up there was to prove to myself that I hadn't killed an innocent man.

Repeating to myself that I had seen blood in the van, I drove as fast as I dared, taking a little over a half hour to drive up two-lane Route 77 and turn right on Tiger Mine Road past a decayed sign that almost welcomed me to San Manuel.

San Manuel is a crummy little town about forty miles northeast of Tucson, off Route 77. A thriving copper mine there made the place quite attractive for a while, to the extent that they even put in a golf course. With the mine petering out, the town is pretty much abandoned, the golf course hardly green. The main road runs between depressed housing on the right and mine tailings on the left, which descend into a milky green lake extending for about a half mile between the town and the Galiuro Mountains farther to the east.

I located Peasil's address and, usual routine, parked my car down the street where it couldn't be identified later. Then I donned a pink terry-cloth turban and my Jackie-O sunglasses, slipped on some three-inch wedgies to make me look taller, and walked to the kind of house that would rent a room to the likes of Gerald Peasil. I wondered for a moment what I would have done if I'd found Max's car there, but there was no vehicle parked in front. A HOUSE FOR RENT sign stuck into the sparsely graveled yard gave me my in. A whiskered old woman who filled her howling-coyote-print caftan came to the door.

Formal introductions were not required. But as we picked our way through drying lantana to the back of her property where a little adobe casita would have afforded Peasil the required privacy, she eyed my turban and the sunglasses.

"You been sick?" she asked.

I mumbled something in a southern accent.

"I been through that, too."

I mumbled something else. Maybe she figured it was her hearing, because she didn't ask me to repeat myself.

"The last guy was here for some months but he hasn't been around for a couple of weeks. He owes me back rent. He paid by the week," she said.

"It looks like the kind of place that would suit me," I said, standing at the doorway of the single room building that looked like it had been trashed with no rhyme or deliberation. It smelled, too, and I closed my eyes, trying to detect whether it was simply old food and bad aim at the toilet or something worse.

"Has to be cleaned up, I guess," said the woman.

"Doesn't look like he did much entertaining," I murmured as if talking to myself, seeing what else I could get from her.

"Now and then I heard some noise, like he had girls in. Maybe a woman yelling once, a fight. None of my business."

For her it was gossip. For me it was crime scene reconstruction. I couldn't pursue the line of thought and only hoped Max would. "Oh, I've seen worse. Would you mind . . . I'm looking for a place away from it all, to finish a book I'm writing."

The woman laughed. "One of those mem-was?"

I looked at the old woman and wondered when Peasil would have made her his next victim. Just before he moved on? Go ahead and make fun of me, lady. I probably saved your life. "Would you mind leaving me alone here for fifteen minutes or so, just so I can see if I feel the inspiration of the place? I promise I won't touch anything."

The prospective landlady grimaced and said, "I wouldn't touch anything in here either."

Once alone, I stepped just inside the door and shut it. From my tote bag I moved aside my gun, which I had placed there prior to leaving the house that morning, extracted a pair of latex gloves, a shower cap, and paper booties for my feet. I put the shower cap back, remembering that the turban took care of keeping my hair from the place.

The room I stood in was ten by ten and served as living room, kitchen, and bedroom all in one. The kitchen in one corner consisted of a hot plate on a card table and a two-foot-tall refrigerator on the floor next to it. A door at the far end looked like it led to a bathroom, which would have the only sink in the place. Even with the garbage tossed about, fast-food wrappers, and unwashed T-shirts, I was able to comb the place pretty thoroughly because I knew what I was looking for.

Not bones, not here, not yet. The place was too small and a quick scan of the hard earth in the undisturbed yard as I walked up told me Peasil hadn't used it as a graveyard. For now I was looking for other things, things that were obviously not Peasil.

I let my fingers travel gently over a chair with faded upholstery that was worn down to the wood frame in the arms. Opened the greasy blinds to see if anything lay between them and the one window in the room. Felt under the metal TV tray that must have served as both desk and dining room table. Looked into the empty refrigerator. Searched quickly for any nook that might contain a laptop computer or cell phone with some incriminating evidence on it.

Finally I found the non-Peasil things tucked under the grimy half-inflated pool float that he had used as a bed in one corner of the room. When he was here, he slept on his souvenirs. They were stuffed into a black plastic bag and used to pad the floor under the float.

From inside the bag I pulled women's clothing: socks with holes in the toes, a sweater more tattered than not, a dirty white blouse with a drawstring at the neck, a skirt with the ghost of what had been a geometric design before the repeated washings had made it fade away. Another skirt with what looked like a bloodstain. These victims had been poor women. Homeless? I thought. Was that what Peasil meant when he said he went after women who wouldn't be missed?

A couple of items had fallen to the bottom of the bag because of their weight. I spilled them onto the floor. A crucifix made of two popsicle sticks on a piece of string and a little laminated prayer card. On the front of the card a picture and the name of Saint Jude. The back contained a prayer in Spanish, which I can read, mostly. The prayer said, "Oh, Holy Saint Jude, Patron Saint of Lost Causes great in virtue and rich in miracles, faithful something of all who request your special something, help me in my present and urgent need."

Causas perdidas. Lost causes. I guess Saint Jude wasn't of much use. Lots of women coming over the border this way, lots of hungry and thirsty women, weakened by the elements and their age, who would gladly accept a ride in a van and the promise of something to drink. A hundred square miles of serial killer smorgasbord.

Peasil had been preying on these women.

Crouching and ready to jump up at the sound of the woman returning, I squeezed the bag once more to see if anything had failed to drop out. I could feel something like a short length of rope through the two layers of the plastic bag and my latex gloves and reached in again to pull out a long gray braid, tied at both ends by twine. One end had bits of pale material stuck to it, bits that, when viewed under a microscope, would most likely be remnants of human scalp. I grimaced at the image of how that might have happened. When I looked closer, I could see that the three strands of the braid were slightly different from each other. One was near white, one a more silvery gray, and the other salt and pepper.

The braid had been plaited after death, with the hair from at least three different women. I placed it with respect on top of the clothing. The gesture felt like leaving Max a note that said, "Look for the bodies."

I looked at my watch. I hadn't dared ask Max when he was coming up this way. He could be right behind me. I stuffed everything back into the bag and replaced it under the pool float for the crime scene techs to find. Once Max discovered the clothing, the artifacts, and the hair that had been ripped from victims' heads, his focus would turn away from me and toward investigating Peasil not as a victim but as a perpetrator.

As I was turning to go, I happened to see a bit of black shine from under an edge of the pool float. Thinking it was the garbage bag, I touched it with my finger to tuck it out of sight and found a cell phone instead. I pulled it out and felt my heart start to bump as I opened it. Torn between whether to pocket it in order to check later for phone numbers or leave it here for Max to discover. A sound behind me made me jump, hold my hands close to hide the fact I was wearing latex gloves.

"Finished in here?" I heard the woman say.

Shit. "Almost."

She must have noticed that I was crouching in a corner, asked, "You being sick?"

"I'm fine. I just dropped my cell phone. Give me a few more minutes."

I listened for the sound of her stepping out the door and screen creaking shut, and hoped she hadn't noticed my paper booties. I clicked on the photo album.

I saw the victims. Bodies. Close-ups of arms, legs, bones pushing up the flesh like tent pins. And faces. The faces, though unmarred, were worse. Mostly when I see victims they're dead. It's better that way. These women, not yet dead, were looking at me. You didn't need to see what he'd done to their bodies; you only needed to see their eyes.

There were several dozen photographs that I clicked through at speed before I found several more of me, likely sent to Peasil's phone from someone else.

I couldn't leave the phone here. Even if I deleted the images of me they'd still be there for some techie to discover. I put the phone in my tote bag. Another crime, taking evidence from a crime scene, added to my running tab.

I left without speaking to the old woman again, cutting across the back of another's property to my car parked on the street behind. I had left behind enough evidence so Max could discover on his own that Gerald Peasil was the scumbag I knew him to be.

THIRTY-ONE

Rather than going home and having to pretend, I drove straight down into the city, stopping at a Bruegger's for black coffee and a plain bagel to absorb its acid. I tried Coleman's phone again, still no answer, still no message. She had contacted the office just the day before, but why not me? Why was she avoiding me?

I flipped open the phone I had found at Peasil's and checked for phone numbers he had called. I tried them all, and they were all on the level of food delivery. If he had spoken to anyone more sinister than Papa John's Pizza, he had deleted that number. Yet I thought about how a deleted number could lead to the Route 66 killer. For an experienced digital technician the phone in my hand might hold both the identity of the real killer as well as the evidence to get me arrested for Peasil's murder. I tucked it back in my tote, making a mental note to find a good hacker outside the Bureau.

I killed an hour calling all the numbers on the phone, getting more and more frustrated with a powerlessness I had never known when I had a badge. Feeling like a pressure cooker was getting me nowhere, so around ten thirty I headed over to the federal courthouse, where I knew Floyd Lynch was being brought to make his official plea.

Parking at the courthouse was a bitch, and so was finding a place to stand on the steps. Tucson hadn't seen the likes of a serial killer since the sixties when an Elvis-looking young man dubbed the Pied Piper of Tucson was picking off high school girls. Everybody was at the courthouse, local and national news teams, and it was pretty funny to see Three-Piece Morrison; Adams Vance, the federal prosecutor; and Royal Hughes, the public defender, all jockeying for position in front of the cameras.

From where I stood I could only hear Morrison's answers to the reporters.

"—proud of our fine local and federal law enforcement agents, including Deputy Sheriff Maxwell Coyote and our own Special Agent Laura Coleman, who succeeded in the capture of the man who will no doubt prove to be one of this century's most active serial killers."

"—that's correct, initial interrogations quickly led to a voluntary confession of no less than eight murders dating back to 1998, the last victim found on his truck when we arrested him."

I scanned the crowd for Coleman.

My eyes lit instead on Zachariah Robertson.

At first there was that same cognitive disconnect that I had experienced when I saw the photos of myself taken from Gerald Peasil's van. My brain had to catch up with the sight of Zach and realize that he had not gotten on the plane back to Michigan after all.

He was nearly hidden behind a cameraman from Fox News Tucson. He was watching me.

Zach and I had been together at one of those times in life when there is raw feeling with no skin on it. You get to know people at those times like you do at no other. We both knew what was happening now. I could see it in his eyes, in the sag of his mouth, open slightly, panting like a nervous dog.

"—Floyd Lynch was twenty-six at the time of the first murder."

"—yes, except for two of the victims, we have identification. One of the unidentifieds is a Mexican alien who had been picked up after crossing the border illegally. It's for reasons like this that the FBI has been so intensively involved, besides the fact that the crimes crossed state lines and therefore fell under federal jurisdiction."

"—correct, all the victims were women."

It became imperative that I make my way through the crowd to reach Zach's side. I struggled to get through the press of the crowd, muttering "FBI, FBI," which had an effect on the regular bystanders but not on the journalists, who held fast to the space they had managed to acquire and would not give way an inch if I was the pope with a case of diarrhea. Still, I was pushing my way through as best I could when a wave of recognition went through the crowd, a sheriff's car pulled up, and Max got out, followed by a handcuffed Lynch.

"—Lynch has provided enough detailed information at quite extensive interrogations, some of which was withheld from the public, so that we have no doubt of his confession."

"Max," I called. He was closer to Zach than I was. I wanted him to be aware. Max looked around at the sound of his name, but didn't see me.

A couple of extra sheriff's deputies forced a path through the crowd.

"—that's a question better suited for Federal Prosecutor Adams Vance."

Morrison stepped out of the way for Vance, who, being a short man, adjusted the microphone slightly. "—yes, he has been declared competent to make those confessions. Floyd Lynch is not insane."

"Max," I called again. This time he found me, but his recognition wasn't the way it would have been a couple days before. Beyond meeting my eyes, he didn't acknowledge me, didn't nod or wave or lift his chin to question what's up. If anything, he looked a trifle apprehensive as if I might be the dangerous one. He said something to a deputy standing close by. The deputy looked at me.

"Zach," I called more loudly and pointed at the man. But Max had already turned away and moved out of earshot, and the deputy didn't seem to make any sense of what I said.

I started to see the scene in different ways, all twined together. Maybe it was Lynch's upper lip that triggered this, the way it protruded a bit. My attention following the rest of the crowd's, I turned to watch him for the first time since seeing his interrogation video.

"—Floyd Lynch is scheduled to make his plea before Judge Sewall at eleven thirty this morning."

I remembered the Lynch I saw at the dump site, and how he now looked more like a sickly animal who doesn't know why the dogs are snapping at him.

Next to that memory there was another, much older one, from well before my days with the Bureau. I was sitting in front of the TV waiting for Mom to get us some sandwiches. We'd been to the eleven o'clock service, what Dad called the Alka-Seltzer Mass, because he said all the people with hangovers went to that one. It was just a bit before Thanksgiving, and because this was Florida we pretended it wasn't so hot and had the windows open.

The program I was watching was broken into by a news bulletin.

A rare live broadcast. Outside shot of an armored car. Inside shot, lots of photographers with those cameras where the flashbulb attachment is bigger than the camera itself. All suits except one dressed in a white shirt and thin pullover sweater.

Not a white hat; no one was wearing hats at the courthouse. Then, not enough security, I thought, and pushed harder, trying to decide whether it was better to get to Zach first or Lynch first or make a big enough scene so Max would be forced to pay attention.

In the broadcast I was remembering, a man stepped out of the crowd of reporters, a thickish man who got too close. He raised a weapon and fired it into the other man's stomach. Someone in a white suit who was leaning forward, clearing a way through the reporters, jerked his hands back to his body, his head back over his chest and even his lips back from his teeth as if every part of his body was intuitively drawing back from the line of fire.

I was the only one who knew, in a way, that this was happening again, and I failed to stop it.

Too late, as Lynch got halfway up the steps, Zach broke from the crowd, ran forward, and yelled, "Lynch!" As the man turned, Zach fired a single shot at Lynch's gut. Lynch closed his eyes, opened his mouth in a soundless groan, and clutched his stomach. And there was the lip, curled up over his teeth. Startled, Max jerked his hands back to his body, his head back over his chest and his lips back from his teeth as if every part of his body was intuitively drawing back from the line of fire.

Too late to reach Lynch, I turned my attention back to Zach. He looked at me again, gave the first smile I'd seen in seven years, which made him a totally different man, lifted the gun again. The crowd went wilder, the camera crews simultaneously ducked and raised their equipment over their heads to capture someone getting killed.

At the Texas police station it had been a snub-nosed Colt Cobra .38, the victim had been Lee Harvey Oswald, and the killer had been a small-time Nevada crook named Jack Ruby. Unlike that weapon, the one Zach used was just a .22, not much of a gun. But different from that time, rather than allowing himself to be taken by the police officers, Zach pressed the trigger and shot himself in the head.

THIRTY-TWO

Once Zach dropped and the gun fell from his hand, photographers and cameramen swarmed forward while crouching down, staying low for fear of more gunfire but keeping their equipment raised overhead for the sake of a Pulitzer. Security from the courthouse swarmed back, linking arms, able to at least keep an opening for the emergency med techs who showed up within a long two minutes, one ambulance taking Lynch away and the other taking Zach. I wormed my way onto the latter and sat with Zach while the EMTs worked. He wasn't used to firearms, the gun must have kicked, and he was aiming high to begin with, so death wasn't immediate. He wanted to talk. I tried to shush him, but the paramedic told me it was better, with a brain injury, to keep him conscious.

"Got 'im," Zach said, with a physical effort that went beyond anything I'd personally known.

"You sure did, buddy." I glanced at the blood on his shirt, the blowback from Lynch mixed with that of his own head wound. You could still see the package creases in this shirt, too. He had put on a new shirt to kill Lynch.

Zach ran his tongue around the inside of his mouth, moistening it enough to speak. "No life."

I assumed he was talking about Lynch's sentence just

then, but he could have been talking about himself, that his own just wasn't worth it anymore. I took his hand in mine, stroked it with the other. "Zach, dearest, why didn't you talk to me?"

His eyes started to go up into his head and then came back down again. He grimaced with a sudden pain. "Dead?" he asked.

I wasn't sure. "Sure Zach, he's dead."

He was having a harder time moving his tongue but managed to get out, "Gla?"

"Totally glad," I said, though it was just another lie because now I'd never find out who really killed Jessica. "Zach . . . Zach? Stay with me, Zach."

Then Zach died.

I leaned back out of the way so the paramedics could do what they were supposed to do, but I knew it wouldn't do any good. You could never change Zach's mind once he'd made it up. I saw a bit of plastic protruding from his shirt pocket and drew out Jessica's photograph. I spit on it and wiped it off against my own shirt, the lamination keeping the blood from sticking to it. I rode the rest of the way to the hospital, and helped with the paperwork. Told them how to get a hold of his estranged son, who was the closest next of kin and who I imagined would be the person to deal with his body. Jessica's body, too.

THIRTY-THREE

I stopped in the bathroom off the emergency room lobby to wash the blood off my hands and got a ride back to my car at the courthouse. Driving back up to Catalina I wondered what it would be like if I could talk about all this with Carlo. Forty-five minutes later I pulled into the garage and went into the house to get slammed anew.

I barely noticed that Carlo was not his usual serene self. Shoving the Pugs away with my foot, with a quick hi to him where he sat at his desk, not noticing he had his head in his hands and even if he did whether it was because he couldn't get his checkbook balanced, I went into the bedroom to change my clothes before he saw Zach's blood on them.

Jane's satin bedspread was tossed onto the reading chair in the corner of the bedroom and the bed was stripped.

The bed was stripped and the sheets were nowhere to be seen.

The bedding must be in the laundry room.

Without trying to appear normal I ran from the bedroom to the laundry room, where I saw the bedding in a heap on the floor. I opened the washing machine and saw the clothes that I had been wearing and forgotten about the day I killed Peasil. They weren't smashed against the sides of the basin the way you usually see clothes after the spin cycle; they had been moved. They had been examined.

I was aware of Carlo standing behind me, not touching me.

I wanted to tell him everything, starting from, oh, about thirty years before and ending with the suicide of my rookie's father, but instead, "You don't do laundry," I said stupidly, looking at a still-pale-burgundy-colored patch that the bleach had failed to remove from the denim blouse.

His voice sounded aggrieved. "I was trying to help out," he said. "You haven't seemed yourself after your ... fall."

I turned around and faced him, no longer thinking of the fresh blood on my blouse. Compared with what he knew now, it was trivial. Carlo didn't seem to notice the blood. I wanted to lift my hand to touch his face in comfort or supplication, but I had drained out of myself and couldn't take the chance of trying to touch him. I didn't have to ask what he knew. He was very helpful and gestured toward the washing machine.

"I was going to put them in the dryer, but they were already dry after so many days. And then there were. Stains. I don't know if you'll get the stains out."

He was saying these little mundane things, but his eyes were begging me for something else, something much bigger, like an explanation that would erase what he was thinking.

"He," I began, perhaps intending to explain how I had been assaulted and killed the horrible man in self-defense. But something told me none of that mattered.

What mattered is that I had killed a man and hidden it from Carlo and I couldn't deny that looked bad.

I turned back and opened the door of a cabinet and pulled out the box of garbage bags we keep there. I took one and collected the clothes out of the washing machine, including the hat, gloves, and shoes, and crammed them into the bag. I turned the washing machine back on, poured some bleach in to get out any remaining residue of Peasil, and shut the lid. Then I took the garbage bag into the bedroom, where I added a couple pairs of jeans, half a dozen T-shirts, and everything in my underwear drawer. Very methodical, I opened the drawer in my nightstand where I keep my prescriptions, took the bottle of Tylenol in which I hid my sleeping pills. Carlo didn't follow me into the bedroom. I didn't expect him to.

I came back out and grabbed my car keys and my tote bag, making this as fast as I could for both our sakes. He was collapsed in the recliner where he usually reads, still begging me for something I couldn't give, a woman I couldn't be.

"Please. Tell me," he said.

"You know what?" I said, as harshly as I could while my heart got another painful little crick that took some of the harshness out by making me gasp at the same time I spoke. "This isn't working out for me."

I turned away despite the pitiful sound of his whisper that may have been "please don't leave."

And I left. I left.

THIRTY-FOUR

I should have realized it would happen sooner or later, but I was still surprised that relationships end so fast. You spend more than a year getting to know each other, building trust, and in three minutes it's over. In my defense, I might have been thinking more clearly if Zach hadn't just died in my arms. Standing in the laundry room I had been like a boxer still reeling from a jab to the gut, being decked with a sharp right to the jaw immediately after; that one-two punch got me. My mind seemed to slip out repeatedly, have a look at whatever I was doing with a detached interest, and slip back in when it was good and ready. That sensation of draining out of myself.

I didn't fully realize my state until I was out of the house and driving south on Oracle, in the left lane, about ten miles under the speed limit. A Chevy flatbed, red and tricked out with all the extras, tailgated me, maybe had been tailgating me for a while without my noticing. When that didn't make him feel any better, he expressed his concern with his horn. I glanced at my tote bag beside me and considered putting a bullet in his front tire, but decided on restraint instead—besides, there were witnesses. When I got to the stoplight at Tangerine Road I put my car in park, got out, and went to the driver's window of the truck. It was closed; in this heat windows would always be closed and the AC on full tilt. I hit the tinted window once with the palm of my hand.

It slid down slowly to reveal a neatly dressed man who should know better than to honk his horn indiscriminately in traffic. He stared at me with apparent alarm.

I thought it was because he'd never had a woman respond to his honking in quite this way. "Okay, you got my attention. Now what the fuck do you want from me?"

He looked at my chest, involuntarily raising his hands as if to protect himself. In that moment I saw in his eyes what he saw, a crazed woman wearing a blouse with blood on it. Without saying more he raised his window, backed up, and drove around me. He did not squeal his tires.

As I watched him pull away, I could feel my heart pumping in my ears and my breath rasping. Road rage that, motherfucker.

I got back into my car; pulled it off the road to let the rest of the traffic go by; and, taking a whimsical shirt with dancing javelinas from the plastic bag, did a quick change with the top I was wearing. I wadded up the bloody one and shoved it under my seat. Then I pulled into the traffic again and, without being fully aware of where I was going or how I got there, ended up at the Sheraton downtown. Maybe I was flying in the direction of my last simple encounter with someone who knew the real me and wanted that place to run to ground. Upon my arrival at the reception desk I asked if Zach's room, room 174, was still free.

Eyeing the garbage bag I held, the girl at the reception desk told me it was. Glad I had had the presence of mind to at least change my shirt, I gave the girl my credit card, got my little plastic swipe key, and scuttled my bag into room 174 before anyone could spot me. I had to get a room somewhere. If I kept driving, I risked killing myself and someone else with my car.

Zach had taken everything with him the morning before when I dropped him off at the airport. He'd probably left his bag there. I wondered for a moment what he had done all last night—drank in some bar, or just wandered. I could feel his presence in the room, sad but at least honest. I sat down on the bed, thought what I would have done to that guy on the road if he hadn't backed down, and tried to get a grip.

You'd think all women must get suddenly serene, their anger draining away with their estrogen. That the rage at even a lifetime's worth of death such as I had known will dissipate into scrapbooking and volunteer work with Humane Society fund-raisers.

Well, maybe I'd been kidding myself that I could be that woman. Maybe that's not how it always is, maybe not how it should be. Of the half dozen lines of poetry I know by heart, there's, "Do not go gentle into that good night. Howl, howl . . . or rage, rage . . . against the dying of the light."

This is Brigid Quinn, a woman of a certain age, raging.

How to express my feelings in that moment, my hatred for that man who had destroyed so many lives and had come back all these years later to destroy mine as well. This man, who was responsible for destroying my life and the only real happiness I'd ever known, was making me mad.

Mad enough to kill him.

Kill him and gnaw his still-warm flesh.

Whoa, Quinn. Slipping off the grid, are we? It's something Dad used to say, along with twenty–thirty years from now, you'll laugh at all this.

Well, Dad, just think. Twenty–thirty years from now, we'll both be dead. Ha, ha. Isn't that a scream?

I paced back and forth, back and forth in the room, wanting to connect and not wanting to connect with another soul. Brother, a Fort Lauderdale cop with a wife with MS, no. Sister with the CIA, who knew where, no. Mom? Not Mom. I dialed their number at the Weeping Willow Retirement Center anyway, the drifting part of my mind slipping out and watching me hit the numbers.

"It's Brigid, Mom."

"Are you all right?" Her voice took on that tone of someone who suspects that bad news is the only kind there is, that I was calling from a hospital and the only moving part left was my mouth. Maybe that's how it is for a mother when everyone in your family is some kind of cop. She always said, "are you all right?" rather than "hello."

"Sure, Mom."

"Good, because sometimes just the sound of your voice gives me an attack of colitis. I worry about you all the time." Before I could make this something like a dialogue she went on. "I won thirty dollars at bingo last night."

"That's great. Congratulations."

"So how's Carlo?"

My voice caught in my throat, and I couldn't speak. Why the fuck did I call her before I was strong enough to hear about how I got to be fifty something and still couldn't do a grown-up thing like keep a marriage together? Or remember that I gave her nervous colitis at the best of times? But it was okay because I didn't have to go into any of that. She turned from the phone, and I could hear her talking to Dad, could almost hear the impatient ice cubes in his glass, almost smell the bourbon. When she turned her mouth back to the receiver, she said, "Listen, honey, it's dinnertime. Daddy wants to take me down to dinner now. Could you call back?"

"Sure. Sure, Mom." I hung up, trying to get back the several decades of maturity I'd misplaced during our few minutes of conversation.

That exhausted family. I couldn't trust myself to call Sigmund, afraid I might tell him things he would have to testify to later at my trial.

I looked around the room for the first time. I was sitting on one of two double beds. I tried not to imagine the body fluids that would show up on the bedspread under an infrared light. Over each bed was a large print showing a watercolor of a cactus, one a prickly pear with dark red fruit practically bursting from the paddles. I pictured the fruit popping like blood blisters and running down the wall. The other was a saguaro, that tall kind of cactus with arms, capped with little white blossoms at the top. I won't say what that picture made me imagine.

Despite this being the safest place for me, I didn't want to be here. I figured I could keep myself from draining out of my head long enough to reach a bar.

234

THIRTY-FIVE

The whole Quinn family was well known for their drinking. Mom and Dad would have parties and my brother and sister and I, mere tikes all, would roam through the house the next morning finishing off the warm highballs left by guests. I pretty much went off the hard stuff for Carlo's sake, but without Carlo sobriety was just a waste of good liquor.

I sat at the bar of Emery's Cantina, on my second vodka over ice in a short tumbler so I didn't have to worry about knocking over a martini glass. The first sip created that captivating tingle at the base of my skull, then radiated warmth down my spine. By the second drink I was just high enough to remember the waitress told me the owner was Hungarian, and I said, "*Egészségedre*," as I raised my glass to Emery.

He laughed, said, "It sounds a little like you are saying 'up your ass,'" his Eastern European accent making the *little* come out like, *lily*. He tried to help me pronounce the toast correctly so it sounded more like *to your health*. While I was having a language lesson I scoped him out better than I did the first time I was in here. Not so much an overweight baby as I had at first observed, but definitely the sort of man people call Big Guy, he carried his weight so that even his belly had an odd sexual appeal.

235

Contact with a living human being felt good, so I asked, "When did you come over?"

"About twenty years ago," he said. For a moment he went inside himself as if watching memories of his own, then told me he emigrated with his family just after the fall of the Iron Curtain. I understand there is, oddly, an unusually large Hungarian population in Tucson so it was easy to find a sponsor. He asked me about my professional life.

I said, "Copyright infringement."

He looked skeptical. "But Cheri has told me you are famous."

I lost the inclination for further conversation. Careful to avoid looking into the mirror that runs behind the whole length of the bar, I turned my focus to the bottles of Tarantula Tequila (no fooling) and something called Cabo Wabo. A stained cardboard sign with the witticism SHOTS HAPPEN, a double pun in a cop bar.

I looked at the jar of pickled pigs' feet on the bar a few feet away. It reminded me of what you'd see in a medical examiner's office after a mass fatality. The pink flesh and white gristle of the feet mashed against the glass as if they were looking back and, if they got out, would slime across the bar at me. There was . . . the way I had imagined with the water sparkling on the mountain, or with the cactus prints back in the hotel room, I started to imagine seeing something else, more violent, more hideously grotesque than before. I couldn't take my eyes off the jar and felt a bit of the vodka rise in my throat.

If it wouldn't have sounded crazy I would have asked Emery to throw a bar towel over the jar. I was sick of seeing these things and disgusted by my own thoughts. You

236

are one fucked-up woman, Brigid Quinn. When all this is over I'm going to go back into therapy, I think. Then I thought, what for?

I finally wrenched my eyes away from the jar, searching for something that showed life was worth it. A vase with a single red rose next to the cash register made me wonder what Emery and Cheri were celebrating.

Emery must have sensed my mood and started doing that thing that expert bartenders do, pretending to ignore me but wiping glasses just close enough so that in case I wasn't just talking to myself he'd hear my whisper and head over. He was that bartender that every detective needs, someone I'd be able to talk to now that I was alone again. He went briefly into a room off the bar, probably his office, and when he came back he smelled like cherry-bourbon pipe tobacco.

There weren't many people there on a weekday night so I felt okay asking Cheri to turn off the jukebox that was playing a combination of 90s pop and guitar country. She did.

Since when did I develop this pathological hatred of music?

Since I could name one asshole or another who's partial to every kind there is, from Bach to hip-hop. Since when music is playing it's harder to hear someone coming up behind you. Since Paul played the cello and every time I hear a stringed instrument it makes me feel like the performer is jabbing the bow down my throat. Certainly I hated music long before listening to Kate Smith belt, "When the Moon Comes Over the Mountain" on a hot summer night, the night I lost Jessica.

I asked Cheri to tell me about herself. "Did you come

here from someplace else like the rest of us?"

"No," she said. "My people have been ranchers here for nearly two hundred years. We were never slaves."

She sounded proud, like she wanted people to know that about her, to see something more than the fact that she was black. I'd heard about that, that small percent of the Arizona population, African American, who found their way here through some means other than slave ships. "Are you and Emery together?" I ask.

She smiled and nodded.

"How did you meet?"

"I needed a job to help pay for school. He knew my family."

"How are your studies going?"

"Good." That's all she said, and then flickered sad. Everybody lies.

I changed the topic again by ordering a burrito with guacamole to absorb some of the liquor, which was getting to me after not eating anything since that bagel in the morning.

My brief exchange with Cheri about her relationship with Emery made thinking about Carlo unavoidable. Because that seemed somewhat preferable to thinking about mass pig fatalities, I gave in to the memories.

THIRTY-SIX

I hadn't spent that much energy standing in my closet staring at my clothes in a long time. For my first date with Carlo, I ultimately chose a floor-length sleeveless black jersey with a low-slung cowl neck that showed off my relatively firm triceps while hiding my monkey-face knees. I let my hair hang naturally instead of pasting it to the back of my head in a twist.

Sound of a knock, he didn't use the doorbell. When I opened the front door it didn't take a trained eye to see the effect I had. His retinas dilated, and his pulse throbbed in the side of his throat. Surprisingly, I could feel my own pulse accelerate in response, as if our hearts were souped-up engines and we were revving for a drag. I tried to remember the last time I had sex, thought I'd rather go straight to bed, dinner was going to feel interminable. He helped me into his unimpressive Volvo, the back of his hand grazing my bare shoulder.

But dinner wasn't at all what I expected. Oh, we went over all the usual backstory. He shared that he was an ex–Catholic priest and had been teaching since he left the Jesuits in his forties. And he talked about Jane, his wife of twenty years, with a seasoned grief that somehow made his face only more attractive. I told him my story as well, the sanitized version, how I was in law enforcement, just a desk job really, retired, not much else to tell.

"Federal or local?" he asked, ignoring the hint that I didn't want to talk about it.

"Federal. I investigated copyright infringements," I added to forestall any more questions about myself, with a small regret that the first lie happened so soon. To turn the focus back on him I gave him a compassionate stare mixed with a "come on, you can tell me" twinkle. "Was it too hard to be a priest? Dealing with so much horror in the world?"

"No, that wasn't it. I found people to be essentially good. That was my problem with the church."

"Since when?" I said, taking an ever so small sip of wine and glancing appreciatively at the soft-shell crab appetizer placed before us. He had brought me to a very nice place.

"Since when have people been good, you mean?"

I nodded, dipping a little leg into a cream sauce and nibbling on it.

"Since always," he said. "That original sin business is crap," he said, but in a mild tone, lacking the intensity with which people usually debate matters of faith. He sipped his Manhattan, with no intention of saying more about that. A little sissy, that Manhattan, but nobody's perfect. Then he asked, "Why, what has been your experience?"

He wasn't bad at focus-turning himself.

"Who knows what evil lurks in the hearts of men?" I asked.

"The Shadow knows," he said.

We both laughed, that kind of moment when you agree to admit how old you are. But then I saw that he really wanted me to answer, and I needed to tell him something.

"My experience has been ..." I nearly said something flip, then found myself wanting to impress him, to show I could keep up with him on an intellectual level. "Most good is just a way of hiding an agenda."

"Interesting. You're familiar with Max Beerbohm."

While trying not to look like I should have been, I admitted I was not.

Carlo managed to tell me without sounding patronizing. "A writer. He wrote a story that agrees with your point of view, only with a different result. Do you care to hear it, or would you prefer to shift back to quips and flirting?"

I was momentarily stunned, a rare experience with any man. Carlo DiForenza had my number, and he was by no means going to let me control the evening. I was uncomfortable with that, but the discomfort felt, in its own way, kind of delicious, and for the first time I went into an emotional free fall without looking for the net. I employed the name that would become my favorite term of endearment, a character in an old cartoon strip called Pogo. "Have it your way, Perfesser."

He smiled to show he got the allusion. "Thank you." He paused to eat his maraschino cherry thoughtfully before going on. "A very wicked man falls in love with an innocent young woman. He declares his love, but she can see he's wicked. His degeneracy is stamped on his countenance. She says the only man she can love will have the face of a saint. So he goes to a mask shop and finds exactly that, a saint's face. She falls in love with him and agrees to marry. But now comes the challenge. In order to keep her love, he must keep up the charade. So he gives money to the poor, is kind to children and small

241

animals, visits the sick. All to convince her that he is the saint she assumes him to be. And every morning, before the sun comes up, he puts his mask back on before she can see what he really is. As you said, hiding his agenda.

"Only one morning, after they have been married for some years, he reaches under the bed where the mask is hidden. He feels nothing but shredded paper. Mice must have nibbled at it during the night and left nothing for him to wear. He begins to weep, knowing that this is the end of his great love. When his wife discovers he has been nothing but a hypocrite, she will leave him.

"The sun comes in the window, and, as always, his wife rolls over so that his face is the first thing she sees. She looks at him with eyes of love, not the horror he had expected. He cautiously kisses her, gets up, and steals a look at himself in the mirror on her dressing table. And he is shocked to see that his face looks exactly like that of the mask he had worn so long. Ah, the entrée," he finished, licked his lips with anticipation, and fell to his scallops and caramelized onions without seeming to notice that the muscle at the top of my jaw had clenched briefly, or that it took me a moment to control my breathing and fan the tears dry with my eyelashes before I could mutter something suitable about my sea bass.

I was grateful for the warning. In that moment I decided I would never allow Dr. Carlo DiForenza to see me without my mask. The tactic had worked well until today.

THIRTY-SEVEN

I had ordered a third, or maybe a fourth, vodka. Emery didn't pour it immediately, stood looking at me with a question he was used to asking. I spoke to show him I wasn't hammered, could still reasonably operate my tongue and lips. "What happened first, Cheri come to work in a cop bar or Cheri studying criminal justice? Or is it just a coincidence?"

"There is a reason for everything. Cheri lost her older sister in an act of violence. You would understand how victims of violence are drawn to it."

"Was it a long time ago?"

Emery's eyes grew large with sadness. "What do you consider a long time?"

"I'd like to talk to her about it sometime."

"If you continue to be a customer, someday you will. Just not right away. Are you sure you want another drink?"

Seeing the way he cared about Cheri's feelings made me more depressed. I canceled the vodka and asked for my burrito to go. Cheri brought it in a Styrofoam container and tucked it with a plastic fork and extra napkins into a brown paper bag.

The Quinn family was also used to having designated enablers. Emery told me he'd have Cheri take me home if I'd be able to show her where I lived. I was ashamed for anyone to know I couldn't go home, that I was staying within a short drive at the Sheraton, and suggested they call me a cab instead. The cab took about twenty minutes to get there so I reordered my vodka while I waited. By this time the place was empty except for me. The three of us talked a little, that inane bar talk that seems like scintillating conversation when you're half-snockered.

Jokes are good at a time like that, especially if you've told them several times before, because you've practiced the words and can get them out with less stumbling. I told the old one about the guy who's afraid to fly because of the possibility of a bomb on the plane. "His therapist says, 'The odds of flying on a plane with a bomb are a million to one.' The guy says that's not good enough. 'Well,' the therapist says, 'the odds of being on a plane where there are two bombs is a billion to one. So carry a bomb with you.'"

Thirty years ago that joke was funny, but Cheri and Emery looked at me without laughing. "I don't know, maybe bombs on planes are not so funny anymore," Emery said soothingly, placating me as only a bartender could who has avoided attacks by mean drunks on countless occasions. Cheri sat on the bar stool next to me and lightly rubbed my back. I didn't like her for it.

"Everything is funny," I said. "It has to be or we're all fucked."

I don't know if I said something witty or if he was just surprised to hear that kind of talk come from a woman who looks like me. This time he belly-laughed, and he had the belly to do it with. "Now that, that I can agree with."

The taxi finally arrived before I could make an even

bigger fool of myself and they all helped me in and the driver took me to the hotel. I was sobered slightly on the way there by marking the passage of each block, hoping the taxi driver was not an assassin and I had just done something really stupid. I tested the door handle so I could jump out in case he didn't make the right turn on Speedway.

But the taxi driver dropped me off without trying to kill me and I made it into the room without any help. I got a couple of towels from the bathroom and hung them over the pictures over the bed so I could stop imagining what I saw. I nearly fell off the bed, then fell onto it and stayed there while the room spun around me.

THIRTY-EIGHT

I must have eaten the burrito during a blackout, because the next morning when I stumbled into the bathroom I found dried guacamole on my nose and the burrito was gone. I was still dressed so after I washed my nose I went to the hotel restaurant, where they have a breakfast buffet, and got myself plenty of bread and coffee to bring back to the room. While I was eating and wallowing in the remnants of the previous night's self-pity, I turned on the Weather Channel for the week's prediction (hot, hot, hot, rain, rain, hot, rain). Staring at the screen I thought about where my life stood, in no particular order:

Zachariah Robertson, the man who symbolized everything good I had ever accomplished, and everything I had failed to do, had killed himself while in my care.

Floyd Lynch, the closest I'd ever gotten to discovering the killer of Jessica Robertson, was dead.

Despite my best efforts at being the perfect wife, my marriage was ruined.

Max was going to find the evidence that I had killed Gerald Peasil and would make me do time.

Someone had tried to kill me twice and there was no reason to think that someone wouldn't try again.

After having such a hard-on to prove Lynch's innocence,

Agent Laura Coleman hadn't returned my messages for forty-eight hours, hadn't been interested enough to show up for Lynch's plea. No one but me seemed to think there was something odd about that. Something, I was finally recognizing, sinister.

There was something linking it all, but everything had happened so quickly I couldn't stop long enough to think about any one event, let alone how they were connected.

Couldn't just one thing go right? I clicked to local news, and, as if in answer to my question, I discovered that after being shot by the father of one of his victims, Floyd Lynch was in critical but stable condition at the Tucson Trauma Center.

I realize life has to be pretty bad when that was the good news. But good news it was. While Lynch remained alive there was the chance of getting all kinds of questions answered.

Besides, I couldn't sit around a hotel room feeling sorry for myself. I needed to find Coleman, make sure she was all right, and finish Lynch's investigation. I owed that much to Zach. First I needed to find out how long Lynch might remain in the hospital.

Before that I needed a shower. The sweet and sour smells of Zach's blood from the day before mixed with the vodka and the burrito reminded me I couldn't remember when last I had bathed.

I took a long hot one, washed and dried my hair, and put on clean clothes out of my garbage bag.

Next. I called Gordo and told him I wasn't living at home anymore, that he needed to step up his protection. He didn't ask why. Good old Gordo.

Next was no option. Lynch was stable and secure for

the time being, and my concerns for Coleman grew the more I thought about it. It suddenly occurred to me she hadn't even called me after the courthouse shootings. Even if she was at her parents' place, even if one of them was gravely ill, she would have seen it on the news and called me. I phoned Maisie Dickens.

"Maisie, I finally heard from Agent Coleman."

"Good. Last time she e-mailed I told her you were looking for her."

I wasn't sure whether that was a good thing or bad thing, but I'd work with it. "Thanks, having you tell her must have helped. She told me to meet her at her house."

"She's taking some time off, I think. Lord knows she's got the vacation days piled up."

I was glad to see that Maisie was in confiding mode. "Yes, and just between us, she's needing some girl talk."

"Oh, does it have to do with her being taken off the Lynch case? And wasn't that something about him getting shot? I knew she was upset the other day but she never talks to me."

"That's our Laura, always trying to hang tough. The thing is, she hung up without giving me her address, kind of distracted, you know? I was there once but can't remember. You know how it is."

Maisie is menopausal. She knows how it is. "She called you? She must really need to talk."

"Mmm. I tried calling her back but can't get through, and I'm supposed to be over there in half an hour. Can you give me her address?"

"Not protocol, Brigid. You know that."

"Come on, just between us old gals. How dangerous could I be?"

That was alarmingly easy. I heard Maisie tap tapping on her computer, and in a second she gave me an address on Elm Street in the Sam Hughes historical neighborhood near the university.

"Give her my love, would you?"

"What a sweetheart you are. I sure will, Maisie."

I closed the phone, tossed the good clothes out of the garbage bag onto the other bed, and left the bloodstained clothes in it. I had already delayed hiding them to my great regret, and I wasn't going to make that mistake again, even if it meant driving out of my way. I wouldn't even take the chance of a Dumpster.

I carried my tote and the bag with the bloody clothes outside to the parking lot. I looked where I had parked my car last and didn't see it. I panicked. That was all I needed, to have my car stolen.

Then I remembered my car was parked at the bar because I'd been too drunk to drive the night before. I threw the bag over my shoulder and headed the mile down around the corner to the bar, feeling like any other homeless person who traversed this stretch. It was already hotter than hell but the exercise would get the rest of the alcohol out of my system.

I found my car safely parked in their small lot where I had left it. I would have liked to make a discreet exit, but Emery drew up in a beige Hyundai, with Cheri watching me from the passenger's seat. I cringed inwardly but with proper barkeep attitude they simply waved me off, not showing any embarrassing concern.

I headed north on Campbell, up where it turns into one of those roads that you see on a map hemmed by little green dots indicating they're scenic. Usually I enjoyed driving around these twists just a little faster than speed limit, feeling my tires hug the asphalt, but this time I hardly noticed. I turned left on Ina, a short distance, then right on Oracle.

Set against the idyllic backdrop of the Pusch Ridge section of the Catalina Mountains is the U-Store-It storage company. Set within the storage building is my space, about as big as half a garage, where I keep my private collection of weaponry.

I moved aside a few boxes of old case files and shells and tucked the plastic bag behind a safe close to the back wall. Hiding the clothes made me recall how I was not a killer but sure had learned a lot from them. If I became a real suspect in the killing of Gerald Peasil they'd access my credit card, find this storage facility charged to it, and get a search warrant. But for the short term the clothes were safe here until I had the time to dispose of them more thoroughly.

Turning my attention to the dinky .38 I had in my tote, I twisted the dial on the safe and opened it to reveal several rifles, a single-barrel shotgun, and half a dozen small arms. From that cache I selected and loaded a 1911, a .45 that was guaranteed to kick some major ass, to keep in my trunk just in case I ran into something ugly at Coleman's house. I grabbed an extra box of ammo. When I emerged with my tote bag heavier than when I went in, I glanced around to make sure no one was watching me.

Then, feeling just this much more confident that I would not be discovered, provided I could trust my husband to keep my secret, I headed back the way I had come, down into the city, to the address on Elm Street that Maisie had provided. I pulled up in front of a nice, tidy little hacienda with lots of purple bougainvillea out front, but the thing that got my attention immediately wasn't Coleman's house. It was her Prius, parked in the driveway, in front of the closed garage door.

THIRTY-NINE

Had she actually been home all this time and was just ignoring me? Feeling half-stupid and half on edge, I left my car parked in the street, decided on the .38 just to be on the safe side, and approached the vehicle cautiously, the way a cop does when they've stopped a motorist, as if someone might sit up in the backseat and start firing. I could see nothing through the windows and used the edge of my T-shirt to test the doors.

I found the driver's side unlocked, and that put me further on alert. No cop would ever, under any circumstances, leave their vehicle unlocked outside, even in their own driveway. Coleman would probably lock hers if she had it in the garage.

I wedged my pistol into the back of my jeans to give the inside of the car a quick once over and found nothing, not so much as a muffin crumb from breakfast on the road. I popped the trunk, which was similarly empty except for a collapsible lawn chair and a few reusable shopping bags. It was a second bad sign that I was able to get into the trunk.

Nothing more to discover there, so I turned my attention to the house. All window shades drawn both against the heat and as security. The front door was locked. This part was as it should be. To make myself less conspicuous,

I went through a low gate on the right side to the back of the house, where I found a French door leading into the living room.

I didn't bother to knock, just in case someone inside was not Coleman. I broke in, no fancy technique, just used a rock on one of the small panes in the door, reached through to the bolt lock. If someone inside was not Coleman the breaking glass would have alerted them, so I stepped in carefully, weapon drawn, and checked the place out.

The house felt warm and a little stuffy, like when someone goes on vacation and leaves the AC on eighty-five. I wandered quickly through the rooms, growing quickly aware that I was alone, and taking just a few minutes to get some sense of her that might help me. Coleman decorated the way she worked, by the book, or in this case, by the catalog. The place was strictly Bed, Bath, and Beyond, white towels, and bed-in-a-bag. Everything except the towels were shades of brown and geometry.

The bedroom was plain and spare, with a window overlooking the front yard. A collection of photographs including one of her family, presumably, hung on the wall. It made me doubt that Coleman brought Royal Hughes to her bedroom. As a rule, people do not have sex in the same room with photos of their mother smiling on them.

The small walk-in closet held two more suits like the ones I'd seen her wear and a dozen long-sleeved silkish blouses that all looked too hot for Arizona. Some casual clothes, too; jeans, cotton blouses, and a raggedy maroon bathrobe with the chenille ridges wearing away.

Nothing but over-the-counter drugs in the medicine cabinet in the bathroom, and she went for the cheap moisturizer, shampoo, and toothpaste. The shower was very clean, the plastic shower curtain had no water drops, which I found neat to the point of weirdness but that's just me.

Back in the living room I noticed a put-together desk with a blotter that made me smile despite my concerns. Only Coleman would still use a blotter. On top of it rested a laptop computer and a few black binders whose edges were aligned parallel to the edge of the desk, all the clutter Coleman would allow. I recognized the cardboard box containing Floyd's reading material that we had brought from the Lynch's, set neatly beside the desk. Heaven forbid Coleman would fail to bring it in from her trunk.

It should have been pretty easy to find what I was looking for, but I rifled through the two small drawers finding nothing but pens and pencils—oh God, they were lined up side by side by length in descending order. She was more compulsive than I'd thought. Calculator, roll of stamps, a can of compressed air for cleaning her keyboard. I went into the larger file drawers beneath. Tax returns filed by year. They still weren't paying agents what they were worth. A six-year-old passport, with only one stamp for Cancun five years ago, listed her birthplace as Henderson, North Carolina, and her birth date as May 12, 1979.

I finally found what I was looking for next to the phone in the kitchen, on a small bench at the end of the counter. I flipped through the lime-green leather address book. Like me, she didn't seem to have any friends. The entries, written in pencil, were few. Her dentist and doctor. Eva's hair salon. What looked like her brother back in

North Carolina. Page after page of blanks. Not even anyone from the office. Except under the Rs, there were the initials RH and a number. Coleman was so afraid of being found out she wouldn't even write his whole name in her address book.

I used her home phone to call the number. Royal Hughes answered very quickly.

"Yes?"

"When was the last time you saw Laura Coleman?" I asked.

"Who is this?"

"Brigid Quinn."

"What are you doing . . . ?"

"Where?" I asked.

"There," he hedged.

So he knew her home number by heart when it appeared on caller ID. "When was the last time you saw Laura Coleman?"

"I don't want you calling my home, Agent Quinn."

"I'm getting a little angry here. When was the last time you saw Laura Coleman?" I repeated.

"At the Lynch crime scene. I told you. You shouldn't call my home. I'm hanging up now."

I heard a voice in the background, "Honey? Can you do Bill's piano lesson today?"

I had no idea where he lived, but I pressed my advantage. "You're a liar, and I'm close enough so if you hang up I'm coming over there to put a tire iron through your double-paned windows before you can call nine-one-one, and let you do the explaining. When was the last time you saw Laura Coleman?"

He paused, must have felt that in his position it was

wiser not to resist me, plus those double-paned windows are really expensive. He lowered his voice to a whisper. "I swear to God, not since the crime scene. It was all over more than a year ago. Why?"

"I think Coleman's been abducted." There, I said it.

No oh my God, or what the fuck, just, "What makes you think that?"

I heard the voice in the background, less distinct this time. He had probably moved outside as we talked.

"Her car is here."

"Oh for pete's sake, she rented a car or flew somewhere," Hughes said, and hung up.

Like I said, no friends. If that's how Hughes responded, especially given current attitudes toward me, I wouldn't get any more traction with Max Coyote or Roger Morrison. I was on my own.

Assuming she still had her maiden name I looked under the Cs in her address book and found Ben and Emily Coleman at the Paloma Vista Retirement Center, with an address and phone number.

Only I didn't call the number directly. Not wanting to alarm her parents I called directory assistance instead and got the main number at the center, asked to speak with the manager.

"I'm calling to ask about one of your residents," I said.

"I'm sorry. We don't give out any information on our residents."

"I'm a family member, and I'm just calling to inquire after Emily Coleman's health."

"I'm sorry. Perhaps you could call their number directly. We don't give out any information on our residents."

"Could you tell me whether their daughter has been there within the past three days?"

"I'm sorry. We don't give out any information on our residents."

"Is this a real person I'm talking to?"

"Yes, and we don't give out any information on our residents."

Why can't anything be easy? I hung up, took the address book with me, and set out for Paloma Vista.

FORTY

If Arizonans want Mexicans to stay out of the country, why do they give everything Spanish names? It kinda sends conflicting messages. Paloma Vista was a modest but lovely two-story structure with a barrel-tiled roof that stretched on both sides of a long circular drive. A small bus with the name of the center and the word FUN! painted big on the side was boarding a group of mostly women.

I pulled up behind it, got out of the car, and asked the group as a whole if anyone knew Ben and Emily Coleman. All of them did. One woman said they were having lunch in the dining room and then shook her head in a tsking fashion as if my question made her sad. Maybe the mom was feeling poorly after all. I walked through the automatic doors, past the reception desk where the young woman didn't ask who I was, through a spacious sitting area where the upholstery on the chairs didn't match the pillows didn't match the rugs except in some existential way known only to a decorator, and beyond into the dining area. A maître d' of sorts welcomed me and asked if I was there to visit someone.

"Ben and Emily Coleman," I said.

He led me to a table set for four, where a couple sat who, I must confess, appeared to be not much older than me. Both as tall as Laura, even sitting down I could see that, lanky and with thick heads of gray hair. I approached cautiously, introduced myself as a friend of their daughter, and asked if I could join them for a moment though I saw they were still eating. I apologized for that.

"That's all right. It's just dessert," Ben Coleman said as he gestured to the chair next to his wife. He also gestured to a young woman who hovered nearby. "May I get you a rice pudding?"

I thanked him for his hospitality, but no, and the young woman hovered away.

Emily had been staring straight ahead with a placid smile during our exchange. Now she turned her head in a regal sweep and smiled at me. "Laura?" she asked.

"No darling," Ben said. "This is Brigid Quinn, a friend of Laura's."

I started to explain that my own parents were looking for a good retirement center, and that Laura had mentioned to me that Ben and Emily seemed very contented here at Paloma Vista. I wanted to come see for myself and ask them personally about their opinion of the living quarters, the food, and other services, before I made an appointment with the management for a formal tour.

"They've been extraordinary," Ben said, as Emily, interest waning once she found I was not Laura, had turned with gusto back to her pudding. "Not every facility is willing to deal with Emily's needs, so we were especially fortunate."

We were interrupted by my cell phone, which made everyone in the dining room look my way as if they were aliens and that was the signal from the home planet. I dug into my tote and checked before turning it off. It was Max. Rather than find out what new pressure he had devised to torture me into a confession, I let it take a message.

I chatted with Ben a bit longer, my wondering how to broach the topic of Laura's whereabouts, when Ben did it himself. He appeared to lose a little of his Perfect Host quality, seemed to grow a little uncomfortable. "May I ask you a question?" he asked.

"Of course."

"This feels a little odd to ask of someone I've only just met, but our daughter calls every single day to check in on her mom. I've been concerned that she hasn't called in three days. I left a message yesterday on her cell phone but she didn't respond." He seemed to grow more embarrassed. "I hate to seem like that kind of parent, but have you been in touch with her?"

I laughed lightly. "Oh, Laura? She's fine. Fine! I know she's been deeply involved in a huge case that's coming to trial. You know how our Laura is, dotting and crossing everything in sight. She mentioned once that you told her anything worth doing was worth doing well."

Ben seemed like the sort of person who would dispense that wisdom. He laughed, too, possibly trying to remember when he'd said it, but greatly reassured nonetheless. I extracted myself from the dining room as quickly as I could without making him suspicious.

The message from Max, which I listened to once I was back in the car, said to call him, that he'd discovered something that would interest me. And he wanted to hear again about how I'd fallen in the wash and bumped my head. And while he was on the subject, that hiking stick that Carlo made me with the blade on one end . . .

did I still have that stick? His voice had an un-Max-like threatening edge to it. I didn't call back.

Instead, pulling out of the retirement center and driving who knows where I tried calling Sigmund. I was as upfront with him as I could be. "I think I fucked up big time, and I think Agent Laura Coleman is in trouble, and no one will listen to me," I said. I told him about where we were in our investigation of Lynch, about the disappearance of Coleman, even about the shooting in the park. I fell short of talking about Peasil. I didn't think that was necessary given the circumstances of the other attempt on my life. He asked me about the shooting incident in some detail, down to the second shots from the direction of the Pima Pistol Club. He grew quiet.

I let him think, then finally asked the silence, "What should I do?"

"Tell Morrison."

"Morrison doesn't want to hear it. I even called Royal Hughes, remember what you said about the public defender and Coleman?"

"Was I right?"

"Yeah, you were right, but even he doesn't think there's anything to be concerned about."

He came at me from a totally unexpected direction. "It's been hard for you, hasn't it."

"What?"

"I heard that Zachariah Robertson killed himself. That must have been shocking for you, Stinger."

"I know, that was so awful, but I don't even have time to process it just now. I have to find Coleman."

"Stinger, why did you stay in Tucson?"

He wasn't saying anything I expected him to say, didn't

even seem to be listening to me. "Are we having the same conversation?" I asked.

"We never talked about that. I've always thought you stayed in the Southwest to be closer to the case you couldn't solve, like a murderer who can't stay away from the scene of the crime. You never lost your obsession with it."

"Don't analyze me now, Sig, I don't have time for it."

"Frankly, after our last conversation I started to think you may have been experiencing some post-traumatic stress linked to revisiting the Route 66 case, opening those wounds. And now, with Zach Robertson's suicide, well."

Something spun off kilter in my brain and I felt a dizzy sensation, almost vertigo. Too dazed to be angry, I pleaded, "But, Sig, you agreed with us about Lynch, you said to go after that investigation."

"And I still feel that way. I'm just saying these fears about Laura Coleman being abducted is . . ." There was a pause that felt like someone deciding when to rip off a Band-Aid. "Brigid, Laura Coleman isn't Jessica Robertson," he said gently.

My cheeks burned and I said, "You think I'm delusional."

"I wouldn't put it that way at all. You've been beating yourself up for years over Jessica's death. Now you have another agent, the same gender and approximately the same age that Jessica would be today. Only this one is, shall we say, a little unreliable. Or maybe she just doesn't need you anymore. Because she doesn't return your calls, you break into her house and decide she's been abducted. Stinger, you're playing back Jessica."

"You mean there's no telling what I might have imagined, right down to the attempt on my life."

"I'm just saying you seem to be the only person who's concerned," he said.

"You think I'm paranoid," I said.

"Stop it, Stinger. I'm not saying anything. I'm just saying you need to pause and think a moment. I'm not worried about Laura Coleman. I'm worried about you. I was worried about you the last time you called. I should have stayed out there so we could talk more about you."

"Son of a bitch," I said, and hung up.

Statistics show that, in an abduction, the trail goes cold after forty-eight hours and the chances of finding the victim alive are greatly diminished. I looked at my watch and remembered the last sure contact I'd had with Coleman: *BTW, you were right!* That was around 8:00 A.M., a little over seventy-two hours ago.

FORTY-ONE

I felt like a blind mouse in a maze, making some small progress like finding out that Coleman hadn't gone to visit her sick mother after all, and then hitting a wall, not knowing which direction to take next. The wall was where I was right now. Coleman was missing and all I had to prove it was her unlocked car, the fact that she didn't call her mom for three days, and lying to Morrison. Apart from that, she was still sending e-mails to the office. All my instincts were screaming that she was in trouble, but if Sigmund thought I'd gone off my rocker, Morrison would laugh me out of the office.

Sometimes it helps if the mouse doesn't aim directly for the cheese. Rather than jumping on my horse and riding off in all directions, I called Gordo to find out if Carlo was safe. He didn't answer the phone and didn't call me back in the next ten minutes, so I headed back to the house to check on Carlo myself, stopping on the way for a coffee and a roast beef sub with everything.

I took a roundabout way into the development, via Bowman, rather than turn down the street closest to the house. That way I could approach more slowly and stay at least three houses away, where I parked and waited, engine idling and AC on, so I wouldn't pass out in the heat.

Munching on the sub, doing surveillance on my own

house, I sat there with no better place to go, sensing Jane's ghost beside me throughout the evening, yet feeling like I had a little purpose in guarding Carlo while I figured out what next in my search for Coleman. We sat there, Jane's ghost and I, the two women in Carlo's life come and gone.

The light next to Carlo's reading chair went on inside the house as the sky finally darkened. My own novel would be sitting on the table next to my own chair. I struggled and failed to remember what I had been reading the day before; I was that overwhelmed and mindsore.

Later Carlo emerged once more to take the Pugs out for their evening walk in the opposite direction from where I parked; it was too dark for him to see my car. Was he stooped more than usual? Were the dogs a little subdued? I was beginning to feel like a ghost myself and wondered if they were all missing me as brutally as I was missing them.

I had long before now turned off my engine as the clear sky allowed the heated earth to cool more rapidly. Drank the third of four bottles of water I'd brought along, and which now tasted like bathwater. I kept telling myself it was silly to sit there all night, but found myself unable to drive away. What if? I thought. And if not that, what if? All kinds of imaginings. Then I thought that maybe if I just did a bit of a perimeter check I'd feel better about dozing off for a bit. Besides, I had to pee and could do so in the darkened arroyo behind our property.

I took a small flashlight out of the glove compartment and walked the short distance down the street, turned right, and hugged the high cinder-block wall of the neighbor's property, playing the light over the ground ahead of me to surprise any snakes before they surprised me. No snakes, but once I came too close to a hunting tarantula that did some threatening push-ups to scare me off, and succeeded.

The yards are separated from one another by the concrete walls, but down the property lines it's all fence made of thin wrought-iron rods. Regretting that I didn't have a spare walking stick with me I held on to the fence for balance as I picked my way over the uneven ground until I came to our own backyard. Ran the flashlight over the ground. Everything seemed safe here, no signs of human activity in the dirt. The back of the house, seventy feet from where I stood, was dark, and I could just barely make out the back door that Carlo sometimes forgot to lock. And was that bedroom window open? How many times I'd chided him about that. Civilians have no real sense for security.

I put the flashlight in my pocket, stopped to relieve myself in the dark, and stepped up on the low part of the concrete wall that was supposed to keep bobcats and coyotes from slipping under the fence. I scrambled ungracefully over. It hurt, landing on the gravel slope and skidding down to sit hard on my butt. By this time I noticed that the flashlight was overkill. The clear sky and a full moon gave the yard a monochrome feel, the trees, the walls, the gravel, the house all pale blue-gray. I was able to see well enough to move quickly past Jane's yard art, the full-size Saint Francis statue and the stone birdbath, without knocking into any of them.

A quick check of the back door to make sure it was

locked and an escape out the side gate would have been easy if I hadn't been spotted by one of the Pugs. Without my knowing, through the glass back door he (or she) had been watching me approach and now set off a barking that attracted the other Pug, who joined in. Then I saw the bedroom light go on.

I ducked behind the Saint Francis statue just as the porch light went on. I didn't dare look, only listened as keenly as I could as he opened the door, told the Pugs to stay inside in case there was a coyote out there. I glimpsed his shadow as he came to stand in the middle of the yard, making himself an easy target to whoever I might have been. It was all too much like a scene from one of the comic operas he loved. Disgusted with myself, I stood straight and stepped out from behind the statue, because keeping him safe was more important than my pride.

"Jesus!" he shouted, and dropped the flashlight that he carried and, like mine, had not turned on.

We both sleep in the buff, and I couldn't help but notice he had taken on the same color as the rest of the yard, his flesh like cold gray marble in the moonlight, or like death on a slab. Another image I could do without. "Since you came out, I need to ask you for something," I said without greeting or apology.

He stared at me through the gloom, his fingers clenched at his sides, looking the kind of pissed that comes just after being startled out of your wits. My whole being wanted to rush to him, to take him in my arms and comfort him, but my pride couldn't go quite that far. He would push me away, had already cut himself off from me, I could feel it.

Keeping my voice as level as possible, with the tone

267

you use when you're giving directions to a motorist, I said, "Give up the evening walk for now. Keep the doors locked and windows closed. If the Pugs bark, don't come out of the house like this. Stay inside. Don't even raise a blind to look out a window. If someone you don't recognize comes to the door during the day, don't answer."

"Enough melodrama!" He threw his hands up in the air as if finally he'd had enough. "This is crazy, and ever since, since that day you said you fell, you've been behaving like some character in a Mike Hammer novel."

That stung, especially coming from the man I had loved, but I understood his anger. I said, "You may be in danger. I don't mean to sound dramatic, but serious danger. I don't know how else to tell you that and I don't have time right now to work on it."

"How long?" he asked.

"I don't know. I have to find someone who I think has been kidnapped. I'm the only one who believes that, and if I stop looking for her she could die. She disappeared three days ago, so if she's not dead already I'm thinking she's got less than twenty-four hours. That's the only truth I can care about at the moment, Carlo. Go back inside now."

He bent over to pick up the flashlight and raised it as if he would hit me with it, then he got control. "You think that's it?"

Now it was my turn to just stare, waiting for more.

He tried to speak with the same level tone as I, and nearly succeeded. "You think you can just come here, give me a cryptic warning, and leave? That isn't how things operate in the real world. There are other people involved. There's me." He paused, took a deep breath, "Max was here."

There was an echo of Paul in his words about how things operate in his world, such a different world from mine. "When?"

"This morning."

"What did he want?"

"He asked me a lot of questions about you, where you were, what I knew about the day that man was killed in the wash. He asked if you still had that hiking stick I made you. He wasn't himself."

"What did you tell him?" I asked, genuinely curious. There had been so many stories invented I wasn't sure which ones he knew.

"The truth."

My pulse sped up at the sound of the word. "What truth?"

"Everything I remembered. That you said the stick broke. The odd way you'd been acting ever since that day you came back from the wash and said you'd fallen."

Said I'd fallen. The roundabout way of accusing me of lying was the worst thing of all. It made me defensive. "You don't know shit about the real world, do you?" I said.

He didn't look offended, just sadder if that was possible. He said, "I actually thought I did, but apparently I was wrong. Max told me a lot, about how you killed an unarmed suspect when you were an agent. The circumstances were equivocal; I think that was the way he put it." He waved the flashlight as if to dispel a sudden wave of smoke. "It's incredible to discover how little I knew you."

FORTY-TWO

Without waiting for any response from me, without saying good-bye, Carlo went back into the house, shooing the Pugs as they tried to come out to me. I left through the side gate rather than look like a jerk scrambling back over the fence. Everything seemed secure here, and if Carlo followed my instructions he should be safe with or without Gordo's protection.

I sat in the car, thinking some. It seemed more logical that the killer was trying to silence me and wouldn't bother with my husband. My absence would draw fire away from the house while I searched for Coleman and tried to find out who was trying to kill me. Even if everyone else thought I was either crazy or bad, I was more certain than ever that these two things, the attempts on my life and Coleman's disappearance, were connected.

I stared at the street in front of me, unable for the first time to avoid the thought that there was no reason to suppose that Coleman was still alive. I mean, if they tried to kill me, why not her? Thoughts heading in that direction, already on edge to the point of falling off, I was shocked by a face in my window.

"FUCK!" I shrieked, and grabbed for my gun on the passenger seat, where it should have been, but found only my flashlight. I flicked it on and aimed it through the window, hoping to at least blind my assailant.

Max stood there, blinking. "It's me," his muffled voice came through the glass. I slid the window down and, uncaring about the neighbors or Carlo, yelled, "You want to get yourself killed?"

"I don't think that flashlight is loaded." Trying to maintain his tough-guy expression but unable to suppress a small smile, he walked around the front of the car and tried to get in the passenger seat, but the door was locked. He waited. I had no choice. I leaned over and flicked the lock.

When he had made himself at home, he said, "Why are you staking out your own house?"

Either I was still in a bit of shock from the surprise, or I was just getting fed up. It seemed I was out of new lies. Also the dark does something for honesty. "Why'd you have to discuss my past with Carlo?"

"I was surprised he didn't already know. It's the kind of thing you share with your spouse."

"Share it with your own spouse. Max, someone is trying to kill me and I'm worried about Carlo's safety because I think someone has abducted Agent Laura Coleman."

"Yeah, right," he said.

So much for honesty. But then it sounded kind of wild to me when I heard myself say it. Kind of trumped up.

He didn't ask why I was just bringing this up only now but kept his focus on the mundane, "You didn't answer why you're out here."

"I came by to keep an eye on him. We're breaking up."

"I'm sorry. He told me you took off suddenly yesterday but I didn't know it was permanent. Why did you leave?"

"Why are you here?"

"You didn't return my call. I pulled up and saw you sitting out here watching the house, so I was watching you, wondering how long you'd stay. Except for when you got out of the car just then you've been here a long time."

"What can I do for you?"

"Gerald Peasil."

I had some sense left even after my shock. "Who?"

Max gave his head an impatient jerk. "Don't pretend you don't know who I'm talking about. I'm still waiting for the DNA analysis, but in the meantime I ran the prints we retrieved against your own, the ones you have on file with the Bureau."

"And?"

"You didn't match any of them."

"Of course not." I cracked open my last bottle of water, buying time. "Want some?"

He took a swig and put it in the cup holder between us. It reminded me of a lion and a gazelle at the watering hole. "So we went up to where he'd been staying. Found evidence of sexual violence, certainly rape, probably murder. At least three. They're sending cadaver dogs up there on the chance he hid the bodies in the vicinity, in the mine-tailings ponds or somewhere. We found clothes so the dogs have a lot to go on."

"Is that good news?"

"That the guy appears to be a serial killer or that he's dead?"

"You tell me," I said.

"No, you tell me. I still can't think of more than one reason why you didn't report it."

I took a drink from the bottle. We both had dry mouth

from the tension of the conversation, and pretended it was simple thirst. "I told you, Max. I was going to call you; I would have called you; I just got scared." I knew what was coming next. I wondered what I would say.

"Scared, you. Did you kill him, Brigid?"

There it was.

"Not me."

"Let's say you did."

"Let's just say."

"How would—"

"Ah, the classic interrogation question. You really think I'm going to do a hypothetical?"

"It was worth a try."

It was a night for honesty all around. "You ever work a sexual homicide case, Max?"

"Yes."

"Accidental, quick, or truly brutal?"

"You know the answer to that. Somebody gets too rough, somebody dies. Somebody suffocates getting themself off."

I nodded in the dark. "But never serial sexual homicide with mutilation. Most people go through their whole career without seeing that. Those images you carry for the rest of your life."

"Oh, here we go. The great Brigid Quinn has seen it all. And I'm just a poor country sheriff's deputy from Bumfuckaz where nothing ever happens except maybe cattle ruslin'. Give me a break."

"Well, I can tell you women's breasts look a lot more attractive when they're still attached to the body."

Max's body twisted. "Jesus Christ, Brigid, do you joke about everything?"

273

"Was that a joke? I'm sorry, sometimes I can't tell the difference anymore." I took another swig of water, and offered him the bottle, which he didn't bother to acknowledge this time. "So now you've got Gerald Peasil," I said. "A real serial killer . . . you say."

"And what a coincidence in this small town where there were only thirty-five homicides all last year that we have both Gerald Peasil and Floyd Lynch within weeks of each other, huh?"

"I guess that's a pretty big coincidence."

"You might think that. Only because it's a small town where there were only thirty-five homicides last year, I started thinking about it. I got to thinking about all these dots we have." Max leaned forward and started making dots in a row with his wiener finger on the dashboard as he listed each one. "There's you not reporting the van in the wash, Gerald Peasil being a serial killer, Floyd Lynch being a serial killer. Then I got to thinking about this hair we found in Peasil's apartment. It looked like hair from three different women, but all shades of gray, white, mixed, braided together. See, that's another dot. I got to thinking about the color, awful lot of gray hair going around, you know, that maybe there's no coincidence about Peasil attacking older women and you being an older woman and about two serial killers operating in the same area. And you being somehow connected to them both." He drew an imaginary line connecting the imaginary dots. "Then I got to thinking about how the ME found that Peasil's artery had been slashed and how you had that stick with a blade on the end. Carlo said you lost it."

"It broke."

"What did you do with it?"

"I threw it away." I paused. Max didn't say anything. "In the garbage," I added.

I turned to see the moonlight shining off Max's eyes. When someone has a temper, like my father for instance, you get used to the slamming and the shouting. It's the calm and controlled people who unnerve you.

Max didn't avert his gaze. I could tell he was looking at what he was convinced was a rogue agent and it was useless to try to change his mind just now. He said, "Of course, right now I just got lots of dots. But I know your connection to Lynch, the Route 66 case. Next is finding out your connection to Peasil. Maybe it's not through Lynch. I'm beginning to think maybe a chance encounter, you were trying to disable him, and things went out of control. You didn't mean to jab his artery. We don't have to call it murder, Brigid. We could call it self-defense."

While trying to act like he had my best interests at heart, Max was still fishing. That told me, for all that Carlo had professed to no longer know me, to no longer love me, he hadn't yet told Max about finding the bloody clothes in the washing machine. If he had, Max would have taken me downtown. I didn't even care anymore about being arrested, except I knew that once that happened Coleman would almost certainly be lost. And that reminded me I was wasting precious time. I needed to get out of this conversation.

"*You* could call it self-defense? You and I both know you have no power to cut a deal on this, Max. If it happened like you're suggesting, the DA would probably go more for involuntary manslaughter. And that's if the defendant was lucky. Hard to argue that a trained agent with a shady past punctured an artery by accident. Especially with a subsequent cover-up. No, I bet that DA would go for at least murder two. But I didn't do it, Max." I tried to keep my voice steady, soft, noncombative. I needed to not push him over the edge, just out of my car. "If you took me in now, the most you'd get is hours of typing up a very long and complicated report. You don't have any witnesses or forensic evidence. You don't even have the murder weapon."

Max leaned close enough toward me that I could feel wet breath and smell the Whopper he had for dinner. I took it without flinching but without fighting back either. With the same calm tone he'd use for pointing out a cloud in the sky, "Carlo is good people. That's why I want to be very careful before I do something that will ruin his life."

FORTY-THREE

Max wouldn't get out of the car until I told him where I was staying. So I told him I was staying at the Sheraton on Speedway, room 174.

Then I drove to the hotel, got my stuff, and left without checking out.

As I loaded my garbage bag of belongings into the trunk I remembered the bloody clothes in the storage facility. Once Max turned this into a full-blown investigation, he would routinely track my credit card bills and find the monthly charge for the storage. I would need to take the clothes into the desert with some gasoline and a match pretty soon.

In the meantime, Coleman's house was the perfect hiding place for me. It had far more amenities than the hotel. It had food. No one would go there because no one gave a damn about her. And if by some chance she made her way home I'd be the first to know.

She also had a computer. I keyed in the word *Password* first, of course, and when that didn't work, combinations of her first and last name. When that didn't work, I tried to remember her pet's name. Eighty percent of people use their pet's name on their home computer, and she had told me hers in the bar. Then I remembered a miniature schnauzer. Duncan.

That didn't work either. I went through her desk again and this time found a list taped to the inside of a drawer. It had about two dozen different accounts, each with a different password made up of what appeared to be random numbers. Coleman and her experience in the fraud division, investigating identity theft. I should have figured.

At the top was the password for booting her computer, 4597358. While I waited for the computer to fire up I took a look at the things on her desk and in the drawers that I had passed over when searching for her address book. There was a sheet of return-address labels courtesy of Alzheimer's Research Fund. A box of androgynous note cards, the geometric design ambiguous enough to serve as both congratulations and condolence. A coaster from her trip to Cancun. That must have been a big deal, that trip.

I went to her e-mail account next to see what messages had appeared in the last three days and whether any had been opened. Among the ads from Ann Taylor Loft and the daily news bulletin from the Bureau, I found two personal messages in her sent folder. The first was the one she had written to me early in the morning, *BTW you were right! Sort of* and one later in the afternoon telling Maisie she was spending time with her sick mom. If she wasn't the one who sent that second message, I wondered what they did to her to get the password and send the message through her account.

Incoming mail showed one other personal message, the one from me, giving her a bit of "what for," and asking where the hell she was.

My message had been opened and read.

It would have been read by whoever was using her

account to send messages to her office.

If I was still with the Bureau and anyone trusted me it would be easy to find out the IP address of whoever sent the message to Maisie and read the one from me.

I played out the various possible scenarios. Maybe whoever took Coleman disabled her and took the time to use her computer. Or he took her to another location where it was safer and accessed her account there from his own computer. Without a good techie I couldn't know.

Frustrated, I turned back to the desk and spotted the neat stack of three black binders I had passed over earlier that day because they weren't what I was looking for. I hauled the one on top to the level of the desk. The three binders constituted the entire record of the Lynch case, not the scaled-down single-binder copy she had given me, but the complete original, including Lynch's journals and all the crime scene photographs. Coleman hadn't told me she had the whole thing, and she was in serious breach of protocol taking it out of the office.

But if she was in the kind of trouble I thought she was in, protocol was the least of her concerns. What did Coleman and I know that was such a threat? I had to find out and confront Lynch. Then maybe he would give me something, anything, that would help lead me to her.

The pad on which I'd made all the notes was still on my desk at home. But I had also sent them to Coleman as an e-mail, so I retrieved that message from her deleted file. I looked at the notes that seemed from a lifetime ago, when I was still a different person. I compared it to the reports in the original books, the crime scene processing, the lists of evidence, the personal effects. Only this time I had the photographs, too. Lots of photographs of victims, both on the scene and on the autopsy table, including the shots taken at the abandoned car site.

If the case was an open one, if Lynch hadn't made his deal so quickly, and if Morrison hadn't been so hot to get the credit for what seemed to be an eight-time serial killer, there would have been more than just three binders; there would have been boxes.

Still, so much here, I grabbed at the second binder and flipped through the pages, reading summaries of Lynch's testimony. Not much on the woman Lynch had mummified other than his statement that she was a Mexican illegal. Like Manriquez had said, he had so many of those unidentified in a refrigerated truck in back of the medical examiner's office, the numbers were overwhelming.

Now the Route 66 victims: there were pages and pages on them, and Lynch had gotten all the details right, give or take a few memory lapses. Except for the one he called the lot lizard. The transcripts of his interviews didn't reveal much about her or the night he killed her. I looked at the picture of what was left of her, photographed inside the car in a fetal position before they pulled her out and her head and leg fell off. I remembered Morrison at the courthouse had announced that all the American victims had been identified. But in the glow of his success, perhaps in the success of finally finding Jessica Robertson, he had forgotten about this one.

"Who are you?" I asked her. "And why hasn't anyone cared about you?"

Maybe that was the right question, that this one victim maybe could help me, the only victim who had not been identified. Maybe the lot lizard was in the database Sig told me about, and I was asking the right question when I asked her who she was.

I looked at my watch. Three hours later on the East Coast at this time of year because Arizona doesn't do daylight saving time. Two thirty A.M. in DC. I called Sig. He picked up on the second ring and didn't sound sleepy. It felt like old times.

"Brigid. I got a question," I said.

"Hello, Stinger. How are you feeling?"

He really wanted to know, but I was still smarting from his insinuation that I was suffering from post-traumatic stress disorder and refused to answer. "What's that site you told me about for searching missing persons?"

"I was going to call you tomorrow. I had Lynch's interrogation video checked against the tapes from Jessica's wire, to do a voice comparison, especially the part where both Lynch and the abductor raised the pitch of their voices to sound like women."

"And?"

"Inconclusive, I'm afraid."

"Thanks. The site?"

"NamUs. It was started about two years ago after you left the Bureau. One database compiles all known information about missing persons and matches it up to another database on unidentifieds. People can find out if a person found dead or alive matches a person they're looking for. And they can provide information as well."

"What's the URL?"

"www.findthemissing.org. Is it Agent Coleman you're still looking for? Because I don't—"

"No. You say it catalogs unidentified remains, too?"

"Yes. I don't know if the person you need is there, but it's been growing exponentially, and anyone can access it. No special clearance needed. Stinger."

"What?"

"You're angry."

"You think?" I hung up. I wasn't sure if NamUs could help me. I wasn't even sure what "growing exponentially" means precisely, other than a shitload of information.

Conscious that this could be just another dead end in less and less time, I keyed in the address.

Once there, I entered what I knew about the lot lizard, which was precious little. Female. Caucasian (I guessed she wasn't one of the illegals). Under twenty, change to under thirty to be on the safe side. Date range, the twelve months of the year prior to the first murder we knew about. Missing from . . . let's try all of Arizona.

A dozen different names came up, most with photographs. There was no time to follow up on all these women. I clicked back to the beginning to see what other options there were. Distinguishing marks. Could those still be seen on the mummified flesh? Had the ME even bothered to autopsy her body, or had he just bagged her and put her in the morgue for the time being?

To see if the autopsy report was there, I grabbed the third binder and opened the cover. Just inside was a cream-colored booklet about six inches by nine inches, bound at the smaller side, smudged with grease and soil, its corners dog-eared by repeated use. Part of the original material or something extra? I opened the book. Floyd Lynch's name written on the first page, followed by pages and pages of information. Trucker logs, kept just in case he was audited.

The box we had taken from the Lynch trailer was still resting on the floor beside the desk. I flipped open the cardboard top and saw more of the same logs. They must have been at the bottom of the box. Coleman had rearranged them, looked through them, selected one. I remembered her text message to me, about meeting at the jail and having found something she was excited about.

The log she had pulled out was for 2004. Just seeing the year started my pulse to throbbing. The meticulous records showed everything, when the truck was weighed, when Lynch switched cargo, even the amount of time he spent eating and sleeping. Most important, it showed routes and the dates he traveled them. I flipped through the log that followed his route, day by day, from the start of the year to August, finding such detail it would have taken a genius to create so elaborate an alibi. I was convinced I was reading the truth.

I finally got to the date I was looking for. On August 1, 2004, the night Jessica Robertson was killed somewhere between Tucumcari and Albuquerque, Floyd Lynch was nowhere near Route 66/Highway 40. He was in Texas at a Flying J on Route 10 near El Paso, five hundred miles to the south and west of the crime scene. Definitive proof that Floyd Lynch did not kill Jessica Robertson, was not the Route 66 killer.

FORTY-FOUR

During those years we hunted for the Route 66 killer, we always knew approximately where the victims would be nabbed, within several hundred miles of Route 66, or on some nearby cross-highway. And we knew approximately when they would be taken, sometime from the beginning of June to the end of August. Conceivably you could set up a perimeter and watch the whole area during that time, but that was absurd. Son of Sam couldn't be captured within the vastly smaller area in which he operated. Instead, we tried to pinpoint different stretches of the road where we figured the killer would be passing through. We posted warnings not to hitchhike at all the local stops, including public rest areas. Our boy seemed to enjoy the challenge.

The historic Route 66 had been transformed into Interstate Highway 40, well paved and well traveled. We thought he might be a trucker who drove that route regularly, either a long-haul eighteen-wheeler cross-country or a smaller rig between nearby towns. We checked with every single company that ran trucks through that route and checked out every goddamn trucker who drove them. Found nobody we could pin it on. Over the years I was going a little nuts, thought all during the year about those summer months and how I was going to get him before he killed again. I thought that way for four years before Jessica signed on and we trained her to do what I no longer could.

Black Ops Baxter was dead by that time, but I trained Jessica myself. While we were engaged in the usual crime fighting, from January to June at any available time Sig worked with her on unmasking a killer and I showed her all the techniques for subduing him—where to apply fourteen pounds of pressure to break a collarbone, that kind of thing. By early June I was convinced she was ready for the job. At least by early June I told myself she was ready for the job. I really wanted to catch that asshole.

The afternoon of August 1, 2004, seventy-nine miles west of Tucumcari, New Mexico, there I was sitting in one of those vans all decked out with electronic surveillance equipment and two other agents who knew how to use it. We had the AC on but it still smelled like sweat, the kind I used to remember when Dad would take us fishing off the Hillsboro Pier. It was the sweat not so much from the Florida humidity as from waiting for the barracuda to strike the bait. That was what we were doing that night, waiting for the fish to strike the bait we'd put into the water. Trolling Jessica. Like in Florida, where you seldom got anything but angel fish off the end of the pier, our chances were slim that this one girl would meet up with the killer. But this had been going on for four summers, and we were willing to spend the man hours and dollars to keep it from happening one more time.

We had Jessica wired for sound and on GPS. She could hear us through a device that posed as a CD player with a headset. I remember how we laughed when she rocked her head to the beat of the music she pretended to hear. We had the van parked a half mile off the road so that no one driving by would see it and get suspicious. Keeping just close enough to her to preserve the signal. If she got picked up by a suspicious individual, we were ready to go after her and alert highway patrol down the road as well.

I remember now another smell in the van, Doritos, Cool Ranch. Tony Vinzetti, one of the supertechs on loan from the Albuquerque Bureau office for the summer, munched bag after bag of Doritos to relieve the monotony. Jessica liked them, too, and had taken one of the bags with her to eat as she walked the stretch of highway.

You might think we'd have her dressed like a hooker, miniskirt and spangled halter top, but that would have been like hanging a sign on her that said Victim. With her diminutive size we went for the runaway look instead, easier pickings than the college girls who sometimes traveled together and not as suspicious as a prostitute walking in the middle of nowhere. Besides, it was easier to hide the wires under jeans and a T-shirt just tight enough to be naive. Her shirt was vintage Rolling Stones, that tongue.

To complete the ensemble she carried a backpack with some clothes in it, under which we hid the GPS tracker. She had painted a peace sign on the back with red nail polish, a nice touch. A small pistol was strapped to her ankle underneath the flared jeans. No need to be really discreet because it wasn't like she was going into a Mafia meeting. Whoever picked her up wouldn't frisk her, and if he tried, she would immobilize him immediately and wait for us to catch up.

I remember those Doritos that Tony was eating drove me crazy that night.

"Must you crunch like that?" I asked.

Tony crunched harder if that's possible.

I turned to the other guy, around the same age as Tony but more mature. I can't remember his last name, Yves Something-French. The whole time we waited he kept his nose in a paperback novel. Émile Zola, I recall. *L'Assommoir*. I remember that name because I kept whispering it, liking the feel of it on my tongue. I had asked him what it meant and he said "Hard to translate." I was just making small talk, so I didn't ask him to try. He was born in Montreal, was angling for an international posting. I remember everything from that night.

"Doesn't that drive you crazy?" I asked him about Tony's crunching.

He turned slightly glazed eyes up at me so I could see he hadn't really left the book, was possibly still thinking in French. "Huh?" he said.

"Never mind."

Yves went back into the world he could put down when he needed to.

"At least suck on them a little before you bite down, would you, Tony? Soften them up so they're not so loud. How do you expect to hear Jessica with all that racket?"

I heard a crunch through my headphones as Jessica responded to my words. She could hear us as well as we could hear her. "Hey, Tony," she said around a mouthful of Doritos, and swallowed so her next words were a little easier to understand. "Let's do an experiment. See how much sucking it takes to soften one of these things. Mark the time and . . . go." Then there was a loud sucking sound

287

that was worse than the crunching. Even Yves laughed. They were all against me that night, the little bastards. And they were both in love with Jessica.

We couldn't be sure the killer operated only at night so we'd been there from the late afternoon when it cooled down a bit and a hitchhiker out on the road was a little more believable. The hours dragged by, alleviated by spots of high alert when something might happen but didn't. Jessica and I talked a little but mostly she and Tony talked, about musical groups and television shows and celebrities I didn't know.

Then Jessica said a car was slowing down. She took a look at it. "Looks like a man, twenties, driving a small flatbed. Should I?"

I have her face in my head, can picture the way she turned it slightly from the truck so there would be no chance of the driver seeing her lips move.

"Go for it," I said. "You're close to the truck stop so it doesn't have to take long if you exclude him."

He pulled up. Jessica waited for his window to go down. I can picture her easing her little backpack off her shoulder as if in preparation for getting into the car. "Give me a lift?" she said in her little-girl voice.

We heard the guy say, "Give me a blow job?"

Jessica was silent; I can imagine her pretending to consider. Because of Sig I knew we were looking for someone with better conning skills than that, someone with charm and apparent sympathy. I whispered, "Not our man. He wouldn't say anything that stupid before he got you into the car. Throw him back."

"Up yours," Jessica said, and the man drove off, laughing.

She kept walking. A number of cars she thought might be possibilities, those with men driving alone, passed her by. The record shows that at 9:17 P.M. she was picked up by another young male, this one more polite than the last. I use the generic *young male* because that was all she had time to murmur before she got into a car. No way to give a description without tipping him off that she was wired, of course.

The three of us listened to banal conversation for a while.

"What's your name?"

"Natalie. What's yours?"

"Richard. Richard Rogers."

"Oh, come on," I whispered, but none of the others seemed to think this name was fake.

He said, "What are you listening to?"

"The Ramones."

"That's a pretty old group. How old are you?"

"Seventeen," she said after a pause that made it seem like a lie.

Pause. "This road is a pretty far distance from any place."

"So?"

"What are you doing out here?"

We had determined in advance this part of the script. I could see Tony mouth the words as Jessica said them. "Things got bad at home. I'm heading out."

"Things would have to get pretty bad to do that; it's never been that bad for me. I guess I've been blessed."

Open-ended comment; Jessica kept her mouth shut. They drove on for a few more minutes. Then he said, his tone lower, slower, more serious. "Tell me, Natalie, do you think you're prepared to die?"

Tony and Yves jerked as if the surveillance equipment had short-circuited. I bit down hard and was aware of my right thumb trembling all by itself. "Easy, Jess. We're here with you," I whispered. "Take it to the next level. Put the pressure on him."

Jessica sounded more than a little nervous. If she was putting it on she was a damn good actress. Her voice had a little tremble in it to make her sound weak, victimlike. "Would you please let me out here, Richard?"

"We're in the middle of nowhere," he said.

"Stop the car. Let me out."

"What's wrong?" he started.

"You're scaring me." She sounded vulnerable.

There was a long pause, and then he laughed. "Wait a minute, did you think I was threatening you with that dying business?"

"He could be toying with you," I whispered. "Keep up the pressure."

"I want to get out of the car now," Jessica said.

The male did not slow the car. "I'm sorry. I'm just doing my missionary duty. I'm with the Church of Jesus Christ of the Latter-Day Saints. You know, Mormons. I didn't mean to scare you. Honest. I mean, look at me." Apparently he risked turning his head from the road ahead so she could see into his eyes.

"You totally creeped me out, dude," Jessica ad-libbed.

"I'm sorry," he said again, and really did sound contrite. "I was just trying to find out if you were secure enough in the Lord to ensure everlasting peace."

"Sweet," Jessica said, still sounding suspicious.

There was a pause. I could tell Jess was waiting for

instructions. "Not our fish. Throw him back, Rookie," I said.

Richard said, "I messed that up, didn't I? I guess I don't have my pitch quite right yet." He really did sound stricken, like if we could see him he'd be banging his head against the steering wheel.

Jessica said, "Look, just drop me off at the next truck stop."

"I swear I'm cool. I won't hurt you and I could use the company. It's kind of lonely out here when no one wants to talk about God."

"I feel you, man. I need to make a phone call."

"There's a Flying J about five miles ahead. But would you like to use my cell?"

"Uh, no," Jessica said, not bothering to make up an excuse.

I whispered to her, "Even runaways would have a cell phone. Next time tell him you're meeting a friend there." I could imagine her give a tiny nod though we couldn't see.

Richard Rogers dropped Jessica off at the Flying J and headed on. After checking to make sure she wasn't spotted making the switch, she started walking in the opposite direction from where they came. No killer would pick her up at the truck stop when it was still light out, the possibility of witnesses. But they might follow her from here. As she walked we talked a bit.

"Hey Rookie, did you by any chance notice that kid was wearing a short-sleeved white shirt and thin black tie?" I asked.

"They always ride bicycles, so fuck you, Coach," she said mildly, in a companionable way. I could feel her smile echoing mine. She was into this as much as I was when I was her age. I knew then she was going to be good.

We alerted again when she got picked up by a nice-looking older male (for Jessica that would have been somewhere in his late forties). He came on to her but didn't make threats or try anything rough. "Too obvious. Let him go," I said. She asked to get out on the side of the road. He didn't slow down. I felt the nerve spark in the side of my neck. Breathing in the van stopped. He offered her a beer.

We heard her say, "I shouldn't. I'm only fourteen."

We heard the car stop and a door open and shut, then the car start up again. Jessica yawned loudly.

"Are we boring you?" I asked.

"Nah, I'm just getting warm. It's a warm night, isn't it?"

None of us answered, wondering whether it was warmer inside or outside the van. She sounded like it didn't matter if we answered her; she was talking more to herself. "It's kind of nice knowing you're all there even though I'm totally in control. Sort of like being a stunt double with a safety harness." She walked a bit more. "I don't think he's out here," she said.

"Oh, he's out there," I said. "You ever see the movie *Jaws*?"

Back over the wire we all heard, "Na, na. Na, na. Na-na-na-na-na . . ."

Tony and Yves both laughed again. Jessica said, "How young do you think I am, Coach?"

"Just a slip of a girl," I said, and stretched, thinking of getting back to the hotel and pressing a cold scotch on the knot on my back. "We should pack it in for the evening. Gets any later and anyone will be suspicious of a young girl in the middle of nowhere."

"Want to pick me up? Wait, so you don't have to make a big swing maybe I can do one more ride to the truck stop at the other end."

"We can come and get you, no problem." I gave Tony a nudge to get his attention so he'd shut down the surveillance equipment.

Before Tony could snap the button that would shut down the radio Jessica said, "Woman slowing down. Gonna get another dose of religion, I bet."

"Send her on her way. We'll come get you."

We heard a door open and Jessica whispering, "She's got AC."

We were tired, we were fooling around, we were getting punchy, we were letting our guard down—maybe ten excuses would serve to explain what happened next.

I held up a finger to stop Tony from shutting off the radio and said to Jess, "You are so bullheaded. Okay, when you get to the truck stop get out but walk a little more east so you're out from under the lights when we pick you up."

"Ten-four, Coach," in the same whisper as before.

"Over and out."

We both chuckled at the cop speak and I took off my headphones. Yves put the van in gear and bumped us out of the patch of hard sand onto the highway. He took his time driving because Jess was at least twenty miles west of us and would take a little time to catch up. In about ten minutes' time we pulled into the truck stop. Yves and Tony went in to stock up on more junk food for the ride back to the hotel, came out with a large bag, and asked if I wanted some raspberry Twizzlers. I declined that, but took a Coke. Yves got gas for the van. You could tell he was looking forward to the day when gassing up vans wouldn't be part of his job.

We drove through the parking lot, past a dozen eighteen-wheelers parked in a row, all dark, their drivers either sleeping or in the truck stop eating, taking showers, checking e-mail. All the truck stops offered free computers.

We found a spot to pull off on the shoulder just before the exit/entrance ramps. Yves turned on a small flashlight and went back to his book. Tony shut his eyes and sucked on a Twizzler. Twizzlers he sucked on, go figure. I kept an eye out the back window of the van for Jessica, who should have been walking up the road at any moment.

Only she didn't. I looked at the digital clock on the van's dashboard. 10:52 P.M.

"Something's wrong," I said.

Maybe from the tone of my voice, even Yves looked up. Without asking what or why, he put the van in drive and made a U-turn that took us back into the parking lot. While he did that Tony turned the radio and the GPS back on.

"Jessica, come in," I said.

Nothing.

"Jessica, are you there?"

Nothing.

"You got her?" I asked Tony.

"I do," he said, and scowled. "Her coordinates are further away than they should be."

"We traveled some, too," I said, arguing foolishly with the expert.

"She's further west than she was when she last reported in. Looks like she headed in the opposite direction."

"How fast is she moving?"

"Stationary."

"Is she too far away for the radio? Is that why she's not answering?"

"Could be."

"Yves, let's go."

Yves revved up the engine and busted us out of the truck stop heading back west the twenty-five miles or so to the spot that the GPS tracker indicated. I talked to Jessica along the way, hoping each time I spoke that it was just a matter of distance that we were closing, that the woman had needed to go in the opposite direction and Jessica couldn't say anything to let us know. She would trust we'd be on her.

Then I did hear something. Music.

"What the fuck," Tony said.

"When the moon comes over the moun-ta-a-a-ne . . ."

"It's either a CD playing or the driver can do a really good Kate Smith impression," I said.

"Who?" Tony asked.

"I'll tell you later," I said, listening intently, made only slightly less nervous by thinking of the kind of person who listens to Kate Smith.

"Is this one of Jessica's practical jokes?" Tony asked.

"I'll kill her if it is. Be prepared to call for backup," I said. "Yves, punch it."

He did, holding at about a hundred, while the singing

continued, now "God Bless America, my home sweet ho-o-o-o-me."

"Closing in on coordinates," Tony said, in about fifteen minutes of the time we left the pickup point. "Stop," he said.

"Stop where?" Yves said, losing his cool, irritation in his voice. "I don't see anything."

He was right. The highway was black, and the moon such a sliver you couldn't see off-road outside of the high beams. Still, Yves pulled off onto the shoulder. We sat for a second, quiet, as if we'd be able to hear her. All we heard was Kate Smith singing "Born free, as free as the wind blows . . ."

I wanted to tell Tony to make Kate shut the fuck up, but we had to keep the volume up in case Jessica's voice came through.

A semi rumbled by, rocking the van with its air and sound. Then nothing again. We got out with our flashlights, no longer trying to disguise ourselves. We brought our weapons, too, though I imagine I was the only one who actually knew how to use one with any skill. Those guys were techies through and through.

Tony ran across the road to see what he could find over there while Yves and I searched off the right shoulder. I think we all knew pretty well what was going on, but none of us wanted to be the first one to say it.

A shout from Tony. We looked up, couldn't see anything but the glare of his torch, not only across the road, but far off the road, and lower as if he was coming out of a gully. His light bobbed across the road to us. He had Jessica's backpack. I wanted to shoot myself right there, but then I would have been even more useless than I already was.

When he reached us, he pushed the clothes around a bit and dug out the GPS device at the bottom of the bag. I drained out of myself. The device must have been found shortly after Jessica was picked up, the bag thrown from the eastbound lane. If it happened that easily it was either a woman with a gun or a man disguised as a woman who caught Jessica off-guard. If this was the killer that Sig profiled, he'd be smart, he'd know Jessica was a plant even if she didn't admit it, and he'd head in the opposite direction from the one she was walking in. At least that assumption was better than fifty-fifty. "Let's go," I said.

We jumped back in the van. "Which way?" Yves asked, only too happy to follow my lead. I gave my chin a shove in the direction we were facing and he took off. I had Tony get radio contact with all law enforcement jurisdictions.

"APB. FBI agent Jessica Robertson kidnapped and heading west on Route 66 or feeder roads. Vehicle unknown. No verbal contact, Robertson undercover, probably immobilized." Not dead. Not dead. "Unsub either a woman or posing as a woman, probably male."

We heard the crackle on the radio, all points jumping into the fray, mobilizing for the hunt. After asking us about the likely perimeter of the scene we heard road-blocks ordered allowing a twenty-mile radius. A lot of territory, and bigger by the moment. Ten minutes down the road we caught sight of a high beam up above and saw two search helicopters illuminating the desert around us.

"Sign up ahead, side road," Yves said, jerking his head to the right. "Says Dahlia."

I thought of the old case with that name, but didn't

know if those guys would have heard about it; nobody commented. "Go straight." The killer would want to put on as many miles as fast as possible and wouldn't chance getting caught on a small road ... unless he had studied this stretch far better than we had, but there was no time to think about that.

Kate Smith was belting "To dre-e-eam the impossible dre-e-eam ..." when the radio connected to the New Mexico Highway Patrol reported, "We have a vehicle."

"Location," Tony barked.

"Just off U.S. 285 about a mile before you get to a small town called Clines Corner."

"North or south, for Christ's sake?"

"North. North."

"That's just a little further up the road," Tony said, and gave me a grim smile. "You chose the right direction."

We pulled up to six cop cars with flashing lights surrounding a black SUV pulled off on a narrow shoulder.

"Ran the plate. Rented," said a patrolman without wasting time identifying himself.

"Thanks," I said. He was de facto in charge. "Anyone in there?"

"We didn't look inside yet. Seems to be abandoned."

"How close are the techs?"

"They're on their way."

"How about you string some tape to stop all your guys from fucking up any footprints or tire tread in the area?" I said.

He looked chagrined, but something told him this was no time to buck the Bureau.

I went back to the van and got out a pair of latex gloves, told Tony and Yves to stay put for a few minutes and then we'd likely be on our way, that this could be nothing.

I just had to look inside, to see if Jessica, or her body, was still there.

I approached the SUV from the passenger's side and opened that door to avoid corrupting the driver's fingerprints. The overhead light went on. There was no one inside the vehicle. I saw nothing except Jessica's wire rigged to look like a CD player, picking up Kate Smith's voice, which was still belting from the car's player, "You're nobody till somebody loves you ... nobody till somebody cares ..." Fuck crime scene protocol, I mashed the back of my hand against the button to turn her off. That's when I saw the smashed Dorito chip mixed with some blood on the floor in front of the passenger seat. The perp had wasted no time disabling her so there was no chance of escape.

In a manhunt the size of the whole Southwest, people were interviewed, rental-car-agency records scanned (the SUV was rented by Elias Smith, a little play on the word "alias" that proved to be a dead end), and the reports came back quick from the DC forensic lab, best in the country. Jessica's fingerprints sprinkled liberally around the passenger's seat in an agent's version of dropping crumbs to leave a trail. Other fingerprints found but none checked out against any in AFIS. The Kate Smith CD and its container discovered under the driver's seat were clean. There was trace all through the vehicle, it was a rental for God's sake, and the killer had no doubt deliberately chosen one that had enough miles on it to show it had been used a lot.

He made one small mistake, put the headphones on

and left his DNA on them, but it was mixed with Jessica's, and even if we had him on file it would have been so contaminated it would be hard to prove it was his. As it was, I never knew if he could hear me saying, "Jessica? Jessica, are you there?"

If he heard that, I was the one who blew her cover.

We continued the hunt, but at the same time expected to find the body posed at some point on the side of the road the way the others had been. After a week we figured the killer wasn't going to take that much of a chance, that he'd gone into deep hiding.

The aftermath was all consultations with experts back in Washington and dealing with the Robertsons, Zach and Elena, when Elena was still married to Zach and alive. We all knew Jessica was dead but the Robertsons didn't give up for months. For years.

And then of course there were the postcards. Zach's agony was kept alive by postcards sent by the killer with the cruel joke about having a wonderful time. No further clues.

The loss of an undercover agent is largely kept out of the news. I kept looking for the killer in the following years, but I never found him. As far as we knew, Jessica was the last victim.

My full report and the audiofiles of my radio contact with Jessica, including her last words to me, "Ten-four, Coach," and the Kate Smith CD in its entirety, looped three times, are in the Bureau archives. And that's all I ever knew for sure until I saw Jessica's body in the car on the road to Mount Lemmon.

Lynch's trucking logs could be verified, but there was no time for that. I thought about the progression of recent events again: Lynch is captured and makes his confession . . . Coleman is suspicious of it . . . Peasil is sent to kill me . . . Coleman goes missing—who else did Coleman tell besides me? . . . There's a second attempt on my life. Who would want to stop us from investigating and why? Who was Lynch protecting? If he didn't commit the Route 66 murders, whoever did had Coleman.

I'd failed to save Jessica Robertson. I'd failed to save Zach. Regret can be a great motivator. I wouldn't fail to save Coleman. If Lynch wouldn't willingly tell me what I wanted to know, I'd beat the truth out of him with his own trucking log.

But it was now the middle of the night: no way into the hospital without being noticed, and Lynch almost certainly had round-the-clock security outside his door. If I had any perspective on this bloody mess, I'd be amused to think Max had set up the security partly to protect him from me. Lynch would be in intensive care, close to a nursing station but apart from the rest of the patients. No patient would want to know he was next door to one of the more notorious serial killers in U.S. history.

I worried for a while about how I would find him, set my brain clock for six, then fell asleep for a few hours on the couch. That was something Black Ops Baxter had shown me how to do, force yourself to sleep when you're in a combat zone.

I even dreamed. This time it was my recurring dream where I'm chasing on foot after a van that I know contains Jessica. It's not always the same vehicle, sometimes it's a dinged-up old Volkswagen van and sometimes an

SUV, something dark and expensive-looking, and I'm frustrated because I can't determine the make. I'm on city streets or a country road, and I yell to other drivers to go after the vehicle because I can't keep running forever. The things that remain constant are that it's always night, I never catch the vehicle, and I can hear Jessica screaming, "Coach."

FORTY-FIVE

I woke up at six, showered, changed my clothes, and neatened myself up so I wouldn't look and smell like a crazy woman. I was wild to get to the hospital, but it was located only a few miles from Coleman's house and showing up before eight would be suspect. To kill some time I nosed through Coleman's fridge and came up with little bottles of liquid yogurt that had the word "probiotic" written on them. I took three and lined them up like the little vodka bottles they give you on a plane, tearing the foil top off each one and sipping it while I sat at a table on her shaded back porch, my cell phone with me just in case Coleman finally called to tell me I was all wrong.

It rang. I watched Max trying to reach me. When he was done I listened to the message. He'd been by the hotel to confirm I had a room there. I took the battery out of the phone.

Coleman had some mouthwash, deodorant, and makeup in her bathroom. I covered up the dark circles under my eyes and chose a lipstick with the pale name of Barely Caramel. I brushed and rearranged my white hair in an unbecoming twist. I tucked my T-shirt into my jeans, then pulled it out again. Needed to put my gun there.

There are benefits to being small and faded. A glance in the mirror told me I was just right for blending into the background of a hospital. I put the trucking log that showed Lynch's routes in August 2004 in my tote and headed over to the hospital, along the way passing through a McDonald's drive-through for coffee and a sausage biscuit so I wouldn't get the caffeine and carb shakes.

The Tucson Trauma Center on Campbell is four stories, complete with a helipad on the roof for transporting patients. The directory in the reception lobby told me that the first floor was all administration. I stopped a volunteer, told her my husband was in the hospital, bad traffic accident. I trembled. She tsked.

I said I had heard there was a dangerous killer somewhere in the hospital and should I be nervous about that? My husband was staying on the fourth floor. She said I shouldn't be concerned for my husband's safety—the killer only killed women, and from what she had heard, wasn't in a condition to kill anyone right now. Conveying a sense that this was the biggest thing that would happen to her all year, she also whispered confidentially that everyone knew Floyd Lynch was on the third floor because of all the policemen coming and going, but she didn't know in which room.

That was easy; it would be the room with the guard standing outside. I planned my next move on the elevator, came to a vestibule with turns to the right and left. Turned to the right, looked down hallways heading in both directions, didn't see anyone who didn't look like a nurse.

Came back to the elevator area and headed in the other direction. Sure enough, there was the metro police guard standing about midway down the hall, barely paying attention. Looked like he had been there all night and was waiting to be relieved. It was hard to be sure precisely which room Floyd was in because the guard was standing between two doors, one open, one closed. If I had to take a chance, though, I'd bet my money on the door that was closed.

I ducked into the closest room on the opposite side of the hall, luckily empty so I didn't have to make up a story, and found a clean hospital gown. I drew it on and doubled my slacks up over my knees. Tucked the trucking log into the front of my jeans and hid my tote behind the door after taking out my cell phone and a pocket mirror. I put the battery back into the phone. More like a patient now, I stopped at the edge of the open door and held up the mirror to reconnoiter prior to making my next move.

But before I could put the mirror down to dial the phone, a chubby nurse with proportionately fat hair and feet turned out like a duck emerged from the elevator with a full intravenous-fluids bag. Wary of being spotted, I drew further back into the shadow of the room and only stepped toward the door when I saw her waddle by. I watched her reflection in my mirror as she opened the door to Lynch's room and closed it again behind herself. Now I knew it wasn't locked.

Still watching, I waited patiently for three or four minutes until the nurse exited the room with a half-empty IV bag. She nodded at the guard, who didn't look up, and exited via the stairway to the side of the elevator.

On my cell I dialed information to get the main hospital number and asked to be patched into the nurse's station on the third floor. When the nurse answered, I said, "This is the Tucson Police. Would you please put Officer Joe Btfsplk on the line?"

"Do you mean the policeman standing guard at four-twenty-six?" she asked.

"Yah, that's the one. Thanks."

In a moment I heard her, "Officer Bit ... Officer there's a call for you on the hospital phone."

He looked puzzled but took the bait. I grabbed a rolling intravenous rack from the room on my way out, and hung by the wall as I approached, just a patient getting a little exercise. I slipped through the door before the deputy could find out whoever was on the phone had hung up. He would take a little time calling the office and trying to find out who wanted to talk to him.

Lynch was resting with the back of the bed slightly raised, his head rolled a little to one side, his hands on the cover. He was thin when I first saw him at the body dump site, but prison food followed by twenty-four hours of nothing by mouth had made him a mere sliver of a man. Tubes ran fluids in and out of him, including one leading to a colostomy bag that might or might not be permanent depending on the seriousness of his wound. A tube for oxygen led from his nose, and an IV was attached to his hand that was providing him with hydration and megadoses of antibiotics to stave off peritonitis. Besides the monitors that allowed the nurses to keep tabs on him from their station down the hall, he was also hooked up to two machines that dispensed painkillers, one a morphine pump he could press himself, and the other an epidural.

I recognized it all; I had been in this position once myself. If infection didn't set in, he'd live. I shrugged off the hospital gown, rolled down my jeans, and pulled out the logbook.

He appeared to be sleeping. "Hey, Floyd," I said, reluctantly nudging his shoulder. There was something about this man I didn't want to touch.

He looked up at me, groggy. "Wha?" he said. The morphine was going to make this a little harder. "Who're you?"

"Brigid Quinn. We've met. I'm working with Agent Laura Coleman."

"Now I'm shot, everybody wants to see me," he said.

That gave me pause. "Who else?"

"My father was here yesterday. He didn't care I was attached to this shitbag, all he wanted to know is what I did to his fuckin' dog. Christ, you don't think I'll have this thing hanging out of me forever, do you?"

"I didn't think you were allowed to have any visitors."

"He got in. The cop threw him out."

Lynch giggled, a hiccupy kind of laugh that appeared to hurt. "My hand hurts," he said, and fumbled for the button of his self-administering morphine pump.

Rather than continue talking about his father or his ongoing medical condition I held the logbook in front of his eyes. "I need you to look at this. Do you know what this is?"

His eyes grew a little more alert, either from the mysterious presence of this woman in his room or rising pain. He ran his tongue around the inside of his mouth and then licked his lips. "I'm thirsty."

"That's because you're not allowed to drink anything. Answer my question and I'll get you a wet swab for your mouth."

"Where's the guard?" He reached for the nurse call button but I got there first and covered it with my hand.

"Wait a sec. Look, Floyd. I'm not here to hurt you. I don't care one way or the other about you anymore. I don't care about you fucking mummies, or about your colostomy, or even whether you go to prison for life. There's something more important for me just now."

He made contact with dull eyes that were still a little unfocused, but I could tell I had his attention.

"This is your logbook that places you far away from the scene of Jessica Robertson's murder. I've got all your logbooks. I didn't take the time to match up all the Route 66 murders, but the chances are you weren't there when they happened.

"That means you're covering for someone. I think the someone you're covering for tried to kill me and has kidnapped Agent Laura Coleman because we got suspicious about your confession. I want the answers to some questions and I know you can give them to me."

He licked his lips again before he could speak. "Why do you think I know anything?"

"Let me ask the questions for now. How do you know Gerald Peasil?"

"I don't know any Gerald Peasil."

"Then try this one: who's got the ears?"

He grew as pale as I remembered him in the interrogation video. He started picking at the IV in his hand the way he had picked at his wart. You could tell he didn't want to talk, but the morphine might have been acting as a kind of truth serum. "He'll kill me, man. He said he'd kill me if I went back on my confession."

"He. You mean the real Route 66 killer."

He shook his hand. "Goddamn thing burns. Feels like a bee sting." He giggled again. "Aw shit man, all I wanted to do is get a life sentence. Live. Is that too much to fuckin' ask?"

"Maybe not, but right now the chances are against it. You're not safe. None of us is safe. Even if you go back to jail he can get you there because you can't run. It's easier to kill somebody in jail than on the outside."

The giggling turned abruptly to blubbering. When faced with the truth they often blubber.

"You're not a killer, are you, Floyd Lynch?" I said.

"No. I'm a loser." He looked at me with big sad eyes, like he thought he should apologize. He went to grab my hand, which was resting on the pull-down metal side, but jerked back as if appalled to encounter live flesh. "You know how you want to be somebody else so bad. I thought I could go slow, build up to it. You know?"

I looked at him a moment, and then got back on track. "Tell me the truth now, Floyd."

And this guy who felt sorry for himself because he didn't have big enough balls to kill people started talking the way people do when they're drinking, like he'd found in me a new best friend. "I met him, 66, in one of those Internet chat rooms. Then we went out of the room and started to write. I'd use the computers at truck stops. He was writing to just me. It was just me. He was like, you know, the real thing. At first I told him no way was he the Route 66 killer. He was pissed. He wanted to prove he was the one. He told me all kinds of details that weren't in the news and it sounded right to me. I pretended I was killing women, too, but I wasn't. I made up stuff. I was ashamed to tell him I was just ... just ... a little dizzy ... whoa."

As if it were too heavy for his neck, Lynch's head lolled suddenly back onto the pillow. His eyelids flickered. When he felt me take the morphine pump out of his hand he came back to me. "I didn't kill nobody, but that body I found ... making it into a mummy, that was all my idea. I ordered that stuff off the Internet. That Natron business. Nobody else thought of that but me."

"What about 66, what else do you know about him?"

"Nuthig." It came out slurred. I hoped nobody would be coming in to adjust his pain meds until I was finished with him. "I jush needed a little more ... time ... to do it."

"Come on, Floyd. He took you to the dump site to show you the bodies."

He shook his head and looked like the act made him dizzy. "He shed he'd hidden 'em in this old abandoned Dodge on a mountain road. I knew about that car and went to see if ... maybe that was the one."

"So you've never seen his face."

Floyd shook his head, more carefully this time. "I saw the bodies and I used 'em. But I got tired of going all the way up the mountain." He walked the fingers on his right hand over his chest and smiled at them.

"Why didn't you just move one of the bodies onto your truck?"

"I tried. It came apart when I tried to move it. I didn't like it that way."

I guess even necrophiliacs have an aesthetic sense. "You used both the bodies? The one you called the lot lizard?"

"Uh-huh," he said in kind of a singsong.

"He didn't tell you how or when he killed that one, did he?"

"Nuh-uh," in the same singsong and did that childish zipper thing across his lips. "He was pretty closemouthed about it. Jush-ed she was different."

I alerted. The killer blabbed about every detail of his other kills but didn't want to talk about that first one. If he wouldn't talk about her maybe it was because he hadn't been as organized with her. Maybe he knew he'd made some mistakes, done something that could connect her to him. "Different? How?"

"Jus, diff . . ." he said, trailing off. I wished I knew how to punch in the codes that would cut off his drugs, but other than ripping the epidural out of his back, which was sure to cause a stink, I was at a loss.

"How different, Floyd? Physically? Mentally? Tell me what you remember, Floyd."

Lynch wasn't paying attention to me, just telling the truth. It must have felt good. "Then I studied about how to make a mummy and I was going to kill someone, I swear I was, but I didn't have the time to work up to it. I printed out his e-mail messages and pretended I was the one who did it all. I sent some postcards to the father of the FBI agent like he did. I even sliced the body I found to pretend it was one of his victims. Then they picked me up. He got a message to me in jail. Shed if I ever denied it he'd have me killed."

"Route 66."

Lynch put a finger to his lips, "Shh. Don't even say it." Then he giggled.

Oh God, I didn't have time for this. "I'm near certain he's got Agent Coleman. Floyd, she was nice to you. She was trying to get a fair deal for you. Can't you help me find her?"

He licked around the inside of his mouth as if he wanted to speak but his tongue was catching on his teeth. "I don't know anything else. I'm sleepy. Let me . . ." His eyes closed and his mouth dropped open so I could hear his breathing. It struck me that there wasn't much breathing, shallow and much, much too slow. Suddenly worried, I slapped his face lightly.

As if in response to my touching his face, a loud ping from the monitor beside the bed made me jump. It felt like the timer going off to tell me my interview was done.

About two seconds later a male doctor and two female nurses came through the door. One of them glanced my way but then all focused on bringing Floyd Lynch back from what they apparently considered the brink.

The doctor shone a light in Lynch's eyes. "Can you hear me, Floyd? No response. Respiration?"

"Shallow, six per minute, pulse rapid, thin."

"Looks like an overdose." The doctor punched at the panel on both the morphine pump and the epidural to stop the flow. "Nurse, check his IV. You, go get a crash team."

One of the women dashed out, the other stayed, checked the IV. "I hung the bag myself but I didn't open it to full. It's all the way open now. Maybe there's an obstruction," she said. She fiddled with it, trying to be useful until the emergency response team arrived.

"He was complaining that his hand was burning," I said, but no one paid attention to me.

Three guys crashed through the door pushing a metal cart filled with emergency gear. Without asking for directions one of them grabbed a board while the other two lifted Lynch off the bed so the third could push the board under him. At the same time that Lynch was being lowered onto the board the guy who had put it on the bed got a syringe off the cart and plunged it into Lynch's chest. That would be the epinephrine. It had no effect.

They were getting the defibrillator off the cart to try that next when the guard poked his head in the door, cell phone held uncertainly, not having been given instructions about this eventuality. He saw me standing against the wall, watching the activity. "Who are you?" he asked.

"His mother," I said, and turned back to watch the heroics of the medical team even though something told me that, being the last person to see Floyd Lynch in a stable condition, I should be hightailing it out of the hospital.

"Clear."

I watched the nurses standing by, powerless to help. One still tapped at the chamber connecting the IV bag to the tubing. Neither of these women was the one I'd seen earlier.

I thought about that nurse who had gone into the room before. Carrying the empty fluids bag. No, not empty. Not by half. Nobody ever switched to a second bag until the first one was empty. Then I thought about Lynch complaining shortly after that his hand was burning as if he'd been stung. Then I thought about how he had seemed to get drunker by the minute while I talked to him.

"It's in the bag," I said, pointing to the stand where the fluid dripped into his IV. "It's in his bag," I shouted and tried to fight my way to where I could rip the IV out of his hand or at least knock the stand over. I got as far as the side of the bed. A member of the crash team who wasn't working the paddles held me back.

"Get this woman out of here," the doctor shouted, "Get her out of here."

The bag continued to drip. Keeping Floyd alive might help me, but it wasn't helping to find Coleman. I thought he had told me everything he knew. I left the room while the guard was distracted by the drama.

FORTY-SIX

You have to get your priorities straight. What they boiled down to at this point was Coleman's survival weighed against my liberty. Top priority was finding Coleman. The way I saw it I only had one option to get Max to believe me and help me. The odds were against it, but I had to try.

I drove to Sabino Canyon Park in the northeast part of the city. You can park your car and take a tram that goes about three miles in and up. It's beautiful: canyon walls on both sides and actual running water. At this time of year, during the monsoons, the water flowed right over the tramway in places where the road crossed the stream. I paid my ten bucks, got on the tram, and rode it up to the ninth stop, the last. There weren't a lot of other people on the tram, the day being hot as hell.

I fished around in my tote for the cell phone—not mine, the one I had taken from Peasil's place. I got off the tram and sat on a low wall that overlooked a canyon and a cliff beyond it.

When Max picked up, I said, "This is an anonymous tip."

"I recognize your voice, Brigid."

"I know, I'm fresh out of clever. Is Floyd Lynch dead?"

"Yes. I was called to the scene because I originally brought him in."

"He was murdered," I said.

"I know. The guard described his mother. I knew it was you."

"It wasn't me, Max."

"I've got you on motive: revenge. Opportunity: you were in the room when he died. So what was the means?"

"I didn't kill him, Max. Tell Manriquez to have a tox test done on the contents of his IV bag. Some sort of opiate. He was poisoned by the Route 66 killer."

"So you're saying the means was poison."

"Goddamn it, Max, listen to me. The real killer's gotten desperate, I think. Somehow he found out that Coleman and I were investigating the possibility that Floyd Lynch had made a false confession. We've been getting too close." I quickly described how I knew, the nurse going in with a full bag, coming out with one half-empty. How Lynch complained about a burning sensation in his hand where the needle went into the vein. How Lynch appeared to be under the influence of a heavy narcotic just before he stopped breathing. How it had to be something slow acting so the murderer could get well away from the hospital before anyone noticed. I wondered if Max had started to have my call traced yet.

Max said, "No one reported seeing a nurse go into the room. Not even the guard."

"If they did, they'll deny it. Covering their asses, Max. The guard's green and scared of losing his job. But that's not the important thing. Lynch confessed to me, Max. A real confession this time. He didn't commit the Route 66 murders but he was in contact with the guy who did them. And the more time goes by, the more I'm convinced the real killer has Agent Laura Coleman."

"And I should believe you why?"

I sucked in a deep breath, knowing I was playing my last card. "Because I'm telling you I killed Gerald Peasil."

He was silent. I knew I had very little time until the trace pinpointed my location. He said, "Why?"

"You were right. He attacked me in the wash. I let him take me into his van so I could find out how many women he might have raped and killed. The kind of thing it would take you days of interrogation to find out, if ever. We fought, and I accidentally killed him. Then I discovered he wasn't just a serial killer. He was specifically sent to assassinate me."

"And why are you telling me this now?"

"You're not paying attention. It's Coleman. Too many hours have gone by since anyone has seen Coleman. I don't know how else to convince you of how serious this is except to tell you the truth about Peasil."

"You'll tell us what you know. We'll start a search."

"Right. First you'll have to explain everything to your boss and spend about ten hours interrogating me and if my instincts are right we don't have time for that. Start the search now. I'll work it from my end. And I'll turn myself in after she's found."

Silence. "We're at kind of a standoff, aren't we, Brigid? I have no reason to propose we start a search for Laura Coleman, just your say-so. You don't come in, and I have no choice but to kick this upstairs. I can't keep it to myself any longer." He didn't sound triumphant, just sad.

"I'm so sorry, Max. I'm sorry to put you in this position."

"Right."

"Really. Listen, if you won't help find Coleman, do me the favor of just holding off the dogs until tomorrow morning. I promise you I won't run. Can you believe that?"

"No. I can't."

I had hoped this would work, but that's why I already had a plan B just in case. So I didn't spend any more time trying to convince him. "Okay. I give up. I'm coming in."

The next tram was coming. Before Max had time to further voice his disbelief, I disconnected and leaned the cell phone against the back of the low wall where it would be unnoticed by hikers but found by Max. I knew Max wouldn't trust me; he'd trace the phone instead and follow me here rather than wait for me to come to him.

Once I knew he had the phone, I'd tell him to look for the deleted numbers. If something happened to me, maybe he would. But I wasn't sure what he would do immediately. Would he have the phone traced on the QT? Or would he report our conversation up the line? Would they issue an APB on me? Probably. Possibly. Just to give me the eighteen hours or so that I asked for was playing fast and loose with procedure. With Max I couldn't tell anymore what he'd do.

But I had enough time to get back to Coleman's place so I could find out if there was an autopsy report on the lot lizard that would narrow my search on NamUs. I wanted to see where it took me.

FORTY-SEVEN

The fifteen-minute tram ride down out of the canyon, plus the drive through back roads to make being spotted less likely, gave me a little time to think about what I had learned from Floyd Lynch.

He was innocent of murder.

He had met the real killer in a chat room. We all knew that the Internet had created a paradise for pedophiles and other perves. You google *serial killer chat room* and you get a quarter million hits. I know because we've tried to monitor them. You can't do anything with that amount of intel, let alone tell the difference between the fantasy and reality from that many sites.

By doubting Lynch's confession, Coleman and I were on to something that threatened the real killer to the extent that he sent Gerald Peasil to get me. He probably met Peasil the same way he met Lynch, had shared information and knew that Peasil had a taste for older women.

When that failed, he tried to kill me himself in the park and then kidnapped Coleman.

Even if I could convince Max that Coleman had been abducted, if all the efforts of the sheriff's department and FBI were thrown into finding her, there was no guarantee it would accomplish any more than I could.

The search could even scare the killer. He seemed to know what we were doing and would just go deeper than he'd ever been. One thing he knew how to do was hide. And if he hadn't already killed Coleman, he would now.

But who knew of Coleman's analysis and our investigation? Not even Morrison knew everything we were doing. Not even Royal Hughes. I couldn't imagine who would know that we were investigating off the reservation, let alone leak the information to someone who wanted to harm us.

Who would that person be, connected to both of us, to Floyd Lynch, and to Gerald Peasil?

The only answer was no answer at all. The real Route 66 killer.

I ran over these thoughts with the regularity of the pistons firing in the car's engine. "Round and round we go, and where we stop nobody knows," Peasil had said as we circled in his van. Except we had never stopped, Peasil and I. The mystery kept on going round and round well after he was dead.

The only clue I had to follow up on was the fact that the first kill, identified only as a lot lizard, was "different." Whoo-hoo.

I was back at Coleman's house by early afternoon. I let myself in through the back door, grabbed a box of organic cereal from her cupboard, and spilled some onto her desk to eat while I opened one of the binders to the section labeled Victims.

At first I wanted to scream that it was just too much to cover and I felt like I was running out of time. I wished I had Sigmund here with me. I was more of a kick-ass-take-names kind of person. He'd be able to see what was different about one of the victims. He could see the part of a picture that was missing.

He would not feel pressured, or panicky, or worried. He would not feel at all. I imagined him sitting somewhere, staring at the pages, blinking. That's all.

I turned the pages without reading, the words dancing, unable to process, aware of the time slipping by. Then I got to the photos and things got easier. I skipped over Floyd's mummy; I was after the other Jane Doe. When I got to the old crime scene shots taken over the five years that the Route 66 murders were committed, I slowed down, forced myself to let the answer come to me rather than hunt for it. Maybe I would discover a pattern of similarities or differences that would help me find out what was unique about the Jane Doe in the car.

Despite various differences in hair color and length, these newly dead victims all looked alike in some respects, young white girls, their eyelids not quite closed, their faces settling into what some call peace but what I see as final resignation, the blood-encrusted wound that had been their right ear, and of course their nudity. But before this happened they were not victims, not evidence, not entertainment in a crime drama, but *people*, and I remembered all their names without having to look at the labels.

Here was Patricia Stanbaugh, found June 26, 1999. She had a twin brother, Patrick, who proved her platinum-blond hair was natural. Hurriedly thrown facedown from a car rather than posed, the first known victim.

Here was Anna Maria Carrasco, found August 12, 2000. A kindergarten teacher in a private school, having an adventure she could share with the children. She bled more than the rest, the second victim.

Here was Kitty (really Kitty, not Kathryn) Vaught, found June 30, 2001. Engaged to be married and this trip her last hurrah, the third victim.

Here was Arline Blum, found July 19, 2002. A wisp of a girl, she was Jewish but had a tattoo of an Egyptian ankh, the symbol of eternal life, on her ankle. The fourth.

Here was Mary Sneedy, found June 4, 2003. She was from Arlington, Virginia, and had the biggest funeral I'd ever attended. The fifth.

Here was, here was ... repeating like a litany in those novenas at Saint Anthony's that Mom used to drag me to on Monday afternoons after school. The smell of incense, the chime of the handheld bell, the adoration of the host, the mournful singing of the *Tantum Ergo,* the murmured responses in the prayers of repose for the souls of the dearly departed. I could hear the dearly departed talking back.

Have mercy on us.

Have mercy on us.

Have mercy on us.

Nothing was coming to me, goddamn it. I clutched the photographs as if I could squeeze something useful from them. Work with me, girls.

Lastly I got to Jessica's picture. Disappeared August 1, 2004. This photo was different from the others in that it was taken years rather than days after her death, her body a brown husk. There was nothing of the woman I had known in that picture.

Only lastly was not Jessica after all. Here was the photo of the other mummy that had been found in the abandoned car. The only victim of the Route 66 murderer that had gone unidentified, unnamed. I remembered wondering who she was, and why no one cared about her.

You were the first, we know that now, that Patricia Stanbaugh wasn't the first after all. You still have both your ears and your tendons weren't slashed. You were killed before the killer had designed his MO and signature. That was different. Was that the difference the killer meant? Too obvious.

You were killed before the killer knew he could get away with killing. Maybe it was unplanned, maybe it was spontaneous. Maybe he knew you. If I knew who you were, I might know him.

I remembered George Manriquez from that morning when Zach arrived to view Jessica's body, how kind George was to Zach. How he had said with a sigh that he'd moved here from Florida looking for a change of pace, but only switched from Haitian floaters to Mexican mummies. It had given him pain, I could see. He was one of those people in the business who hadn't lost their feelings. He might care about this woman whether she was a prostitute or not. I flipped to the medical examiner's report. Sure enough, he had done a complete autopsy on the Jane Doe.

No organic disease that could be ascertained. The other victims were healthy, too.

Method of death: strangulation. That wasn't different either.

X-rays showed her dental work in the event records could later be found to match them. George pronounced her teeth and state of her jaw in keeping with good hygiene and nutrition. So far not the sort of thing you'd find in a low-class prostitute, certainly not an addict. No difference there—all the victims had been wholesome sorts.

The body had been dumped in a car and naturally mummified in the dry desert heat. Different.

No noticeable marks, tattoos, or the like. Pierced ears. Arline Blum had the tattoo on her ankle. All the victims had pierced ears.

Bone structure indicates ectomorph, a small, slim build even before her flesh had desiccated.

Skull indicates African American descent.

I read the line again. Now that was different.

I swiveled Coleman's chair back to the computer and went back to www.findthemissing.org. In the unidentified-remains database I keyed in the little information I had before: sex, geographic area, year she went missing. This time I changed Caucasian to African American.

Then I cross-checked my entry with the missing persons part of the database. There was only one African American missing in that year. Just to double check, I keyed in a date range of three years. She was the only African American to go missing from the area during that whole time. There was a photograph of her, a high school graduation photograph. And she had a name. Her name was Kimberly Maple.

She was not an unknown prostitute. At least she had a name. Kimberly Maple.

I had an inkling, but quick went to a population-statistics site and searched for African Americans in Arizona. Less than four percent. If you reduced that by half to eliminate the males and reduced again for Kimberly's probable age at time of death, it was less than one chance in fifty. The waitress at Emery's Cantina was black and had a relative who was the victim of a violent crime. Not quite two bombs on a plane but maybe close enough.

I picked up Coleman's phone again and dialed directory assistance. Yes, there was a number for a woman named Cheri Maple. But why would Emery say that her sister was the victim of a violent crime? Why wouldn't he say she had disappeared? Unless Cheri told him that because she knew Kimberly was dead.

A female serial killer? Cheri killed her sister and found out she liked doing it enough to keep doing it?

You're tired and you're desperate, I thought. Stop and think some more. I breathed in and out a few times, pictured Sigmund. Always reject your first assumption. I picked up the photograph of Kimberly Maple taken at the crime scene. I thought how, if she was the first, as Lynch had said, that her corpse would have been in that car for at least thirteen years. How old would Cheri have been, fourteen at the most? Absurd to think she had anything to do with all those deaths far from Tucson so long ago. She couldn't even get a driver's license, let alone rent a car. I looked at the photo again and watched as my blasted imagination switched Kimberly's face to Cheri's and back again.

Once more. Go through the sequence. Coleman suspects a false confession when Lynch tells her he threw away the victim's ears. She goes to her superior, and to Royal Hughes, and God knows who else, to make her case. They all ignore her. Or do they? Could the killer be someone on the inside?

Morrison takes her off the case when she goes around him to bring in me and Weiss.

Frustrated after being suppressed by Morrison, Coleman backs off, but gives me a careful analysis applying Sigmund's profile and the video of the interrogation. Who knew she was continuing her investigation without authority? Coleman and I only talk about it in her car on the way to and from the Lynches'.

And in the bar. Twice. I scanned my memory to see everyone who was in the bar during those meetings. Cops, Cheri, Emery, other people I didn't know. Who were those other people? Who might have heard us talking?

I scanned the rest of the bar in my head, the dusty bottle of Tarantula Tequila on the top shelf, the rose next to the cash register, the jar of pickled pigs' feet. People at tables, guy at the end of the bar. No one had been close enough to hear us talking except for the couple of times I raised my voice and people looked over. What had I said?

Still on the NamUs site, I clicked on the police reports and was tickled to see how much information had been entered there. Not by law enforcement, the girl had gone missing years before the database was started, but by Cheri, who had learned so much from her criminal justice studies. Parents lived on a ranch near Durango, Colorado. Kimberly had been attending the University of Arizona, working on an undergraduate degree in anthropology. They started a search after three days. Everyone interviewed in the case was entered into the database, including all her professors, her classmates, a roommate who was the last to see her, and her boyfriend. Cheri had entered all the names. I scrolled down each one, reading a synopsis of their interviews, recognizing none until I got to the boyfriend.

Who was listed as Imre Bathory.

He would have known Cheri while he was dating her sister. He was good at showing sympathy. He would have befriended the whole family and the seduction of Cheri was insurance. Did Cheri tell him about NamUs, and how she had fed all the information into the site? It was a calculated risk, not selling the bar and leaving town. Doing everything that an innocent man would do. He couldn't change his name without anyone asking why. But he could tweak it a bit. Just like I knew that *egészségedre* was the Hungarian toast, I knew that Imre was the Hungarian form of Emery.

It's those little pieces of information you collect because you never know how they'll be useful until they are. And how did I know for sure that Emery was the connecting link to everything?

That night I'd gotten drunk at Emery's Cantina, what I thought I'd seen, had convinced myself I had only imagined, in that jar of pickled pigs' feet. That jar covered with dust because no one ever asked to eat them. That jar that must have sat on the counter for years.

I should have trusted that image of those things that were not pigs' feet. Because sometimes imagination is not imagination.

FORTY-EIGHT

Again taking side streets and keeping an eye out for cops along the way, I pulled into a parking lot adjacent to the bar. Rather than risk being spotted in the car, I took my 1911 and a bottle of water and sat on a shaded bench at the end of the strip mall, pretending to ponder a real estate circular, to keep an eye on the entrance to the bar.

As I watched, customers came and went, most of them cops. Emery wouldn't do anything to Coleman while there were cops around. Neither could I. I wished I could enlist their help, but by this time there might be a warrant out for my arrest and they would hardly help me search the place. So I waited.

By the time the small parking area in front of the bar indicated there were no more customers inside it was early evening, shortly after the dinner hour, which is about five P.M. in Tucson. There was one remaining car out front. It wasn't the same car I had seen the day I came to fetch mine and Emery and Cheri had driven up. This was a nondescript black Subaru. Probably a rental. He was on the move.

I got up from the bench and walked up to the car. Rapped on the trunk once, hard. There was no answering rap. If Coleman was in there, she was dead. Game over. I told myself she wasn't in there.

I stepped around the front of the car with my back against the wall of the building. The civilian traffic went on its way in the fading light of the summer evening, bent on its normal pursuits, without any idea of what was happening in this place.

Rather than charge into an unknown, I first made my way around the perimeter of the building, quickly so I could enter before another customer walked in, a cop who would foil my search or a civilian who could be collateral damage if things got ugly. The windows of the place were all placed high, up by the roof, so there was no seeing in or out. A single door at the back must lead to the kitchen. When I tried it, quietly, I found it locked. Across a small patio a storage shed that appeared to belong to the bar was locked as well. I rapped lightly on that, too, but heard no moan or responding knock from within.

With more urgency now, I made my way around the other side of the building and had no choice but to come in through the front door. I held my 1911 poised as with the other hand I pushed open the thick wooden door of the bar, glad that Emery hadn't yet locked it. The doorjamb felt good against my back as I peered into the interior lit only by the lights over the bar. I locked the door behind me and flicked off the neon OPEN sign.

If a law enforcement officer is seasoned enough, has witnessed enough violence, he can smell a crime scene. It's not just the coppery smell of blood you read about, or the more obvious rotten-meat odor of decomposition. There are aromatic subtleties. Most homicide investigators will be able to say the same, that a homicide scene carries its own distinctive scent, the lingering aroma, something like a mix of asparagus urine and olive oil, the smell of the person knowing they're about to die. They say it's the smell of terror.

No one coming into a crowded, noisy place, not even if they were a cop, would notice it. I did because I was there alone, in the dim light, with no sounds to distract me. Behind Emery's signature scent of cherry-bourbon pipe tobacco, behind old fried onions, behind a thousand bodies, there was the smell of stale blood, too. And bowel. Somewhere there was also an odor of gasoline. Not your typical bar smells.

There were three places that smell might be coming from: behind the bar, in the kitchen to the back, or in the office off to the right. I dropped down for a second to scan the floor underneath the tables, found nothing, and came back up to find some comfort again in the feel of the wall against my back. I was about to take a chance moving to my first target behind the bar when I heard whistling from the office area. Emery emerged looking genuinely startled to see me standing in the shadows with my weapon pointing at him.

"Hello, Emery," I said.

Once he'd gotten over the initial surprise of seeing me standing in the dim light of the restaurant area with a drawn weapon, he didn't seem surprised at all, and that was what made me certain. The sight of my weapon must have told him I knew everything. He nodded, apparently intending to work with that.

"I'm glad you're here," he said. The light over the bar illuminated his face so I could see that one of his front teeth was missing.

Without speaking, I moved a little closer, stumbling

once with the stress and fatigue of recent days. My brain was sending my body instructions to recharge the muscles because my brain didn't give a shit how out of shape I was.

When he saw me fumble, Emery's eyes gleamed in the light from the bar. He was taking my measure, whether I was really dangerous. I had my doubts as well. "Don't go behind the bar," I said. "Stay where you are, hands in view."

He lifted a calming hand and pushed himself an arm's length from the far end of the bar so that he stood unguarded, midway between the bar and the door of his office.

"Is Coleman alive?" I asked. I wanted to keep my eyes on him, but for a second I glanced at the jar of pickled pigs' feet at the end of the counter.

He noticed my shifting glance. "She's right in here," he said, and on the last word he ducked out of sight to his left, through the door of his office.

"Shit," I muttered for having lost my advantage, but I still had the gun. There was no sound from inside the office, but my quick search had told me there was no exit from it either. I had to move fast and hope he had left his shotgun behind the bar. Knowing the flimsy paneling between us was no cover at all, I crouched as low as I could and moved quietly to the door of the office.

Standing just to the side of the entrance thinking, *It's so simple—stay alive, find Coleman.* Spotting the far left of the office: no one there. Trying to slow my heart down with my breathing. Whipping around to the other side of the door, still no shots fired, scanning the other side of the room—desk, chair.

My glance caught Coleman slumped in the chair, lots of blood.

Anger taking control, I started to charge into the room to kill or be killed, and then I heard a moan. I turned, tunnel vision kicking in, and almost fired. Then I saw another Coleman.

All the muscles in my body strained against the absolute imperative to press the trigger, the way they do to save yourself when you're falling. At the same time my brain took a split second to process the second Coleman—which came at me like a puppet tossed across the room. Her body hit me hard across the legs without giving me time to brace myself. We both went down. The gun slipped out of my hand, and I watched with despair as a man's hand picked it up. You don't ever want to lose your gun.

I hoped Max had put out that APB on me and that they were finding me, closing in. I could use a good cavalry charge about now.

The man I knew now as a killer trained the gun on me. "Roll her over," he said.

Coleman had a piece of clear packing tape across her mouth, which mashed her lips in a grotesque way. I sat up and started to help Coleman do the same, but she emitted a muffled roar from deep in her throat. She seemed out of it either from pain or drugs.

I removed the tape as gently as I could and asked her, "Where are you hurt?"

She whimpered and her hands moved between her knees, which she had drawn up to her chest in a fetal position. Then she passed out again. I noticed a little blood on the floor.

"You cut her tendon," I said.

"Both of them," he said, staying a safe enough distance away from me. Even with the benefit of a weapon, he was taking precautions.

But Coleman was alive. And the one thing I would do is save her. Gently, with as little pain to her damaged legs as possible, I helped her out of the line of fire, to the far side of the room where she could rest against a battered gray metal storage cabinet. Her eyes silently pleaded with me, and I wanted to tell her my best lie ever, that there was nothing to worry about. I wanted to tell her whatever she'd believe, but I didn't think that was much. Then still heedless of the gun in Emery's hand, I turned my attention to the body I had first thought was Coleman.

I saw now that it had been one of those disconnects when you're imagining one thing so hard that's what you see. I expected to see Coleman's body there, and that's what I saw. But the body was that of Cheri Maple, and she was just as dead as the smell that led me to her. She was sprawled in an old chair next to the desk, facing me. From the faded look of her pupils and the impossible tilt of her head, I could tell she was gone even if she hadn't taken a frontal shotgun blast.

"You need to be dead, man," I whispered aloud. "You really need to be dead."

Emery didn't respond as he moved behind me and patted my back for the presence of another weapon. He gestured with his free hand to another chair in front of the desk. The desk was very tidy, nothing but an old-fashioned landline, a stapler, a few menus, a humidor with pipe holder, and a pencil cup crammed with everything but pencils.

Emery took the chair behind the desk for himself and said, "Sit."

Wondering why he was in no hurry to eliminate or at least immobilize me, I sat down across from him while Cheri's body sagged in the chair to the right of me. Even with a psychopath like Emery, it felt macabre to have Cheri in on the conversation.

But it helped, too. The sight of Laura Coleman lying helpless across the room and Cheri dead before me made me drain out of myself in much the same way as when Carlo had found my bloody clothes in the washing machine. Only this time it was good, that I could stay as collected, as free of sympathy, as the killer before me. This is what I had tried to explain to Coleman, that we all must become what we want to conquer, and it was welcome, because it meant the Brigid Quinn I needed to survive had just kicked in.

"Why did you kill Cheri?" I asked, stalling for time until I could figure a way out of this mess. "Because she saw what you did to Agent Coleman?"

"No. Because she saw this in the walk-in freezer." He kicked a booted leg out from behind the desk. He looked disgusted, as if he blamed the corpse for his lover's death.

My resolve slipped for a moment before I could get it into my head that Carlo didn't wear boots. "May I?"

"Be my guest. Just move slowly." He kept my pistol trained on me as I stood slowly, steeled myself for what I might see, and moved to the side of the desk for a better view. The body was fairly intact except for a little dried blood around the mouth.

"Who is it?" I asked, relieved that I did not know.

"Who knows? It took a while to find someone with

334

decent teeth who was apparently homeless so no one would be looking for him."

"Was there a reason, or just for kicks?"

He looked offended. "A very good reason. He is going to be me when I blow the place up."

I managed to avoid reacting, kept to the key information. "What about ID, fingerprints, dental records?"

Emery knocked at the side of his face. "There aren't any dental records. I have a jaw like a rock. That's what the cops will remember me saying. Plus, just in case, I had this happen in the bar earlier today . . ." He lifted his front lip to show me the gap where his tooth was missing. Then he lifted the lip on the corpse to show it had one missing, too. "No fingerprints on record," he said. "But thank you; just in case, I'll make sure to obliterate them in the explosion. Anything else I may have missed?"

"How long have you had him?" I asked, to keep him talking and discover whatever mistakes he might have made.

"Oh, he is fresh enough. He wasn't in the freezer long." Still holding the gun on me with one hand, he opened a desk drawer and took out some clear packing tape. "Amazing how useful office supplies can be," he said. He tossed me the tape. "Sit on the floor over there and wrap some of that around your ankles, would you?"

"Go fuck yourself," I said to him without rancor, without any feeling at all. I said it to test the effect.

Emery picked up a metal stapler from the desk with his left hand and stepped over to where Coleman lay listlessly on her right side, her head on the floor. I shouted, but not fast enough to stop him from stapling the edge of her ear. The pain brought her around and she screamed.

"There, I do make myself clear, don't I?" Emery said with a patience that sounded almost sincere.

I took the tape and wrapped a strip around my ankles as he directed, thinking all the while how I could buy time to save us both. When I had disabled myself to his satisfaction, he took the tape from me, stood me up from the chair, and wrapped my wrists and hands behind me in the same fashion, so that my fingers were covered.

"Tying up loose ends," he said, and, despite his being behind me, I could almost feel him smiling to himself, his confidence growing. "Being able to make puns in a second language is very smart, don't you think? I thought I had lost any chance of taking care of you. And here you are." He threw me onto the floor.

After catching my breath and gaining some balance, I said, "Did you meet Peasil the same way you met Lynch, over the Internet?"

Emery shrugged his assent. "I thought Floyd Lynch really was another killer. He told me he was not when I saw him in the hospital. I assume he did die?"

I nodded.

He said, "Lynch was the mistake that has led to my losing this bar. But I can always buy another one in another place. With a different identity. And now that Cheri's gone, start all over."

Without explaining what he meant by starting all over, Emery tucked my pistol in the back of his pants and left the room. I turned my attention to Coleman. I needed to know what she knew, what the possibilities were. I scootched closer to her so I could speak more softly.

"Talk fast," I said. "Are you on something?"

Coleman nodded, her eyes closed. "I'm sorr—"

I would have slapped her if I had the use of my hands. Instead I leaned my forehead against hers and said, "Look at me, Coleman. I'm going to get us out of this. We're both going to live. So get tough now. Did he drug you?"

She stuck to essentials in staccato bursts. "Roofie. Worn off."

"How did he get you here?"

With more strength in her voice she said, "He was waiting outside my house. Tasered. I didn't see it coming."

"Happens. Keep looking at me. Weapons."

"The shotgun he used to kill Cheri. I don't know where it . . . and yours. That's all I know of."

Coleman's teeth started to chatter and her eyes grew vague. It looked like she was going into shock.

"How much pain?" I asked, keeping my tone as bland as if I were asking for the time.

"Not too bad," she said.

"You're doing great. You're doing great. Stick with me, kiddo."

She kept trembling, but her eyes were back on mine as she shook her head. "He kept me locked in a storage room somewhere." I could see her struggling to think of anything else that might be useful.

"Why are you still alive?" I asked.

"He said . . . he said he wasn't sure when he would need to get out of town and he needed my body to be fresh."

I nodded, then heard a footstep in the hallway leading to the kitchen.

FORTY-NINE

Emery walked into the office with his shotgun and the jar of pickled pigs' feet. He stood the shotgun in the far corner leaning against the wall and placed the jar on his desk. "I don't want to forget to take this," he said, and went on as if in mid-conversation. "Even though, after Kimberly's sister—you found they were sisters, right?"

I nodded.

"—came in about six years ago looking for a job," he ran a thoughtful hand down the side of the jar, "it lost its appeal. The whole business lost its appeal, and besides, Cheri alive made a much better souvenir. Every time I made love to her she reminded me . . ." He stroked Cheri's dead hair on the way to his chair behind the desk, where he filled his pipe with the cherry-bourbon tobacco whose smell I could never hope to forget.

"You know what they say about the seven-year itch." He lit the pipe, puffed it a few times, and pressed a button on what looked like the stereo console behind his desk. We all listened to our voices:

"Talk fast. Are you on something?"

"I'm sorr—"

"Look at me, Coleman. I'm going to get us out of this. We're both going to—"

I said, "You made your point: the whole place is bugged."

Emery obligingly turned off the recorder and put a fresh piece of tape over Coleman's mouth. "I've been listening to you for a long time, Brigid Quinn."

"You could hear us talking wherever we were in the bar just by pressing the right button."

"Oh, I don't mean just recently in the bar." He raised his voice into a mockery of a female, "Jessica? Jessica, are you there?"

He meant to taunt me. But remembering that night, thinking of how he had put the radio receiver headphones on and heard me call out for her, strengthened my conviction that one of us would die before much longer.

Emery watched me while relighting his pipe. He puffed, the smoke coming out the sides of his mouth like stray thought. "I couldn't foresee that Floyd Lynch would know about that abandoned car, get himself caught, and use the bodies to make a deal. It would have worked out perfectly if you weren't here to support Coleman's suspicions."

"And kill Peasil."

"You did kill him?" Emery laughed, hiccuping a puff of pipe smoke out his nose. Seeing his plan come together without a hitch except for Cheri's messy demise was making him feel more comfortable. "You know, I wasn't absolutely sure about that, could only guess it was what happened."

"I guess I spoiled that part of your plan."

"Yes, but here you are again, so that's okay," he said. "Is there anything you don't know? Have you told anyone else?" Emery frowned at the thought.

Keep him guessing. Even though Coleman was passed out on the floor, she still looked alive. Keep her alive. "Floyd Lynch wasn't a genius. But he could remember what he read pretty well. And he had all your e-mails. Copied them over by hand to make it look like his own words."

"Isn't it funny, Brigid Quinn?" He smiled to himself, as if he relished saying my name to my face after all these years. "You made me do this. I was contented with my little black souvenir for years until you and the agent came in here talking about how Lynch didn't do the crimes. That was when everything started to unravel."

His words had made me nearly lose my cool no matter what the consequences, but just then his attention was diverted from me to a knock at the front door.

FIFTY

The two of us both listened harder for the second knock. Only Coleman, still in a stupor from the pain and drugs, had not reacted. I would have taken the chance of bolting out the door if it hadn't been for the tape around my ankles. I had time for one loud yelp that probably couldn't be heard all the way outside before Emery back-handed me across the face. While I was stunned, he put a strip of the tape over my mouth before going into the public room of the bar, closing the door behind him.

After trying and failing to shout through the tape, I let my head drop, my cheek resting against the blood-soaked thin carpet. I quieted my ragged breathing as well as I could and listened with all my might, while rubbing my face against the rough nap of the carpet to make the tape come loose.

"Hold on just a moment," I heard Emery call loudly enough for us all to hear. Footsteps seemed to go away from the bar, and that was confirmed when I heard a motor go on, possibly the dishwasher in the kitchen. That muffled the sound of the footsteps further, until the sound of music blended with the dishwasher, but softly so it wouldn't appear he had just turned it on. I don't know what was playing, some old twangy country western thing. Then his voice again.

"Well, hello there. We'll be open in just a bit; I had to take care of a small problem. An appliance."

Whoever was there must have stepped through the door because I could hear a man's voice, barely distinct over the music if I held my breath and listened with all my senses. "I'm actually looking for someone."

"Nobody here but me right now."

"Just the same, I was wondering if I could ask you a question?"

"What's that?"

"Ever hear of a man named Gerald Peasil?"

Pause. "No, I'm sorry. I haven't. Who is he?"

"We're following up on a half-dozen phone numbers and this is one of the places he called."

Pause. "You know, I'm not being hospitable. Please come in and have a drink, Officer . . ."

"Coyote. Deputy Sheriff."

A longer space of quiet as Max must have moved farther into the bar.

"I'm Emery Bathory. I've seen you here before."

"It's a popular place."

"Come."

"Mr. Bathory, I don't have much time."

"And neither do I. But it is civilized, as well as good business, to offer you hospitality. Come."

The dishwasher and the jukebox blotted out the sound of footsteps, so I couldn't tell where they were, but the quiet made me assume they were moving in the direction of the bar. I imagined Emery going behind, angling carefully so Max couldn't see the gun shoved in the back of his pants, Max standing at attention or sitting on a stool.

"Soda?"

"No, thanks."

"So you think this, who did you say?"

"Gerald Peasil."

"You think this Gerald Peasil might have called here?"

"Well, yes, we know he did, but he's not the one I'm looking for. It could be a coincidence, but there's a car parked in the lot just behind your place. Belongs to a woman I'd like to talk to."

"Why do you think she's here?"

"She's a short woman with very white hair. Older but fit."

Was Max playing Emery? No, he had managed to get the deleted phone numbers off Peasil's phone, but he would have no reason to suspect that Emery was the one connected to Peasil, let alone a killer himself. Max would see the number of Emery's Cantina as just a bar on a list of takeout joints, a routine check. At best, Max might have suspected that Peasil was contacting one of the patrons here and had been about to follow through on that lead when he saw my car.

The door was hardly more than a sheet of paneling. If it was thin enough to hear their conversation easily, it might be flimsy enough to bust open with one good kick if I put all I had into it. I jerked my body, trying to roll closer to the door. I managed to get onto my back, pain shooting up my spine and down my arms, which were pressed at an unforgiving angle into the floor. All the while straining desperately to listen.

"You must mean that little older lady who started coming in here with someone from the FBI, I think. A tall, very pretty young woman with short curly hair."

"You saw them together here?"

"A couple of times, yes. But you're interested in the older woman?"

"Yes."

"She was here earlier. Why do you want to see her? Has she done something wrong?"

"I just have some questions about an ongoing investigation."

It was hard to move and hear what was happening at the same time, but I managed to roll over twice, getting halfway to the door. Not fast enough. Rolling onto my back again, and using my knuckles behind me for leverage, I sat up.

"So when was she here?" Max asked.

"It has been a busy day, so I'm not sure I can say with any precision. She didn't stay long. I think she met that FBI agent and they headed off together, left her car in the parking lot. You could leave a message for her, though, on her windshield. And of course if they come in here later I'll tell her you're looking for her."

There was a small silence, then Max again: "I don't think she could be that far away."

"Why is that?"

"The tote bag she usually carries is on the front seat of her car."

"How careless."

I was inching my way forward now, nearly to the door, and could see that the lock was on my side, which meant Emery couldn't have locked the door. That would make it even easier to kick open. Falling to my side and drawing up my knees. Kicking at the door, but not close enough to connect. Inching forward a little more. I happened to look in Coleman's direction and her eyes were wide open, staring into mine, knowing what was happening.

"Level with me, Mr. Bathory. Is she here? Did she talk you into cov—"

I'd only have one chance to surprise them both. I drew up my knees again and crashed the door open.

Max turned to look, and even Emery was distracted for a second before drawing my 1911 from the back of his pants and shooting Max in the chest. ·

FIFTY-ONE

Emery was pissed. He looked at Max bleeding and still on the floor where the .45 had knocked him off his feet. He slipped Max's gun out of its holster, stepped over the body to lock the front door, then ran the few quick steps needed to reach me where I lay on the floor, having rolled over onto my stomach to ease the agony of my arms taped behind me. I couldn't see him, only hear him as he stepped on my neck and punched the gun into my temple. I felt a spray of his saliva. With the part of me that could drain out and witness myself, I heard myself whimper like a muzzled dog.

But Emery was scared, too, and losing his cool. The surprise of Max's appearance came out in a rasping, screaming voice. "Did you leave your purse in your car as a signal?" He punched the gun against me again, harder. I gasped with the pain. "Who else is going to show up here?" When he saw I couldn't answer because of the tape over my mouth, he ripped it off.

All I said was, "Go ahead and fire that weapon, you motherfucker. Someone is bound to hear one of the shots and call the cops. They'll see Max's car outside."

A greater sense of concern seemed to have overtaken Emery. He grabbed his pipe from the desk and puffed so steadily that if I lived I would never again be able to separate the smells of cherry, bourbon, and clotting blood.

I pressed my small advantage. "What's the plan, Emery?"

He thought. He paced a bit. "They'll think somebody who hates cops bombed the place. Or they'll think there was a gas leak and it was accidental." He spoke faster, clearly assuming that any delay was increasingly risky but wanting to make sure he thought everything through. "No, that won't do, they'll find evidence of a bombing." He looked triumphant. "Here you go. They'll think someone was after you and the rest of us were just collateral damage."

"What about the bullet in Max? They'll find it."

"Maybe they'll think you went berserk and shot Coyote and then killed the rest of us to hide the fact. It was your gun."

"And then blew myself up with the whole building? You're too smart for this, Emery. You know they're going to be able to figure out that something is wrong with this whole setup."

He pondered that a moment, gave a final decisive puff, and put his pipe back on the desk. "You know what? It doesn't make any difference how they reconstruct the crime just as long as they think an innocent bartender is dead." He put the pistol into the front of his pants. "I have to position the bodies and get this over with."

He moved toward the homeless man, grunted with the effort of trying to drag a body weighing in the neighborhood of two hundred and fifty pounds. It didn't budge on his first try.

"Want some help?" I asked.

"Didn't the profile of me tell you I'm not an idiot?"

"You've got a lot of bodies to move. You're running out of time. You're going to have to cut this tape off me anyway before you leave so they don't find it on my body. You still have the gun."

It was fairly convincing. You lie really well when you think you're about to die. Trusting in his own brawn and the weapon he grabbed an X-Acto knife out of the pencil cup on the desk and sliced through the tape on my wrists and ankles, knicking me a couple times in the process. He put the knife back on the desk. "You get the heavier end so I can hold on to the gun," he said.

"I don't think I can lift that end," I said.

"The hell you can't," he said. "I've been watching you."

I stood up and moved behind Emery's double, grasping him under the armpits while Emery hooked an arm around his legs. I lifted, then dropped him, which distracted Emery for a moment.

"Sorry," I said.

Emery glanced over at Coleman. "No delaying tactics or I'll staple the agent's other ear."

We both went at it again, half moving, half dragging the corpse toward the kitchen, where the focus of the explosion would be. Only now, thanks to the distraction when I dropped the body, I had the knife tucked into my jeans and covered with the edge of my shirt.

We moved into the kitchen, where lined up on a stainless-steel counter were six liter-size bottles of alcohol, a twisted rag protruding out the top of each. Now I knew where the smell of gasoline was coming from. He handed me one of the homemade bombs and directed me.

"Slide it under his throat so it destroys his face," Emery said.

I got down on my knees and did so. I tried to stand, but my back suddenly cramped and I gasped with the spasm. This was not a good omen for my getting us out of this scrape.

Emery looked around at the bodies. "Five within twenty-four hours. To think I used to make elaborate plans to do one woman once a year." He shook his head, seemingly embarrassed at the mess he had made.

Still on my knees, I made my plan. Emery was taller than I, so an underhanded slash across his stomach with the knife would surprise him, and then a quick jab to his right temple would finish him off. The biggest problem was my back. The move was fairly simple, but I did not know how the hell I was going to be able to get up off the floor to accomplish it. I could only hope that the adrenaline building in my system would do its job.

Emery walked over to the counter by the sink where the rest of the Molotov cocktails waited in bottles of Bombay gin, Grey Goose vodka, and Crown Royal. Top-shelf explosives. They had longer strips of cloth than others I'd seen, and these were all connected by a single strip, presumably so he would be able to place them distant from one another, have enough time to light all four, and dash out the back door before the place blew. "I definitely have to place one of these by the agent's feet," he said. "I don't want them to see that her tendons were cut."

"Was it vodka?" I asked.

"What?"

"In Lynch's IV bag."

He put my gun down on the counter and picked up the bottle of Grey Goose. "I figured with all the pain killers he was on, a liter of alcohol going straight to his brain would finish him off but allow me plenty of time to get away from the hospital. How did you know?"

I started to tell him I saw him posing as nurse with the half-empty IV bag and how the alcohol stung going into Lynch's hand, but Emery wasn't interested. Still thinking, his eyes drifted off to the primitive IED in his hand and I could imagine him imagining what it would all look like, the sequence in which he would light the fuses before he bolted. He was close enough to me, and I now had my fingers wrapped around the front of my shirt that covered the knife, carefully up on one foot, keeping my abdominal muscles tight and my spine as rigid as possible while prepared for the pain when I leaped on him for our one chance at survival. I just needed to get him to come a little closer, but he backed up instead.

"Brigid Quinn," he said, "I saw you take the knife. Did you think I would let you get close enough to use it?"

We were very still then, he standing about six feet away and able to move quickly, and I on my knees before him. I was out of options and wondered how it would feel to die. We watched one another for a moment, guessing each other's next move, and then were both distracted by the soft but unmistakable sound of a shotgun shell being racked.

Cha-chin.

It came from the direction of the doorway between the kitchen and the bar. Emery's back was to the door and from my position on the floor I could just make out the gun in Coleman's hands though I couldn't see her body.

"Don't!" I shouted, because even in that second I knew what would come of it.

Emery tried to turn but didn't make it halfway before the roar of the shotgun blast, a surprised look, and the front of his belly blew over me.

Emery was a large man. He didn't immediately fall, but looked at me, then looked at his midsection, from which the blood started gushing. He was even able to stumble a step and reach out to me before toppling to his knees and falling flat out with his face turned partly in my direction, resting in his own body fluids.

Just to be on the safe side I dropped, too, so my face was about ten inches from Emery's. I could tell he was still alive.

I could see that the bowl of his pipe was close to his lips. He must have fallen on it and jammed the pipe stem into his throat. That was only insult. The shotgun blast was injury enough. He was coughing up blood around the pipe, and I knew I should move before the trickle reached me. He tried to suck in air as if he wanted to say something, but, besides the pipe in his throat, the shot might have shaved off the bottom of his lungs and that would make talking hard.

"Damn it, Emery, I wish I could have killed you myself," I whispered, staring into his left eye, the one that was turned toward me.

A little more blood burbled from his lips. His fingers scrabbled a bit on the linoleum. But I could see consciousness fading from that one eye. I wished there was an afterlife so I could kill him forever.

Then he was dead. I could say the dying didn't take nearly long enough or entail enough pain, but you have to keep a positive attitude. I raised myself up and looked over the top of his bulk. I saw Coleman on the floor behind him, lying on her back, holding her arms rigid so that the barrel of the gun was parallel with her body, its muzzle still trained in my direction. I fell on my back then, so all of us, the dead and alive, were down, all but Emery staring at the fluorescent lights on the ceiling.

"Laura!" I yelled, rocking back and forth in my anger and frustration. "You idiot. You had to go shoot him in the back when he wasn't armed."

Coleman had managed to pull the packing tape from her mouth before crawling into the kitchen and now lay chattering things like, "You fuckin' die. You. Die. You fuck."

I don't know how long she would have gone on like that, but, "Laura, he's dead," I whispered as gently as I could, while hoping her hysteria didn't tend toward chambering another shell and firing indiscriminately. "He can't get any more dead."

She quieted, sobbed into herself, but seemed unwilling or unable to lower the gun.

"Can you point that thing somewhere else?" I said. She didn't respond either in word or deed, so I rolled over, crawled out of the line of fire, and hoisted myself to my feet. I went over to her. Her arms were still locked in the same position from which she had fired the gun. I took the gun from her, threw on the safety, and leaned it against the doorway. Then I gently lowered her arms to her sides. "I'm sorry," I said. "Thanks. But I was going to take care of him."

She continued to cry, started to shake, then managed to get out through chattering teeth, "Bullshit. I saved your fuckin' life."

"Shh," I said. "Okay, you're right. You saved my fuckin' life. Are you stable?" She shook her head no, then yes.

"We're not done here," I said.

Then, Max.

Max. I stepped over Coleman's body and ran into the front of the bar and knelt beside him, where he lay on his back. There was blood on his chest and pooling underneath him where the gunshot had knocked him backward onto the table and then to the floor. I pressed a finger to the side of his neck, though I didn't expect to feel a pulse. Nobody survives a .45 center-mass shot even without the double tap.

In the space of time that I felt for his pulse, I remembered everything I knew about Max. Poker player, philosopher, Native American, lawman, husband, enemy, friend. I never thought that at their death another person's life could flash before your own eyes. I wanted to cry at the thought that there wasn't nearly enough of it, and I knew very little of what there was. But no time now. Later, after I had seen to Laura Coleman, there would be more time than I wanted to think about Emery's last victim.

I took a second to rip the plug of the jukebox out of the wall. Then I used the phone in Emery's office to call 911.

"Officers down," I said, and gave them the location. I didn't bother describing the exact situation. It would have taken too long and they would discover soon enough.

I made a quick assessment and knelt down again next to Coleman. "Okay, I think we've got the facts now. I need to get you away from this part of the scene. Roll over on your side so your ankles don't drag."

"I don't understand," she moaned.

"I'll explain in a minute."

Confused but obedient, Coleman rolled over. I lifted her by the knees to avoid as much pressure on her ankles as possible, while she inched forward on her elbow into the restaurant area, where I propped her head on a stack of paper napkins I got from the bar. I tried to put her far from where Max's body lay in front of the bar, but the place isn't that big. Coleman turned her head to look between the legs of the chairs at him and wiped the back of her hand over her eyes.

"You just rest there a minute while I finish staging a scene," I said.

My back starting to spasm, making me move like Jed Clampett on speed, I went into the office, dabbled my fingers in Cheri's blood, then went to the kitchen and picked up the shotgun to cover any other fingerprints with my freshly bloody ones to leave no doubt as to who fired the gun. With a towel I wiped off the 1911 that Emery had used on Max, making sure there were none of my prints on it. Then I pressed his fingers against it before resting it next to his right hand.

I knew it wasted a second, but I kicked the man who killed Jessica. I kicked him in the head. It didn't make me feel any better, but then nothing ever would.

I went back into the bar and, mindless of the remaining blood on my hands, got down two glasses, opened the bottle of Tarantula Tequila. I poured a couple of

354

healthy slugs, knocked back mine, then went back and sat down next to Coleman, noting from the alarmed look on her face that she had come out of her drugged state and just noticed I was covered with gore.

"Here, drink this." I raised her head and forced down as much of the tequila as she would take to stave off the shock. "We've got less than two minutes to talk fast before this place is all sirens and flashing lights and shit, and here's how it's going to play out. I killed Emery. You didn't see it happen because you were out here trying to crawl for help."

"Why would you do that?" she asked.

"We can go over the whys later. Just listen."

Coleman's head rocked back and forth on the pile of napkins. "Emery was a serial killer. They won't do anything to me."

"Yes they will," I said. "I know you're half in shock and you can't see the way things will play out. But I can, so you have to listen very carefully. You shot an unarmed man in the back, Snow. It was a righteous kill, but you did it while investigating a case after you were taken off. Second: because no one paid attention to your suspicions of Lynch, Max Coyote is dead. The Tucson Bureau made a royal mess of this case and Special Agent in Charge Roger Morrison is going to be looking for a fall guy to deflect attention from himself so he doesn't look responsible. You'll be that guy."

"I don't care anymore."

"So what are you going to do, teach high school or do security for some corporation? Coleman, sweetheart, you're one of the good guys. You need to do this."

I could hear the sirens now. "Don't think I'm going

altruistic or noble, Coleman. My life is already in ruins and this won't make it any worse. I just don't want to give Morrison the satisfaction of drumming you out of the Bureau."

"I'm going to tell them the truth."

"No you're not, because you can't do anything but crawl, which means I'll be out the door first. I'm going to tell them what happened, and if you give them a different story after, they'll get me for obstruction of justice and I'll go to prison. I'm putting myself into the perfect lose-lose situation, my dear, so you have no option but to win."

"You can't do this."

We were running out of time. "Oh yes I can. As an added incentive to you, I'll also tell them you fucked Royal Hughes."

There went the flashing colored lights through the high windows near the ceiling.

But before facing the SWAT team, I had to spend two more seconds on one more thing. I quickly went into Emery's office and picked up the jar of pickled pigs' feet from his desk. There was that little cream-colored edge pressed up against the glass on the inside that I had seen while sitting at the bar, a form and color that almost jibed with the rest of the contents. What I had thought was another instance of my bizarre imaginings.

A voice on a megaphone said, "You are surrounded. Come out slowly with your hands up."

I brought the jar of pigs' feet back into the bar, raised it well over my head, shut my eyes, and threw it so that its side hit the cash register. It shattered beautifully, with most of the shards falling behind the bar, the pungent vinegar odor meeting me as I climbed up on one of the stools to peer at my handiwork and see that I'd been right about what had been displayed there all these years.

Six well-preserved human ears.

I grabbed a handful of the white paper napkins and went to the front door, carefully opened it, sticking the napkins out first. When I opened it wide I saw the array of squad cars, everything from Tucson Police to Arizona State Highway Patrol. Interspersed among the cars were the SWAT guys, rifles up and ready. Some last little spurt of adrenaline I didn't know I had left kicked up when I stared into a half-dozen expert muzzles and another less-than-expert couple dozen I thought could go off accidentally at any moment. The faces reminded me what I looked like at this moment, unrecognizable.

"Brigid Quinn, FBI," I shouted, hands in the air and moving forward slowly. "Two downed officers inside. Hurry."

FIFTY-TWO

Coleman had tried her best to act tough, but was too much in shock to speak much, which was just as well. I spent some hours with the investigators and, to give the devil his due, with Roger Morrison, who showed up and played nice with both the metro cops and the sheriff's deputies. I agreed to come in on Monday for interviews with the officer-involved-shooting folks, though it was going to be a little dicey given the fact I was decommissioned.

But before any of the conversation, Coleman and Max were both brought out on stretchers. Both on oxygen. Good lord.

"Max?" I asked. "He didn't have a pulse."

The paramedic nodded. "Slight. He's barely stable. But alive."

There's that nightmare where you've accidentally killed someone. You can't bring them back to life and you know you're going to have to spend the rest of your life with that on your conscience. Then you wake up and you realize they're alive after all.

And they're probably going to send your ass to jail. My sense of euphoria upon hearing that Max was alive was only slightly tempered by that realization. Probably later I would care more about going to prison for Peasil's death and the subsequent cover-up, but in that moment I was one hundred percent glad that at least I had finally stopped the dying.

I went back to my conversation with Morrison, and when I finally thought to look at my watch I saw the time matched the darkness I was just beginning to notice. The paramedics urged me to get into the other ambulance for a ride to the hospital, but I only wanted to get back to Coleman's place. Just when I thought it was all over but the shouting, I spotted Carlo's Volvo parked well beyond the crime scene tape, lights off, his face leaning forward and peering intently through the windshield as if he was trying to watch a drive-in movie in the rain.

Despite having his hands full with keeping the media away from the scene, Morrison must have been keeping a close eye on me. "Are you okay?" he asked, probably meaning whether any of the carnage covering my body was my own.

I nodded without looking away from Carlo.

"Your husband," he said. "I met him when he arrived and told him he could stay as long as he didn't get out of the car."

"Do you remember when that was?"

"Yes," Three-Piece said. Before answering further he took uncustomarily harsh care of a pushy reporter. "Sir! Please remove your fucking camera from the agent's face. She's not going to say anything. Get this man out of here." He gestured to a nearby patrolman to escort the reporter out of the scene. Then he looked at his watch. "It was about three hours ago."

"He's been sitting there for three hours? Just sitting

there? How did he know I was here?"

Morrison shrugged, having spent his supply of nice guy. "How the fuck should I know?" he snapped. "I've been a little busy." Then, possibly recalling I'd been a little busy myself, he said, "I called him. You should go now," sounding like letting me go was against his better judgment.

"No. Coleman," I said. "I should stop by the hospital."

"Don't worry, she won't be left alone tonight, and her brother is flying in tomorrow."

"Nice. Family is nice. She's a hero, Agent Morrison. I want you to know that."

He made a kiss-kiss sound and shoved his thumb in the direction of the Volvo. "Get the hell out of here. Go on."

Muttering "prick" softly and without any energy, I left the scene and approached Carlo's car, weaving once or twice like a drunk. He got out, helped me into the passenger's side without comment, and got back behind the wheel. The Pugs had been in the backseat and now tried to scramble through the space over the console to get to a lap, any lap. I blocked them with the towel one of the paramedics had given me.

"I probably shouldn't have brought them," Carlo said, and started to shoo them back, "I thought . . . I don't know what I thought."

"You thought right. I just don't want to get . . . on them."

"Are you okay?" he asked, meaning the same thing Morrison had meant.

I shifted my right shoulder tentatively to check on the rotator cuff, which I had wrenched a bit dragging the corpse of the homeless guy. I joked, of course. "Sure, just a hard day at the office."

He didn't smile, sitting there staring briefly at the real me for the first time. "I mean you should go to the hospital. I mean ... is that your blood?"

I looked down at what was mostly everyone's blood but my own. "No. And I'm not in shock and not hurt beyond maybe some torn cartilage." I could hear my voice beginning to slur. "I'm just a little nauseous from the adrenaline drain."

"I watched you moving around for a long time and it seemed you were so in control of yourself, but if you have any doubts we should go to the hospital."

"Not tonight."

"You're sure?"

"Right now all I need to do is clean up."

We pulled out of the packed dirt parking lot and into the street heading north, in the direction of his house while I sat quiet, with the horrible images of events just passed already playing in my head in preview of coming attractions. It was a twenty-mile drive to the subdivision in Catalina, but I don't remember it. I came back into focus when he pulled the car into the garage, and I told myself I should get out and go inside but just sat there. He came around to the passenger side and opened the back door first, taking the Pugs one at a time and placing them on the garage floor because it was too high for them to jump. I had neglected to fasten my seat belt and he put a hand under my elbow to help me out, but I shrank from his touch so he backed away and I got myself out of the car.

I staggered through the door into the house, where the

Pugs danced around me, sniffing the blood on my jeans. That did it. Not wanting to further taint the place, without pause I kept going through the living room and out the back door, shutting it behind me so the dogs couldn't follow, into the depths of the yard which by this time was lit by a full moon overhead.

Some people's lives aren't meant to include relationships. Innocent people can get hurt that way. I had always been right about this.

I was looking at all the rocks that Carlo and I had collected, and which I had laid out in meandering lines around the yard like a labyrinth. By some grisly serendipity known only on nights like this I spotted, of all the hundreds of rocks, the piece of rose quartz I had picked up the day I killed Peasil. I picked it up. I pitched it as hard as I could over the back fence. Because of the moonlight I could see it smack into a prickly pear and knock off one of its burgundy fruits.

"What are you doing?" Carlo asked.

I hadn't been aware that he had followed me out back, and now I didn't care that he could see I was crazy. It didn't matter anymore and it was almost a relief that I didn't have to pretend to be normal.

"I need to get rid of all these," I said. "I have to get them all out of this space." So I started throwing them. I picked up a small granite rock shot through with mica, and tossed it, too. Then I picked up a piece of gneiss and threw that. Then something I couldn't name—something metamorphic. It wasn't like I was angry or nuts or making a dramatic statement, just very methodically giving the place back to Jane. It seemed like a good idea at the time. I can't tell you how long I was at it or how much of myself I'd gotten rid of over the back fence before Carlo figured it was time to stop me.

He took my wrist, uncurled my fingers, and made me drop what was in my hand. "There are so many rocks here," he said, "and it's late. You can do the rest tomorrow."

I obeyed. Walking back to the house I stopped at the garden hose, trying to turn it on so I could hose myself down outside, but Carlo led me inside the house and straight into the bathroom, where he unbuttoned my stained blouse and tugged down my blood-dampened jeans that had tightened onto my skin. I let him, putting my hand on the edge of the counter for balance rather than touching his shoulders when I lifted my feet one by one. He put me into the shower and turned on the water. I stood there, my brain sending out messages that I should be washing myself, but the rest of my body wasn't responding. Then the shower door opened and Carlo stepped in with me, his own clothes off.

I don't know why I flinched.

"I won't hurt you," he said, his eyes as glistening as the shower walls.

There was nothing of man and woman in the act of cleansing. While I stared at the floor of the shower he washed me very gently, two or three times over, horrified, I imagine, by the residue of blood on my body and yet obeying some greater call of servanthood. He rubbed more gently over the rose tattoo on my chest as if seeing it for the first time and afraid of smudging it. He tilted my head back just enough to wash my hair without the suds running into my eyes and only considered his job done when he looked down at our feet

363

and saw that the water was no longer running pink.

He turned off the water, opened the shower door, and stepped out, returning quickly with a towel with which he dried me carefully while I stared at an unknown woman in the mirror over the sink. Carlo must have found places on my ankles where Emery had knicked them with the knife when he cut the tape off me. He got some antibiotic ointment and a couple of Band-Aids from under the sink and took care of the cuts. He didn't realize how spent I was until my knees buckled. He held me up despite my feeble protest.

"It's a warm night," he said. "I don't think you'll mind your head being damp, yes?"

I didn't answer. I let him move me like a mannequin to the bed, which he had turned down on my side, and help me in. He went away but returned with a little water. He opened my nightstand drawer where I hid my meds and rifled through the bottles as if familiar with them.

"I can't find your sleeping pills," he said.

It was not a time for denial. "I left them where I was staying," I said, shivering a little as I felt the cool pillow against my wet scalp. "But I have some Valium in the top drawer hidden in an aspirin bottle."

"I know." He put one pill in my hand, then a second one when I didn't lower my hand. For good measure he got an antihistamine out of the medicine cabinet in the bathroom and gave me that, too, like a sleeping cocktail.

The Valium started to kick in. He looked at me before he flicked off the light. Last thing I remember is looking back at him, feeling the satin of Jane's pink bedspread under my fingertips and thinking, without knowing why, *say my name*. Not Honey, or O'Hari. Preferably not Jane.

Even if you regret marrying me, at least please say my name so I know what woman I am.

He did not. He said something else. The light went off. He didn't get into bed with me before I fell asleep and the next morning when I woke up I could tell from the straightened bedding on his side that he hadn't slept with me.

You don't get much of what you want. It's surprising that there can be any happiness at all if it's a matter of getting what you want.

FIFTY-THREE

The next day felt oddly normal except that it took much longer than usual, prolonged by politeness. I expected at some point Carlo would deliver the coup de grâce, but I wasn't going to put my head on the block for him. He had seen me unbalanced the night before and was probably finding it hard to know when and how to talk to me, but I'd show him I was tough enough to take it. It was so incredibly sad. We didn't speak much, hardly even looked each other in the eye; two people being alone in the same house only intensified the loneliness.

I knew he would always carry the image of me from the night before in his head and that it would color everything between us. I knew what that was like. I had a lot of those images I couldn't get rid of.

Morrison called, asked how I was, confirmed that I would be at his office at nine A.M. the next day. He was very solicitous and didn't sound like he was going to go after me for killing Emery. He sounded nervous.

I next called Gordo Ferguson and told him thanks for watching Carlo and that I wouldn't be needing him anymore.

I went back into the NamUs Web site and found the contact information for Kimberly Maple's parents.

Someone would have to tell them their daughter's body had been found and that Cheri had died. If not me, then who?

I called Max's wife Chrystal. She must have been at the hospital; I left a message.

Laura Coleman: not a phone call for her. Despite feeling depressed and stiff, I lugged my body into the car and down to the same hospital where I had visited Floyd Lynch the day before.

When I got up to her room on the second floor, I found her family—mother, father, and older brother—draped around her bed like a cordon. I started to go away again, but Coleman spotted me in the crack between her parents and called me into the room. I was introduced all around as the person who saved her life. Ben Coleman flickered with recognition, but Emily didn't remember me at all. Her brother, Willis, of heftier build than the willowy Val, mashed me into his substantial girth and praised his god for me.

I didn't speak of who had saved whose life. We still needed to get all the facts right between us before either of us submitted to interviews. I guess she was kind of right because, although she was the one to shoot Emery, if I hadn't shown up at the bar she'd definitely be dead. See what I mean about the truth? Hard to pin down sometimes.

Coleman asked her family to leave us alone for a few minutes, and they departed to the hospital cafeteria after more kissing on Coleman and repeated thanks to me.

I noted the bandage on her ear where Emery had

stapled it. "Boo-ya," I said to her. "You were one tough broad. Did they stitch up your tendons okay?"

She looked proud at the praise, more like an agent and less like the daddy's girl I saw when I first entered the room. She nodded and said, "They're going to let me go this afternoon. Doctor says it will take some time with a lot of therapy, but I should be able to reassume all my duties just fine. And with this Percocet I'm more than fine."

"Ah, good stuff. I've enjoyed that myself on more than one occasion."

"But I'm not too groggy. Tell me what happened and how you found me."

I explained how I'd been suspicious when she didn't contact me, what I did to try to track her down. The clue that was only significant to me, the unlocked car. Breaking into her house. The logs. Floyd's murder. There was a lot to tell. Then it was her turn.

"I told you how Emery captured me, kept me drugged. He had my phone. He was sending text messages to the office. Then he got into my Yahoo! account and . . ." She paused, ashamed. He would have needed her password, and she didn't want to talk about what it took to get it from her.

"And Morrison never asked to talk to you directly because he was pissed at you and was happy to have you out of the way until Lynch made his plea. Nobody could take what you took, Coleman. I would have given him my password, too." I told her what I'd figured out. "Emery Bathory, Floyd Lynch, Gerald Peasil. They were connected, and Lynch only knew what happened in the Route 66 murders because Emery told him."

"How did they meet?"

I told her about the chat-room connection. "You were right from the start, Floyd Lynch just pretended to be a killer and got caught up in the celebrity of it when he was nabbed. If you hadn't pulled out that logbook that showed he wasn't there when Jessica was killed, I wouldn't have had anything to confront him with. That was what made him tell me the truth."

Coleman's brain swam through the painkiller haze, focused temporarily. "Three guys, you said."

I nodded. "In a loose confederacy. Trading stories, mostly, until things got messy."

"And Emery heard every word we said in the bar."

"And knew we were a threat to him." I stopped before spilling about his sending Peasil to kill me. "Through the cops' talking he'd know everything that went on. It was a great way to keep tabs."

Either the Percocet was really taking effect or her mind was watching some of the tapes from the night before. Then, "Who's Gerald Peasil?" Coleman asked.

"Who?"

"Gerald Peasil. You said that name."

"Coleman, try not to think about it."

She paused the tape and looked at me. "That's the best advice Brigid Quinn can give? Try not to think about it? If I were feeling stronger I'd slug you."

"Trust me, it works." I straightened a wrinkle in the sheet. "Are we in agreement then? You're not going to accuse me of perjuring myself when there's a hearing?"

"Brigid."

"You were crawling in the bar. You didn't see what

369

happened in the kitchen. You heard the gun go off. Maybe you passed out. That's all you need to say."

"Brigid, you'll be in too much trouble. You're not even an agent anymore."

"And you're not snow. You kept investigating a case you were no longer assigned to. You breached all kinds of protocol. Plus, you shot an unarmed man in the back. But the only way you can ultimately find justice in all this is to be snow. The homeless guy, Cheri, and Emery—three people died at the bar and there will be questions. If this whole situation gets hot and they do a real investigation, Morrison could be in trouble. He'd blame you, spin the situation so you're the one who suffers any fallout. Do you understand?"

I didn't add that I was already in big trouble, so taking the rap for this didn't matter much. Coleman didn't have to know that. She stared at me with neither assent nor disagreement.

"I've gotten out of worse situations," I said. "This is nothing. And besides, I'm pretty much at the end of the game. You have a lot of scumbags left to catch."

"One thing I still don't understand," Laura said.

"What's that?"

"How did you know I had an affair with Royal Hughes?"

I decided not to tell her about Sigmund sensing it, or going through her address book, or about my conversation with Hughes where he admitted it. "Just a guess. I would have."

She considered that, then said, "Do you want to know why I switched from Fraud to Homicide?"

Not that much, actually. I had other things on my mind. Carlo. Max. "Why?"

"Because I kept hearing so much about you and the cases you worked, the bad guys you caught. When I heard you were retiring I figured somebody had to keep catching those guys."

"Aw, that's sweet. The fact is, I retired because I caused the Bureau trouble over shooting that suspect."

"That was political bullshit. I wanted to take your place because I admired you so much."

Why do people always get this way in hospitals and airplanes? I said, "Oh, one other thing I forgot to tell you. I smashed the window in the back of your house and broke in the other day, so when you go home don't be alarmed and think you were burgled. I didn't take anything but some of your yogurt." She opened her mouth with a question, but I stopped her with, "Trust me, Coleman. I'm the agent you don't want to be."

Finally, I made a quick stop in Max's room. He was in intensive care, considerably worse off than Coleman. His wife, Chrystal, a woman who had nothing in common with her name, hovered on the far side of the bed in full stand-by-your-man mode.

Max was barely conscious but saw me as I approached. He tried to take a breath, to speak. You could tell it hurt. Chrystal stroked his arm and told him not to try. She said, "They told me it was a miracle, the bullet missed his right lung and didn't hit any bone, something about the angle of his body, he didn't take it dead on, otherwise it would have done much more internal damage. He's also concussed because he hit his head when he went down."

Max turned his head and I leaned over the bed to get closer. I heard him whisper, "I heard, you killed the bartender."

"That's right. I saved your life," I said helpfully. "You should have believed me about Coleman. It was your own damn fault you got shot."

Chrystal let out a shocked, "Brigid!"

Max took another smaller breath so it would hurt less, with just enough air to get the words out before he sank into the pillow, exhausted. "I'm surprised you didn't kill me. You had the chance."

Chrystal, who had been leaning over from her side of the bed, jerked upright and looked wide-eyed, expecting me to assure her he was hallucinating from the painkillers. I could have told him I'd rather have died myself than be responsible for losing him. Instead, I smiled and patted his hand. "That's just because, .45 to the chest, I assumed you were already dead, sweetheart."

He reflected my smile with a weaker one of his own. He said, "The phone. Peasil's cell."

"I know. I left it for you to find, and you traced one of the numbers to Emery's bar."

He shook his head as if he had something else to say and I was keeping him from saying it. He took another small breath. "Those faces."

This was where we finally met, Max and I. We met in what was really important, in the victims, and seeing justice served even if we sometimes didn't follow the manual. "I saw them." He was almost worn out from our exchange, so I answered the question in his eyes without his having to ask it. "It was still an accident,

Max. That's the goddamn truth."

"Good."

There would be time later to find out what he meant by that word. He closed his eyes and Chrystal told me flat out to go.

FIFTY-FOUR

By not immediately reporting his suspicions about me, Max had already crossed the line. With any luck he'd stay there. Now that I was certain he was safe, it was time to save my own skin. I'd remind him again later that if he had believed me when I said Coleman had been abducted, he wouldn't have gotten himself shot. Like I told him, it was his own damn fault. I'd also point out the noise I made by kicking out the door distracted both Emery and him, so Max turned and the shot was off. And I'd remind him I killed Emery to save his life. Okay, so that last part wasn't quite the truth; at the time I thought he was dead and I was only taking the blame to save Coleman's career and atone for some of my own mistakes. But if the lie could do double duty I wasn't about to stop it.

The only thing that remained was getting through the rest of the afternoon with Carlo, going through the motions of preparing dinner, eating, reading, as if life would go on the same. But after the Pugs' evening walk, at the time when we would slip into our bathrobes and have some warm milk and a bit of boring television to quiet down, the mood turned edgy. He took the car keys from the hook by the door that led to the garage and said, "Come on, it's time to take a ride."

A giggle leaked out of me, the kind you hear with a rising hysteria. "Holy Jesus, that's what they say when they're going to whack you."

With more sadness than anger Carlo said, "Please put down your defenses, dear. Our marriage hangs in the balance," and opened the door for me to go first.

I got into Carlo's Volvo without appearing overly meek. We drove in silence down Golder Ranch Road, and he turned south on Oracle, and I thought, no, he couldn't let me hang around the house all day and now dump me back at Coleman's place.

And he didn't. Just after passing the Oro Valley Marketplace on Oracle and Tangerine, Carlo suddenly turned left, toward the mountains, into the darkness of Catalina State Park. It was where we had hiked before, and where I had been shot at, but this was the first time I'd been in the park at night. I didn't even know you could get in after sunset.

Without switching to his brights Carlo drove slowly along the winding black mile to the parking lot, from where, if it were daylight, we could have seen all the trails leading off from the single trailhead. As it was, the last thing I saw was a spider as big as your hand crawl through the headlights' beam just before he turned them off.

We sat in the total dark for a while, the blackness obscuring us from each other. If this was his show, let him talk. I was too depressed and tired to help him. As I waited, my eyes adjusted to the dark, and, while I still couldn't see Carlo's profile, I started to pick up the outline of the mountains in the east, appearing only as a starless silhouette. I noticed for the first time there was no moon yet tonight, or it had come and gone. Then, as if it was seeping through the dark, a pale gray smear appeared from left to right across the sky, what Carlo had once told me was the Milky Way. That's how the Milky Way is; you can't see individual stars so much. It's a big-picture kind of thing.

"It's hard to begin," Carlo finally began.

"You'll be kind. You can't help it."

"What I mean to say is, when you've lived with lies for so long, it's hard to know how to express things so that they can be trusted. It's hard to know what the truth is."

Nobody knew that better than I. "I have to tell you I'm very tired, and still achy, and not thinking clearly."

"Yes," Carlo said. "I'm well aware of that. It's why we're doing this tonight, while it's dark and your façade is still down. It may be the only time in our relationship that I've had the upper hand, and don't think I'm proud of it."

"You never wanted to know," I said, hating the whine in my voice. "I just did what you wanted me to do."

He sounded aggrieved, too. "It wasn't what you might have talked about that bothered me. It was you."

For the time being I nodded, just to keep him talking. As I proved with Emery, when your life is threatened, as long as you keep the other person talking you have a chance of survival. Most people can't talk and kill at precisely the same time. Think about it. You close your mouth before you pull the trigger. I was prepared to keep the Perfesser in lecture mode just as long as he wanted, until I figured out what the rest of my life looked like.

Only then he pulled the trigger.

"That time I talked to Max? He didn't actually give me all the details of your past."

"He didn't know all that much," I said.

"I asked him about you. You know, you."

"What did he tell you?"

"Like you say, not much. He gave me the phone number of someone at FBI headquarters in Washington. A psychologist friend of yours, he said. David Weiss."

At first I hardly knew I was shot. There was that numbness that comes before the pain, when everything drains out of you in your shock. There was no telling what Carlo knew about me.

"Weiss?" I said, and heard it as kind of a squeak. Knowing in advance that I was dead, I said, "I told you I was going to tell you everything. Didn't you trust me?"

"No. Yes. I couldn't wait."

I was suddenly so not tired. "He told you all about me killing the guy, didn't he? Not the last one, the other one when I was still with the Bureau. Sig knows more than anyone."

Whether or not Carlo was keeping up with the death toll, he only scoffed. "Forget that. Tell me about this Paul fellow."

Again my reality tilted and I felt like I was slipping toward the abyss, going into emotional free fall. But sitting there, both of us facing the windshield as if in a confessional, and having no choice, I told him everything. I told him how every person I was close to, family and friends, was a cop in one form or another. I told him

377

how I suspected myself of driving away every civilian I'd known. I told him how I had been half-afraid of driving him away and half-afraid I couldn't. I told him so much more than I'd ever told Sigmund, including how Paul was nothing like Dad, and how that meant he must be good.

I told Carlo I was terrified that he would leave me if he knew who I really was.

When I was finished, Carlo stayed silent, as if I'd been talking too fast and he needed to catch up. Then he said, "What an asshole."

Stunned, stricken by his response, I turned my head away. "Maybe you had to be there," I managed.

"Not you," Carlo said. "I mean Paul. Paul sounds like a real asshole."

I sat blinking, processing that, wondering why it didn't sound like either absolution or penance. One perfect man in my life calling the other perfect man an asshole. I didn't know what to think anymore.

"And you thought I was like him," Carlo said. I could feel him humphing mildly on his side of the car. "I did part of my pastoral training as a prison chaplain, for Christ's sake. I've given last rites to someone who was shanked in the ear. I've walked someone to their execution when they still used the electric chair and stayed to watch his body melt. What do you take me for, some kind of pansy-assed cleric with Communion wine where his spinal fluid should be?"

"No?" Only I was careful to remove the question mark.

"Fuckin' A. Because that would be offensive."

I still had my doubts. "Wait, this isn't one of those stooping-to-conquer maneuvers, is it?" I asked.

He ignored that. "I can't understand why you've withheld so much of yourself from me."

That pissed me off. "You didn't want to know! Remember our first date? You told me that story about the man with the mask. Your message was loud and clear."

"What did you think I was saying?"

"Whether you knew it or not, you were saying that you were good and I was bad." Peasil's body flashed into my head, probably not for the last time. "That I needed to hide all the things I'd seen, all the things I'd done, and pretend to be as good as you."

"Good Lord, you thought I didn't imagine what you might have witnessed? I've got a PhD and a doctor of divinity, O'Hari, and I'm not stupid. You're just going to have to, what do you call it, come clean with me."

"Please don't make me tell you the truth, Perfesser. It never turns out well. You won't like me afterwards."

"Well that's a chance you're going to have to take, because I don't see any other option."

"Do you think there's a chance you won't dump me?"

Carlo knew better than to simply reassure me, knowing how anyone can lie. "This is not a healthy relationship."

"I'm beginning to see that, but in my defense, I've never had any other kind."

"Maybe with a lot of honesty I think there's a strong probability that I will not leave you, yes."

"Before I start a major confession, would you tell me first everything Sigmund told you?"

He paused to consider before shaking his head. "Listen, we can go slowly on this, but for starters—and forgive the aphorism, but for the past twenty-four hours I haven't been able to come up with a different way to say it—you have to trust the people you love. And you have to trust their love for you. And just to set the record straight, I might add that when I told you the story of the man with the mask I was talking about myself."

In that moment I had a glimpse of all the men that Carlo had been, all the masks he had worn. I liked this Carlo who was talking now, this powerful man who met me on my own ground. Maybe that's why I had married him, because I saw this version that first day in his classroom. Until now all the rest between us had just been trying on different people. Maybe we do that at any age.

"Daphne," I blurted.

"What?"

"My name isn't really Brigid. I was baptized Daphne, but I changed it when I joined the Bureau so the guys wouldn't tease me."

"That's a start." Carlo put his hand on mine, the touch throbbing in my viscera. I had not realized until the touch how dangerous the moment had been. His grip tightened and he pulled me closer to him with an aggression that showed me I had underestimated so many things about him. I was close enough now to see his face even in the darkness.

"Now come kiss me, wench," he said.

I did.

And then so seriously, in some low register I didn't know he could reach, almost baring his teeth as he said it, "I love you, Brigid."

He said my name. He hadn't until now been calling me by name. The raw exposure of a man in love is frightening, even to me. I trembled and pulled back and felt my eyelashes dampen. "Why?" I managed to say, still doubtful, still fearing the intimacy.

He knew. Seriousness put aside as suddenly as it had flashed upon him, his old light touch returning, Carlo beamed at me and shrugged, "Damned if I know."

I started to retort, something like don't go getting all sappy on me. Instead, I leaned again over the console dividing us and kissed his shoulder so gently I'm sure I didn't even bend the skin. The feel of my upper lip on his shirt was salvation for the real me, whatever that would be. I allowed the intimacy, whispered bravely his real name. "I love you, too, Carlo."

Carlo's gentle fingers reached into my hair and pulled out a pin. A white curl fell down the side of my face where I could see it.

"I'm afraid I'm feeling a little old, darling," I said.

He nodded. Again, no lies, and I rather liked it. He said, "That comes and goes for me, too, and probably will until we die. But you know what else David Weiss said about you?"

"What?"

"After young men see you they dream dreams without realizing why. A very astute man, your Dr. Weiss." He put his arm around me and kept it there for a little while.

I knew I wasn't out of the woods with Carlo yet; there was still a lot of truth to tell, and, to tell you the truth, decisions to be made about how to tell it. I wasn't sure, for example, how he would react when I told him I might be going to prison for killing Gerald Peasil. No, Max wouldn't say anything. Would he?

We drove back to the house, where I dropped wearily to the floor with the Pugs. They frisked about me, hesitant, laughing. With that feeling of unreasoning giddiness at being alive and, for the moment, safe with the pack, "Group hug," I yelled. The Pugs jumped me. I returned their assault with head noogies.

The Pugs got bored and ran off, leaving my jeans studded with pale short hairs, but I stayed on the floor a few more minutes, staring at the living room from this unique angle. The strip of wallpaper with mauve grapes near the ceiling was just as ugly from here, though.

"Jane?" I whispered. "Jane? You here?" It was ten thirty, an hour past our bedtime, and Carlo had gone off to get ready for some long-delayed sleep. Only the sound of the Pugs' lips smacking at their communal water bowl disturbed the silence. I guessed Jane's ghost was not in the house. Maybe it never had been. I rolled onto my stomach and pushed myself from the floor to a standing position. My first stop tomorrow, before the start of my official interrogation, would be at Crate and Barrel—no, make that Pottery Barn. I needed to pick out a new set of dishes with no similarity to antique Bavarian china. And a new bedspread, not pink and not satin.

When I went into the bedroom, I saw Carlo had pulled down the whole bedspread. And I noticed now the dining room chair that had been placed near the foot of the bed, where he must have sat through the night before, keeping vigil.

I needed to begin again, for I had discovered I could have one happy year in my life. What god, no matter how vicious, would deny me a second? I remembered confessing to Carlo in the dark, my emotional free fall into the abyss I'd always dreaded. Only this time there was someone to wait at the edge, wait for me to come back.

Exclusive
Bonus Content

Read on for author interview,
book club questions and much more...

RICHARD AND JUDY ASK
BECKY MASTERMAN

We note you work in a forensic science publishing house. This has obviously inspired your debut novel, which is at times gruesome in its details of rape, murder, mummification, and necrophilia. When you were writing, did you ever find yourself unable to sleep at night?

Forensic scientists can talk about blow fly larvae over dinner and it all gets to seem matter-of-fact. And a presentation with PowerPoint slides is a lot different from a movie with screams and incidental music. At the same time, there's no doubt of the trauma they deal with and they use gallows humour to stay sane. For example, at the yearly US medical examiner's meeting, they call their golf tournament the Cadaver Open. I've been working with them for a long time in this spirit, so if I have trouble sleeping it's because of plot problems.

It's interesting, compelling and original to have as your protagonist a feisty 59-year-old woman. Did you see a gap in the market?

I created Brigid Quinn after reading a lot of mysteries with kick-ass dames in stiletto heels. I thought: what if my protagonist was more of a 'Miss Marple meets

Bruce Willis' character? In the earliest versions she was tongue-in-cheek, because I didn't take her seriously. No one else did, either. That was around 2004 and all the agents said nobody wanted to read about a woman over 40. But after a few years, I think the market caught up to me. My agent, Helen Heller, encouraged me to allow Brigid Quinn to be more real, more intense, and sometimes heartbreaking. Now I get lovely messages from women who thank me for acknowledging that we don't necessarily go gentle into that good night.

Did you base the story on any particular serial-killer case, or cases?

A writing mentor once told me that authors are like garbage scows. We store everything we encounter our whole life long and then sift through it to create our stories. To create my villains for *Rage Against the Dying*, I remembered reading that the FBI had started a Highway Serial Killer Initiative; I knew someone who was a long-haul trucker (though as far as I know he never killed anyone); one of my authors is an expert on mummies; another wrote a book on necrophilia. See what I mean about using it all? When Brigid Quinn and her profiling buddy, David Weiss, reminisce about past cases, some, like the Grim Sleeper, are real. Others I made up.

What next? Will your second book also be a thriller? And will Brigid Quinn be in it?

I am hard at work on the second Brigid Quinn thriller, still untitled. I wanted to call it *Unterminated: Rise of the Boomers*; my agent and editor both nixed that. They keep me focused on the dramatic aspects of the work, and I do so want to move your heart, but if I couldn't laugh—like the medical examiners do—I'd go nuts.

Download our podcast at http://lstn.at/rageagainstdying

Do you have any questions that you would like to ask Becky Masterman? Visit our website whsmith.co.uk/richardandjudy to post your questions.

Richard and Judy Book Club
QUESTIONS FOR DISCUSSION

The Richard and Judy Book Club, exclusively with WHSmith, is all about you getting involved and sharing our passion for reading. Here are some questions to help you or your Book Group get started. Go to our website to discuss these questions, post your own and share your views with the rest of the Book Club.

- Discuss the character of Brigid and her difficulty in building relationships.
- The tag line for this novel is 'old case, new rules'. How significant to the plot is the partnership of, and the age difference between, Brigid and Laura?
- The key to this book is the pace and suspense. How does the author build up the pressure to the end of the novel?
- Do you react differently to thrillers with a female lead?

For information about setting up, registering or joining a local book club, go to www.richardandjudy.co.uk

IN CONVERSATION WITH BECKY MASTERMAN

Q. Brigid Quinn is such a brilliant character. How did you go about creating her?

A. I took everything I always wanted to be: fiercely loyal, physically powerful, attractive to men, quick-thinking, witty, and I pushed all that to maximum capacity. Of course, there's no way to keep the author out of the characters, so insecurity, remorse, and occasional poor judgment crept into Brigid, too.

Q. What do you think having an older, female protagonist does to the thriller story?

A. I'd like to think that having an older female at the heart of a thriller plot is the best way to show boomers what it looks like to retain our will and vitality long past our youth, to not go gentle into that good night. Also that Bruce Willis isn't the only one out there who can still kick butt.

Q. You get a real sense of the landscape in your novel, is this a part of the world that is important to you?

A. I moved to the southwest desert after living most of my life in Florida, so maybe I see things about the landscape that desert dwellers take for granted. Like color.

Coming from a lush tropical environment, when I first looked at the desert I thought, 'It's so BEIGE!' I found out you just have to pay better attention. Eight years later, I still pull off the road to look at a cactus flower and stop writing to watch a hummingbird.

Q. How did you go about plotting the story? Did you let your characters lead you, or did you know how events were going to unfold?

A. I think I always do the 'what if' first, which is the problem of the book. Then I think of characters who interest me. Then I throw the problem at them and see what happens. Then when I have the first draft done, I throw the whole damn book out, eat a pound of chocolate, and start again.

Q. What sparked the idea for *Rage Against the Dying*?

A. Novel Writing Month. My husband had just retired and I challenged him to a competition. His novel was about a sentient plant that evolves and wants to even the score against the animal kingdom. Mine was a mystery called 'One Tough Broad'. That's when Brigid Quinn was born.

Q. You've created such a strong, female lead. Which other literary heroines do you admire?

A. Jane Eyre. It shames me to admit this, but I wouldn't have had her moral backbone. I would have told Mr. Rochester, that's okay, I understand. We can just live together. In a different house. No, on second thought, of course I wouldn't have done that. When I think it through, I would have left, too, but you see how I waffle?

I also like the smart women of Jane Austen and George Eliot. And Olivia Benson.

Q. What kind of research did you have to do before embarking on writing *Rage Against the Dying*?

A. For the past fourteen years I have had the exciting day job of being a forensic science commissioning editor for a reference publisher, so you name a topic and I know the expert. They're all so kind to me. My favourite story is about Dr. Anil Aggrawal who wrote a book for me which includes a list of 527 sexual paraphilias. When I asked him what arousal by mummies would be called, he said he didn't have it on his list but would create a term in my honour—*moumiophilia*.

Q. Have you always wanted to be an author?

A. It never occurred to me that I could learn to write stories until after I turned forty. By that time I had developed the passion, discipline and, most importantly, the compassion necessary to write. But maybe we are born authors. My dad always said my favourite phrase was, 'Let's pretend . . .'

Q. What has been the most unexpected aspect of being published?

A. (Laughter) That I didn't beat Michael Connolly my first week out. Another valuable lesson in humility learned.

Q. Do you listen to music when you write? If so, which artists?

A. Do you think it would help? Right now complete silence in the house. No music, no TV, sound turned off even on the computer. If I pay attention, I hear the dog behind my chair licking his paw and the cactus wren outside who sounds like one of those ratchety new-year's noisemakers.

I have been known, however, to belt show tunes in bars.

Q. Where do you get your inspiration to write from?

A. I don't know!!! Someone please tell me so I can get it more easily! Until then, I wait. Someone has said what it takes to be a writer is the patience of a cat. And moving your fingers. You move your fingers over the keyboard and the inspiration sometimes follows, more often in that order than the other way around.

BECKY MASTERMAN'S
TOP READS

Choosing ten favourites is hard. This is a list of some that blew me away with a perfect combination of great writing, heart and clever concept. Most of the books listed here are the first books I discovered by the authors. They may not be the author's most acclaimed work, but reading that first book is like falling in love the first time. The rest are great, too, but you never forget the initial infatuation. I regret that my tastes run more to male writers than to my sisters who deserve great praise, but there are some women on this list. Maybe it's because one of my delights in reading is to understand what is outside my ken. I already know the mind of a woman.

Rebecca by Daphne du Maurier
And Then There Were None by Agatha Christie
Nancy Drew: The Hidden Staircase by Carolyn Keene
Rain Gods by James Lee Burke
The Hank Thompson Trilogy by Charlie Huston
Killshot by Elmore Leonard
The Night of the Hunter by Davis Grubb
The Curious Incident of the Dog in the Night-Time by Mark Haddon

Shutter Island by Dennis Lehane
Bangkok 8 by John Burdett
No Country for Old Men by Cormac McCarthy
Once Were Cops by Ken Bruen
The Comfort of Strangers by Ian McEwan
Master of the Delta by Thomas H. Cook
The Forgery of Venus by Michael Gruber
The Girl with the Dragon Tattoo by Stieg Larsson
Our Mutual Friend by Charles Dickens
Gone Girl by Gillian Flynn
The Silent Wife by A. S. A. Harrison

Ways to get involved

The two of us are absolutely passionate about reading and there's something immensely satisfying about discussing books amongst friends and family.

We'd love you to be part of these conversations so do please visit our website to discuss this book, and any of our other Book Club choices. There is so much to discover and so many ways to get involved – here are just some of them:

- Subscribe to our author podcast series
- Read extracts of all the Book Club books
- Read our personal reviews and post your own on our website or post your short review on Twitter #RJBookClub
- Share your thoughts and discuss the books with us, the authors and other readers
- Set up, register or join a local book club

For more information go to our website now and be a part of Britain's biggest and best book club – whsmith.co.uk/richardandjudy. See you there!

Richard and Judy Book Club

@RJBookClubNews

Our latest Book Club titles

THE NUMBER ONE BESTSELLER

JODI PICOULT
The Storyteller

'Gripping' *Grazia*

LOUISE DOUGHTY
APPLE TREE YARD

Two wrongs don't make a right.

A COMMONPLACE KILLING
SIÂN BUSBY

BECKY MASTERMAN
RAGE AGAINST THE DYING

OLD CASE. NEW RULES.

RICHARD AND JUDY
Thorntons
BOOK CLUB
2014
EXCLUSIVE TO
WHSmith

ESCAPE IS JUST THE BEGINNING
THE NEVER LIST
KOETHI ZAN

CURTIS SITTENFELD
Bestselling author of *American Wife*
SISTERLAND

LONGBOURN
JO BAKER

THE ROSIE PROJECT
GRAEME SIMSION